RED DEATH . . .

Both monitors bloomed with the image of the tank. In the magnified view, a tiny red dot appeared on the side of the tank's hull.

"There's the targeting laser," Abrams said.

The dot moved forward and upward, found a starting point near the base of the turret, and steadied.

Abrams looked up at the Ruby Star weapon. It had tracked with the targeting laser, adjusting itself on top of its heavy tripod. Only the increased roar of the generators heralded the event.

Without warning, a thin ruby beam emitted from the nozzle end of the laser, instantly snapping across the half-mile of distance to the tank . . .

As Abrams watched, the end of the beam advanced, touched the turret, then moved to the right.

"Boost the power to seventy percent," Abrams called out.

Again the targeting laser found the side of the tank, this time picking out the center of the hull.

It was so quick, it was almost unnoticeable. . . . A flash of bright ruby red at the tip of the laser.

Silent.

Then the tank nearly vaporized.

BOOKS BY WILLIAM H. LOVEJOY

COLD FRONT

BLACK SKY

DELTA BLUE

ULTRA DEEP

ALPHA KAT

DELTA GREEN

PHANTOM STRIKE

WHITE NIGHT

CHINA DOME

RED RAIN

William H. Lovejoy

PINNACLE BOOKS
KENSINGTON PUBLISHING CORP.

This one is dedicated, with love,
to my sister,
Pam Beaumont

PINNACLE BOOKS are published by

Kensington Publishing Corp.
850 Third Avenue
New York, NY 10022

Copyright © 1996 by William H. Lovejoy

Pinnacle and the P logo Reg. U.S. Pat. & TM Off.

First Printing: February, 1996
10 9 8 7 6 5 4 3 2 1

Printed in the United States of America

THE PEOPLE

General Technologies Inc., Myanmar

Christopher Carson - Vice President, Director of Myanmar Modernization Project

Jack Gilbert - Director of Technology Acquisition, Assistant to the Director

Martin Prather - Director of Disbursements

Don Evans - Air Fleet Manager

Tracy Hampton - Surface Fleet Manager

Sam Enders - Director of Microwave Systems

Billy Kasperik - Manager, InstaStructure

Kiki Olson - Director, Personal Computer Systems

Becky Johnson - Secretary to the Project Director

General Technologies Inc. Subcontractors

Stephanie Branigan - Assistant Vice President, UltraTrain, Project Director

Craig Wilson - Chief, Motive Power and Rolling Stock, UltraTrain

Dick Statler - Chief Roadbed Engineer, UltraTrain

Janice Cooper - Secretary to the Assistant Vice President, UltraTrain

Delbert Creighton - Project Manager, Hygienic Systems

Robert Mickeljohn - Supervisor, IBM Computer Services

Phillip Draft - Myanmar Division Director, Bluebird Bus

Ronald Vermont - Chief Engineer, Cable Engineering

Charles Washington - Manager, Hydrofoil Marine Corporation

General Technologies Inc., Headquarters, Palo Alto, California
Dexter Abrams - President and Chief Executive Officer
Mack Little - Director of Laser Technology
Dennis Larkin - Chief Auditor
Troy Baskin - Chief of Security

Government of Myanmar
U Ba Thun - Minister of Commerce, Supervisor of Modernization Proclamation
Lon Mauk - Colonel, Myanmar Army, Commander of Security Services
Tawn Yin May - Major, Adjutant, Security Services
Lin Po - Major, Commander of Railroad Security
Chit Nyunt - Colonel, Myanmar Air Force Intelligence

Hypai Industries
Hyun Oh - Director of Material Sources, Director, Myanmar Contract
Kim Sung-Young - Assistant Director, Myanmar Contract
Mr. Pai - President, Hypai Industries

Chieftains
Khim Nol - Shan State
Daw Tan - Northern Shan State
Nito Kaing - Southern Shan State
Shwe - Western Shan State

Others
Pamela Steele - freelance writer, London

THE HOT SEASON

ONE

The road to Banmo, Kachin State, Union of Myanmar

The Razor—which was the only name by which he was known—waited patiently in the natural defilade. He squatted on his haunches, his arms resting on his thighs. He could hold the position for hours if necessary, without cramping his leg muscles, and be prepared to spring instantly into defensive or offensive postures.

Like the tiger of his native region. The Razor had always liked the image.

He was alone on this, the west side of the road. The other three were nestled into hiding positions among the trees crowding the eastern side of the dirt track that wound through the forest. Two of them, he could see—pale blobs of faces shining through the leaves, and later, he would chastise them for their negligence. Then he would instruct them.

The Razor also considered himself a master teacher, though he was but twenty-two years old.

He himself stayed well back from the road, depending upon his ears to tell him when the quarry approached. The tree directly in front of him, nearly strangled by vines and shrubs, protected him from the sight of others. On his left, a granite outcrop nearly three meters high shielded him from any counterfire he might expect to come from the north.

Behind him, the bluff fronting the hill was thirty meters tall, but a crevice crowded with roots and vines would allow him to scamper like a monkey to its summit, then disappear into the all-but-impenetrable rain forest.

Squatting there, the Razor studied his knees and concentrated on the sounds around him—the chirps and squeaks and squalls of insects and wildlife in the forest. An angry mosquito buzzed nearby, but did not attack. A parrot called to a potential mate. Somewhere, a monkey chattered to himself. A thrashing above and behind him could have been created by a black bear or civet cat.

He was dressed simply in Western-style jeans and a black T-shirt. The armpits of his shirt were damp with perspiration, the product of the humidity that smothered the forest. He had long ago abandoned the locally fashioned sandals and switched to running shoes, also black, but fitted with a slim piece of protective steel in each sole. His belt was a military weave, olive drab, and carried the handmade leather sheath that housed the razor for which he was noted.

The razor was a barber's, finely honed, and antique. It was likely a relic of the British colonial era, and its handle, into which the blade folded, was made of ivory. A Bengal tiger was gracefully engraved into the ivory on one side, and an Indian elephant was carved into the yellowed surface of the other side. He had always assumed that the image was of the elephant that had given up the ivory.

All of his other supplies were stored in a pouch slung over his back: a plastic bottle of water, five magazines of 7.62-millimeter ammunition, a portable radio, a plastic sheet, a first-aid kit, two chocolate bars, and a bag of rice. Anything else he might need for survival could be claimed from the jungle.

He raised his head when he heard the diesel engine. It was straining under load, reaching a higher pitch when the transmission was shifted down. A truck.

But coming from the south. It would be of no interest.

The Razor stared through the veil of tree leaves across the road and willed his comrades into immobility.

No one moved, and fifteen minutes later, the truck groaned by on the road. It was ancient and rusty, and its bed was covered with patched canvas. The blue-black cloud of its exhaust trailed after it. It was not notable.

Twenty minutes later, he heard more automobile engines, this time coming from the north. Their hum carried down the tunnel of the road smoothly. They, also, were in a lower gear, but the intent was to retard their speed on the downslope of the rutted and narrow cart track.

The Razor rose gracefully to his feet and picked up the assault rifle leaning against the rock. It was a Kalashnikov AK-47, made by the Chinese and dated, but in excellent working order. He treated it as kindly as he treated his razor.

Constricting his throat, he cawed softly, like a wounded myna, to alert the others.

After retrieving three extra magazines from his pouch, he went to his knees and crawled, using his elbows to pull himself forward, under the spreading branches of the tree and alongside the rock. Yesterday's short rainfall had left damp, fungi-smelling loam under the foliage. It released the odor of mildew when his elbows and knees disturbed it.

The massive piece of granite reached fully to the road's edge. The road, in fact, had been hacked out of the forest so as to avoid the rock, and the curve around it was relatively sharp.

He laid his weapon down carefully and advanced his head over it, peering around the rock and up the road.

On the other side of the track, he saw his men taking up their positions, one six meters high in a tree, one below the brow of another outcropping, and the third situated as was the Razor—flat on the ground behind a boulder.

Because of the curve of the road, he still could not see the approaching vehicles—there was more than one. But he heard them, and that was enough.

The road to Banmo

Christopher Carson was in the passenger seat of the second Land Rover, next to the Union of Myanmar army noncom, who was driving with what Carson frequently considered reckless abandon. Colonel Lon Mauk was sitting in the back with Stephanie Branigan of UltraTrain. Carson thought Mauk's manipulation of the seating arrangements a bit transparent. He wanted a few hours in close proximity to Branigan.

In the lead utility vehicle were two well-armed Myanmar soldiers, in addition to Hyun Oh of Hypai Industries and Jack Gilbert, who worked for Carson.

Mauk had told them that their tail-end position in the two-vehicle convoy was safest, but after the first couple of hours, Carson would have traded safety for fresh air. The dust raised by the lead truck floated in the still air for miles, and though they were a half-mile behind it, the fine particles whipped through the open side windows and coated them with grit. Given the heat at ten in the morning on a mid-May day of the hot season, rolling up the windows was not even a consideration.

They had taken the road out of Myitkina, following the Irrawaddy River valley, but it was not the road Mauk had recommended. It was, in fact, a relic of the Stone Age as far as Carson was concerned. Still, it was he who had insisted upon meeting villagers in remote settings like Sinbo and Dumsu Yang. After climbing into the hills leaving Dumsu Yang, they were now descending along a stretch of rugged hills to the valley. It was hot and dry, and they were now traversing a pocket of thick tropical forest sprinkled with conifers and teak.

The sky was brassy blue and cloudless, but the horizons were limited by the rain forest, which encroached from both sides and threatened to leap the road and rejoin, crushing anyone caught in between. Carson also thought that defining the narrow, two-tracked ruts as a road defied common sense. A few minutes earlier, they had had to stop completely and nose the trucks into the forest in order to let a truck slip by.

Though he had been in the Union of Myanmar for over two years and had toured the country several times, the previous trips had been accomplished in the air. This was his first view of the northern provinces from ground level. Mauk had been skeptical of the need, but Carson thought it was important to his own feeling for, and sense of, the country. He wanted to know what the locals thought of the presence of foreigners.

So far, in the three-day trek, he hadn't learned much. The tribal members and the peasants he had spoken to through Mauk's interpretation were remarkably uncommunicative. If they had dreams or desires beyond basic survival, they weren't going to reveal them to a *farang*—as the neighboring Thais called a foreigner. Or perhaps they weren't going to reveal them to Mauk, who may have been more an obstacle than a facilitator in translation since he represented the central government. Carson had known Colonel Mauk for the same amount of time he had been in-country, but had yet to be able to read him with reliability.

The Land Rover bounced out of the furrows it was following, clipped a tree trunk with its bumper, then banged back into the ruts. The driver grinned maniacally as Carson grabbed a handgrip on the dashboard to keep himself more or less in his seat.

He looked back at Branigan, and she rolled her eyes at him while licking the dust from her dry lips with the tip of a pink tongue. She had given up on makeup in general after the first day and lipstick after the second. To Carson's eye, she didn't need either, anyway.

The road that they were moving down was steep, and the driver had the transmission in second gear. The engine complained at high whine.

"Another thirty kilometers, then we will reach the main highway," Mauk warned them from the backseat. "From there, it is but twenty kilometers to Banmo, where we will stop for lunch."

"If I have stomach enough left," Branigan told him. "There's an airfield in Banmo, isn't there?"

"You wouldn't want to bail out on us, would you, Steph?" Carson asked her.

"Only the first chance I get."

Mauk smiled. Carson supposed it was his I-told-you-so smile. He turned back to stare through the dusty windshield.

The Land Rover ahead of them disappeared as it went around a tall rock outcropping on the right. Carson looked up through his window and saw that steep hills were visible above the tops of the trees.

The driver braked as he approached the curve.

And the windshield exploded.

TWO

The road to Banmo

The safety glass starred and crazed. Two slugs caught the driver in the face, and his body whipped backward, his head slammed into the headrest. Blood sprayed against the roof and into the back.

Branigan yelped.

The Land Rover skipped out of the ruts and slewed into the dense foliage on the right, tipping up on its left wheels before banging back to all four wheels.

A flight of startled and brightly colored birds flashed out of the trees, climbing for the sky.

Carson slapped his palm against the gear shift to throw it into neutral.

"Down!" he yelled. "Get down, Steph!"

He grabbed the muzzle of the driver's assault rifle from where it rested on the floor as he pulled the latch and threw his door open. He rolled out of the seat and onto the dry earth of the road edge, spinning around flat on the ground to look down the road from beneath the vehicle.

Another volley of automatic fire—distinctively that of AK-47s—chattered, and geysers of earth stitched across the road. A dozen metallic bangs indicated hits on the truck.

He couldn't see where the fire was coming from, but was certain there were several rifles in operation. The first Land

Rover, which had been allowed to pass by the point of ambush, was probably under attack also.

Lon Mauk leaped from the door of the truck, pulling Branigan after him. He shoved her down behind the protection of the right front wheel, then spread out on the earth next to Carson. He had his automatic pistol in his hand, and he ran the slide back to chamber a round.

"Do you know how to use that, Mr. Carson?"

"I believe so, Colonel."

The rifle was a Kalashnikov AK-74, the most recent example of the durable and reliable Russian design. It had a full clip of 5.45-millimeter ammunition. Carson thumbed the selector to single fire. He wasn't going to waste what he had.

Another burst rattled the far side of the Land Rover.

A crescendo of automatic fire sounded from around the big rock, and Carson assumed that the soldiers of the lead truck were returning fire.

"Any ideas, Colonel?"

"Bandits, I believe. They may have thought they were smart, letting the sergeant pass by first, but now we have them pinned between us."

"We won't get around that rock on this side of the road."

"I will cross the road and advance on that side. You will cover me."

"I'll go with you."

"No. You are a guest in my country."

"I'll relax here then. You'd better take the 74."

They exchanged weapons, and as soon as Mauk rose to a crouch, Carson elbowed his way forward, under the truck, so that he had a better view. He thought he saw the muzzle wink of a rifle high in a tree, and he raised the automatic—a Browning nine millimeter—to sight on the middle of the tree.

"Now, Colonel!"

Carson squeezed off a round.

The muzzle jumped a little, and he pulled it down and fired again.

Mauk sprinted across the road and disappeared into the forest.

Carson pulled back and rolled behind the rear wheel as return fire peppered the Land Rover. He looked over at Branigan, who had scrunched herself up against the front wheel. Her color didn't look good.

"Chris?"

"Stay where you are, Steph. This won't take long."

Carson rolled to his feet and ran around the open door of the truck to slip between two trees and into the jungle. He didn't have a machete, and he had to fight his way through the tangled growth. Branches and vines grabbed at him; he ducked his head and plowed his way through them. Several times, he was forced back by the thick vegetation and had to change his route.

The earth rose steadily beneath him, and within a dozen yards, he ran into the side of a cliff. He looked up, but didn't see any way he was going to scale it. Turning south, he stayed close to the cliff and pushed his way toward the firing he could still hear. The growth was thinner and the going was easier next to the rock face.

The loose soil of the ground seemed to rise some, but by the time he reached the promontory of granite that abutted the road, he was still some twelve feet from its top.

The gunfire had abated. The shooters were taking single shots, conserving their ammunition now.

Since he didn't see much advantage in returning to the road and exposing himself by going around the rock, Carson decided on heading up. Shoving the automatic into the back pocket of his jeans, he pushed his way through the branches of a conifer to its trunk, which was about fifteen inches in diameters. The needles stung his face and bare forearms, drawing some blood.

He had to shove some growth out of the way, but he found footholds on dry, bare limbs and began climbing. It took him four or five minutes to penetrate the maze of vines wrapped around the branches before he found a branch headed in his direction. He gripped a higher grouping of leaves with his hands and worked his feet along the bough, one behind the other.

It sagged the farther he got out on it, but his head emerged from the foliage, and he saw he had a four-foot jump down to the top of the rock. Rather than think about it, he released his grip and leaped.

The branch went down about a foot as he launched himself, costing him leverage, and he landed half on the solid granite surface, his legs dangling down. His chin slammed the hard, bird-dung-covered surface.

He started slipping backward.

Scrambling, digging his fingers into shallow fissures, he pulled himself up until he was lying flat on the top, breathing hard.

He felt the Browning slip from his pocket.

Heard it hit the side of the rock and scrape along as it plummeted to the ground.

When Carson looked up at the cliff face on his right, he saw that it continued upward for another twenty feet.

And in a vertical crevice of the cliff, pulling himself upward on the vines with apparent ease, was a man in black.

Carson clambered to his feet, ran across the eight-foot top of the rock, and grabbed for the man's leg.

He caught the ankle with his right hand.

The man swore in an unfamiliar language and tried to kick himself free.

Carson got his left hand wrapped around the man's ankle, lodged his knees against the cliff, and tried to tug him out of the crevice.

"Come on, you son of a bitch!"

The bandit released his right hand, dropped his shoulder, and let his AK-47 sling slip free of his shoulder. The weapon slid down his arm, and he grabbed the stock.

· Using his left hand, Carson pulled himself up the man's leg and took a swipe at the rifle with his right. His fingers caught the sling.

And his feet slid from the rock.

For a moment, he hung there from the sling of the rifle. He released the ankle and grabbed blindly for a hold on a tree root.

The bandit let go of the rifle.

And Carson plunged fifteen feet to the ground, next to the rock.

He hit soft earth with a solid thump on his left side and shoulder; his breath whooshed from his lungs.

Inhaling deeply, he rolled onto his back, bringing up the rifle to aim at the man frantically climbing the cliff, and squeezed the trigger.

Nothing.

The safety was on.

He thumbed it off, but he was too late.

The man in black had disappeared.

Cursing softly to himself, Carson rolled back onto his stomach and looked around. There was no one else with him in the cavity of rock and trees, but the sporadic gunfire still sounded from across the road. On his hands and knees, he crawled quickly to the safety of a tree trunk near the road, then peeked around the trunk.

He counted three men firing from concealment, picking them out by the thin bursts that escaped their flash suppressors. He chose the one in the tree, the one he had first shot at, as his first target and brought the muzzle of the AK-47 assault rifle to bear.

He didn't know how many rounds were left in the magazine, but he used single fire and pulled off one round.

Dropped his aim to a man on the ground and fired again, searched for the third.

The first man dropped out of the tree, tumbling end over end, and crashed to the earth.

The second man stopped firing.

The third threw his rifle out onto the road.

After a few more shots from the soldiers on his right, it was quiet.

From somewhere in the tangled tropical forest to Carson's left, Mauk barked a few orders in Burmese. A minute later, one of the assailants came out of the trees and sprawled face-down in the middle of the road. He put his hands on the top of his head.

It was quiet.

Carson could hear the Land Rovers' engines idling.

Then one of Mauk's men from the first truck walked up the road, staying to the side of it. He probed the foliage with his rifle barrel as he advanced. When he found two bodies back in the shrubs, he called out to Mauk.

Mauk emerged into the road, and Carson got up and pushed his way through the tangle of tree limbs. He was hot and sweaty, and rivulets of perspiration had created tracks in the dust on his face. He tried to wipe it away with his forearm, but only smeared his face with the blood from cuts on his arm. His blue knit sport shirt was ripped in several places.

Down the road, the first Land Rover was parked at the side of the road, and it, too, was pocked with bullet holes. Gilbert and Oh rose from behind the hood and started walking toward him. The second soldier joined them.

Stephanie Branigan came around the rock and looked at him. "My God! Are you all right, Chris?"

He grinned to show his lack of pain, which was only a little fib. The scratches were more irritating than painful.

Mauk reached the bandit in the road, rolled him over, and studied his face, which remained stoic. The colonel told his men to tie the man's hands. Carson had the distinct impression that, if the foreigners had not been present, a swift and brutal interrogation might have taken place.

Jack Gilbert, a solid specimen of the male gender who loved his morning workouts, asked, "Friends of yours, Chris?"

"Possibly, but I never remember a face."

They gathered in the road as the soldiers dragged the bodies of two bandits from the foliage. Branigan turned her back on them. He was watching her for a reaction to the killing, but apparently there was to be none, or, at least, no reaction that was visible.

Carson felt Mauk's eyes studying him carefully.

Carson gave him the assault rifle and told him about the escapee.

"And I probably scratched your pistol, Colonel. I'll buy you a new one."

"It will be unnecessary, Mr. Carson. I see that you are familiar with the Kalashnikov."

"More with the M-16. I used to be an army reservist."

"Ah."

Until he got so busy that he had had to resign his commission, Chris Carson had served in the army reserves as a UH-60 Blackhawk helicopter pilot. He had made captain when his aviation company had been called up for the Persian Gulf War. None of that information was on any résumé that Mauk might have seen.

Mauk studied him some more, openly and curious, but not necessarily with suspicion.

Carson put the man in his late forties, and they were hard-earned years, he judged. He was about five feet seven inches, and his wiry body appeared fit in his khaki uniform, but his face was weathered and lined, and his deep brown eyes appeared as if they had witnessed a great deal. Which, since he was in charge of the country's internal security for Carson's project, they probably had. Under his service cap, his head was shaved, reminding Carson of a Buddhist monk.

Hyun Oh, whose company was responsible for the installation of local telephone exchanges, shuffled his feet as the silence grew longer. Oh's face was pallid, and the man looked like he might vomit at any moment.

"I believe," Mauk said, "that we must terminate this tour. I will radio for helicopters."

Carson was going to protest, then decided against it when Branigan's face displayed her relief.

"I could use a shower," he said.

Ahlone Road, Yangon, Union of Myanmar

U Ba Thun was the minister for commerce, and he had been given additional duties that rightfully belonged in the interior ministry. The overt reason was simple enough. Ba Thun spoke fluent English as well as Burmese—the official language—and half-a-dozen of the one hundred distinct languages utilized in the country. As a result of centuries of intermarriage between ethnic groups, the people of Myanmar were more easily defined by their languages than by their ethnic origins. The language of the lowlanders, surrounding the Irrawaddy River valley, was predominantly Burmese, but Shan and Mon were primary languages in the northern plateau regions.

Ba Thun, with his mastery of English, had become the government's spokesperson when it was decreed that the gates of Myanmar would be partially opened to a controllable horde of foreigners. It was not only his linguistic ability that made him the logical choice, of course. Until two years before, he had also been an army general. His military bonds with other members of the State Law and Order Restoration Committee (SLORC) automatically made him both loyal and reliable.

When the cities of Burma were in chaos in the summer of 1988, with student protestors overrunning the streets of Rangoon, General U Ba Thun was one of the military leaders who seized power on September 18. General U Saw Maung assumed control of the government—chairmanship as well as minister of defense and minister of foreign affairs—and viciously reacted to any dissent whatsoever. In June 1989, the government changed many long-standing names: as declared in the United Nations, the Union of Burma became the Union of Myanmar; Rangoon would henceforth be known as Yangon.

Maintaining control had not been easy. In May 1990, the opposition party known as the National League for Democracy and led by Aung San Suu Kyi achieved a landslide victory at the polls, but the junta delayed the installation of a civilian government until the constitution could be rewritten. In December, the SLORC outlawed the National League for Democracy and kept San Suu Kyi under house arrest at her parents' home in Yangon despite the fact that she had been awarded a Nobel Peace Prize.

International pressure on the government had increased steadily. In 1993, the American President made a personal plea for San Suu Kyi's freedom. Six Nobel Peace Prize laureates traveled to Bangkok to voice the same prayer. The United Nations Human Rights Commission pressed for Myanmar's suspension from the UN. Arms and economic sanctions and embargoes were proposed.

Internal economic problems also threatened. Sixty-five percent of Myanmar's economy was based on agriculture, and the country's imports easily doubled its exports.

To alleviate the situation, the members of the State Law and Order Restoration Committee reluctantly agreed among themselves that change was required to boost the economy if they were to maintain control. On the domestic political front, some freedoms were granted to opposition parties, though not yet enough freedom to mount a serious threat to the incumbents. A restoration of the People's Assembly had been promised for the near future. Most of the members of the SLORC resigned from their military positions, presenting the face of a civilian government.

And foreign investment was suddenly encouraged. Dollars and francs and pounds were desperately needed.

In fact, once he had been given the charge of modernizing the country, U Ba Thun found that he relished the idea. After consulting for several months with foreign experts, Ba Thun proposed a program that, after many more months of debate, had achieved approval.

The Modernization Proclamation issued by the SLORC was met with suspicious but optimistic favor by dissidents in the urban areas. The rural population seemed indifferent, and the tribal peoples in the back reaches of the country were positively antagonistic. Ba Thun thought that reaction ironic, since the program was intended to benefit the tribes as well as anyone else.

Along with his stewardship of the foreign nationals, Ba Thun found himself to be, amazingly, something of a social being. Previously, his life outside the military had been confined to deep friendships with other generals and colonels. Now, he found himself responsible for entertaining, not only the contractual personnel, but also the representatives of governments that placed tentative consulates in the capital. The premier, as minister of foreign affairs, preferred to avoid contact with foreign agents.

Today, it was a luncheon for a committee of the International Airline Transport Association. With twenty-four months of steadily improving conditions in the country, several airlines were showing an interest in adding Mingaladon Airport to their schedules. Ba Thun intended to encourage them despite reservations among some members of the SLORC.

His steward, Chin Li, who had once been an army lieutenant and his aide, rapped lightly on the door frame of his study.

"Yes?"

"It is almost time for the guests to arrive, Minister."

"Very well. Let us examine the preparations."

He pushed himself out of his chair and went around the writing table to claim his suit jacket, thrown over the back of a couch. Ba Thun thought it important to make his guests feel comfortable, and he had readily adapted to wearing Western suits. This one was a summer weight worsted in a pale ivory shade. They were tailored to fit his somewhat rotund figure, and he felt as presentable, perhaps more so, than in the military uniforms he had worn for thirty-six of his sixty-two years.

In the grouping of pictures on the wall above the couch was a small, gilt-framed mirror, and he bent over slightly to check his image in it. His closely barbered black hair was in place, and the nick in his chin, which he had made while shaving, was not apparent.

Satisfied, he donned the jacket and asked Chin Li, "Do you suppose I am ready for the cinema?"

"To watch it, or to participate in it, Minister?"

Ba Thun smiled and followed Chin Li from the study. They crossed the wide living room, passed through the entrance foyer, and entered the dining room. The house, which he had lived in for over ten years, had been built by a British civil servant in 1910 and was situated on a sizeable lot on Ahlone Road on the western side of Yangon. The Thailand and Indonesia Embassies were but a few blocks away. A tall brick wall encrusted with bougainvillea and vines enclosed the property, and access was gained through one of two wrought-iron gates on either end of a circular drive. The two-story house was actually modest in size, with four bedrooms on the second floor, and only the study, living room, dining room, and kitchen on the ground floor. A garage in back, which had once been a stable, contained second-floor rooms for Chin Li and for the woman who cooked for him.

The dining room was not as elegant as it could have been. Finely grained teak, more than plentiful at that time in Burma, had been fitted as wainscoting and topped with a heavily textured wallpaper. The paper was now faded badly, and the sheen had disappeared from the teak paneling. In Yangon, or anywhere in Myanmar, it was very difficult to find qualified craftsmen to make necessary repairs.

The table, made of walnut and capable of seating twelve people, was covered with a linen tablecloth to hide the mars and scratches in its surface. Places were set for eight, and the dinnerware was at least presentable. Ba Thun had purchased it in Bangkok.

He checked the layout of the silver and glassware at each place, then nodded his approval to Chin Li. His steward showed him the wine he had chosen, a chardonnay, and Ba Thun agreed with the choice. He knew next to nothing about wines.

From the kitchen, he detected the slight aroma of seafood. They were having a light lunch, a salad with shrimp and lobster.

"I believe a dash of the air deodorant would improve the air."

"Of course, Minister."

He wandered back to the living room and stared through the big front windows at the yard. It was overgrown with trees and shrubs that were no longer trimmed to the same specifications as the colonial overseers had once demanded. Ba Thun preferred the wilder appearance. The shade provided by the huge old trees cooled the yard, and the breeze drifting through the screens of the open windows and doors was scented and soothing.

As he watched, a white Citroën drove through the northern gate and pulled up before the portico. Behind it was a beige Chevrolet sedan. Both automobiles were at least ten years old. A few newer cars were beginning to appear in the city, but they were rare. Ba Thun's own automobile, provided by the government, was a 1982 Ford station wagon.

When he heard Chin Li open the front door, he straightened his suit jacket and walked to the foyer.

"Ah, Mr. Witherton! I am pleased to see you again!"

GTI compound, Yangon

General Technologies Incorporated (GTI) had arranged to lease an entire block of buildings off Bogyoke Aung San Street in central Yangon. All of the buildings faced in on a central courtyard accessible by three gateways between buildings on the north, west, and south; the courtyard was frequently crowded at night with the vehicles used by project personnel. GTI had devoted a considerable amount of money to rehabilitating the buildings into offices and living quarters for those assigned to the years-long project. GTI policy, which in Myanmar meant Christopher Carson's policy, was to make the employees of the company and its subcontractors as comfortable as possible.

To the inhabitants, the compound was known as the Zoo.

Stephanie Branigan got back to the Zoo at eight o'clock at night. Colonel Mauk had sent them home from Mingaladon Airport in a military staff car.

The four of them—Branigan, Carson, Gilbert, and Oh—got out of the car in front of the administration building, toting their carry-on luggage. There were few people at ground level in the compound at that time of night, but the upper level veranda, which circled the interior, was lit by yellow antimosquito lamps, and in the amber light, she could see quite a few folks, who were sitting outside their apartments taking in the balmy night. The soft voices engaged in conversation carried on the evening air. The dozen bug-zappers spaced around cast blue light and chortled as they consumed their prey.

Oh bid them a good-night and headed across the compound toward his quarters. He still looked shaky, she thought.

Carson said, "How about if the three of us have dinner together? I'd like to have a kind of debriefing."

"Give me an hour, would you, Chris?" Branigan asked. "I'm going to have to find a shovel to get the dirt off."

"Nine o'clock, then."

Hoisting her duffel-bag strap over her shoulder, Branigan walked the half-block to the northeast corner of the compound where her office complex was located. It was closed down for the night, and she used her key to open the main door.

The reception room was tiny, room enough for only three chairs, a couple tables, and a few plants. There was no receptionist. Her office was to the right, and the business office was on the left. The door in the back wall led to a rabbit warren of work spaces reclaimed from a building that had once served as a printing plant. The constricted areas were made bearable by light-colored paint on the walls and good commercial carpet with a tweedy beige woven into brown on the floors. Someone on her staff had framed cartoons and comic strips and hung them on the walls as decoration.

There were two desks in her cramped office—her own and

that of Janice Cooper, who served as secretary to too many people. Branigan stayed only long enough to grab the stack of phone memos on the corner of her desk, then went out and locked the door.

Near the northern portal of the compound, next to the Ultra-Train offices, was a stairway, and she took it to the upper floor. The second flight of the stairs brought her back to a railed deck that faced the courtyard and provided a sun shelter for the ground-level offices. The deck had a roof made of tin, and when it rained, the constant drumming could be soothing or maddening, depending on one's mood. The second floor was subdivided into living units, small but comfortable. According to their ranks, people were assigned to apartments as singles or as roommates of two or three people. On the south end of the compound was a dormitory available to project personnel in town for one reason or another. Most of the people under Branigan's supervision were located at other sites in the country.

As the chief engineer in Myanmar and an assistant vice president for UltraTrain, a subcontractor to General Technologies, Branigan rated an apartment that didn't include a roommate. It was sixty feet down the deck, and she had to dodge rattan chairs and tables and charcoal braziers on metal stands to reach it. She also had to dodge a dozen people who were sitting outside their apartments, drinks in hand, enjoying the balmy breeze. She said hello to all of them, but didn't bother to relate her adventures. The rumors would begin flying by morning, and she'd let Carson handle them.

Unlocking her door, she stepped inside. The red light of the answering machine was blinking, and she let it blink. She was too tired to deal with any minor crises. The more she was faced with answering machines and voice mail, the more she favored the philosophy, "If it's important, they'll call back."

Her apartment had a fair-size living room, a bedroom, a bath, and a kitchenette. Tossing her bag and her purse on the double bed in the bedroom, she crossed to the kitchen and opened the window, which looked over Bogyoke Aung San Street, a main thoroughfare jammed with people, cars, and tuk-tuks, the three-wheeled, motorscooter-engined people movers. It was colorful and bustling, the people constantly on the move. Sometimes, she would sit and watch the scene, trying to compare it to her upbringing in Seattle, but nothing seemed to correspond.

The air started moving a little. She turned on the ceiling fans above the kitchen table and in the center of the living room, then closed the venetian blinds to shut out the people on the deck.

In the bedroom, which also overlooked the street, she stripped off her safari outfit, as she called it, dumped everything in the hamper, and headed for the shower. A half hour with warm water, soap, and shampoo did wonders for her vital signs, though she still felt a little drained by the trip. Its violent end wasn't designed to make her optimistic.

She dressed in a wraparound denim skirt and light-blue blouse, then took her phone memos to the kitchen table and sat down to leaf through them.

Stephanie Branigan did not often wonder how she had come to be a railroad builder in the Union of Myanmar. She had brazenly asked her bosses for the assignment when it came up two months after Richard Branigan, her husband of sixteen years, walked out of their home in Encino for the last time. He was headed for greener pastures with something in strawberry blonde.

She had known it was coming. Richard, a journalist with some decent credentials, had put up with her moves for all of their married lives. First, it was Seattle, her hometown, while she finished her master's degree at the University of Washington. Then it was General Dynamics in Los Angeles, then Grumman where she became immersed in rail technology. When she moved to Martin Marietta and transferred to Colorado, Richard resigned from the *Los Angeles Times* and followed along. Then, finally, the hiring and substantial promotion by UltraTrain.

And back to Los Angeles.

Richard quit the *Denver Post* and found his old position at the *Times* still available.

But he wasn't happy.

And she, apparently, wasn't blond. Branigan's tresses, which she cut short for the tropics and her work, were auburn.

Her transfer out of the United States was a welcome one. The new environment and the heavy workload kept her mind busy with details unrelated to her personal life, and she appreciated it. At thirty-eight, she thought she still had plenty of time for another marriage, if one happened to come along. At the moment, she wasn't looking for it, and she certainly didn't miss it.

She decided there was nothing too pressing among the phone memos, and after one more glance at the answering machine, feeling a bit guilty about not listening to the twelve messages on it, grabbed her purse and let herself out of the apartment. Several people invited her to have a drink, but she begged off and made her way across the compound to the cafeteria.

Carson had done well with his cafeteria, which she used often. Because of her frenetic schedule, she didn't keep much more than eggs, milk, lettuce, and tomatoes in the small refrigerator of her kitchen. It was easier to walk to the cafeteria, which was open from six in the morning until ten at night. The menu had a few choices each from Burmese, Thai, Chinese, and American entrees. From time to time, Mexican and Italian dishes were on special, but the primarily Burmese kitchen staff wasn't yet totally qualified on those recipes, though they thought they were.

Carson and Gilbert were already there, seated at a round table near an open window. About twenty late diners were scattered around the room. Half-a-dozen ceiling fans in the dining area kept the warm air on the move.

She approached the table, waving the two of them back into their seats as they started to stand. Both of them had had mothers who ingrained them with old chivalries, she assumed, but she was too tired to appreciate it.

One of them had gotten her a drink, pale amber surrounding welcome ice cubes, and she sat down to taste it. Scotch.

"Good," she said. "Thanks, someone."

"You look like the kid next door again," Jack Gilbert said.

"How are you holding up?" Carson asked.

"You mean the gunfight at the O.K. Corral? I'm all right."

"Sure?"

"I couldn't get particularly upset by the dead men. They were shooting at us, after all. Maybe that's a cold reaction."

"Good enough, under the circumstances."

"I know it's a tough country. My objective was to melt into the ground while you guys played Wyatt Earp. How *did* you learn that role, Chris?"

"Cowboys and Indians in the backyard."

She doubted that. She knew he was from somewhere in Iowa and had attended the University of Iowa as well as the Wharton School of Business. The same blurb she'd read reported that he had been with GM before moving to GTI. He had told Mauk he'd been in the army reserves, but she didn't know about that. He had probably learned to fly helicopters in the army, since she knew he flew them.

He was young for the responsibilities he held, about four years older than she was. Ash-blond hair combed straight back and deep sea-blue eyes. She guessed him at just short of six feet and the weight was about right for his build. There were flat planes in his cheeks, which reflected the overhead light in different directions. His nose was slightly bent, and she'd have figured it for a football injury. Some kind of athletic injury.

Gilbert said, "Those two soldiers I was with wouldn't give me a gun. I was disappointed, but not much. Oh and I spent our time staring at the radiator of the truck."

"About as much fun as a close examination of a hubcap, I expect," she told him.

Gilbert was her age. He had deeply tanned skin, which didn't set off his chestnut-brown hair and brown eyes very much. He reminded her of a California beach bum, but she knew he had an engineering degree from the University of Denver. His Oklahoma rearing showed up in his accent. His title with GTI was director of technology acquisition, but in Myanmar, he was acting as Carson's assistant. He had asked her out a couple times, but she had put him off. Instinct told her he was a womanizer with a long list of experiences.

She turned her attention back to Carson, who was lounging back in his chair, his glass held lightly in both hands. From the slant of his mouth, she thought he had found the whole affair slightly amusing, as if he had spent the morning in a video arcade. Maybe it was supposed to be like that, but she didn't think so.

"You *are* in the reserves?"

"Was," he corrected.

"Chris was a hotdog chopper pilot in the Persian Gulf thing," Gilbert volunteered.

She raised an eyebrow.

"My aviation company got called up for Saddam's festivities," Carson said. "Lots of stand in line and wait. What I was more interested in was what you two thought of today's episode."

"In what way?" she asked.

"How about motives?"

"Motives? A bandit's a bandit. Isn't he? Or they?"

"Sometimes. What were they after?"

"Our valuables?" Gilbert asked.

"They skipped the truck that passed us. It probably had a more valuable cargo than our wallets."

Branigan thought about that, then said, "And they let the first Land Rover go by, then picked on us."

"You think you were targeted, Chris?" Gilbert asked. His tone said he was a bit skeptical.

"Seems to me," Carson said, "that someone was specifically singled out. Maybe it was Colonel Mauk."

"This is scary," Branigan said.

"Mauk may have it figured out, but he hasn't said anything

to me. Until we know more, I think we ought to tell all of our people to be overly cautious. Even when they're not traveling."

"I'll get a memo out in the morning," Gilbert said.

"And I will, too," Branigan told him.

"We've always known that there are some factions who don't like having us in the country, even with the jobs and money we're spreading around. Maybe we've just been lucky so far, but let's not get complacent now."

Branigan had been thinking of the attack as a random one, peasants with guns after *kyat*. The thought that someone might want her dead, simply because she was an American, was chilling.

She was afraid she'd spend the rest of her tour looking over her shoulder.

"I'll pose as a dapper waiter," Gilbert offered. "What can I bring you? The blackboard says that enchiladas and tacos are on tap."

Branigan decided she wasn't very hungry.

Myanmar army barracks, Yangon

Colonel Lon Mauk had eaten a quick meal in the officers' mess, then returned to his headquarters administration building to find his adjutant, Maj. Tawn Yin May, waiting for him.

Yin May had become too comfortable with his posting in the capital. His jowls sagged, and his large eyes appeared depressed in his face. His stomach pressed hard against his khaki uniform shirt, straining the buttons. With his small stance, the effect was ludicrous, Mauk thought, though he refrained from saying anything. Yin May was loyal to him, and Mauk would do nothing to place stress on their relationship.

Mauk's office was stark. Only a desk and chair, two straight-backed chairs in front of the desk, and two filing cabinets rested on the worn beige linoleum. The walls were bare—not one memento from his days as an infantry officer, then as a military policeman was displayed. Through the window behind his desk, aircraft could be seen taking off or landing at Mingaladon Airport, also the headquarters for the Union of Myanmar Air Force. The airport was four kilometers distant on Prome Road.

The old army post dated from the 1920s, most of the old barracks and administration buildings constructed of red brick with white-trimmed windows and doors. The windows stuck in their sashes, and the doors frequently displayed gaps between the doors and the jambs. With the onset of the project, Mauk had been assigned one building on the post. His administrative functions were carried out on the ground floor, and living quarters for himself and the small contingent of men he had in the city were provided on the top floor. Most of his command was spread throughout the country, dependent upon where the contractors had a need for security.

Yin May followed him into the office, and Mauk waved him to one of the visitor chairs as he walked around his desk and sat down. A stack of memos was centered on his green blotter, and he pushed them aside.

"Well, Major?"

"There was no identification on either of the dead men or the prisoner. Despite some persuasion, the prisoner refuses to give us his name."

"You took his picture?"

"Yes. We showed it to other prisoners, two of whom suggest that he is known as the Boar and works for Daw Tan."

Mauk placed his elbows on his desk and interlaced his fingers, letting his thumbs battle each other as he thought. Daw Tan was a warlord with a relatively large organization in the northern sector of Shan State. In addition to his interest in controlling his own territory of about one thousand square kilometers, Tan had connections with Khim Nol, who headed one of the larger opium-processing systems. Both Tan and Nol had well-bribed ears in many niches of the military and civil services. Chieftains Shwe and Kaing were included in the social structure of Shan State.

For years, the ruling government had coexisted rather peacefully with the organizations of all four chieftains. Why would Daw Tan seek to change that balance at this point in time?

"You are certain of this information?" he asked.

"The prisoners were not pressured in any way, Colonel. I do not think they would lie."

Mauk dropped his hands to the blotter. "It would mean that Tan has made a change in his attitude toward the government."

"How so?" Yin May asked.

"This was not an accidental event, Major. Someone knew the route we would follow, and that route was not determined until the night before, when we stayed in Myitkyina. At dinner, Carson persuaded me to leave the main road to Banmo and follow the track along the river. He wished to talk to peasants along the way."

"Could we devise a list of those who knew of the change?"

"It would be difficult," Mauk said. "I radioed the alteration in itinerary to headquarters last night. Anyone could have been listening to the conversation, at either end, or through monitoring the frequency."

Yin May rubbed his heavy jaw with a plump hand. "What would Tan have to gain?"

"By killing me? Or by killing the engineers?"

"Either," the major said.

"We have not harassed the man, and I do not believe he would endanger his position by killing me. I assume he was after Carson."

"Could his men have been operating alone?"

"As an outside contract?" Mauk asked. "It is possible, I suppose, though unlikely. Tan rules with an iron hand."

"Yes. I will put the question to our informants."

"Do that. And increase the level of awareness with the guard contingent commanders. We do not want to lose any of the Americans or Europeans while they are our responsibility."

When the Modernization Proclamation had gone into effect, Lon Mauk had been detached from his police duties and assigned to Minister U Ba Thun's office as director of security for the foreign contractors. He had had to rob, steal, and cajole detachments of soldiers from regular army units in order to mount a sufficient network of protection for the construction sites. Currently, there were sixty-seven such sites throughout the country, and each had a minimum of three soldiers performing sentinel duties. The average guard unit had fifteen men assigned to it. Mauk's total personnel strength was close to one thousand men, and that had other commanders demonstrating either resentment or some degree of fear.

He had been careful to keep his activities, in the eyes of anyone who counted, completely overt and free of corruption. Most of the field officers now appeared to accept his assignment for what it was.

"Should we also increase the surveillance at the General Technologies compound?" Yin May asked.

"We have six men assigned now?"

"Yes."

Christopher Carson did not know that his compound was watched.

"Use twelve men," he decided.

The major nodded, but did not take notes. He had a phenomenal memory, another reason why Mauk appreciated him.

"And the next time you are in the orderly room," Mauk said, "you might mention that I am attempting to meet with Daw Tan."

The two of them knew that the company clerk Corporal Syi was on Daw Tan's payroll. It was more convenient to use the noncom as a communications conduit than to arrest him.

"You will talk to him?"

"Who knows?" Mauk said. "He might well want me dead. I will give him the chance. In any event, meeting with Tan is preferable to reporting this incident to the minister."

THREE

Near Man Na-su, Shan State

Daw Tan was not the richest man in the province, but he arguably qualified as the ugliest. His face had been battered so many times in the fifty years it had taken him to be born, survive puberty, and outwit and outfight his way to prominence that it was a multicolored mass of lumps, bumps, and depressions; the scars ran deep. Three almost evenly spaced gouges ran from high on his right forehead to just below his right ear. They were an awful purple and lavender against his mottled brown skin, and they had been deliberately inflicted by a rival when he was twenty-five years old. The rival was now dead, dying over a period of sixteen hours at Daw Tan's hand.

Tan was now fifty years old, but the scar tissue above the brow of his left eye was still a discolored landmark on his forehead. He did not have a right eye, and he did not disguise the fact. The skin had grown together over the empty socket. There were other scars—knife, bullet, and club—on his cheeks and left ear, but the harelip was one feature with which he had been born. His dark brown hair was limp and long, worn in a ponytail at the back of his head, but still hanging well below his ears. He was relatively tall, but lean, as if he had never had enough to eat. When he did eat, he wolfed his food as he had always done, a habit born of the time when his next meal was not a certainty.

The difference now, of course, was that he *was* rich. Only

two or three others in Shan State could boast of more *kyats, bahts,* dollars, francs, pounds, or deutsche marks parked profitably in banks from Bangkok to Hong Kong to Switzerland. He was a millionaire many times over, but he only thought of his wealth as a means to buy the power that his ragged and private army could not secure for him. His only aim in life was to secure his fiefdom.

His standard of living, while considerably better than that of his youth, was not particularly remarkable. Six kilometers from Man Na-su, he had built a conglomeration of sheds, huts, and houses deep in the forest. Though the airstrip was noticeable, the houses were not visible from the air because of the dense canopy of the forest. There were nineteen structures, ranging in purpose from garages to dormitories to single units for his chief lieutenants to his own residence.

Tan's house had three sleeping rooms, a Western-style bathroom of which he was most proud, and a huge communal room furnished with six couches, a dozen matching easy chairs, a large round table, and his desk. There was no kitchen, since Tan and his young wife of twelve years took their meals in the centralized dining hut of his personal village. The walls of the house were constructed of native stone and mortar, thick enough to insulate against the extremes of temperature, and the roof which extended over the wide front veranda was thatched. Far back in the woods, to diminish the sound, was a small shed containing two diesel generators—one a backup—which provided electricity for lights, refrigeration, and communications.

One of Tan's principal assets, which kept him far ahead of his contemporaries, was his communications system. He had a microwave-relay antenna which tapped him into the antiquated and frequently inoperative Myanmar telephone system, but far more important was his UHF radio network. From his powerful base station, he could reach the men who commanded his bands of soldiers almost anywhere in northern Myanmar. He had paid nearly a half-million dollars American for his electronics in order to obtain radios with uniquely coded scramblers incorporated within them. Needless to say, there was no one in his retinue who knew how to maintain them, and Tan paid a hefty annual retainer to a man in Bangkok who traveled to Man Na-su quarterly to make needed repairs.

He had also paid for the schooling for the four of his men who operated the base station twenty-four hours a day. They could handle minor problems, and with their separate living quarters and their slightly better salaries, they commanded a special status within the Daw Tan army.

It was one of his communications specialists who made the intercom buzz in the middle of the night. It buzzed angrily three times before Tan's wife shook him awake and told him.

Irritated, he rolled over and stood up from the mattress, which rested directly on the polished wood floor. He plodded naked through the large room, lit only by the cold moon shining through the large windows, to his desk. There were three instruments on his desk: the telephone, the intercom, and a radio repeater.

He mashed the button on the intercom.

"What do you want?"

"I am sorry to awaken you, Chief Tan, but the Razor wishes to speak to you on the telephone."

Without replying, Tan picked up the telephone and held it to his right ear. He did not hear well through the left ear.

"Yes?" he said. On the telephone, no names were ever used.

"It is I," the Razor said. "I am calling from Bhamo."

Like Tan, the Razor preferred the old names. Bhamo was now Banmo to the new regime in Rangoon.

The connection was terrible. Static rattled in the background, and the voice ebbed and flowed in volume.

"Where is your radio?"

"It was broken."

Another one to fix.

"Report."

"The event was unsuccessful."

Tan had already guessed that. There had been no mention of an attack on the radio news that evening.

"How unsuccessful?"

"Two of our own are terminated, and the Boar has been taken."

"Alive?"

"At last sighting."

"Will you have another opportunity?" Tan asked.

"Not immediately. He left the area by helicopter."

Tan swore to himself while thinking of the next step. "Go to the house in Bhamo and get another radio, then go to the capital. Complete your assignment as soon as possible."

"I will do that," the Razor said. "Should I also take care of the loose end?"

The man who had been captured. The Boar. He was a good man, but he was in the wrong hands.

"Do that, also," Tan said and hung up.

He did not go back to bed immediately. He sat on the softly cushioned cool leather of his desk chair and lit a cigarette.

He regretted the missed chance, but he would not second-guess the Razor. The man was Tan's sharpest tool, and if the mission failed, it was not for lack of courage or purpose. Tan saw the Razor as a perfect imitation of himself in his younger days. He could have been a son. The Razor, in truth, might have been his son. The assassin had come to him, disenchanted with his mother, Nito Kaing, when Kaing executed her husband, the man the Razor perceived as his father. Over twenty years before, Tan and Nito Kaing had engaged in several assignations, outside of her husband's knowledge.

Anything was possible.

He never dwelt on it for long, but occasionally, Tan regretted that he did not know more about the Razor's genealogy. Nito Kaing had never discussed it with him.

He also regretted the failed attack because the target was an ideal symbol of the change the government was forcing on Tan's life and country. For centuries, his people—known as the

Shan, but related to the Tai group—had managed to fulfill their destinies without interference from outsiders. He and his fellow chieftains did not need a government that dictated the way they must rule or with whom they must do business. Tan did not wish to have his authority undermined by the introduction of his people to Western ways and commodities. What could Coca-Cola or sliced bread do for him?

Nothing.

At these times of introspection, Tan ignored his use of electricity and radios and Toyota Pathfinders. He could be selective about those things that furthered his business and those which did not.

Daw Tan knew that he was not alone in his resistance to the changes Rangoon would have them make in their lives. It might mean the formation of coalitions of power, but there were those in the hills, and even in Rangoon, who saw telephones and railroads and helicopters as swords of their own destruction.

He would not give in to it, and he was powerful enough, with some minor assistance, to prevent it.

He knew this to be true.

City Hall, Yangon

U Ba Thun's office was located in City Hall on the corner of Sule Pagoda Road and Maha Bandoola Street. The building lionized the architecture of the British colonial years, but provided him with elegant, if aged, quarters for his operations. Next to his office was a large conference room, frequently utilized by the SLORC for short meetings.

As this was to be.

The seven men sat around the single table, and though they each were filled with their own hopes and desires, there was not much to distinguish one from the other in age or politics.

They were all within five years of Ba Thun's own sixty-two years, and he had known each of them for most of his life, their earliest contacts made in the army or the air force. Had he had brothers of his own, he knew that they would be exactly like these men. There was a singleness in the goals they set for themselves and for their nation that transcended mere discussion. They all knew what was important, though each held distinct views about how the end might be achieved. From time to time, vociferous arguments might arise, but these were generally settled in consensus.

And unfortunately, they had all come to know what was necessary.

When they had been young and naive officers, the aims had been all too clear. To their credit, they had achieved the first objective, control of the country. To their dismay, they had learned late in life that Myanmar did not stand on its own. It was part, and an amazingly small part, of a global community. Their continued existence within that community had dictated an adjustment in their goals, and Ba Thun thought that most of them had accepted the requirement well. Some, like the interior minister and the cultural minister, resisted change and debated merits with seemingly endless resolve. So far, they had been outvoted.

The highly polished surface of the oak table held seven glasses for the three tall pitchers of ice tea, seven ruled notepads, and seven ballpoint pens. Rarely did any of them take notes.

The premier said, "Tell us of this incident."

Ba Thun related what Colonel Mauk had told him of the attack.

"And Mauk feels that it was directed at someone in particular?" the minister of the interior asked.

"Yes. His conviction on that point seems sincere. He suggested the target would be himself or Mr. Carson, though he would not be pinned down further."

"Why Mauk? As the target?"

"In his role as commander of security for the Modernization Proclamation, he does represent a distinctly different role for the army," Ba Thun said. "The chieftains may well think of his activities as directed at them. Never before has the army spearheaded a suppression of the warlords."

"There have been civil wars," the premier said.

"Yes, but once we pushed the dissidents back into their territories, we abandoned the battle. For the first time, we are capturing disputed lands in the guise of transportation and communications corridors, then holding onto them."

"Perhaps we should not," the minister for the treasury suggested.

"No," the premier decided for them. "If we allow that to happen, all that we hope to accomplish will be for naught. In our agreement with the chieftains, we have acknowledged their autonomies in their particular regions, and they have granted to us the control of communications and transportation centers, as well as the corridors which connect them. If we forego that right, what we are building will be destroyed through theft and neglect within a year."

Ba Thun agreed with him aloud.

"Mauk thinks that Daw Tan is behind this?" the minister for culture asked.

"He does."

"What is Tan's objection?" the minister of the interior asked. "Of all the chieftains, he is least affected."

Daw Tan controlled a large part of northern Shan State. Two other tribal chieftains had control of plateau country in the southern and western parts of the state, some of it within the area known as the Golden Triangle, which also slipped into Thailand and Laos. All three of the warlords maintained a relationship with Khim Nol, who might have been considered as the supreme chieftain in the state, headquartered in Keng Tung, the supposed capital city of the Golden Triangle. Nol's fabulous wealth was based on the opium trade, of course, and Tan and the others all had a piece of that flow of money.

In southern Shan State, the existing national railroad went only to the state capital in the southwestern sector, Taunggyi. It was to be extended across the state to Keng Tung, some forty kilometers short of the Chinese border. In the northern part of the state, in Daw Tan's dominion, the existing railroad connected Mandalay with Kyaukme and Lashio. In addition to the upgrading of that railroad, new lines were to be constructed northward to the silver mines at Namtu and northward, along the old Burma Road, from Lashio to the Chinese border. The new construction affected only the northern edge of Daw Tan's empire.

"Daw Tan," the treasury minister said, "is afraid of the encroachment of civilization."

"And he has a point," the cultural minister added. "Not all that modernization brings us is a godsend. Not too long ago, I might remind you, we all felt as Tan continues to feel."

"Then, too," Ba Thun added, "relinquishing those corridors the premier speaks of can only be seen as a personal attack upon their holdings and their persons, if not by the populace, then by the chieftains themselves. It is a loss of face."

"Nevertheless," the premier said, "we have agreed that the high-speed trains will give our people greater access to markets and trade, as well as to education. Increased national communication will, in the long term, result in a greater national unity and cohesiveness. The consequences for commerce and improving gross national product are obvious. I do not see us compromising further with the likes of Daw Tan."

U Ba Thun did not fully agree with that position. The warlords were necessary for the near future, for they could control the population. In the greater span of time, say ten or fifteen years, their power would erode out of existence, leaving full governance to the central administration, however that might shape itself over time. A hard-line stance taken against the warlords at this time would be foolhardy. The agreements between the government and the chieftains, never written down, were delicate and traditional. Each side had expectations about their treatment.

"Daw Tan should be eliminated," the premier said. "He may serve as an example to the others."

"Perhaps easier said than done," Ba Thun said.

"We have but to arrange a meeting with him."

Publicly, the government never acknowledged the chieftains in any manner; they were outside the law. In practice, however, accommodations with them were frequently negotiated.

"Before we adopt a final resolution," Ba Thun said, "let me speak with him. Perhaps reason can prevail."

The premier scanned the faces at the table and found enough positive nods. "Very well. Be certain he knows that he may no longer try our patience."

"I will."

"Now, for the immediate response. Are we to increase the level of protection for the foreigners?"

"I am reluctant to provide additional army units to Mauk," the interior minister said. "Already, he commands a large force, and loyalties may be shifting."

Loyalties among military units were watched carefully. It would not do for the balance of power to tip in favor of any one particular unit.

"Has Mauk requested more troops?" the premier asked.

"Fifty men, yes," Ba Thun replied, "but not as added protection for the contractors. They are to be assigned to permanent guard duties, and in that respect, he does have a rationale. As more installations are completed, and he is forced to protect them, his troop strength is stretched thin."

Again, the premier surveyed the men around the table, then said, "Give him the fifty men for facilities duty. For the time being, the contractors will have to take care of themselves."

GTI compound, Yangon

Carson's Thursday in General Technologies' administrative offices located in the Zoo was a typical one of meetings, too many telephone calls, and crisis intervention.

His offices on the eastern side of the compound housed

forty-two people, most of them GTI employees and the others representatives of some of the subcontractors on the Myanmar Project. His own subordinates were construction management specialists, auditors, field inspectors, and the typical array of accountants, computer people, and support staff. In addition to the overall management of the Myanmar Project, his department had oversight for GTI's own InstaStructure construction firm, the heavy-equipment division administered through the surface fleet manager, the air-transport section, the microwave systems company, and the personal computer systems division. At various points in the seven-year run of the contract, he would also have control over road-building, pipeline construction, and hopefully, mining companies—all owned by GTI.

The responsibilities were heavy, but Carson relished both the control and the obligation.

The office suite had been rehabilitated from a pottery factory, and while it was a poor second cousin to the GTI headquarters in Palo Alto, California, Carson thought it was comfortable enough. His own office was finished in Southeast Asia—teak floor, tightly woven and colorful rug, bamboo furniture with blue and white cushions. The large window which fronted the compound had its panes opened wide to capture whatever breeze might come by. One wall held a grouping of ten- by thirteen-inch color photos of some of the far-flung construction sites for which he was responsible. A telephone console and a computer rested on the credenza behind his desk. Beside the computer, a half-dozen pictures framed as a collage featured Merilee, his twenty-year-old daughter who was a junior at Rice University. She had his blond-and-blue-eyed fair coloring and her mother's rounded facial features. Whenever he studied the pictures long enough, he saw Marian in them, and the old aches and guilts rose in his throat.

Merilee was on the phone, twelve hours in time away from him.

"It's two o'clock in the morning there," he said. "Aren't you supposed to be in bed?"

He had inelegant and fearful images of just who she might be in bed with. He wasn't ready for her to grow up.

"I'm studying, Dad."

"You could have skipped summer school and come over here, like I suggested. You'd like it."

"I want to graduate in December. I've got things to do," she told him. Again. "Besides, it's too humid where you are."

"And it's not humid In Houston? Baby, you need to travel a little."

He put his hand over the mouthpiece when Becky Johnson, his secretary for the past six years, stuck her head through the doorway from the outer office.

"Marty wants to see you," she said.

"Tell him five minutes."

"And don't forget you've got to be out of here by three."

He gave her a thumb-to-forefinger okay sign and went back to Merilee. "You called for a reason, right?"

"Ah, yeah. My car got a little wrecked."

"What! Are you okay?"

"I wasn't in it, Dad."

His heart came back to normal altitudes. He could imagine her agonizing over the decision to call him. It might explain the timing of the call.

"What's a 'little wrecked,' Merilee?"

"Like, the right side is crunched."

"Front to back?"

"Yeah."

He groaned to himself. Her Prelude was less than two years old.

"How did it happen?"

"Well, see, Jerry had it. . . ."

"Who's Jerry?"

"Jerry? He lives in the apartment next door and his car was in the shop and he had this dentist's appointment—on the other side of town, you know? Where his parents live?—and he got back and there wasn't room in the parking lot and he kind of parked it on the street, but not very close to the curb and . . ."

Carson tried to picture the car parked at the curb, with the *right* side exposed to side-swiping traffic. No doubt there would be tickets involved for improper parking.

After she ran down, he said, "Okay, honey. In the morning, you take it out to the adjustor and get it appraised. Tell Jerry he's going to be responsible for the deductible and any tickets."

"But, Dad . . ."

He knew what was coming.

". . . it's going to take a week to fix it. How am I going to get around?"

"Fix the tire on your bike," he suggested. "Or borrow Jerry's car."

Martin Prather came into his office while he was saying his goodbyes. Prather was a studious-appearing man, thick glasses magnifying his hazel eyes, and a receding widow's peak rapidly giving into baldness. He was a perfectionist and coldly serious, exactly the kind of man Carson wanted as his chief auditor and director of disbursements.

Pulling one of the straight chairs up to the edge of the desk, Prather sat down opposite Carson and plopped a heavy file folder on the desk.

He tapped it with the slim fingers of his right hand and said, "Delbert Creighton."

"Creighton? What now?"

"Baksheesh, I think. On his latest statement, he billed us forty-five hundred in the contingency fund, but I don't see anything to back it up. He's paying off someone."

General Technologies, in the person of the president and chief executive officer, Dexter Abrams, had been right up front with the State Law and Order Restoration Committee when they were negotiating the contract. Despite a centuries-old custom of everyone in the nation—from customs officers to high-ranking government officials—soliciting bribes from everyone in sight, GTI would not pay bribes unless the SLORC wanted to double the amount of the contract.

At twenty-one billion dollars American over a seven-year period, the contract was rich enough for the committee, and it opted to begin reforming the mores of its employees instead. In spite of a great deal of resentment, GTI's policy of no bribes had become accepted in most of the country, though it had taken nearly a year for the reality to set in.

For its money, General Technologies served as the general contractor in upgrading the infrastructure of the country. GTI was installing most of the electronics, such as microwave relay, and satellite-uplink and -downlink technology. All of the bureaucracy was undergoing transformation to the current century as computer systems were emplaced and governmental employees submitted themselves to GTI-managed educational seminars. GTI also worked closely with the contractor Hypai Industries, which was engaged in replacing the telephonic systems in the major cities. Del Creighton, of Hygienic Systems, Inc., was a subcontractor to GTI, who was charged with upgrading the sewer systems and sewage plants in Yangon, Mandalay, Taunggyi, Myingyan, Pakokku, Bassein, Prome, Pegu, Thaton, Moulmein, Henzada, and Tavoy, all cities of one hundred thousand or greater population.

"I'm not going to start questioning your judgments now, Marty. Cut them a check less the amount you're questioning. Creighton can take it out of his salary if he wants his budget to balance."

"I'll write you a memo-for-file to that effect, Chris."

"Damn. I wish these people would adhere to the party line. Every time we seem to be on track, someone like Creighton screws up. I'll chew his ass the next time I see him."

"It could be something else," Prather said, "but I doubt it."

"It's okay, Marty. Anything else pressing right now?"

"Oh, there's always a few suppliers trying to gouge the subs, but we're cutting them off as fast as we catch them. It's been running pretty smoothly the last couple weeks, so that's scary."

Becky Johnson rapped on the door frame. "Airport, boss."

"I know, Becky. I'm going."

Prather left while Carson shut down his computer and found his carry-on bag behind the office door. He always kept a bag packed, since he never knew when he'd be called out for one emergency or another.

In the outer office, which was verdant with Johnson's tropical plants hanging from the ceiling and stacked on most horizontal surfaces, he told her, "I should be back by tomorrow afternoon. Please don't call me."

"Not unless it's a world-class, invasion-quality snafu."

"Those, I know you can handle."

She was expert at juggling a dozen incoming telephone calls while holding off seven or eight irate people at the same time. She was thirty years old, pert and clear-eyed, and she hadn't wanted to come to Myanmar with him, but Carson had gotten her husband a job with Educorp, the GTI subsidiary responsible for training the Burmese citizens who would eventually take over the systems being installed all over the country.

As he headed for the door, she said, "Hey, boss! Don't fly too low or get shot at, huh?"

"Promise," he told her.

The Strand Hotel, Yangon

The hotel had been built in 1901 and had once been owned by the Sarkie Brothers, who had also owned the Raffles in Singapore and the Eastern & Oriental in Penang, and had been regarded as one of the finest hotels in the world. Before it fully decayed in 1991, Dutch-Indonesian hotel magnate Adriaan Zecha entered into a thirty-six-million-dollar deal with the Myanmar government and restored the grand old hotel to five-star elegance. The Victorian bathtubs and open-cage elevators disappeared, along with the 1936 annex, which was replaced by an eight-story addition.

The hushed and richly furnished lobby was one of Hyun Oh's favorite places in the city, and he often met with others in the lobby or in the lounge. He had even stayed in one of the luxurious rooms his first night in Yangon. When Mr. Pai, his superior, learned of it, he had been ordered to leave immediately. The company was not paying six hundred dollars American a night for Oh to live like a king.

Now, he lived in a one-bedroom apartment at the General Technologies compound, which was considerably better than the four-room flat in Pusan in which he had grown up with three sisters, his parents, and his maternal grandmother. Still, he liked to come to the Strand and feel what it would be like to have mountains of money. The menu had been restored to its original magnificence, also, and every couple of months, Oh made reservations and indulged in a sumptuous meal.

Hyun Oh, though he wished to one day have mountains of money, was less than well compensated by Hypai Industries. Certainly, his income was not comparable to that of other foreign executives. He imagined that Christopher Carson, Stephanie Branigan, or Delbert Creighton of Hygienic Systems made two or three times the salary Hypai afforded him.

And this was despite the fact that he was married to a niece of Mr. Pai. In fact, he was hampered by that relationship. Two thirds of his salary was taken from him each payday and delivered straight to his wife. He could barely afford the extensive wardrobe he maintained, nor the personal Toyota Celica he drove around Yangon, both of which were absolutely necessary to the fulfillment of his duties. In the hierarchy of the company, he was normally the director of material sources; for the Myanmar contract, he had been assigned as project director. He knew little of telephone technology, but he was an excellent administrator. Despite this, the magnificent job title was his only reward. Hypai Industries did so well for itself because it did so poorly for its employees.

Oh was thirty-nine years old and handsome enough to attract many women. His straight black hair was trimmed full on top and carefully edged over the ears and across the back of his neck. His eyes were alert and sincere; he was a good listener, able to keep his full attention directed to whomever his conversant might be. He was quick to smile, as he did to a pretty Asian woman who glanced his way as he crossed the lobby.

Unfortunately, Oh was married and had two children. His family had remained in Seoul to be near Mei's elderly mother and to consume most of his salary. Quarterly, he was able to spend a few days with them, and that renewed his faith and his love for Mei. Once he was back in Yangon, however, he felt his resolve slipping with each day that passed. There were many beautiful women about, seemingly receptive to his smile, and he found it more and more difficult to resist them. Having to account, not only to Mr. Pai, but also to Mei, for the way in which he spent his money helped to restrain him.

In the lounge, he found a table near the door and ordered coffee. Oh did not drink many intoxicating beverages. He liked to feel that he had control of himself.

Mr. Gyi arrived precisely at three-thirty.

Oh stood up to greet him, then signaled for more coffee.

Gyi was an elderly man, a Burmese merchant of jade and other gems. He was, Oh thought, quite wealthy, a necessary ingredient of the pact Oh was attempting to assemble.

Hypai Industries was installing state-of-the-art telephone exchanges in the major cities, and those systems would become the property of the government—the Union of Myanmar Telephone Company. For the outlying areas, however, the government had agreed with Hypai Industries' reasoning. A limited amount of free enterprise was to be tolerated in the telephone system, and syndicates would be allowed to form for the express purpose of extending the system into remote areas. Fourteen syndicates would be licensed, and none could have cross-ownership. It was Hyun Oh's secondary job to facilitate the funding of the syndicates so that they could buy their equipment from Hypai Industries.

"I trust that you have had a fruitful day, Mr. Gyi."

The man dipped his head and shrugged at the same time. "My day has been uneventful, Mr. Oh."

"Were you able to speak with your friends?"

"I was. But let us enjoy our coffee, first."

It was ever the same. Oh had been courting Mr. Gyi for over two months, but Mr. Gyi and his Burmese friends were in no hurry. It took forever to overcome the small courtesies and get to the business at hand.

He smiled at his guest and said, "Of course."

Mingaladon Airport, Yangon

Jack Gilbert enjoyed the hell out of life.

Except when people were shooting at him, of course. That had never happened to him before, and he was still shaken by the incident. He wasn't the kind to confide his fears in anyone else, so he had spent the last twenty-four hours brooding over it.

He had been around the world a couple times, and he had found himself in some iffy parts of town in London, Paris, Singapore, all places where the threat of a mugging was very real. In those situations, he had always taken care to be extra alert, aware of the people around him, ready to bolt and run. In Yangon and some of the other cities and towns of the Union of Myanmar, where he knew some strange people carried guns and liked to use them, Gilbert had maintained that awareness.

Still, the actuality had come as a shock. He had never *really* thought anyone would try to kill him. Reviewing his actions now, he thought he might have been braver, though he didn't quite know how he'd have accomplished it. He envied Carson his seemingly natural instinct to take action.

Gilbert genuinely liked Chris Carson. They had worked together for four years, beginning in Palo Alto on the Ruby Star Project, and he was gratified that Carson had selected him for the Myanmar job. Much of what he was doing was a true challenge, and Gilbert liked challenges as much as he liked women, many of whom he had loved, and none of whom he had married.

The Myanmar Modernization Project had imported a lot of women, a very international cast, and Gilbert had dated quite a few of them. He had even made a lighthearted pass at Stephanie Branigan, which she had deftly deflected. She seemed to have little interest in men, much less one like Gilbert, whom she might have suspected as being something of a gadabout. He did like the trial of a new female target.

For example, he thought, he might love the young woman two people ahead of him in the customs line. He would probably have to meet her first.

He kept his eyes on her back, peering around the man and woman in front of him; as the line shuffled forward, Gilbert kicked his battered duffel bag along the floor every time the Asian man ahead of him bent over to move his four suitcases. One of the things he couldn't understand about life was how a trip to anywhere in the world required four suitcases.

The woman had one suitcase and an oversize purse. That was a check mark in the plus column, right there.

She was blond, the smooth cascade of her hair reaching almost to her shoulders before it flipped outward. She was five or six inches shorter than his five ten. There was a nice hourglass configuration to the pale yellow linen dress she wore. When he got a glimpse of her left calf below the hem of the dress, his instinct was verified. The rest of the leg had to be as good.

When the man ahead of him lifted his bags to the table for inspection, she got away from him, moving smoothly down the linoleum floor towing her hardside suitcase on its built-in wheels.

He watched the customs inspector rifle through the man's luggage, converting neatly folded clothing into heaps of flannel and linen and cotton. When the inspector spoke, it was with a gruff barking brevity.

Gilbert had his left hand in his pocket, gripping a fifty-*kyat* bill, just in case. While he waited, he scanned the crowd around the customs tables and spotted a Myanmar army officer. The man was watching the customs operations carefully, and Gilbert released the bill in his pocket and withdrew his hand.

Sometimes, one got away with not having to augment the customs inspector's salary. The presence of the army officer would explain the inspector's short temper and beleaguered manner.

When it was his turn, Gilbert tossed his duffel bag on the table and unzipped it. He had beat the inspector at his own game, stuffing the bag haphazardly instead of wasting his time folding and packing.

The inspector peered into the bag and frowned.

Gilbert smiled.

The man poked around, took a close look at the shaving kit and can of shaving cream, then nodded his reluctant approval.

Gilbert zipped the bag and headed down the concourse to his gate.

The young lady was standing at the desk, waiting for her seat assignment. Gilbert got close enough to see the fine curve of her cheek; a pert, tip-tilted nose; and the seat number, B-14.

Through the window overlooking the tarmac, he saw that his plane was a Fokker-VFW F-27 Friendship. Myanmar Airways had no doubt picked it up secondhand from a more progressive airline.

He waited patiently, and his smile and request got him the seat next to the blonde.

On board the airplane, he stuffed his bag in the overhead compartment, then settled into the somewhat-worn upholstery of the seat. He got a good look at firm, Cupid's bow lips, barely touched with a cinnamon lipstick. The eyes were a vivid blue. He overcame the urge to check out the rest of her body.

She gave him the barest hint of a noncommittal smile.

He stuck his hand out. "Jack Gilbert."

With apparent reluctance and a definite London accent, she said, "Pamela Steele."

She shook his hand with the merest pressure of her fingers.

"Bangkok your destination or a stopover?"

"Destination," she said.

"What a coincidence."

GTI operations, Mingaladon Airport, Yangon

Carson had taken nearly an hour to fight the traffic with his company Blazer. The four-wheel-drive truck with the big tires tended to intimidate the smaller cars on the road, but the ramshackle one-and-a-half and two-ton trucks and the tuk-tuks didn't care a lot. They darted into whatever spaces appeared in traffic, and if his Chevy happened to be a bit too close, they didn't care about a dinged fender.

The entrance to the airport was torn up by road construction, and he had to wait until a Burmese girl dressed in Western jeans and a halter top—a disgrace to the government, no doubt—dropped her flag and let him drive ahead. He bypassed the parking lots in front of the passenger terminal and took the access road to the general aviation section of the airport.

Mingaladon shared its runways with commercial aviation, general-purpose freighters, and the air force. Carson didn't say so in public, but he didn't think the air force was very impressive. They had a few thirty-year-old Lockheed AT-33s, some Cessna T-37Cs, a few SIAI-Marchetti SF.260MBs, and a dozen Pilatus PC-7 Turbo-Trainers for fixed-wing aircraft. Douglas C-47s—at least sixty years of age—and some Fokker F-27s served as transport. The rotary-winged complement included Kamans, Kawasakis, Aerospatiale Alouettes, and even a few trusty Bell UH-1s. It was a mixed bag to say the least.

On the far right of the general-aviation section, on the east end of the airport, Carson parked in the lot reserved for GTI. He grabbed his bag, locked the truck, and went into the office.

Don Evans, GTI's air fleet manager, notable for his completely bald head and generous, flowing walrus mustache, was behind the counter and looked up as he came in.

"Hey, boss!"

"You have an aircraft for me, Don?"

"The best of the lot, naturally. Ready to go."

If it hadn't been, Becky Johnson would have taken his head off.

Evans let him through the counter and led him through the doorway into the hangar. A couple dozen men were working in the hangar, tackling chores ranging from turbine rebuilding to instrument calibration. A Beech Super King Air and a Bell JetRanger were in the hangar for maintenance. The King Air was their only fixed-wing airplane and, under the terms of the contract, the only aircraft allowed to cross over national borders.

On the apron outside the hangar, five helicopters were parked in a single line. One was a mantis-appearing Sikorsky Skycrane, one of nine GTI had in the country. Two of the helos were Sikorsky heavy-lift S-65s, and two were Aerospatiale/Westland Gazelles, five-seat utility helicopters. General Technologies operated twenty-seven helicopters in support of the Myanmar Project. Don Evans was kept busy scheduling personnel, cargo transport, and heavy-lift missions for GTI and its subcontractors. His air force was considerably more up-to-date and better maintained than that of Myanmar.

They walked out to the first Gazelle.

"You sure you don't want me to send along a pilot with you, Chris?" Evans asked.

"No. It'd just take him off something more important."

"Sleep, maybe. I do have reserve pilots, you know."

There were sixty-four pilots and twenty-five maintenance technicians in Evans's department. They lived in quarters two miles from the airport, and they commanded a large piece of Carson's in-country payroll.

"This is just a skip and a hop," Carson told him.

They went around the chopper as Carson did his preflight inspection, then Evans backed away while Carson pulled open the door and crawled into the right seat. He strapped in, then propped the plastic-coated checklist on the instrument panel and went through it carefully as he fired up the single 590-shaft-horsepower Turbomeca Astazou turboshaft power plant. It caught with a high-pitched whine, and Carson pulled on his headset to dull the sound.

He dialed in Mingaladon Air Control on the primary Nav/Com radio.

"Mingaladon, this is GTI zero-six at Hangar G-4."

"GTI zero-six, Mingaladon. What are your intentions?"

"Zero-six. We will be VFR for Prome."

During the hot season, which ran from the first of March until the beginning of June, the flying weather was almost perfect, and most of their flights were made under Visual Flight Rules (VFR).

"Zero-six, you are cleared for takeoff to three hundred feet AGL, then departure on nine-zero to five miles."

Carson acknowledged the instructions, reading them back, then pulled collective and rose straight off the concrete until he had 300 feet above ground level (AGL). He rotated the nose to dead east, got 90 degrees on his compass, then dipped the nose and picked up speed.

Evans waved to him from the ground as Carson shot away from the hangars.

Five miles east of the airport, Carson got clearance to duck under inbound traffic and head north. When he was well clear of the airfield, he turned to the northwest and, forty miles later, picked up the Irrawaddy River.

The river, which ran almost the full length of the country and was navigable for nearly eight hundred miles, was jammed with traffic. Freighters, barges, small passenger vessels, and fishing boats plied the smooth waters in both directions. All that freight and grain moving by water seemed archaic to Carson. He hoped to see less congestion on the river when Branigan got her trains running. And he hoped that, after a few years, the river would be a hell of a lot less polluted than it currently was.

He stayed to the east side of the river, and using it as his guide, turned north. He held his altitude at two thousand feet.

He was north of the delta region around Yangon, which was some of the most fertile farming area in the world. Since about 1987, when retail-trade barriers were lifted and new fertilizers, seeds, and irrigation methods introduced, the agricultural productivity had increased substantially. Here, in the Lower Burma plain, which reached northward to Prome, Carson saw mostly rice fields. The Upper Burma plain, stretching around Mandalay, was much drier.

Because it was late in the hot season, the greenery below him seemed to have a yellow tinge. On his right, he could see the Pegu Yoma, a mountain range that divided the Irrawaddy River valley from the Sittang River valley, which also ran northward. The mountains weren't high, with peaks around eight hundred feet, but they were rugged and heavily forested, and there were almost no roads running east and west between the rivers.

Prome was 140 miles north of Yangon on the river, and when he had covered half the distance, Carson let the helo drift to the right until he spotted the railroad right of way, which mainly followed the route of the paved Highway 2. Between Prome and Yangon, the roadbed had been widened and the installation of UltraTrain's rail guides was all but complete. There weren't many construction crews left on this stretch of the line.

Most of the crews on this division were now working southward, out of Prome into the delta region on the west side of the Irrawaddy.

A few minutes later, Carson saw the outskirts of Prome, a town of nearly fifty thousand people. He banked to the east and soon found the GTI park, a cluster of modular houses utilized as offices and living quarters for the people working in the area—direct employees and subcontractors' workers. From the blank spaces on the north side of the park, he deduced that many of the trailers had already been moved on to the next construction site. The trailer homes were shifted around the country as necessary, and when the project was completed, they would be contributed to the government to be used for housing those currently in substandard living quarters.

Six yellow-fabric crosses were staked to the ground on the east side of the encampment, two of them occupied by Sikorsky S-65s. Carson chose an empty space and settled the Gazelle onto it.

He cut the power and killed the ignition, and as the rotors wound down, two ground crewmen ran out from the temporary operations shack to tie the helicopter down. Sam Enders appeared in the door to the shack and waited while Carson got his carry-on and crossed the weed-strewn field.

Enders, who had brilliant white hair that was long and left to blow wildly in the wind, was sixty-five years old. His mind was as brilliant as his hair, and he had a bass voice that sounded as if it rumbled up out of a 55-gallon barrel. He was director of microwave systems.

"Hey, Sam!"

"Hi'ya, Chris."

"Have we got a system?"

"I'm going to let you be the judge. Come on."

They climbed into Enders's Chevy pickup, and Enders pulled away from the operations hut, spitting dirt and dust from under the rear wheels. He drove like a West Texas rancher, which was how and where he had grown up.

As he headed into town, Enders said, "We ran the last tests at three o'clock and got greens all the way. You can tell your Mr. Ba Thun he can start pulling down landlines."

"Prome to Yangon."

"And next week, we'll have Mandalay on-line. By the end of August, I expect to have every one of the major burgs hooked up."

As each city was connected to the system, Ba Thun intended

to recover the antiquated copper wiring between cities and re-
cycle it. The idea had been Carson's, but Ba Thun took to it.
He needed every cent he could find.

Fifteen minutes later, near the river, Enders parked in front
of a brand-new concrete-and-steel building finished in pale
green and identified with a simple sign:

MYANMAR NATIONAL TELEPHONE COMPANY
General Technologies, Inc./Hypai Industries—Contractors

The two of them got out of the truck, said hello to the two
guards standing beside the steel entrance door, and went inside
to find twenty people milling around, waiting for them.

Carson knew most of them, and Enders introduced him to
the local officials he hadn't met before.

The whole group took a tour of the building, which was a
copy of others going up in other cities. The structure in Mandalay was five times the size of this one and had been built by
the GTI subsidiary InstaStructure. In Yangon, the major microwave center had been installed on the second floor of the large
Kemendine Railway Station. Hypai Industries had been responsible for the local telephone equipment, and while the major
portion of Prome had been rewired with fiber-optic cable, many
of the local service installations would continue for well over
a year. The priority customers were government and commercial ventures.

Sam Enders's part of this venture was the microwave-relay
equipment and its interface with the Hypai components. When
the entire system was done, all of the major cities would be
linked by microwave, with satellite uplinks located at Mandalay
and Yangon. The satellite-link system was already operative in
Yangon.

Once the cities were on-line, Enders's and Hyun Oh's crews
would branch out to the smaller towns, placing prefabricated
structures—now being built in Yangon—on prepared sites and
installing the electronic equipment. That part of the program

was expected to go relatively quickly, and with its completion, GTI's responsibility would have been met. From those towns into the outlying regions, the syndicates Oh was trying to establish would take over.

Carson was impressed with the neatness and cleanliness of the installation. He hoped it stayed that way, and with the right training of indigenous personnel, there was a fair chance. At the moment, a class of ten students was touring the rows of steel cabinets, watching intently as their instructor pulled open doors and pointed out switching banks and fiber-optic transponders, which were essentially small lasers that generated coded light pulses. The fiber-optic transmissions were far superior to the old electric signals sent down copper wire. A 144-fiber cable could carry forty thousand simultaneous voice and data transmissions, and do it at the speed of light.

Carson spent a few minutes congratulating everyone on the quality of their work, which in fact did impress him.

"But does it work?"

Enders pointed to a telephone on a desk at the front of the room, and Carson went over to sit down.

"About five in the morning in Menlo Park, right, Sam?"

Enders looked at his watch. "That it is, Chris. Shit, you aren't going to get the boss out of bed?"

Menlo Park, California

Dexter Albert Abrams jolted upright in his bed when the phone rang.

He'd had a late night with the board's finance committee, the night before, and hadn't gotten to bed until two in the morning. He had also planned to stay in it until about ten on Thursday morning.

Alicia raised her head from the pillow next to him and mumbled, "You going to get that, Dex?"

"Damn it! Why don't we have a truly unlisted number?"

He leaned over and grabbed the phone from the nightstand.
"H'lo."

"Morning, Dex. Didn't get you up, did I?"

"Chris?"

"Me."

"You son of a bitch!"

"Just imagine this, Dex: Every little syllable I utter bounces from here to Yangon, to the GE ComSat 504, to the San Francisco downlink, to Menlo Park. And not a noticeable lag time in the whole process."

For a fact, Carson sounded like he was next door.

"Where's here?" Abrams asked.

"Menlo Park. Don't you know?"

"I mean you, damn it!"

"Prome."

"No lie? You're on-line?"

"First one," Carson said. "You got the first call."

"I'm overwhelmed," Abrams said, but wasn't. This was exactly the way it was supposed to go. He wouldn't expect less. "And congratulations, by the way."

"I expect a little something in my next pay envelope."

"Very little, I hope. Look, Chris, what kind of progress are you—"

"I do have about twenty people in the room with me here," Carson said.

Which killed that conversation. They chatted a few minutes more, and Abrams hung up.

He was awake now.

And Alicia wasn't.

Slipping out of the bed, Abrams headed for the kitchen to make coffee. Now he'd have to sit up and worry about the damned laser.

FOUR

Prome

The twelve- by forty-foot trailer had two bedrooms and was used for transient personnel. Carson was transient tonight, but he didn't get himself locked into it until after eleven.

The celebratory dinner and speeches with local government and business leaders had run longer than Carson had hoped for, and there was nothing to be done about people who liked to talk. Half of his job amounted to keeping the functionaries happy and therefore amenable to alterations in the program if and when they were necessary, and there were *always* minor changes to be made.

Back in his office, Carson had a master timetable for all of the projects. Currently, the telephone system was eleven days ahead of projections, and the railroad was twenty-one days behind schedule—Branigan was going to have to eat some hefty per-day penalties if she didn't catch up in the next five years. The sanitation systems were four days ahead, and the freshwater pumping and filtration stations—eleven of them—were all but completed. Overall, Carson was just about on schedule, maybe four days behind if he melded all of the projects together, and that was an amazing feat. He was proud of it, but he also knew that, as they got farther into the backcountry, they were going to run into problems, and his schedule could go to hell in a hurry.

He turned on the lights in the small living room, tossed his bag in the back bedroom, and shrugged his way out of his sport coat and tie. In the kitchen, he rummaged in the refrigerator and found an icy bottle of Michelob. The trailer was air-conditioned, so it wasn't particularly warm, but he opened the beer, anyway.

He flopped on the couch, toed his shoes off, and turned on the television, which was hooked into a single-satellite system. All of the trailers got the same channels on the satellite locked into the antenna, and since his choices were an old Spencer Tracy movie, a home-shopping guide, or a rerun of *Gilligan's Island,* he shut it off. The preliminary planning was under way, and a year from now, GTI would be initiating the television expansion part of its contract, bringing international programming to regions in Myanmar that were barely aware of radio.

Carson didn't like long nights by himself. They invited introspection, and he had done so much searching of his mind and soul in three years, he felt as if he knew every little niche and hidey-hole. He sipped from his icy bottle, set it on the coffee table, and then leaned back and placed his stocking feet on the table next to the bottle.

He ought to take some time off, he thought, and fly to Houston to see Merilee. He could always use the excuse of overseeing the repairs to her car. The problem with that scenario was that, though he loved being with his daughter, he always suffered a bipolar reaction. Merilee reminded him so much of Marian. And that always brought back the sound of screaming tires, flashing headlights, and crying in the night.

He knew that Vietnam vets suffered flashbacks; he had never expected that he himself would succumb to the same phenomenon, and if he did, it should have been as a result of some of his sorties in Iraq.

Even the time his Blackhawk was shot down over the desert never bothered him. But the February night on Highway 101, heading home to Palo Alto from a GTI shindig in San Francisco, came back to him regularly.

Carson was a fast driver, usually holding his Jaguar sedan ten miles above the limit. Because he'd downed three scotches

*after dinner, he consciously held the speedometer at five above
the limit and stayed in the inside, fast lane. Traffic heading
both north and southbound was heavy, and he was being careful. He and Marian both had their seat belts snugged into
place.*

*From the passenger seat, Marian talked to him about cor-
porate politics, ". . . you noticed Janet Thomas buttering up
Milo?"*

"I did, love."

"She's after the personnel director slot."

"Think so? Last I heard, Jim Deal was still director."

*The steady stream of headlights on the other side of the
highway was mesmerizing. Except for a few jerks driving with
their brights on.*

"Not for long, the way she's knifing him."

"I don't listen to the gossip," he told her.

*"Well, she's dropping innuendos about mistakes he's been
making."*

"Jim's got a pretty firm grasp on his . . ."

The headlights came right over the median.

*Carson was stunned by the alteration in the pattern for a mo-
ment, then slammed on the brakes and eased to the right, trying
to force the car in the lane beside him to the right shoulder.*

*Another fast driver, behind him on the inside lane, banged
into the rear bumper of the Jag. The sedan whipped around,
sliding backward down the highway, and the northbound
pickup broadsided Marian's side of the car.*

Carson woke up in the hospital.

Every time he relived it, he zeroed in on that millisecond of
hesitation before he stepped on the brakes. A fraction in time
earlier, and the pickup might have missed him entirely, or at
worst, clipped the back end of the Jag. Hell, he was a pilot; he
had great reflexes. But they had been slowed by three shots of
Black Label.

It didn't matter that the pickup driver's blood alcohol content had been twice the legal limit, or that he'd been fishtailing his way through traffic all the way from San Jose. Carson was too damned slow.

And Marian Carson died because of it.

He and Marian had been together since they were both six and in the first grade in Des Moines. They had married after both of them graduated from the University of Iowa, and she had traipsed along with him to Wharton, then to General Motors where he eventually became an assistant vice president. When Dex Abrams, an executive vice president, moved to GTI as CEO and wanted Carson to go along, Marian hadn't complained a bit, just started packing.

She had had infallible instincts, and she had always been his good right hand, keeping tabs on the social and peripheral parts of his jobs that he hated coming to grips with. He had never been in love with another woman and couldn't really fathom that concept. It had always been Chris and Marian.

And he killed her.

Carson never drank more than a beer or a single drink anymore.

In the year after she died, he had nearly blown his job, and would have, with anyone other than Dex Abrams in command. Despite his lack of experience with a project as grand in design as the one in Myanmar, Carson was told by Abrams that he would supervise it.

Carson begged off.

Abrams booted him out of the country, anyway.

And he had pulled it off.

So far.

But the nights were still long.

Seven kilometers north of Mogok

On Friday morning, Hyun Oh had awakened very early and caught a ride on one of the General Technologies' resupply flights—they flew almost daily—to Mandalay, where he met his escort, an army captain named Suu. Driving a Hypai company pickup, they had arrived at the Mogok mines, 160 kilometers north of Mandalay, just after eleven o'clock. The mines were situated above six hundred meters of altitude, on the edge of the Shan plateau, where the air was cool and dry.

The Mogok mines were world-renown for their production of ruby and jade and sapphire gemstones. For centuries, the finest in colored stones had been unearthed here.

Oh had visited other mining sites in the country, and he had had his name on a list in Yangon for over a year, seeking the right to tour Mogok. He had not been certain his wish would ever be granted.

With a copy of Suu's written orders, they were allowed past a chain-link and electrified fence that looked to Oh to be of recent construction. He suspected that the fence could be part of Lon Mauk's new security program. The two guards that emerged from the shanty near the gate appeared particularly menacing, and they were armed with small machine pistols. He did not doubt for a minute that they would use the pistols at the merest provocation. Such visions of violence could incapacitate Oh. He was not given to the physical aspects of life.

The mines were, naturally, a target of the insurgent groups—who could be anything from Karens to Mons to Shans, depending on which rebellion was in the upswing, and minibattles between the army and the rebels could erupt at any time. These wars had subsided to some extent in the two years of the Modernization Proclamation, but still, Oh sensed a tension in the air that did not help his peace of mind.

Once they were through the gate, they drove another mile until they reached a cluster of buildings. After he found a place to park, Oh and Suu got out of the truck, but the army officer did not take him toward any of the buildings.

"We will be limited as to what we can see, Mr. Oh. Did you have a preference?"

"Just as stated in my application, Captain. I am interested, merely to satisfy my curiosity, in the techniques of mining gemstones."

"We will go this way, then."

Suu led him along a path through the trees.

Oh had been half-expecting to find a major surface-mining operation, with huge trucks carting hundreds of cubic meters of gravel and dirt, massive sieves, deep quarries.

It was a great deal more unsophisticated than that. After a short trek, they came upon a pit dug into the ground. The pit was perhaps ten meters across and five meters deep, full of dirty water accumulating from ground- or rainwater. A dozen shirtless men waded knee to waist deep through the pool scraping gravel from the bottom with shallow pans. When they had a full pan, they carried it to the side of the pit and dumped it into a screened sieve.

A man with a high-pressure hose then washed the heap of gravel.

And another man sifted through the remains, picking out by hand the sapphire and ruby rough. The harvester had to have a good eye for many of the pieces simply appeared to be black-and-rust-streaked gravel.

Oh followed Captain Suu around the perimeter of the pit to the sieve, and the two of them bent down to watch the selection process. The man worked fast, spreading the gravel with coarse and callused fingers, snapping up promising stones and dropping them in an openmouthed cotton bag strapped around his waist.

Very few of the pieces were large, and when one appeared, Suu reached out and took it. He handed it to Oh for examination.

The coating felt rough under his fingers, and he rolled it between his thumb and forefinger. One side seemed to carry a pink tinge, so Oh rubbed it with his thumb. The coloring seemed to become deeper, more of a cherry color.

"Ruby?" he asked.

"Exactly, Mr. Oh."

Suu took the stone back and gave it to the collector, who dropped it in his pouch.

Oh was aware that the entire process was closely scrutinized by an Army major standing some five meters away. The mines of Myanmar were all government owned and, therefore, operated by the military. He had learned from Christopher Carson that, in the past, an army officer or soldier assigned to a mine could expect to become rich in a very short time by merely pocketing a few stones for later smuggling across the Thai border.

The Modernization Proclamation had ended that traditional practice. Colonel Mauk had revised the security procedures and completed a one hundred percent exchange of personnel at all mines—expelling the old and possibly corrupt, and bringing in trusted men. Since the trusted men could not be entirely trusted, loyal field officers, like the major, watched over the process. They were, according to Carson, rewarded with promotions and bonuses to temper the urge to steal or to overlook theft in exchange for a commission.

The subsequent statistics suggested that, in prior years, more than half of the nation's annual revenues through gems had been lost to thievery. The revised control of gems had been absolutely necessary since jade and sapphire and ruby sales were to provide the bulk of the funding for the modernization program.

Oh had also figured out for himself that someone in Yangon was in charge of determining just how many of the colored gemstones would be released for sale in a given year. To flood the international market would only drive the prices down, so carefully calculated numbers of stones were offered to dealers in auctions conducted in February and August.

To date, global prices for jade, sapphires, and rubies had remained stable or increased a bit, underscoring the validity of the Myanmar program.

Oh watched the deft fingers culling the gravel, saw a large stone plucked out and dropped in the bag. The man said something to Suu.

"Yellow sapphire," Suu interpreted.

Oh had a momentary vision of that fabulous stone warming his pocket. In the rough, it might be worth fifty thousand dollars American. Four times that when cut, faceted, and polished.

When he and Suu backed away from the sieve, he felt as if he should be holding his hands out, palms up, to demonstrate to the major that he was innocent of greed or lust.

The two toured another pit, then Suu showed him the building where the gems were collected, boxed, and stored for transportation by an armed helicopter. There were quite a few boxes—crates made of wood, and though he could not translate the Burmese writing, Oh did note that two boxes, much smaller than the others, appeared to be set aside. He automatically presumed that they held the most precious of the stones.

On their exit from the mining site, the pickup was searched thoroughly by the guards, including the undercarriage by way of mirrors mounted on long handles. Oh stood outside the truck and did not think much of the search. He was busy calculating how many rubies could be crated in a three-hundred-millimeter square box.

Mr. Pai would want some educated estimate in the report that Oh was to write.

Myanmar army barracks, Yangon

An administrative services lieutenant called the group to attention as Mauk and his adjutant, Maj. Yin May, entered the assembly room.

Mauk told them to regain their seats. He marched directly to the podium and leaned on it to survey the six majors and lieutenant colonels who commanded his field operations. They were all attentive, all dedicated men who were loyal to him. He had handpicked them, trained them personally, and promoted them to their present ranks.

"Gentlemen, your reports, please."

This was a monthly meeting, held so that all involved were aware of what was taking place in other sectors. Mauk believed there was a necessary place for secrecy, but not among or between those in his command. He felt relatively certain that none of them held back information.

He listened as each stood and delivered a concise review of the past month's activities in the mines, the railroads, the communications and utilities systems, and the protection service, which included bodyguards for members of the State Law and Order Restoration Committee. Of the reports, he was mildly dissatisfied with that of the major serving as liaison to the border security unit. There was nothing to be done about it since the border and customs organizations were not under his direct control. The major reported that he had personally witnessed a large number of infractions of the new laws regarding bribery and corruption, but all Mauk could do was forward the major's report to the general in command. He did not anticipate that many corrections would be made.

When the major sat down, Mauk expressed his appreciation, then reported on his own encounter on the Banmo Road.

"From the tactics utilized, I deduce that either myself or the Americans were intentionally targeted."

Major Lin Po, the commander of railroad security, asked, "These were Daw Tan's men?"

Mauk shrugged. "Perhaps. The indications suggest as much."

"I had thought that he was very much observing a truce."

"As did I, Major. I will know more after I meet with him."

Mauk had found under his office door a small slip of paper upon which was written a location and a time. It was a standard procedure by which Daw Tan set meetings.

"Despite any strong evidence," Mauk said, "I suspect that we will be facing an escalation of hostilities. I want you to inform your subordinates and increase the state of alert. Should any of our units come under attack, the standing order will be to protect foreign nationals first and property second. If at all possible, we should attempt to capture the attackers."

"What of your prisoner?" the commander of communications and utilities security asked.

"He has given us nothing, not even his name. We have freed him to mix with the general population of the jail."

"Is that wise, Colonel Mauk? Will he be safe?"

"I doubt it, but that is his worry," Mauk said. "We are, of course, watching him to see how safe he really is."

GTI compound, Yangon

The session was a monthly one, normally falling at three in the afternoon on the third Friday, and all of the subcontractors' representatives were present except for Branigan. Her office had called Becky Johnson with an alibi.

Carson usually received a call from Colonel Mauk, who timed his meetings at one o'clock on the same days. Mauk would provide a précis of the military meeting for Carson to relate to his own people. Today, Mauk had had nothing to report, not even additional information about the attack. Carson had hoped to get more from the man.

When he had initiated these meetings two years before, they had been sparsely populated. Now they were larger than he liked. Every subcontractor or department head felt as if he had to bring his assistants, operations managers, financial managers, maintenance supervisors, and in some special cases, public-relations directors along with him.

Because of the size of the group, they met in the largest room in the compound, the dining room of the cafeteria. Coffee and doughnuts were set out on the serving line, and Carson had filled a mug before taking his seat at a table that was more or less the head table. Becky Johnson sat next to him, running a tape recorder and taking notes.

At the tables more remote were the assistants and assistants to assistants. At the closer tables, facing him, were the project directors. Hyun Oh had come in at the last minute, out of breath. He took a seat next to Marty Prather, GTI's disbursements director. Sam Enders of GTI's microwave division munched a big glazed doughnut while talking to Del Creighton of Hygienic Systems. Janice Cooper was sitting with them, in place of Branigan. Don Evans and Tracy Hampton, the air fleet and surface fleet managers for GTI, were arguing about something. Evans loved to argue, for one thing, and Hampton, a fiery redhead with bright green eyes, was always willing to oblige. Ronald Vermont, a civil engineer with Cable Engineering, watched them with some amusement. Billy Kasperik of InstaStructure sat with Phillip Draft from Bluebird Bus, Bob Mickeljohn of IBM, and Kiki Olson, GTI's personal computer systems director.

It made for a hell of a gathering, but then the Myanmar Project was a hell of a job, with a scope that ranged from the integration of computer systems to the rebuilding of bridges—a specialty of Ron Vermont.

Carson banged an empty glass on the Formica tabletop to kill the buzz of conversation.

"Good afternoon, everyone. I hope you've noticed that the agenda is short, and I hope to keep it that way."

Smattering of applause.

Carson briefly related his version of the attack by the bandits, skipping the details of his involvement, and reinforced the memo sent out by Jack Gilbert. "Let's take special pains to see that all the drivers read that memo, please. Vehicles and convoys might make the most enticing targets."

He looked to Evans and said, "Don, I trust the stack of paper in front of you is *not* your report."

Evans stood up, stroking his thick mustache with the forefinger of his left hand. "That's for you to read, Chris. I can give you the gist of it, offhand. First, some of you people are slipping on transport requests. I need your paperwork five days ahead of need, not two or three. Help me out there, and I won't make you unhappy, or foul up your own schedules, by bumping you back. Second, I'm going to have four S-65s and a Skycrane down for periodic maintenance next week. That's going to put my capacity at eighty-four percent of normal, so some of the least priority jobs are going to be delayed a couple days. Try to plan on that, if you will. Last, Prome is coming off the daily schedule of flights. We'll hit there twice a week on the morning flights. I'll have a new schedule out to you by Monday."

"Everybody got that?" Carson asked. "Let's stay together on the scheduling. Tracy?"

She rose, her striking red hair and taut figure clad in white knit blouse and slacks capturing everyone's attention. She managed the scheduling of some five hundred semitrucks, dump trucks, cargo haulers, crew buses, pickups, and automobiles. Additionally, one of her divisions provided bulldozers, landscrapers, cement mixers, and cranes and their support vehicles for the excavation projects of most of the subcontractors. Only Branigan's railroad project had its own equipment.

Hampton said, "As many of you know, at the end of the project, the ownership of all of our vehicles will be transferred to the Union of Myanmar. As part of the planning for that event, we are conducting training schools in Yangon and Mandalay. Last Friday, we graduated our second class of diesel mechanics, the first class of automotive electronics technicians, the fifth class of general mechanics, and the twentieth class of drivers.

"We have now reduced our nonnative workforce by sixty positions and added sixty-seven Burmese drivers and mechanics to the payroll. The corresponding savings amount to twenty-two thousand dollars a month."

The Burmese worked for considerably less than the Americans, Canadians, and Europeans, for whom GTI had to pay union wages and dislocation allowances. And yet, the Burmese selected for the program were all getting a rise in their standards of living. By the last year of the project, the budget called for a native workforce or ninety-eight percent. Next year, Don

Evans would begin a similar program for aircraft mechanics and pilots.

"On the maintenance front," she added, "last month, we show an overall fleet readiness of ninety percent, which is five percent above our optimum. We'll lose some of that as the vehicles become older. The only negative statistic involves sedans and pickups that are frequently on the highways. Our rate of accidents—mostly fender benders and, thank God, no fatalities or serious casualties—is up. Now, I know the locals leave something to be desired in terms of driver skill and highway courtesy, but half of these accidents are the result, in one way or another, of the deficiencies of our own people. We don't have freeways and superhighways here, so please, everyone, tell your drivers to slow down."

Jaguar sailing backward down Highway 101.

"You heard the lady," Carson said. "We don't want any of our employees being forced to leave the country because they can't handle a car. Thanks, Tracy. Who's next?"

Sam Enders reported on the completion of the microwave facility at Prome, his deep voice reverberating nicely through the room.

Billy Kasperik of InstaStructure provided his completion numbers on major facilities, then added, "We've got sixteen of thirty-seven microwave substations finished and stacked up at the airport. Don, I need to get with you and see about moving a few of them closer to their final sites whenever you've got a Skycrane free. We're going to need the room at our Mingaladon storage area soon. Finally, we've completed the sewage plant facility at Henzada, and I've moved those crews and equipment to Bassein."

Delbert Creighton reported on the sewage plants completed, said he was moving crews and materials to Henzada, and emphasized that the water-treatment facilities at Pegu and Sandoway were completed. "And I need to talk to you about a budget item, Chris."

"See me after class, Del. How about you, Phil?"

The Bluebird Bus Company had landed the subcontract for metropolitan transport, and Phillip Draft, their top representative in Myanmar, scooted his chair sideways so he could see the people behind him.

"We've now taken delivery on thirty buses in Mandalay, forty in Yangon, and five each for Moulmein, Thaton, and Amherst. We've put new equipment on thirty of over a hundred routes the government wants to have upgraded. The major stations, thanks to InstaStructure, are complete at the airport and in Yangon and Mandalay. The maintenance shops are sixty percent complete. We're placing bus-stop kiosks as fast as InstaStructure gets them out, and we've got another hundred and forty to go. The driver certification program is lagging behind schedule, and I've added two people to my recruitment staff. On the back end, with about seventy drivers out of training and on the job, we're learning about some areas in which we're deficient. We're revising the training programs to correct those deficiencies."

"You want to highlight them, Phil?" Carson asked.

"Not necessarily, but I will. There seems to be something—I don't know, in the national consciousness of the Burmese, and maybe all of Southeast Asians, when I think about it—that promotes a total disregard for safety. Our brand-new drivers get behind the wheels of brand-new buses and go hell-bent-for-leather. They could care less about passengers, pedestrians, other autos, or themselves. We're attempting to train some of that freethinking out of them."

"Good. Anything else?"

"One more item. Next month, I'll have twenty more buses in Yangon, and I want to establish a route between the GTI compound, the government offices and foreign consulates, the hotel strip, and the airport. To make that successful, and to set an example regarding mass transit for others such as the embassy and consulate people, I need ridership."

"Damned good idea," Tracy Hampton said. "That would have a positive effect on my maintenance, fuel, and, particularly, accident figures."

Carson jotted a note to himself. "Let me know when you've got a schedule, Phil, and I'll get an aggressive memo posted."

"Thanks," Draft said.

Ronald Vermont of Cable Engineering, the subcontractor responsible for civil-engineering projects, reported on the status of bridge and underpass replacements and repairs. The report bored Carson to death, but Vermont was excited about his challenges.

Robert Mickeljohn of IBM and Kiki Olson, the director of GTI's personal computer systems, reported together on their joint operations. Mainframe computers had been emplaced in Yangon and Mandalay to handle governmental and city programs. A network of personal computers was in the process of being linked to each other and to the mainframes. A few city and national departments were now trained and operating on the PCs, and many others were on schedule for training. Half of Yangon's traffic-control system was scheduled for computer-control testing in August.

When they sat down, Carson said, "Great! On schedule and on agenda. That's it, I think, unless you have something, Janice?"

Janice Cooper, Branigan's secretary, said, "I've never attended one of these meetings before, and I don't know what Stephanie would have said. Except that we've got a train off the track."

Fifteen miles south of Taungoo

Stephanie Branigan slid down the embankment, leaped the drainage ditch which had three or four inches of water in it, then climbed to the roadbed. Craig Wilson, chief of motive power and rolling stock, scrambled after her.

Dick Statler reached out a hand, caught hers, and pulled her up the last few feet. Statler was the chief roadbed engineer.

"We've got about a half-mile walk," Statler said. "Sorry we couldn't have dumped it closer to the highway."

"I brought my hiking boots along, since I was damned sure it wouldn't be convenient," Branigan told him.

The three of them headed north, walking on the smooth concrete of the base of the guideway. There was just enough room on the base for them to walk three abreast.

In most areas of Myanmar, the UltraTrain guideway was under construction right alongside the existing main line. In many places, they had had to widen the roadbed, build new trestles and bridges, and block off sidings. Later, after the UltraTrain was maintaining consistent performance, the old lines would be taken up, and in the case of the 380-mile corridor between Mandalay and Yangon, a second line would be constructed next to the first. Myanmar, after all, did have over forty million people, and she envisioned a time when a large segment of that population would become a great deal more mobile than they now were. The traffic between the two largest cities would be heavy.

The guideway was deceptively simple, almost aesthetic, in appearance. Each fifty-foot-long segment was constructed, upside down, by pouring a carbon-carbon and fiberglass fiber-impregnated mixture of concrete into a mold. After the mixture cured, it was broken out of the mold and turned right side up so that the magnetic, electrical, and electronic components could be added. Then it was trucked to the site and craned into position, lowered onto concrete columns sunk to bedrock, and carefully aligned with connecting pins to the segment of guideway behind it. For straight segments of roadbed, the process was fairly simple. It got complicated in the engineering, molding, and placement for curves, especially since almost every curve they encountered had differing radii. She and Dick Statler together had designed a set of flexible molds so that they could adapt to the changing curvature.

A cross section of the guideway revealed a base ten feet wide and eighteen inches deep at the outer edges. The topside was tapered upward until it was twenty-four inches thick in the center to improve the strength and rigidity. Every three sections were separated by a flexible rubber bushing to allow for the expansion and contraction of the earth and the rail segments. From the center of the concrete base, a continuous pedestal was raised three feet high above the base. The pedestal was two feet wide, and along the top and each side were indentations for the magnets and their wiring.

The UltraTrain was a magnetic levitation, or maglev, design. The electrical charge on the superconducting magnets in the pedestal and in the floor and lower sides of the train "floated" the train one inch above the pedestal. The opposing magnetic forces of the pedestal sides and the lower sides of the car which wrapped over the pedestal kept the car centered over the pedestal.

Supertrain designs like the UltraTrain had been on the designing boards for decades, and working models had been tested in Germany and Japan since the early seventies. The German's Transrapid public demonstrations of their sixth prototype had carried over 16,000 passengers in 350 runs at speeds up to 250 miles per hour. Transrapid-07 had a design speed of 312 miles per hour.

The startling aspect of this, to most people, was that the trains carried no motive power. Craig Wilson's title of chief, motive power and rolling stock was as antiquated as the diesel trains stumbling across the rails of America. These train cars had no wheels and were therefore not truly "rolling" stock.

And the power to move the trains at such high rates rested in the pedestal magnets. With electronic and computer control of electrical current, the charges on the embedded magnets was alternately shifted from "north" to "south," from attraction to repulsion between the magnets of the guideway and the magnets of the train. While one section of magnets "pulled" the train forward, another section "pushed" it forward. And then alternated from south to north. The speed of the alternation controlled the speed of the train.

And with no groaning diesels in the night, and no steel wheels on iron rails, there was no noise. Only the flow of the air over the aerodynamic surfaces of the trains created a whisper of movement. Branigan had stood in a German pasture and watched a train go by at 200 miles per hour on an elevated track without disturbing the cattle grazing beneath it.

Dusk was settling, and a few cars on the highway a quarter-mile off to Branigan's left had turned on their headlights. Just as many did not.

They rounded a curve to the right, the highway disappearing behind a thick stand of forest, and Branigan saw the three-car test train ahead. She had been told that it had not left the guideway, of course, but she was still relieved to see it straddling the pedestal.

"How much damage, Dick?"

"Craig will have to tell us for sure, but I don't think it's too bad. It was moving at around eighty when it lost power."

"I'll bet we lost most of the coaster wheels," Wilson said, "and there's probably some magnet and structure damage."

For maintenance and storage purposes, when power was off the guideway, the train cars settled to the pedestal and rested on small four-inch steel wheels located between magnets.

Statler, who had already surveyed the damage, said, "We've got a quarter-mile of guideway to rebuild. Topside magnets were torn up pretty bad."

"How about the pedestal?" she asked.

"That met the design features, Stephanie. There's some gouges, but they'll be repaired easily enough."

Ten men were standing around the stranded train when they reached it. Wilson immediately went under the lead car for an inspection. One of the men, apparently a foreman, went with him, brandishing a flashlight. Ten minutes went by before he crawled out from under the car.

Pushing to his feet, he told her, "It's bad enough. There are enough cracked magnets that I don't think we'll get her back to Yangon under track power."

"Damn it! I don't like the PR image of hauling these cars back on flat cars."

"No way around it, Stephanie."

She looked to the west, where the sun had already disappeared behind the trees.

"Okay, Craig. Call for a crane. If we move fast enough, maybe we can get them back before morning. I'd like to do it at night when there are fewer eyes around, if at all possible."

"Got it. Dawn's our target." Wilson headed for an emergency door to the car to use the train's telephone.

Statler borrowed a flashlight and led her farther north along the guideway. She stumbled several times on the rough surface of the ballast next to the concrete guideway. The cars were twelve feet wide, extending a foot to either side of the guideway, and they had to walk around them.

Past the short train, they regained the concrete, and Statler marched along, sure of where he was going. Branigan tried to match the pace of his long legs.

Three hundred yards past the train, Statler stopped and trained the beam of the flashlight on a metal access door in the side of the pedestal. The door was wide open.

"Right here, Stephanie."

She took the light and bent over to examine the interior. Each section of the guideway had a similar door that provided access to the interior of the pedestal so that electrical and electronic connectors between segments could be attached to each other, maintained, or replaced. The interior of the pedestal contained a one-foot-diameter tunnel to accommodate the wiring. The doors all had quality locks, to keep kids and the curious out, but this lock had been picked.

Within the access hatch, black soot coated the walls of the small concrete tunnel.

When she had seen enough, she stood upright. "Bomb."

"I think so, Steph, yes. The engineer on the train would have known of any disruptions in power or control the minute the wiring was tampered with. This was booby-trapped, or remote controlled, so that it went off just as the train reached the segment."

"Damn it, Dick! We don't want to spend all our time guarding the guideway or looking for break-ins."

"I've thought about it," Statler said, "but the only thing I've come up with is spot welding the doors shut in a couple places on each door. It would make maintenance tougher."

"We shouldn't have much maintenance on most of the main lines. And if we do, the computers can tell us approximately where the problems are."

"The schedule calls for quarterly visual inspections and annual continuity tests."

She thought about it for a minute, then said, "We can tap into the two-twenty-volt line all along here, can't we?"

"Yup."

"Electrify the doors. They're metal."

Statler grinned at her even as he did some mental calculations. "With transformers, I bring it down to, say, a hundred and ten volts, so we don't kill anybody, just give 'em a hell of a jolt."

"We don't want to kill anyone," she agreed. "At least, not the curious kids."

"Hell of a lot of work. And a lot of transformers."

"Figure one out of three doors, but make the installations random. A guy touches one door and lands on his ass, he's not going to touch any more."

"And maintenance?"

"Insulated keys. They open up, reach in, and shut off the current."

"I like it, Steph."

Branigan did, too. She had always been good at on-the-spot solutions.

Bangkok, Thailand

The first thing after breakfast on Friday morning, Jack Gilbert had checked in at the bank and verified that he had some money available. One million dollars by letter of credit, check, or in cash. A great deal of business was accomplished in Southeast Asia in the form of cash. People either liked the hard feel of it in their hands or the ability to shift it to other endeavors without leaving a paper trail.

Only briefly did he consider the fantasy of signing out the entire million in about six different currencies, then booking two seats on a flight for Jakarta. Gilbert flirted with these fantasies from time to time; sometimes, he liked living on the edge in his mind.

The second airliner seat, of course, would be for Pamela Steele of London, England. On the airplane, once she learned that he was a wheel with GTI, she had warmed up to him, and they had shared dinner together at the Tara Hotel. The Tara was in a more moderate price range—that was to say, cheaper—than Gilbert would normally choose for himself, but it was a nice hotel, and he had immediately changed his plans for shelter when he learned Steele was staying there.

After dinner, they had cabbed down to Sukhumvit Road, gotten a table on the patio of the Trail Dust saloon, and listened to live country music. The Thai performers adequately re-created the sounds of Alan Jackson, Garth Brooks, and Bob Wills. Mimicry in entertainment was an Asian art form, Gilbert had often thought.

He was a little disappointed in the fact that Steele seemed at home in Bangkok. His tour guidance was not required. She was, in fact, a bit of a world traveler. A freelance photographer and writer, she was currently on assignment for a London magazine and newspaper. She didn't identify either, and he wasn't certain whether that was a result of modesty or of shame. Some of the London tabloids were edge-of-the-mind examples of journalism. Her task was to deliver a series of stories on the modernization of Myanmar. Her tribulation was that Myanmar would only grant her short visas of three days to a week. So she lived in Bangkok, and hopped over to Yangon with every chance she was given. After three months of pursuing permissions, she had yet to be allowed outside the city limits of either Yangon or Mandalay.

"You wouldn't be any good with a camera?" she asked.

"All thumbs and lens covers, I'm afraid," he had told her.

This Friday, with a daylong series of disappointing shopping behind him, Gilbert was looking forward to getting back to the Tara, showering, and meeting Ms. Steele. He had but one more stop scheduled for the day.

This was at a discreet emporium on Mahesak Road, a short thoroughfare of three blocks of century-old buildings in the *farang* area of Bangkok. It was a center of gem dealers who dealt in stones from both legitimate and possibly shady sources. The place he was looking for was simply a numbered door at street level. He rang the buzzer, identified himself on the intercom, and when the door buzzed, pushed it open. He stepped inside, closed the door, and faced a flight of stairs that had seen better decades. The front edges of the wooden steps were worn into rounded concavities by millions of passages. They groaned and squeaked as Gilbert climbed to the second floor.

At the top, he was faced with another locked door, this one more modern. It was of gray steel, set in a steel door frame.

A tiny window in the middle of the door contained an eye, and after it surveyed him for a few minutes, the door clicked and opened. A small-statured Thai stood his ground, regarding him coolly. Most of the dealers on the street were of a dozen different nationalities, a consequence most likely of the Thai national philosophy of avoiding confrontation. Dealing in gems could be highly confrontational.

"Mr. Gilbert?"

"Mr. Chao?"

"May I see some identification, please?"

Gilbert dug his wallet out of his hip pocket and handed over his international driver's license.

Apparently satisfied, Chao waved him inside and locked the door.

The room was ancient, but the walls were repainted, and

there was an expensive Persian carpet on the floor. A large oak rolltop desk was pressed against one wall, and a massive vault, finished in black with gold pinstriping, dominated the inside wall. There were thick bars on the windows behind a small sofa. There were no display cases. Mr. Chao was a *dealer;* he didn't show his wares to any Tom, Dick, or Harriet coming off the street.

The safe was closed and, Gilbert presumed, locked. A dozen paper folders, called briefkes, rested on the polished surface of the desktop. Chao would have prepared himself for Gilbert's visit.

Chao urged him to a seat on the sofa and offered coffee or tea, which Gilbert declined. He sat down while the Thai gathered the briefkes from the desk and brought them over to the glass-topped table in front of Gilbert. The dealer sat down next to him.

"You said on the telephone that you would be interested in large stones."

"Very large. And in the rough, if possible."

"I have none in the rough state," Chao said. "These twelve are my largest, and while they have not been cut as yet, the surface has been ground to allow a better examination of the interior structure. Do you have a loupe?"

"I do," Gilbert said, searching in his right jacket pocket for the magnifying eyepiece.

He and Carson had taken a short course from an expert gem dealer in the United States, and after much practice—and testing of his memory and his ability by the gemologist—Gilbert was confident of what he was looking for.

Chao opened the first briefke and handed him the stone. It was a six-sided crystal almost two inches long. The cherry-red color defined it as ruby, though some spinel and garnet carried the same characteristics. Right off, he knew it wasn't what he was seeking, but he fitted the loupe to his right eye and sighted into the stone. The fluorescence was magnificent; and deep in the stone, he spotted the silk, a structural arrangement of densely woven needles. African and Thai rubies did not have silk.

"It is a Burma stone," Gilbert said.

"Indeed, it is. The Ceylon silk is more coarsely woven."

"But not as large as I had hoped," Gilbert said, handing the stone back to him.

Chao searched through several of his briefkes, then gave Gilbert another gem.

"This one weighs eighty-one carats."

It was a tad over 2.5 inches—63 millimeters—long. They were getting there.

He louped it.

"Again, a Burma stone," he said, "though there is some distinct zoning present."

Chao seemed to be accepting his knowledge of rubies.

He said, "It could still be cut into two extremely exquisite pieces."

"Yes. Anything larger?"

Without registering any surprise on his face, Chao uncased another, more massive stone.

"That is the best of my lot. It is nearly one hundred and twenty carats. In its uncut state, it measures ninety-one millimeters in length."

Gilbert examined it closely, then handed it back.

"A tremendous ruby, Mr. Chao, but I'm afraid, not quite what I need."

"Could you be more specific?"

"I would always be happy to look at anything in excess of one hundred millimeters in length, and of Burma origin."

"That is rare, Mr. Gilbert. Almost always a product of the Mogok mines, they infrequently reach Bangkok. Most often, large stones would be cut in two before reaching the market place."

"But you do see them?"

"Less and less. We are receiving fewer goods from Myanmar."

Which meant that Colonel Mauk's new-and-improved security enforcement program was having an effect.

"If you were to leave me a telephone number," Chao suggested, "I could call if such a stone appeared."

"I would appreciate that very much," Gilbert said and gave him his card. It listed a California phone number, but someone would pass the message on to him. Giving Chao his Yangon number might seem strange; a man from Myanmar comes to Bangkok to buy Myanmar gems?

"Would there be any other way I might be of service, Mr. Gilbert?"

He pulled his wallet from his hip pocket and leafed through the bills. Extracting twenty one-hundreds, he laid them on the table.

"If you had a small, finished ruby, I'd take a look at it as a gift for a friend of mine."

"Certainly."

Chao returned his heavy stuff to the safe and dug around for more. Gilbert looked at the two thousand on the table, but had no misgivings. He made 120 grand a year from GTI, and after all, it was only money.

He hoped Pamela Steele liked rubies.

FIVE

The Razor waited patiently in the predawn light.

He leaned against the brick side of a barracks building, smoking. He had abandoned his jeans and black T-shirt for a private's jungle fatigues, combat boots, and slouch hat. The former private's body was in back of the motor pool, his slit throat draining his blood into the parched earth.

He estimated that he had thirty or forty minutes before the body was discovered. And in addition to the time until discovery, he had the element of surprise. The effrontery of a rebel foray *inside* an army encampment would bring shock and chaos with it. The government troops would run like headless chickens, blinded and without purpose.

Continuing to smoke his raw-tasting 555 cigarette, the Razor nodded to enlisted men passing between their barracks and the mess hall. None of them paid him much attention.

Fifty meters away was the three-meter-high chain-link fence of the military jail's exercise yard. It was topped with six strands of inward-slanting barbed wire. The exercise yard was small, and the fence ran along only two sides of it; the other two sides were faced with the walls of the administrative, cell block, and dining structures. In the corner where the fences met was a guard tower, and a single soldier leaned on the railing of the tower and studied the brightly lit interior. Perhaps twenty prisoners milled about in the yard, having finished their four A.M. breakfasts.

Miu, also known to the Razor as the "Boar," was with them.

The Boar was nervous. He would know that Colonel Mauk was allowing him freedom of movement within the jail for a purpose. The Boar understood that, as did the Razor.

And the Boar tried to hide himself within the groups of prisoners standing about the yard. His eyes darted frequently toward the fences, scanning them, trying to see beyond the lights shining inward.

There was no place to hide, however.

Pushing away from the wall, the Razor sauntered toward the jail fence, fieldstripping his cigarette, veering off toward the mess hall when he came within ten meters of the fence. He was but one of fifty soldiers following a track worn in the packed ground over the years.

The morning light was beginning to spread, colors becoming discernible out of the shadows.

His own eyes scanned the soldiers around him, the jail, the roofs of nearby buildings. Colonel Mauk would not offer up this enticing prize without feeling certain that he had it, if not fully protected, at least covered. He picked out an armed soldier behind the glass window of one of the barracks, a faint shadow moving against the darker background. Another leaning against the mess hall, the muzzle of his slung assault rifle aimed down.

And yes, another guard in the tower, this one inside the small enclosure, crouched so that only the top of his head appeared above the bottom edge of the window. His attention was diverted outward, away from the jail yard. So, at least three, and perhaps more, were expecting him.

From the corner of his eye, the Razor saw that Miu continued to shuffle about, attempting to shield himself with the bodies of six or seven prisoners.

They were only bodies.

The Razor reached under his fatigue blouse and pulled the silenced Uzi free of his belt. Gripping it in his right hand as he walked, and partially masking it with his left forearm, he aimed toward the enclosure and squeezed the trigger.

Thwt-thwt-thwt . . . thwt-thwt-thwt . . .

The sound was but a shallow cough.

He worked the muzzle left, then right again. And back again.

The prisoners in the yard convulsed, screamed, went down, arms and legs flying akimbo.

Miu was one of them, flat on the ground, his head jerking spasmodically.

The Uzi went silent, its magazine spent.

The unarmed soldiers around him, belatedly aware, went to ground or began to sprint away from him.

The floodlight on the guard tower whipped around frantically, attempting to find him.

The Razor ejected the magazine, grabbed a second one from his pocket, and slapped it in place. He ran the bolt to inject the first cartridge as he darted toward the closest barracks. Spinning around as he ran, he fired a short burst toward the guard tower.

The huge floodlight burst in a tinkling crash of glass, and he was in semidarkness.

He fired a group of three rounds toward the barracks window where the armed soldier had been hiding.

Was aware, finally, of bullets spraying the air around him. He could feel the air compress before their passage, heard the high-pitched whistles singing as the slugs flew past his ears . . .

Many thudded into the barracks wall, and chips of brick spattered him. Geysers of earth rippled along his path.

He spun right, then left, then was behind the corner of the barracks, racing for the other side.

Around that corner, then running at full speed down the alley between two rows of buildings.

Toward the motor pool.

He heard the slap of feet behind him, many men joining the pursuit. A few shots cracked and bullets swished past him.

Someone stuck his head out of a door ahead, and the Razor squeezed off one shot.

The head disappeared.

More shots ringing out now.

He began to zigzag, occasionally firing a shot behind him, to keep them at a safe distance.

Thirty meters of open ground, then the garages of the motor pool. He slid around a corner, out of sight of the pursuers.

And there was Mauk.

He was ten meters away, with six soldiers ranged next to him, all with their rifles trained on him.

The Razor jerked the Uzi upward. . . .

Mauk shot him twice in the legs.

His legs collapsed beneath him, suddenly without muscle or form, and he tumbled to the ground, rolling on his shoulder, trying to spin himself around to aim a burst from the machine gun.

Mauk shot him again, this time in the left arm.

The colonel wanted him alive, of course.

The Razor whirled the Uzi around, shoved his thumb into the trigger guard, and pressed it home.

He did not feel the bullets cutting his stomach in half.

City Hall, Yangon

Minister U Ba Thun greeted his security chief with less than the utmost enthusiasm. He did not bother to rise from the chair behind his desk.

"So. Where we had one useless captive before, we now have two useless captives? Corpses."

Mauk crossed the office and placed an object on the desk. It took Ba Thun a moment to realize that he was looking at an old-fashioned razor.

"I think, Minister, that we would not have learned much from him, were he to have lived. As it is, his death means more progress for the country than if we had captured twenty rebels."

Ba Thun picked up the ivory-handled instrument and flicked

open the blade. The fine steel appeared surgically precise, and it gleamed brightly under the overhead light. When he thought of the blood that had been lost to this inanimate piece of craftsmanship, a shiver ran down his back. He let a little of the disappointment he had inserted into his tone evaporate.

"Sit down, Colonel. This was truly the Razor?"

Mauk slid one of the straight chairs close to the desk and sat, his back militarily straight.

"I believe there is no doubt."

"And he was one of Daw Tan's pets?"

"Only by supposition, Minister. There has never been a provable link."

"I do not understand Tan's actions," he said.

"Nor do I," Mauk agreed. His elbows rested on the arms of the chair, and his hands gripped each other, his thumbs pressed tightly together. It was a habit Ba Thun found suggestive of the man's inner turmoil, though his face never revealed anything similar.

Since the foreigners had begun building, or rebuilding, his country, Ba Thun had developed his own vision of the future. He disliked having his vision, his master plan, revamped for him by others, even those on the committee.

"I must speak to Tan," he said.

"I am to meet him tonight," Mauk said.

Ba Thun did not ask for details.

"If you do not like what you hear from the man, do not oppose him. Rather, arrange a meeting between him and myself."

"Of course, Minister."

The Tara Hotel, Bangkok, Thailand

"This is the first Saturday I've had off in six months. How are we going to make it memorable?"

Pamela Steele's eyes were much less guarded now. The bright and curious blue shades emanated—could it be?—affection.

And ambition, too. He wouldn't forget that she had places to go and things to do, and would likely use any means to achieve them.

She pushed her luncheon salad plate aside and sipped from her half-full wineglass. "You've toured the city before?"

"Too many times. I don't need to see another pagoda."

She was wearing a pleated khaki skirt of cotton drill and a pale-yellow blouse with a high man's-style collar that disappeared under the fall of her smoothly brushed blond hair. The outfit served only to emphasize the Raquel Welch curvature and distract him frequently.

Gilbert was dressed in safari casual, slacks that matched her skirt, a beige sport shirt, and a long-skirted jacket with abundant pockets. He felt as if the two of them were a perfect match.

"How about," he asked, "a nice long cruise up Chao Phraya?"

"We could do that. Or I could teach you how to work a Nikon. I'd even buy you one."

"Or we could go find a setting for this."

Gilbert reached in his baggy side pocket and pulled out the briefke. He handed it to her and watched her eyes as she opened it. When she unfolded the paper, the blue intensified, which he didn't think was possible, and each of her eyes increased in size by about a quarter of an inch, which he knew was impossible. He was imagining things, wasn't he?

"This is beautiful, Jack. It's not a synthetic?"

"It's real. Burmese, they tell me."

She looked at him across the top of the stone. "What kind of setting are you looking for?"

"I don't know. Ring. Or maybe a pendant. What do you think?"

"It's for the girlfriend?"

"I don't know that, either. You want to be my girlfriend?"

Now her eyes narrowed, studying him with suspicion.

"Are you trying to buy me, Jack?"

"Pamela! I'm shocked."

"No, you're not. I asked a question."

"It's a pretty stone. I thought you'd like it. The goodness of my heart and all that."

"I've still got a question pending," she insisted.

He leaned forward, his elbows on the table.

"You just offered to buy me a camera."

"Well, I have a nefarious motive," she admitted.

"A more sinister one than mine, I assure you."

She looked again at the ruby, picked it out of the folder with her thumb and forefinger, and held it up to the light shining through the window.

"Deal?" she asked.

"How's it go?"

"I buy the setting, a ring, I think. And then I buy you the camera and teach you how to use it."

"Deal."

Steele smiled and said, "I love the ruby."

"Good."

Gilbert wasn't sure just how things had turned out. Had he just bought a beautiful girl a present and ended up a spy?

When she took his hand as they were leaving the restaurant, he thought it might have been worth it.

Sule Pagoda Road, Yangon

Carson and Branigan strolled leisurely through the thick crowd on Sule Pagoda Road, a north-south avenue teeming with neon and color.

Carson had waited late in his office for Branigan to get back and fill him in on the details of the derailment that wasn't a derailment. He thought of it as a demagnetization, but he hadn't mentioned his interpretation to her. She wasn't in the best of humor and surely wouldn't buy into his comedy. Instead, he had offered dinner, and she accepted.

They moved easily through the throngs of Burmese and were

rarely jostled by the intense and harried shoppers and shop-keepers. A few small-business proprietors stood in front of their jewelry and clothing and what-not stores and beseeched them with begging eyes. There were very few foreigners in the crowd; the State Law and Order Restoration Committee had not yet finalized a policy regarding tourism, and tourist visas were limited. Though they badly wanted the revenues tourism could provide, Carson thought that they weren't certain they wanted the problems that accompanied the tourist dollars.

He said as much to Branigan as they stepped off the curb to cross Arawrahta Street.

She had her hands stuck deep in the pockets of her pant suit jacket, and she seemed to be focused on internal thoughts as she walked. Her purse, hanging from a long strap over her left shoulder, slapped his right arm as they walked.

"What? Oh. I think they'll give in to the pressure, Chris. And probably within the next year. We'll have so damned many tourists, we won't be able to take these walks."

"You're preoccupied," he said.

"Yes, I am. Sorry."

When they reached Maha Bandoola Street, they skirted the mob surrounding the Sule Pagoda, which stood in the middle of the intersection. The temple was over 140 feet high, and it was unique in that an octagonal shape was maintained from the stupa to the top of the spire. The eight sides represented a bird or animal and eight planets. At least two thousand years old, the temple had been used by the British as the center of the grid they laid out for Rangoon when it was reconstructed in the 1880s. The Sule Pagoda, like the great Shwedagon Pagoda a couple miles to the northwest, was founded on hair relics, and its name honored the Sule *nat,* the guardian spirit of Singuttara Hill.

They were approached by a fortune-teller—prolific around the temple, but Carson waved her off.

Carson was taller than most of the pedestrians around him, and he could see the Rangoon River a couple of blocks down the street. The river, crossing east to west and then curving toward the north, helped to define the southern and western limits of Yangon. On the east side, the Pazundaung Creek set the boundary for the east side of the city.

As they continued walking, Branigan seemed to come out of her reverie.

"Why," she asked, "do these people object so much to the things that can bring them a better life?"

"I'm not sure I can answer that, Stephanie. For one thing, I suspect that the general populace, especially in the hill region, is partially unaware that increased standards of living are available to them. They've been living the way they are for so long, with incomprehensible civil wars raging around them, that they don't know any better. The politics of the national government and of the rebel factions mean little to them."

"If that train had been doing the design speed of two hundred and twenty, we'd have had fatalities."

"Yes."

"Is it worth it?" she asked. "What we're doing?"

"I think it is."

"Why? If nothing's going to change, anyway. The SLORC is going to keep a heavy hand on transportation and communications."

Carson considered his response. He had been impressed with Branigan's performance in the two years he had known her. She was personally aloof from most of the project personnel, but that wasn't entirely negative. She was a boss, and she had difficult decisions to make. Several times, he had pondered the idea that, if he had been a normal flesh-and-blood male, he'd have been panting after her like a heat-stricken hound dog. He suspected Gilbert—knowing Gilbert—had made a pass at her and had been rebuffed. Gilbert was *never* turned down, so he had to believe that Branigan had set herself some boundaries.

Branigan wasn't stunningly beautiful, but she was trim and attractive. All of the right curves were in the right places, and though they weren't lush curves, they could be enticing. Her face was a trifle elongated, but the cut of her hair, which was rich and full-bodied, countered the length. There was a small scar under the left side of her jaw, and he had wondered at the cause a couple of times. He wouldn't have asked about it for anything.

The aura surrounding her was reserved, suggesting an electric fence about two feet away from the body proper. For some, that air of reservation and grace would stand as a challenge. He suspected that, if she were in the right mood, her bright green eyes would turn to dark pools in which a suitor could get lost.

Fortunately, he thought, he had no interest in becoming a panting hound dog. In-office romances were deadly, anyway. He had seen too many of them in his corporate life, and they tended to foul up the worlds of both parties.

So Branigan was simply Branigan. She was a capable administrator, and he admired the way she ran her division.

Also, he felt as if he knew her well enough by now, and had been reassured of her loyalty several times, that he could confide a few secrets in her.

"Steph, if I told you something, could you keep it between us?"

She almost stopped as she looked up at him, searching his eyes. "I hope you know that I can."

They reached Strand Road and turned left, walking past the Bogyoke Zay Market, peopled with thousands of bargainers. Across the street, wharves and warehouses fronted the river.

"Okay. You know that the microwave-relay stations will also carry channels dedicated to the Yangon and Mandalay television stations?"

"Sure. Each station will serve as a relay transmitter for TV signals, to reach farther into the hinterlands."

"Educating more of the population," he said.

"Not necessarily so," she countered. "The SLORC has made it clear that its current policies of censoring broadcasts aren't going to change."

"What if there were a couple of channels buried in all of those electronics that they couldn't find?"

Now, she did stop, pulling him to a halt with a hand on his arm. "You've programmed in some outlaw TV stations."

"Along with a few radio frequencies."

"Jesus. That's great, Chris, but wouldn't they catch on quickly?"

"Oh, yeah. This could be the scenario, Steph: After we all pull out, and if it doesn't look like the SLORC is making much progress, we can activate the channels and pump world news and current events right to the loneliest bandit in the back of Kachin State. Now, the only way the SLORC can stop those broadcasts is to destroy the microwave installations. That would wipe out their own telephonic voice and data communications. It's a Catch-22. To keep their populace from learning about the world, the committee would have to cripple their own military communications and control."

"Damn"—she grinned—"I didn't know you had a hidden agenda."

"There's always hidden agendas," Carson said, thinking about the other one.

They started walking again, her left hand gripping his forearm lightly.

"Now, I'm hungry," she said. "What did you say we're having?"

"There's an Indian place down a block. Something in a curry, madam?"

"The hotter, the better."

Night Market, Taunggyi

Daw Tan felt as if he owned the capital city of Shan State, though, of course, he did not. Of the more than ten thousand people living in the city, however, he could count on perhaps half to respond to any directive he might issue, no matter the position of the government. He had never tested his ability, but the feeling of power was delicious.

His driver piloted the Pathfinder slowly through the darkened streets until they reached the Night Market, which after midnight, was also unlit. The stalls were vacant, and nothing moved except the aromas carried on the air: rotting vegetables, decaying fish and meat.

"Stop here," he ordered.

The driver pulled to the side of the narrow street and shut off the engine. He pulled his Kalashnikov to his lap and sat surveying the street and the rearview mirrors. The street inspired claustrophobia, the houses jammed together, pushing in on them. Tan was accustomed to more open spaces.

He watched the square in which the Night Market was situated, a half-block away.

After five minutes, a shadowy figure emerged from the gloom of one of the stalls. The figure was alone, or appeared to be so.

Daw Tan opened his door and got out. "Be alert."

The driver got out, also, taking up a stance next to the front fender.

Tan crossed the street and walked slowly toward the man. They met in the middle of the dusty apron that fronted the market, and under the half-moon's light, nodded to each other.

"Colonel Mauk."

"Chieftain Tan."

Tan scanned the shadows behind the officer. "You are alone?"

"Of course not. But my men are well away, and you will be left alone."

Over the years, Tan had come to respect Mauk's honesty, at least, to respect it as much as he could that of any government representative.

"It was you who wished to meet," he said.

"The incident on the Banmo Road?"

"I had heard of it."

"And did you also hear the rumor that you were behind it?" Mauk asked.

"That story did not reach my ears," he said, not offering more.

Mauk was forced to ask the question, but asked it obliquely. "Were your men involved?"

"They were not."

There was no hesitation in his delivering the lie. Daw Tan, for several years of his youth, had been raised in the Islamic faith. He would not be considered a strict adherent to the tenets of the Koran, but he sometimes found it useful to apply them as circumstances dictated. As Mauk had been raised a Christian and therefore an infidel, Tan was obligated to lie to him.

"We have an agreement," Mauk said.

"And so we do. The government has unofficially recognized my authority in exchange for the freedom to extend its telephone and railroad lines through northern Shan State. Have your railroads or telephones been harmed?"

"Not in Shan State."

"Nor will they be," Tan promised.

Tan's philosophy was that an agreement was an agreement so long as it tended to benefit him. So far, the new railroad construction had reached only partway to Lashio, along the route of the existing railroad. He would have to reevaluate his position once the construction began to extend beyond Lashio.

And in any case, his agreement was only binding as to construction in northern Shan State. He felt absolutely free to do as he pleased anywhere else in the country.

"I seek only your word in regard to those two items," Mauk said. "One, that you had nothing to do with the attack on Banmo Road, and two, that you intend to fulfill our previous accord."

"You have it."

Mauk's dark eyes searched his own, then he nodded, and turned away.

As if having a second thought, he stopped abruptly and

turned back to Tan. From his pocket, he retrieved an object and offered it.

Tan reached out and took it, then Mauk walked away, disappearing once again into the shadows of the market.

In the soft light of the moon, Tan examined the warm tones of the ivory handle of the razor.

It was too bad, he thought. The Razor could have been a son to him.

He thought also of the message Mauk was sending to him, and he did not think that he liked it. The man was not entitled to deliver veiled threats. His agreement with the government gave him total immunity, and he would never suffer from an oppressive administration.

Not in his lifetime.

SIX

Palo Alto, California

The General Technologies Incorporated plant was set in a 160-acre park a half-mile off of Highway 101. Across the man-made berms and through the thick stand of carefully placed pine and blue spruce, the serene waters of the lower San Francisco Bay could be seen.

There were seven massive buildings—concrete and bronzed windows—on the site, along with six parking lots capable of handling sixteen thousand cars. The parking lots were not obvious; that was the reason for the berms.

From his corner office on the fifth and top floor of the administration building, Dexter Abrams had an unobstructed view of the Bay. He liked his view of the water for it reminded him of his forty-foot ketch, the *Alicia Mae,* which he loved almost as much as the boat's namesake, his wife. Abrams did not often get to sail the *Alicia Mae* because of the constraints on his time, and that made his view of the Bay that much more precious.

Abrams had been a senior vice president at General Motors when he was lured away to become the Chief Executive Officer of GTI. He had brought with him a great deal of valuable experience and four good men, including Chris Carson. Though he had been a hard worker at GM, putting in sixty- and seventy-hour weeks, he hadn't anticipated that his work in Palo

Alto was going to require so much more time. Eighty hours in a week was the norm.

Though he didn't like to admit it, the load was wearing on him. It showed up in his puffy face which made his eyes seem deeper and darker than the hazel they were. His eyelids were droopy and sometimes made him appear less alert than his mind proved to be. He worked out at least three times a week, so his body continued to fit his tailored suits. Still, he felt as if his 185 pounds was about five pounds higher than it should be for his six-foot three-inch stance. His silver-gray hair was styled once a week, right in his office. For fifty-six years of age, Abrams felt his face made him look a few years older. It was nothing that more sleep and maybe six or seven uninterrupted days on the *Alicia Mae* could not cure.

He had arrived at his office at five on Sunday morning, planning to spend four straight hours on backlogged paperwork, but he found Mack Little waiting for him in the administration lobby.

Little was a somber and brainy man with a high forehead and curly hair. Despite his rather lackluster demeanor, he could be animated, especially when working on, or just discussing, the exotic creations that emerged from his lab. He was Director of Laser Technology, lasers being one of GTI's twenty-two divisions, and one of the most active and revenue-producing.

"Mack, I don't see you."

"Sure you do, Dex."

"Go away. I've got work to do."

"This won't take long."

Shaking his head in resignation, Abrams led the way across the lobby and used his key to call the executive elevator. They both stepped into the car when the doors sighed open.

Fearing that Little's problem involved the Ruby Star project, Abrams didn't ask any questions during the short ride to the fifth floor. One never knew where the bugs might lie.

His office and select areas of the GTI campus were about as secure as current technology allowed. His office walls were doubled up, and white noise was piped between the two walls, as it was through the space between the dual glazing of the windows. That prevented telephonic boom microphones from listening through the windows or reading the vibrations of the glass. Additionally, each morning at three o'clock, the security section headed by Troy Baskin swept his office for listening devices.

The two of them walked through the morning-dark vacant space where his three secretaries worked, and Abrams unlocked the first of the double doors into his office. Abrams had never been in the military, but he thought he had better safeguards for his secrets than anything ever developed by the Pentagon.

As soon as he had the doors closed and the white noise turned on, Abrams asked, "This about Ruby Star?"

"Oh, no, Dex. We're still moving forward on that."

"And chewing up all my money while doing it, no doubt."

"You have any money left?" Little asked, grinning.

"Very damned little, as the finance committee is fond of reminding me. Sit down."

He went to the sideboard and turned on the coffeepot, which one of the secretaries prepared for him each night. Then he crossed the nice expanse of plush gray carpet to the corner where his small conference table was placed. He sat in one of the dark-gray leather chairs opposite Little.

With a stiff forefinger, he pointed toward the foot-high stack of paper on his desk. "See that, Mack?"

"I see it."

"Make this as fast as possible, will you?"

One of the qualities that Abrams admired in Mack Little was that, though he was an expert in quantum mechanics, he could always talk to the uninitiated in comprehensible terms. And Abrams was uninitiated; his background was business.

Little said, "We've got a mirror problem on the TNF application."

Mirrors were crucial components in laser devices. The term laser arose from the full title of Light Amplification by Stimulated Emission of Radiation, and was partially based on optical physics. In essence, a laser generated "coherent" light, and did so with an active medium like carbon-dioxide gas, some way of introducing energy into the active medium—frequently a flashlamp, and a set of mirrors mounted on each side of the active medium. One of the mirrors was used to transmit the radiation that reflected from it.

GTI was one of several companies in as many countries engaged in practical research on Thermonuclear Fusion—they called it the TNF Project. Little's research unit was using a pulsed carbon-dioxide laser focused on a miniature pellet of the hydrogen-isotope tritium in the attempt to produce a controlled fusion reaction, hopefully on a scale of less than that of the fission reaction at Hiroshima. A successful fusion process would eliminate energy source problems for the next century as well as producing immense profits.

"As I recall," Abrams said, "we devoted a considerable amount of time to selecting your mirror manufacturer."

The Research Committee, composed of two members of the board of directors and five company employees—including Abrams himself—had argued the merits for a full morning.

"Do you also recall that the committee opted for the lowest bid, Dex?"

"How much was it?"

"Thirty thousand bucks each."

"Well, damn it! It's only a goddamned mirror."

"Remember the vote?" Little asked. "You and the board members went for the low bid, along with Stu Gallagher. And Gallagher, being an administrator rather than a scientist, always swings with the brass. He wants a future."

"It's a mirror, for Christ's sake!"

"It's a mirror that's required to focus a beam precisely to microscopic measurements. The mirrors we got won't perform to specifications."

"Send them back."

"I can do that, but I'll guarantee you that Beckwith Optics will never, ever get them right."

"Christ! What was the next bid?"

"Not the next one, Dex. We need to go with Crayless, which is what we recommended in the first place."

"How much?"

"Seventy-five thousand each."

Abrams groaned. "And how many?"

"Twenty-four."

He ran the mathematics in a microsecond. "That's a million, eight hundred thousand more. For mirrors."

"It's more than that," Little said. "It's lost time, too, with my people twiddling their thumbs until Crayless can grind the first few mirrors. Six weeks, I'd guess, so I guess the total cost will go over four million."

All he needed to take to the next board meeting was another setback. With his new job, Abrams had learned valuable lessons about conforming to governing board expectations. One could fight them, but only so far.

"There's no way you can get by with . . ."

"None. Cheap just ain't gonna cut it," the quantum-physics expert said in the Virginia twang of his youth, which he utilized at will.

"I'll have to call a special meeting of the Research Committee."

Little shoved a sheet of paper across the table. "There's the vote of the three scientists. All you need is one more. Yours would do it."

After Little left, Abrams moved over to his desk and turned on his computer terminal. He called up the budget/expenditures year-to-date report for the Laser Technology Division and found what he expected to find.

The research section was forty-four percent over budget, primarily on the TNF Project and the Ruby Star Project.

The production section was doing relatively well, with increased sales in the compact-disc and video-disc applications, where lasers were used to etch the discs. The medical technology devices—ranging from tissue-cutting instruments to ophthalmic apparatus for noninvasive surgery of the retina to the miniature endoscopic fiber transmitters used in angioplasty to clear cholesterol blockages in the arteries—were performing far above expectations. As projected, range-finding and targeting lasers under defense department contracts were down, though their sales of similar machines for surveying were holding up.

The bottom line, five-twelfths of the way through their fiscal year: The overruns in research were going to eat substantially into the division's profits. If Little was right about an additional four-million-dollar cost in research, and the figures held through the balance of the year, the Laser Technology Division was going to show a profit of less than five million.

The board wasn't going to like it. And understandably, the stockholders weren't going to like it.

Dexter Abrams, the master businessman, might just start looking for another job.

Or get Chris Carson off his ass, and working at what he was supposed to be doing.

Near Man Na-su, Shan State

Khim Nol did not look like a well man. If Daw Tan was the ugliest man in the Union of Myanmar, Khim Nol would be the unhealthiest.

His face had been ravaged by smallpox at an early age—he was now in his early sixties—and the reddened pits starkly contrasted the pale greenish tinge of his skin. His brown eyes appeared protuberant, as if there were a great deal of pressure behind them, gases building up inside his skull. His hair was still dark, but so thin that, from a distance, he would appear bald. He was a tiny man, fitted well in expensive casual clothing, but carried the appearance of frailty.

And that was deceptive, for Khim Nol was the strongest man Tan had ever known. His strength was greater than that of the government of Yangon, supported by rumors of a personal wealth that exceeded ten billion dollars American. Despite the fact that, in person, Nol was a mild and steadfast man, his notoriety included instances in which he had personally directed the removal of the limbs and organs of men and women while they were still alive. In private situations, Tan had twice been witness to Nol's manic rages. At such times, his reasoning became chaotic and his decisions capricious.

Nol preferred to arrive at his destinations unannounced, and that was true of this Sunday morning. One of his six bodyguards had banged on the door to Tan's house and gotten him out of bed. Tan's own guards had not sounded an alert for him, but that was understandable. They understood the hierarchy of power. After Tan let him in, the bodyguard searched the house, ordering Tan's wife to leave for an hour.

Then Khim Nol came in, his face in the dusky morning light of the living room more ashen and pitted than normal.

"May I prepare you something to eat, Chieftain Nol?" Tan asked.

"I have eaten already, Chieftain Tan. It is not necessary."

While four of the bodyguards took up stations around the large room, Nol selected a seat in the center of a sofa and sat down. It was not required that he ever ask permission to do what he wanted. When he nodded at Tan, Tan sat in one of the armchairs placed at right angles to the couch.

"This business of the Banmo Road?"

"A fiasco. I admit it."

"Yes. You should," Nol said in his soft-spoken way. "And I have word from Yangon that the Razor is no longer with us."

"My sources say that he accomplished his mission, which was to silence Miu." Tan did not enlighten his superior as to the other half of the Razor's mission.

"He was a good man, though perhaps less fearful than he should have been."

"A credit to me," Daw Tan agreed. "And very much a son."

Nol may have perceived the possible truth of that statement, for he said, "With the son no longer available, the father must complete the work."

"Personally?" Tan had already been planning a replacement for the Razor.

"Personally," Khim Nol said. "It was your most capable lieutenant who proved unsatisfactory, was it not? If he was the best, then that leaves you. I have the utmost faith in your abilities, Chieftain."

Nol smiled in a fatherly way, his gray-streaked teeth a slash in his face.

"My reflexes are not what they once were."

"I am certain they will live up to your reputation. Or are you saying that you no longer have the confidence you once had?"

"Of course not. I will accomplish what is necessary."

"And quickly, of course. I have an arrangement to fulfill, and I trust in your ability to serve as my capable agent."

"Yes."

Doing as he was ordered by his superior meant that Daw Tan was allowed to continue conducting his own business interests in northern Shan State. To ignore any suggestion of Khim Nol was to slice his own throat.

Still, Daw Tan did not like Nol questioning his confidence. If anything, his confidence was greater than it had ever been. And yet, at fifty years of age, he had expected that he would be allowed to let others take care of the mundane tasks.

But that was all right.

He could still kill.

The Strand Hotel, Yangon

Stephanie Branigan crossed the ornate lobby of the Strand to the dining room and gave her name to the maître d'.

"Ah, mademoiselle, yes. This way, if you please."

She followed him across the sea of white linen to a table by a window where Hyun Oh was waiting for her. The South Korean stood up as they approached.

Branigan thought that Oh must have a wardrobe selection that would raise the envy in any woman. She was certain he must have worn the same outfit more than once, but it was difficult for her to recall it. Today, he wore an ivory suit of lightweight silk, a shirt white enough to blind, with an overlay of a white Oriental pattern on the white background, and a tie the palest shade of yellow. His black wing tip shoes were polished to a high gloss. Among the engineers and construction people who populated the Zoo and who wore anything within the spectrum of casual, Oh was a standout. She had never seen him without a tie knotted precisely in place.

"Good afternoon, Miss Branigan. I am happy you could join me for lunch."

"I wish you'd cut out the Miss stuff, Hyun. Please, it's Stephanie."

The maître d' pulled out her chair for her, and she sat.

"I am afraid that my parents did not prepare me well for the daily regimen of working with a group of Americans. It is difficult, after my training, to be less formal."

"I'll try to un-train you," she said, smiling.

"Thank you."

They both ordered the crab entree, and since it was Sunday and her one day off, Branigan ordered a glass of Chablis.

"I was sorry to hear of the accident with the train," Oh said.

"It wasn't an accident, but I don't think it's going to happen again."

As they talked about the sabotage of the UltraTrain, Branigan looked around the dining room. It was almost full, and the patronage was primarily foreign. She heard parts of conversations in English, French, Spanish, Italian, Chinese, Indian, and—she guessed—Greek. She smiled at a few people she knew, or had met briefly. They were primarily associated with the embassies or consulates, rather than the Myanmar Project.

The Strand was one of those hotels she was always pleased to look at, for its cultural and aesthetic qualities, but usually avoided for lodging and meals. She tended to be more practical. Hyun Oh, however, seemed to relish the place. He knew the waiters by name, and he was entirely comfortable. She supposed he was striving for a man-of-the-world sophistication, and she normally found those aspirations to be somewhat hollow.

It took a little while for Oh to get to the core of this luncheon meeting; she knew it wasn't a date. She didn't go out on dates.

"The reason I asked to meet with you . . . Stephanie, is this: I wish for you to know that Hypai Industries has just completed development of a superconducting magnet."

"Ah!"

"We believe it is a tremendous accomplishment. I have not personally seen the test results yet, but the efficiency factors are excellent, I am told. And I believe the price will be extremely competitive."

She had heard that Oh was a real hustler, making the rounds with proposals to many of the subcontractors and to the Burmese businessmen whenever he had clearance to approach them from the government. And she supposed that he would truly have a good working sample of the magnet soon. Whatever else they were, the South Koreans were top-of-the-line copycats. She didn't know of one original design, in any field, that they had come up with on their own, but give them a car, a television set, or a CD player, and they'd start batting out copies by the millions. The saving grace was that they batted them out a great deal cheaper by placing the onus of the production costs on their underpaid workers.

And what would her bosses say to such a proposal? Would they undercut their American assembly-line workers if they could get the thousands of magnets she needed for half, or even three-quarters, of the cost? Boosting their profit margin for the project by an equivalent amount?

In a millisecond.

And one of the rationales was that they had shaved the profit margin to almost nil in order to secure this contract. If they turned out a working railroad that made the Myanmar National Railway the envy of, at least, Southeast Asia, they would make their profit in the next contract . . . and the next . . . and the next. That was her job, making certain there was a next contract.

"I tell you what, Hyun. Get me a working model and the plans for it, and I'll take a look."

"That is all I ask," Oh said, quite humbly.

GTI compound, Yangon

Hyun Oh had offered Stephanie Branigan a ride back to the compound, but she had begged off, saying she was going shopping. He had driven alone in his Celica back to the compound and had trouble finding a parking space. On Sundays, many of the field teams came to Yangon for the day and used the transient quarters.

The Hypai Industries central offices were located next to the cafeteria, and when he tried the door, he found it open. Inside, with all of the windows closed, it was hot and close. He opened a window in the reception area, then looked into the assistant director's office.

Kim Sung-Young was in the chair at his desk, his back to Oh as he tapped at the keyboard of the computer on the credenza against the wall. Sung-Young was a rotund man of fifty years, an electronics engineer, and unlike Oh, understood telephone systems thoroughly. It was he who managed the day-to-day construction activities of the Hypai field crews and engineers. As assistant director, he was also in charge of the accounting system.

Oh rapped his knuckles against the door frame to get Sung-Young's attention.

He spun around in his chair. "Mr. Oh. You surprised me."

"I am glad to see you at work, but I fear the timing. Is there a problem?"

"No, no problem. It is only the infernal paperwork."

"Yes, I know it well. How is our schedule holding up?"

"At the moment, we are two-and-a-half days behind. It may be attributed to causes beyond our control."

"I am sure, yet let us try to accelerate the pace and return to the planned schedule."

"I will do my best, Mr. Oh."

"Thank you. I also need an envelope."

They had taken to calling them envelopes, for fear that the real word would reach out to Colonel Lon Mauk and offend his policy of forbidding bribes. *Baksheesh* as they called it in the Middle East. In Asia, too, it was an acceptable custom.

"How large an envelope?" Sung-Young asked.

"Thirty thousand *baht*, I think. The man I am meeting is wealthy enough that less would be insulting."

Sung-Young turned in his chair and scooted it across the floor to the big black safe against the wall. Both Sung-Young and Oh knew the combinations for the two tumblers, but Oh preferred to let Sung-Young manage the vault. After he opened the door, he withdrew a steel box from the bottom shelf. It was labeled Petty Cash.

Opening the box, he took out a small ledger and handed it to Oh. He jotted the date, the name of the man he was meeting, and the amount on a single line, then signed his name at the end of the line.

The deputy director fumbled through the rubber-banded stacks of bills. The box normally contained around fifty thousand dollars' worth of American dollars, Thai *baht*, and Myanmar *kyat*. He counted out the amount in Thai currency and handed it to Oh.

"Thank you."

Oh backed out of the office and crossed to his own. He knew that Sung-Young resented him to some extent. The man was older and more experienced, as well as being an accomplished engineer. By all rights, Sung-Young should have been in charge of the Myanmar contract, and he did not care to defer to an obviously inferior and younger man.

There were, however, a great many things that Kim Sung-Young did not know. Among those things, he did not know that he received precisely the same salary as Oh, rewarded as skimpily for his knowledge and expertise as was his superior. He did not know that the project was, in reality, seven-and-a-half-days ahead of schedule. Sung-Young had never read the contract, which allowed for ten additional days. The contract with Hypai Industries was similar to all contracts let by the SLORC; there were daily financial penalties for overruns, and there were daily incentives for completion of projects ahead of schedule. In Hypai's case, that amounted to $100,000 a day, and Hyun Oh had chosen to set a one-million-dollar bonus for ten days' early completion as his standard for the project. If he succeeded, it would please Mr. Pai, and it could only bolster the personal bonus Oh expected to receive at the end of the contract.

In his own office, smaller than Sung-Young's in order to give the man some feeling of his worth, Oh attended to a few minor paper matters of his own while he waited for the clock. Once a week, at three o'clock, five o'clock in Seoul, he was required to call Mr. Pai. It had become an irritating ritual, for it meant that he never had a complete Sunday to himself. Many times, he had called only to find that Mr. Pai was out for the afternoon. Mr. Pai would not ruin his own Sundays if he chose not to do so.

Precisely at ten seconds before three o'clock, he pressed the Speed Dialing button on his executive telephone set. It was programmed for Mr. Pai's home telephone and utilized a built-in scrambling circuit. The telephonic route followed the completed Yangon exchange and the microwave relay to the satellite link. Reception was clear as a bell but for the slight echo of the encryption devices.

Mr. Pai answered immediately.

"Good afternoon, Mr. Pai."

"Hello, Hyun Oh."

He delivered his typical weekly report of the Myanmar contract—exchange completions, shipments of equipment received from the Pusan factories, workforce strength, budget to expenditure ratios, and schedule position, rounding it off to eight days ahead. Certainly, Sung-Young would be able to gain a half-day.

"And the local ventures?"

"I have now identified, and met with, the potential primary investor or general partner in each of the fourteen sectors requiring a private telephone company. In four instances, I have met at least three times with those men. We now have an oral commitment for what would be known as the Arakan Telephone Company. It would be headquartered in Sandoway."

"But nothing in writing?" Pai asked.

"As yet, no."

"And the others?"

"I am to meet with the man from Karen State this week. He, like many of the others—especially in the north, is still reluctant to invest heavily himself or induce others to substantially invest."

Mr. Pai understood that the local businessmen feared that the money they invested in a private telephone company could quickly disappear as a result of the activity of rebel factions.

"What would make them less reluctant?"

"They would like to have a large investor as a silent partner," Oh told him.

"Of course. They want control, but without risk."

"My argument, naturally, is that the Myanmar government wishes to promote local investment with the consequence of local profits, keeping the revenues in the country to bolster the standard of living."

"That is not necessarily true," Pai said.

"I know. The SLORC is encouraging foreign investment, but through partnerships with native companies which will have the operational control."

"I suppose, Mr. Oh, that we could create a separate venture capital company to enter into agreements with the local companies. We might be able to assume, let us say, forty percent of the investment. If they want control, they must provide the bulk of the investment."

Oh wanted to say "our" capital, but he said, "The capital expenditure of Hypai Industries would be placed in jeopardy, Mr. Pai. It is certainly a greater risk than, for example, a venture into India or Indonesia."

"Not all of fourteen ventures would necessarily fail."

"I have been considering this deeply, Mr. Pai, and I have another proposal. What if Hypai Industries initiated an insurance company?"

"To underwrite the ventures?"

"Exactly. The insurance subsidiary would gain premium income, enhancing the profit picture of the company. If one of the telephone companies suffered a loss, the insurance company's reserves would be utilized to offset the loss."

"Do you also suggest a percentage, Mr. Oh?"

"Insurance policies are notoriously difficult to read, sir. What with the fine print and the conditions assigned to claims, the insurance company's liability could be reduced to, perhaps, twenty percent of the loss. I am not an expert in insurance underwriting, but I believe the lawyers could write clauses acceptable to Hypai Industries."

And practically unreadable by the new Burmese capitalists.

After a long pause, Pai said, "This is certainly a commendable suggestion, Mr. Oh. I will look into it. What of EASTGLOW?"

EASTGLOW was the code name for the third, and most important, of Hyun Oh's missions in Myanmar.

"I have now completed most of the research, Mr. Pai. And I am now attempting to identify the best possible person or persons through whom a contract might be secured. It is not an easy task."

"We are quickly running out of time. You must move more rapidly."

"I do not want to make a mistake, Mr. Pai."

"It is a risk you will have to assume."

"Of course," Oh said, but his stomach felt queasy.

Mr. Pai thought he understood the dangers of Myanmar, but that was only in terms of the bandits and the rebels. He did not fully appreciate the ruthlessness of the government itself.

It was not only EASTGLOW that could be in peril; Hyun Oh's life could well be in danger, and of the two, he much preferred to lose EASTGLOW.

Air Force operations, Mingaladon Airport, Yangon

Lon Mauk had always distrusted the air-force branch of the armed services. Simply because they were able to fly obsolete aircraft, the officers were imbued with an arrogance and cockiness that was far in excess of their true worth.

The man with whom he met, Colonel Chit Nyunt, was no different from the rest. Dressed in the standard air-force uniform, Nyunt altered regulations by wearing a blue silk scarf at his throat. It was supposed to give him an air of derring-do, Mauk supposed, but served only to make him appear as foppish as the colonial ruling force had once been. Mauk was not impressed.

Nyunt was not only a flyer. He was also the head of the air force's intelligence bureau, a body with a checkered history of success, and Mauk was prepared to accept Nyunt's revelations with appropriate skepticism.

They did not meet in the intelligence officer's office, but in the operations office on the military side of the airport. A high counter ran across the middle of the operations room, and Nyunt stood on one side of it, his elbows and bare forearms resting on the top. Effectively, the posturing told Mauk that he was not welcome on the other side of the counter, in the air force's domain.

"Thank you for stopping by," Nyunt said. "I have been so busy, I could not get away."

Busy playing golf or chasing other men's wives, no doubt. "I understand completely, Colonel."

"I did think you should be immediately aware of an item that one or my operatives uncovered."

"Affecting the modernization program?"

"As we understand it, yes. The information comes by way of the rebels in Karen State."

The Karens and Kayahs made up about ten percent of the population of Myanmar, and a large faction of them had never been enchanted with the central government.

"It seems that an attack is being planned in Karen State, apparently against the new railroad."

Mauk's mind immediately captured his personal map of the maglev railroad's progress. Construction was under way in various parts of the country, with the major railroad yards all but completed in Yangon and Mandalay. The main corridor between Yangon and Mandalay had been re-tracked south from Mandalay to Pyawbwe and north from Yangon almost to Pyinmana. There was but another hundred kilometers to complete before the Yangon-Mandalay leg was joined. Simultaneously, other routes were under construction—north toward Prome from Yangon, north from Mandalay toward the mines, east and south through Pegu and down along the coast in Karen State toward Moulmein.

There were other segments just beginning, but in Karen State, no railroad construction was currently envisioned.

"It would be against the railhead in Mon State, which is now extended to Thaton?"

Thaton was twenty kilometers inland from the coast.

"That would be my supposition," Nyunt said. "The construction northward from Ye"—the city was the southernmost point of the railroad in Mon State—"is but thirty kilometers in length. If I were a rebel, I should want to disrupt the traffic on the more substantial segment."

Mauk could agree with that assessment, though he hated to do so.

"Who is your source?" he asked.

"Ah, Colonel, I cannot reveal my sources."

"Naturally. You will increase your air surveillance of the railroad in that area?"

Nyunt shook his head sadly. "If I but had the resources, I would be happy to do so. However, night operations are not planned."

Rebel actions almost always occurred at night, but the air force was widely known for its reluctance to fly at night. Part of that reluctance could be laid to inadequate or inoperative instrumentation for night flying, but much of it, Mauk had always thought, could also be placed on pilots who were superheroes in the sunlight and much meeker in the darkness of storms or the night.

"I will speak to Minister Ba Thun," Mauk said. "Perhaps he can encourage the SLORC to devote additional revenues to support aerial coverage of the railroad at night."

The slight flicker in Nyunt's eyes told him the man thought little of that idea, but his bravado was required to speak otherwise. "That would be wonderful, Colonel Mauk."

"When is this attack to take place?"

"Why," Mauk smiled, "my understanding is that the target date is tonight. I suspect you will not get the SLORC to act in time."

Moulmein

When he had received the warning of the possible attack on the railway from Mauk, Carson had called the airport to get clearance for a flight to Thaton. Operations had turned him down, saying that military maneuvers were taking place in the area. He had to hope that meant the air force had been prodded to put airborne patrols into the region.

So he had called Branigan to alert her, then phoned Charles Washington at his apartment. Washington, whose operations were headquartered near the Lower Hledan Street Jetty on the Rangoon River, was in charge of development of the hydrofoil river-transport fleet. His Hydrofoil Marine Corporation was under a separate contract with the SLORC and was not a sub to GTI. Washington, a huge black man who had once played tackle for the Detroit Lions, didn't have anything better to do on a Sunday night.

It was 130 miles, down the Rangoon River to the Gulf of Martaban, and across the Gulf, to Moulmein. They made the trip in just over two hours aboard a sixty-foot hydrofoil and arrived in Moulmein at eight o'clock at night, met by one of Branigan's drivers in a Land Rover.

Washington elected to go along with them, forcing Carson into the backseat with Branigan so that the six-foot six-inch, 260-pound former tackle could have minimal room in the front passenger seat.

Carson had always hated backseats. It made him feel claustrophobic. And not being behind the wheel was another challenge he didn't care to take. He was born to be a boss, and he couldn't stand the lack of control. It reminded him of the Banmo Road.

"Where to, Miss Branigan?" the driver asked.

"We're headed for Thaton."

He slapped the truck into gear, backed away from the pier, and headed for the juncture with Highway 8, which ran north and south along the thin slice of geography that Myanmar owned between the Andaman Sea and Thailand. At its widest point it was sixty miles wide, and it ran south from the main body of Myanmar for five hundred miles. The Thanintari Taundan mountain range was the dividing line between Myanmar and Thailand and dominated the Myanmar side of the line, leaving little arable area along the coastal lowlands.

The driver turned left on the highway, which was in fairly decent repair, and after he crossed a bridge over the bay, Carson saw a sign next to the highway: THATON—67 KILOMETERS.

"Damn," Washington said, "I'm sure glad you're injecting a little excitement into my life."

"If you think flying bullets are exciting, Charles," Branigan said.

He turned in his seat as far as his bulk would allow, to talk to them. "You don't think they are?"

"I've experienced them," she said. "I'm not eager to repeat it."

"Yeah, I heard. What do you think about all this, Chris?"

"Mauk's informant said it was a rebel operation."

"And you don't think so?"

"We haven't had any trouble with the rebel factions in two years," Carson said. "I don't know why they would get upset with us all of a sudden."

"What's hard to know," Washington said, "is what group of nuts might be behind it. You've got a whole bunch of bandits, another bunch of druggies, and five or six organizations of political dissidents to choose from."

"Plus some hill tribes that don't care to march into the twentieth century, much less the twenty-first," Branigan added.

Branigan looked worried, Carson thought. She was a people person in addition to an engineer, and she would be thinking about her crews on the line. The railroad construction was moving ahead twenty-four hours a day, using three shifts of Burmese and international workers under American and European supervisors.

He heard the *thrupp-thrupp* of rotors approaching and leaned against the window to look up.

"What's that?" Washington asked.

"UH-1H," Carson said when he spotted it flying five hundred feet above the old rail line. "We call it a Huey. Mauk told me he was trying to put some pressure on the air force to get some air cover up. Looks like he succeeded."

The helo went on by, its landing light on, following the tracks into the dusk.

"Anyway," Washington said, "we were saying?"

"I don't know, Charles," Carson said. "There's not much to go on. We've got the attack on the road, and we've got the threat of an attack tonight—"

"Don't forget my train," Branigan said.

"And an incident of sabotage. It doesn't add up to a concerted effort to kill the project."

"I'm going to ask Mauk for guards to put on the boats. Or for some automatic weapons I can give a private-security outfit. I've got six hydros on regular service on the river between Yangon and Mandalay now, and next month, I'm supposed to take delivery on another eight. I don't want anyone shooting them up, especially with a load of passengers or cargo."

"I wouldn't count on the guards," Carson told him. "The way I read the political-military scene, I'd guess there's a few good old boys who are getting worried about the size of Mauk's forces."

"What about the weapons?"

"Iffy. They don't like guns in the hands of anyone but friends."

"Hell, every guy in the hills has a gun."

"I'm saying what they don't like, not what the reality is."

"I'm going to give it a shot, anyway," Washington said.

They were halfway to Thaton when the two-way radio blurted, "Hey, Chalkie! This is Dribble. Can you read me?"

The driver grabbed the mike from its dash mount and keyed the Transmit button. "Chalk here, Brent. What've you got?"

"You don't happen to have Mr. Carson with you, do you? Some of his people are trying to reach him."

"Hold on." Chalk passed the microphone back to Carson.

"This is Carson. Go ahead."

"Mr. Carson, your microwave station in Moulmein just blew up."

"Goddamn it!" Pressing the Transmit stud, he said, "Anyone hurt?"

"I've got no details," the voice said.

Carson hesitated, trying to decide what to do.

Branigan solved it for him. "Let's turn around and go back, Chalk."

"I'll bet they changed targets on us," Washington said.

SEVEN

It was almost nine-thirty by the time they got back to Moulmein, a city of around two hundred thousand people. From far outside the city limits, Carson had been able to see the yellow-red tinge against the night sky on the far side of the city that suggested a major fire. By the time they threaded through the city's internal traffic—everyone in town on the way to see the fire, apparently—and reached the site, the fire had lost intensity.

The fire-fighting units were just arriving.

Near the airport, which was farther to the south, Carson saw the lights of several aircraft circling for the approach pattern. He guessed that Colonel Mauk would soon arrive.

Chalk parked as close as he could get, outside the chain-link fence supposedly protecting the building, and they all climbed out of the Land Rover. Carson stretched his back and shoulder muscles while looking at the carnage.

Sixty feet back from the fence, the InstaStructure building was still standing, its steel-and-fiberglass reinforced concrete walls having absorbed the damage. The roof, made of steel, was gone, and flames still licked the air above the tops of the walls. Littering the ground around the structure were sheets of the roofing and twisted structural members.

An argument was taking place near the gate, and Carson walked down to it, skirting haphazardly parked cars which were blocking the access for the fire engines. He found an army soldier arguing with a fireman, and interrupted long enough to find out that the guard wasn't letting anyone in, much less the fire department. After producing an ID for the soldier, he was allowed to countermand the order and have the gate opened for the fire trucks. The soldier ran off to try and find the operators of blocking cars in order to get them moved.

When he stepped back, Washington asked, "What was that all about?"

"Mauk's people are taking their orders seriously. The fire chief, if that's what he is, wasn't authorized entry."

Two pumpers of sixties' vintage pulled into the enclosure, and a dozen firemen began pulling hoses every which way. The closest hydrant turned out to be a quarter-mile down the road.

It took nearly an hour to quench the flames, and they were just dying away when an air force helicopter landed in a nearby field. Its rotors beat back the drifting smoke. Carson's clothes reeked of smoke and his eyes felt as if they were reddened. His mouth felt as if it were coated with soot. Branigan's light-colored jumpsuit was gray with residue.

The aromas drifting on the air were not palatable, either.

Carson, Branigan, and Washington walked toward the chopper and met Mauk when he exited the craft.

"Ah, Mr. Carson. A tragedy?"

"I don't know how bad, Colonel. At this time of night, there should have been three people on duty."

"How did they get in?"

"I don't know that, either. The gate was locked when I got here, and your man seemed pretty intent on keeping everyone out."

The four of them walked back together, and the guard let them inside the fence when Mauk waved him aside. Mauk also spoke to an officer in charge of a truckload of troops who had shown up earlier, and soon, the soldiers began to ring the facility outside the fence.

Carson crossed the unpaved parking area toward the building, trying to stay out of the way of fire equipment and working men, stepping over chunks of steel and girders that had once supported the roof. Firemen were already beginning to roll their hoses. When he reached the open doorway, stepping in a puddle of water, he leaned through the frame and surveyed the interior.

This should have been a small anteroom, its walls dividing the telephone company's installation from that of the microwave station. There was no division now. The walls had gone up in flames, and the equipment rooms were charred and black. Melted plastic dripped over metal components. There was a heavy ozone odor. He saw that the main electric transformers on one wall had maintained their integrity. They were supposed to withstand heat of over 2,000 degrees Fahrenheit. Over it all was a sheen of water, and grayish water was two inches deep on the concrete floor, rushing over the doorsill.

"You suppose the electrical feed shut down?" Washington asked from beside him.

"I hope so. Otherwise, these firemen would have learned new things about using water on an electrical fire."

Just inside the doorway, Carson saw the blackened form of a corpse stretched out on the floor. Its limbs were grotesquely curled up against the torso. He hoped the man, or the woman, had died before burning.

Branigan splashed through the water behind them, and Carson turned around to stop her.

"You don't want to see this, Steph."

She took him at his word and stepped back.

Carson left the concrete slab of the porch, stamped his damp shoes, and walked around to the back, Branigan and Washington following him.

At the back of the building, the antenna complex was located within another fenced area. There hadn't been any fire here, but all of the antennas were bent and caved in, the victims of some kind of detonation. Satchel charges of plastic, he guessed, rather than grenades.

"This is terrible, Chris."

"It is."

They turned when steps approached them from behind. Colonel Mauk joined them.

Mauk looked over the antennas, then said, "You are a military man, Mr. Carson. What would you estimate from the damage?"

"Not hard-cased munitions, Colonel. C-4 or C-6 plastic explosive."

"Yes. Inside the building, also."

"The explosive of choice of terrorists," Carson said.

"Bastards," Washington said.

"Would you estimate the monetary damage?" Mauk asked.

"I'm not sure of the Hypai side. Maybe three million. At least that much on our side."

Under the contract, acts of terrorism were the responsibility of the Myanmar government, and the contractors would be reimbursed for the reconstruction. Part of the price, though, would come out of Mauk's hide, Carson thought, since he was in charge of security.

"I saw one body," he said.

"There are three," the colonel reported.

"They will likely be Burmese. We had turned over operation of this facility to the local telephone administration."

"Mons, then. I hope one of them is the perpetrator," Mauk said.

"What about the railhead, Colonel?" Branigan asked.

"There has been no activity, Miss Branigan. I still have a large security force in place there, and there are three helicopters patrolling the right-of-way."

"Could this be a diversion for an attack up there?" Carson asked.

"Possibly," Mauk said. "However, I suspect that our information about the railroad was a diversion for the activity here."

"Disinformation?"

"Exactly."

"What are you talking about?" Branigan asked.

"Someone made sure the wrong information got into the intelligence pipeline in order to mislead us," Carson told her.

"This is getting very scary," she said.

Carson thought so, too.

"I doubt," Mauk said, "that we will learn much more tonight. After it cools off, our forensic experts will go through the rubble."

"You'll call me if you learn something?" Carson asked, remembering that he hadn't learned much about the earlier incident from Mauk. He felt as if he ought to get closer to the intelligence sources. It was difficult to make competent decisions based on wild guesses.

"Of course."

They went back to Yangon aboard Washington's hydrofoil, putting in at the Hledan Street Jetty at two in the morning. Half an hour later, Carson and Branigan were back at the Zoo.

He went directly to his second-floor apartment, a near image of others in the compound, and mixed himself a light scotch.

Then he sprawled on the sofa and picked up the telephone.

Abrams was out somewhere, but he called back about three in the morning.

Carson brought him up to date.

"We weren't at risk on the financial end?"

"No, but I'm going to have to have another look at the contract to see what it does to our schedule, Dex. I'm not quite sure how it's covered, but if we'd run over schedule as a result of rebuilding the Moulmein complex, we might be liable for penalties."

"Ridiculous! Not our fault."

"I know that, but I don't know if the lawyers thought about it when they were drawing the thing up."

In the back of his mind, Carson was already deciding to move the crew—which had just finished Prome—from Toungoo to Moulmein. He'd have to talk to Hyun Oh about Hypai's end of it, also.

And in the interest of time, rather than tow all of those trailers the 225-mile distance, he'd have to check with Don Evans and see if they could arrange to get them moved by Skycranes. It was more costly, but time would cost him more in the end.

"If they weren't thinking," Abrams said, "I know a bunch of lawyers who are going to be looking for new jobs."

"There were three killed, too."

"Shit. Ours?"

"No IDs yet, but I don't think we had any of our employees on-site. Not at that time of night, anyway. I'll check with Sam Enders in the morning."

"Let me know immediately if we've had a fatality. You're not on a scrambled phone."

"No. I just got back to my apartment."

"Okay. What about the other?"

"We're working on it."

"Time is getting critical," Abrams told him unnecessarily.

"I know what time it is, Dex."

Keng Tung

Minister U Ba Thun arrived in Keng Tung at ten o'clock in the morning by way of a government helicopter. The 650-kilometer trip took over two hours, and he was not happy with his wrinkled appearance when he arrived.

Unofficial capital of the Golden Triangle, Keng Tung lay in the mountainous highlands of western Shan State, at the crossroads of three paved highways. The State Law and Order Restoration Committee ignored the distinction, just as it ignored the comparatively open borders between Myanmar, Laos, and Thailand which allowed poppies, opium gum, and the finished opium product almost unrestricted movement throughout the Triangle.

Closing the border would mean open warfare with the druglords, quite likely a war which the SLORC could not win. There was heavy international pressure on the government to do something about men like Khim Nol. However, the jungles and mountains made effective military action almost impossible. Then, too, the opium trade relieved some of the economic pressure on the central government. A single peasant made little from growing the poppy plants—perhaps a hundred dollars American a year, but that was money they would not otherwise have, and it kept them independent of the government.

For the time, the SLORC preferred to face one problem at a time. Today, the Modernization Proclamation. Tomorrow, perhaps the drug trade.

The population of Keng Tung did not warrant an airport, yet there was one. It would not be found on many maps because it been constructed by Khim Nol for his personal use and for the use of his subordinates. As his helicopter closed for a landing, Ba Thun noted the aircraft lined up alongside the single runway. In addition to two helicopters, there were a half-dozen large cargo aircraft, two sleek business jets, and a Cessna T-37 jet trainer. The government of Myanmar could not afford such aircraft.

When his helicopter landed and the rotors began to slow, a black Toyota Pathfinder drove up and stopped next to the aircraft. There was one man behind the wheel.

Ba Thun opened his door and slid out. His bodyguard started to come with him, but Ba Thun waved him back. He walked over to the Pathfinder.

The driver stuck his head through his open window, "I am to drive you, Minister."

"How far?"

"It is not far. In the village."

He walked around the truck and got in on the passenger side.

He watched the odometer from the corner of his eyes, and the trip turned out to be 1.1 kilometers long. It was a small house on a side street, and there were seven vehicles parked around it.

Leaving the truck, Ba Thun walked up to the door, which was opened immediately for him by someone's bodyguard, a hard man with eyes like flint and an assault rifle on a sling hung across his stomach. He entered, and the door was closed behind him.

The interior of the house was unfurnished except for one large table surrounded by five chairs. There were just enough chairs for the people in the room, all of whom Ba Thun had met many times before: Nol, Tan, Shwe, and Kaing. The last, Nito Kaing, was the only female. As the widow of the man who had once controlled the southern Shan State drug trade, Kaing had been expected to quietly defer the territory to the dead prince's lieutenant, and she had surprised everyone by executing him instead. Or that was how the story went. Other stories suggested that she had arranged her own widowhood. There was supposed to have been a son, in his late teens at the time, who was so appalled by the assassination of his father that he forsook Nito Kaing and disappeared into the hills. In any event, she had unexpectedly amassed a considerable amount of power and was, as far as Ba Thun understood, the equal of Tan and Shwe.

"Minister Ba Thun," Nol said, "I am happy we could arrange this meeting."

"As am I, Chieftain."

Ba Thun thought that Khim Nol looked to be on his deathbed. He also thought that he would have preferred meeting Nol alone, but the man had been adamant about the presence of the others.

They all took seats around the table, and though he probably should have felt intimidated by the number and the proximity of these warlords, Ba Thun was relaxed. No one here would be a hazard to his safety. It was part and parcel of their understanding.

Khim Nol was the only one who smiled. The others remained stoic. Nito Kaing's nose was red, as if she suffered from a cold. Ba Thun doubted that she used her own product; these people were too smart for that. She was a tiny woman, much too small for the power she wielded. Her black hair was pulled back tightly into a bun at the back of her head, and her dark eyes were penetrating and direct. In contrast to the others at the table, her skin was nearly flawless, a pale sheen almost ceramic in its perfection. She wore no makeup. There was a diminutive beauty there, but it was marred by the knowledge, or supposed knowledge, of the atrocities attributed to her.

"It is you who requested the meeting," Nol said.

Ba Thun outlined the incidents of his concern, finishing with the bombing of the telephone facility on Sunday night. He could not and would not accuse anyone here of wrongdoing or of broken promises. Neither could he suggest they were incapable of controlling their subordinates. This meeting was primarily for show and for the record. Anytime a member of the SLORC held a meeting with one of the chieftains, policy provided that he write detailed notes of the encounter for the files maintained at City Hall.

He said, "I am here to enlist your assistance. For the past two years of our agreement, our coexistence has been peaceful and fruitful. I believe we all have benefited from the lack of conflict. Now, however, it appears that someone wishes to disturb that equilibrium. I ask your help, not necessarily in subduing whatever renegades are at large, but in identifying them. The government will then take whatever steps are necessary to restore the accord between us."

Ba Thun thought that nothing would come of this plea, but it was important to the tentative relationship between the SLORC and these five powerful people to verbalize it.

Nito Kaing spoke nasally, as if her nose were indeed blocked. "The equilibrium you speak of, Minister, is not that equal. For the first year, yes, we saw no change in our domain. But word travels quickly, and there are changes taking place that we did not anticipate."

He knew what was coming, but he let her tell him.

"The peasants desert Shan and Kachin States in droves, moving to the cities in search of the work promised by the foreign construction companies."

Not all of them were finding work, of course. The percentage of beggars on the streets of Yangon and Mandalay had increased dramatically. It was a problem the interior ministry was attempting to solve. Still, those who did find work with General Technologies, with Hypai Industries, or with one of the subcontractors, were earning more income than they had cultivating the opium plants in the hills. Ba Thun suspected that the dissatisfaction of Kaing and the others could be traced to their bank accounts. With fewer farmers, and with competition from the foreign contractors, they were required to increase the amounts they paid to the cultivators and collectors. It would be eating, in small ways perhaps, into their millions of dollars of profit.

If the drug lords had not expected the development, they were not alone. The members of the SLORC had also been surprised by the sudden migration from the hills. Those that did not locate employment were becoming an added burden for the state. When they were not automatically provided with the golden jobs, their voices became strident.

"I am aware of the problem," Ba Thun told them, "and I believe it will not endure. There are only so many jobs available, and when, perhaps in a year or less, the people realize that they cannot secure them, I foresee that they will return to their homelands."

Nito Kaing and Daw Tan gave him skeptical looks.

"In any event, I believe that it is in the best interests of both you and the government to maintain harmony. Suppressing the renegade activity should be a priority for all of us."

Khim Nol smiled at him.

GTI compound, Yangon

Jack Gilbert heard footsteps coming down the concrete porch, which fronted the building. His office was a cubbyhole forty feet down from the main entrance to the GTI offices, an afterthought of the renovation. The secretaries, the copiers, and the mailboxes wouldn't be called convenient. He didn't mind, since it gave him a bit more privacy.

The overhead fan turned lazily, barely stirring the hot air hanging in the small space. The fan would go faster, but when he turned it up, it scattered papers to hell and gone.

He looked up as Chris Carson entered through his open doorway.

"Afternoon, boss."

"How was your trip, Jack?" Carson rested a hip on the corner of his desk and folded his arms across his chest.

"Socially or professionally?"

"I'm more interested in the latter."

He leaned back in his chair. "Zilch. I've got a half-dozen dealers on the lookout for me, but I don't think we're going to have much luck. The impression I got from talking to them was that any stone of the size we're looking for is going to be cut down before it ever hits Bangkok. And I also read something more between the lines. The sources out of Myanmar are drying up. Mauk's new security programs are having an effect on the illicit trade."

Carson clucked his tongue against the roof of his mouth a couple times, grimacing.

"Getting some pressure, are you, Chris?"

"Dex did mention it, yes."

"We go to Plan B, then?"

"Have you got a Plan B?" Carson asked.

"I've been thinking about it."

"All right. Why don't you come up to my apartment tonight, and I'll buy you a drink while we lay it out."

Carson left, and Gilbert spun around to his computer, loaded the word processor, and called up the file he'd worked on occasionally.

To get into it, he was required to enter a password, which he did: QX23P78.

The file appeared on the screen.

It was headed, "BURMA ROAD."

Gilbert had named it that because it was the more difficult route.

GTI compound, Yangon

Becky Johnson smiled at him as he entered the reception room. "Go right on in, Mr. Oh. He's waiting for you."

"Thank you, Miss Johnson."

He went into Carson's private office and found the man on the telephone. Carson urged him to sit down with gestures while he continued talking.

Oh sat on the small, two-person couch shoved into one corner. Carson's office was not large, and the desk, couch, and single easy chair utilized most of the space. There was a high stack of correspondence in the basket marked, IN. A few sheets of paper rested in another basket with the small sign, KAPUT.

Carson hung up, walked around the desk, and sat down in the chair next to the sofa.

"Just back from Moulmein, Hyun?"

"Yes. It was not a pretty sight."

"What are your immediate plans?"

"Like you, I am going to divert crews from Toungoo for the reconstruction. I have also ordered the necessary equipment rerouted from the Toungoo facility. Mr. Sung-Young is now preparing a change order, with the appropriate additional charges, to be delivered to Minister Ba Thun."

"I expect that Ba Thun will want to argue with us about another six or seven million dollars."

"It is in the contract," Oh said.

"Yes. However, I might suggest that you take a close look at your contract. It may be different from ours, but we've run into a little snag."

"Snag?"

"A catch that our lawyers missed. The time it takes us to

rebuild Moulmein, or any other facility damaged by terrorist activity for that matter, will not receive adjustment in the total project schedule. The final deadline remains the same. If it takes thirty days to reconstruct Moulmein, we could go over the project deadline by a month. The penalties will cost us a half-million a day. Fifteen million dollars."

"Ah. I see." Oh tried to remember the contract language in regard to terrorist losses, but could not. He strongly suspected that the Hypai contract would be similar to the GTI contract. And there went his seven-and-a-half days of bonus. This could cost him personally a quarter of a million dollars—if Mr. Pai were generous, money he had already spent in his mind.

"The way I'm beginning to look at it, Hyun, is that it might be more favorable to us if you and I went to Ba Thun and suggested to him that we were each going to eat the three-million-dollar cost in exchange for a thirty-day extension of the project schedule."

Oh brightened at that suggestion. It would cost Hypai Industries three million dollars, but still leave him seven-point-five days ahead of schedule and the potential for his lucrative bonus.

"Absolutely, Chris! Shall I make the appointment with the minister?"

GTI compound, Yangon

After a dinner of meat loaf, green peas, and mashed potatoes, Carson climbed the stairs to his apartment, opened the windows and turned on the fans, then took a long shower. Sluicing away the residue of heat and dust from a long day helped to refresh him, though not as much as he'd have liked. He hadn't gotten to bed until after three in the morning, and the first crisis of the day had gotten him out of it before seven.

He had just gotten dressed and mixed himself a Black Label and water when Jack Gilbert knocked at the screen door.

"Come on in!" he called and mixed a second drink.

Gilbert came in, letting the screen door slam behind him, and crossed the living room to the kitchenette. He took the drink Carson offered, and they both sat at the small table.

Gilbert savored his first sip. "Just the medicine I needed."

"Did you know we've got a chopper down at Pegu?"

"Anyone hurt?"

"No. A turbine failed, and the pilot put it down a little harder than normal. Evans is sending a Skycrane over in the morning to bring it back."

"When did it happen?" Gilbert asked. "You think it's more sabotage?"

"It was about six this morning, and I don't know about sabotage. Evans will check it out."

"Everything seems to be going to hell all of a sudden, Chris."

"Seems that way, doesn't it?"

They had had their expected share of equipment breakdowns, especially as the equipment racked up more hours. And there had been accidents, which put a few people in the hospital. Those, too, could be expected on a project of this scale, and Carson was only happy that there had been no fatalities. In the last week, though, the incidents were piling up a little too quickly.

"So," Gilbert said, "you been thinking about Big Mama?"

The company had given the project the code name of Ruby Star, but Carson and Gilbert had taken up the reference of Big Mama. Just in case there were some big ears in the wrong places.

"I have. You?"

"Here." Gilbert pulled several sheets of paper from his coat pocket. They were folded lengthwise. "This is the only hard copy."

Carson laid them flat on the table and smoothed them out. The heading of "Burma Road" caught his eye.

"Rough road, all right," he said.

Gilbert had formatted the report neatly: Goal, Strategy, Tactics, Mission Objectives. As he read, Carson realized that he and Gilbert had been thinking along the same lines, though Gilbert had applied some nice twists to the details. He didn't mind letting Gilbert have the credit; Carson had never been one of those bosses who felt as if only the good ideas should come from himself.

"I like it," he said.

"Before we get into it too deeply, Chris, I need to get your reaction to another topic."

"Shoot."

"This one's social." Gilbert told him about Pamela Steele and her journalistic restrictions à la the Myanmar government.

"She bought you the camera?"

"Well, I gave her a ruby." Gilbert grinned. It was something of a Cheshire grin.

Carson hadn't been in love with anyone other than Marian, but he knew some guys could get a little slaphappy.

"This is serious? Or are you just trying to get in her pants?"

"I don't know. It was a small ruby."

"Is this thing a spy camera?"

Gilbert let the ends of his mouth sag as he shrugged. "Well . . . it's tiny. I could probably hold it in the palm of my hand. I think it's a pretty good one; she paid six hundred for it."

"Then it's probably something you don't want to get caught with."

"Probably."

"But, hell, what do you know about photography?"

"Right!"

"If I were you, I'd devote half of each roll to generic stuff—landscape, kids in the villages, and the other half to anything that might be newsworthy. Then, if one of Mauk's soldiers confiscates the damned thing, you can plead yourself out as an inept tourist with a camera you don't understand."

"Good idea. And correct, too."

"And don't take any pictures of our installations, nor Hy-pai's."

"Not even the trains?"

"No. Stephanie has promised exclusive coverage to some magazine for the inaugural ride on July fifteenth."

"Pamela particularly wanted those shots. She hasn't been able to get a visa for the fifteenth."

"That one, you're going to have to work out on your own. All I know is what I promised Steph."

"I think her exclusive will fall apart, anyway. I've had a look at the guest list, and Ba Thun is getting very generous with visas for correspondents."

"That's kind of surprising," Carson said.

"It is, isn't it? Well, I've got seven weeks to figure it out."

"Okay, we ready to talk about Plan B?"

"Let's."

They didn't get a chance at it. The phone rang, and when Carson went to the living room to pick up the remote unit from the coffee table, he found Colonel Mauk on the other end.

"I hope this isn't more bad news, Colonel."

"Fortunately, it is not, Mr. Carson. I wonder if we could meet, perhaps in the next half hour?"

"Where are you?"

"At the barracks."

"I can come out there."

"If you would."

Gilbert promised to burn the paper copy of Burma Road and lock up, and Carson went down to the office and got the keys to a GMC Jimmy. He left the compound by way of Bogyoke Aung San Street and drove west until he reached the intersection with Prome Road. Traffic wasn't heavy, and he made good time, even managing to pass a couple tuk-tuks and a taxi driven by a guy who thought he was Don Garlits in a funny-car drag-ster. Farther north, Prome Road was also Insein Road, and he stayed on it until a new Prome Road branched off to the right.

There were lights on at the University of Rangoon, and he

remembered that a demonstration by students had been scheduled for tonight. It was supposedly directed at the education
ministry of the government, and all of the foreigners in town
had been warned to stay away. Beyond the University, he passed
the immaculate grounds of the park surrounding Inya Lake. It
was too dark to see much, and he promised himself once again
to take some time off and see more of the city. He was going
to find himself, five years from now, getting on a plane to leave
without having really seen anything worth putting in a scrap-
book.

Maybe Gilbert's new flame would buy Carson a camera?

When he reached the army encampment, he stopped at the
gate. The guard was expecting him and directed him to Mauk's
offices.

The military installation, like many of the public facilities,
had been built by the British, and it was old. Many of the
buildings were constructed of reddish brick, with vines climbing the exteriors. The mortar needed tuck-pointing, but Carson
didn't think he'd suggest a restoration contract. Ba Thun was
overloaded with contracts.

He parked in a visitor slot in front of a three-story building
with a sign out front that read: MODERNIZATION SECURITY
UNIT, UNION OF MYANMAR ARMY.

Inside, a corporal led him down a long hallway, with a worn
linoleum floor, to a corner office.

It was the first time he'd been in Mauk's office, and there
was nothing there to recommend a return. A desk and a few
chairs, nothing on the beige walls.

"Thank you for coming, Mr. Carson."

Mauk stood to shake hands, and then they gathered at the
desk.

"I have some information to share with you," Mauk said,
"but first, I must explain myself. Explain what I have done."

Carson nodded.

"I made some discreet inquiries about you through contacts
I have in the British secret service and the French Surete."

Carson was surprised. He thought he'd already been vetted when he was required to fill out a five-page history before he was issued a visa.

"I learned, for example, that you served very well in the Persian Gulf War. This was not information you provided in your history."

"It didn't seem important, Colonel."

"It is to me. You earned a Purple Heart when your helicopter was shot down. You also earned a Silver Star for bravery when you rescued men from your burning Blackhawk. Your superiors rated you highly for loyalty, performance of duty, and discretion."

"That's all from a time that is behind me," Carson said.

"I was most interested in the discretion," Mauk told him. "Also, I learned that you were driving the car when your wife was killed, and that you feel a large degree of guilt in that regard."

"That's my problem, Colonel."

"Did you know that I was once the target of an assassination attempt? Seven years ago?"

"No, I didn't."

"My wife and three children were murdered."

"Ah, damn. I'm sorry . . ."

"I understand your problem," Mauk said.

And that was all he said about it. He abruptly changed the topic and said, "You will understand that it is often difficult to know exactly who is trustworthy in this country?"

"As in my own."

"I am going to trust you, Mr. Carson. And I hope that what I tell you will go no farther."

Carson wasn't certain he wanted to be Mauk's confidant, but he said, "It will stay with me."

He also knew that trusting started out on a low entry level. They would feel each other out over a period of time before they really shared everything they probably ought to share, if they truly trusted each other.

Mauk rocked back in his chair. "Let us work in reverse, then, starting with the event at Moulmein. There were three fatalities there, all verified to be employees of the Myanmar Telephone Company. Additional investigation reveals that one employee was a Karen tribesman, a man known to accept bribes and to have engaged in some unscrupulous activities in the past. We suspect that he planted the bombs, intending to kill the guard on his exit, but that something went wrong with his timing device. There were timing devices located in the rubble.

"This tells me two things, one of which I will discuss in a moment. The second is that my security section, which is already stretched too thin, will have to take on the task of investigating all of the personnel hired, or to be hired, by the telephone company. I have suspended all hiring of new employees until each applicant is thoroughly examined.

"Now, let us go to the accident with the UltraTrain. That may or may not have involved an inside employee. Still, I am compelled to begin an examination of all nonforeign employees of the National Railroad Company."

"You're talking about thousands of people, Colonel."

"I am well aware of it. I may have to shut down all of your operations, allowing a few of them to continue only after all employees have been given an acceptable clearance."

Carson groaned, but kept it to himself. He saw the schedule coming apart at the seams.

"There is also an incident about which you do not know, Mr. Carson. The prisoner we took on the Banmo Road was killed, here in the prison."

"Jesus! Right in the cell?"

"He was in the exercise yard at the time, and we managed to eliminate his killer, a bandit known to have an association with Daw Tan."

Carson searched his memory. "The warlord from the north?"

"From Shan State, yes. It is obvious to me that someone feared that the prisoner would speak out of turn."

Mauk slid a photograph across the desk.

Carson picked it up and studied it. The image blurred as he tried to place where he had seen the man before. He was certain he had.

Yes.

"I had this guy by the ankle, once."

"I had thought as much," Mauk said. "He was known as the Razor, the same man killed here. So. The evidence is sparse as yet, but it is leading me toward several theories," the colonel said.

"And they are?"

"Follow this, if you will: The telephone facility is bombed. The train is sabotaged. As a result of those events, I believe that you were the target on the Banmo Road. Perhaps Miss Branigan was also a target."

"Why?"

"One of my theories, because Daw Tan may be involved, is that someone unnamed wishes to discourage the modernization of the country. It interferes with centuries-old traditions as well as certain farming activities. Additionally, the farming population is being depleted as peasants find their ways to the cities in search of higher wages."

Carson knew what farming Mauk referred to; most of the officials in Myanmar did not openly acknowledge the drug trade.

"My next leading theory could well mean my downfall if I cannot rely on your reputation for discretion."

"I never take notes, Colonel."

"It seems to me that your death, or the deaths of any of your leading subcontractors, as well as delays in making the trains run or the telephones work to specifications in the contract, has an obvious consequence. Can you tell me what it is?"

Carson hadn't expected to be questioned. He took a minute to think about it, then said, "The schedule won't be met. *Wouldn't* be met."

"Exactly. And then?"

"And then GTI starts laying out fifteen million a month.

RED RAIN 145

That is, GTI would lay off part of that on any subcontractor involved."

"For ten months? Fifteen? Twenty?"

"If it ran long enough, it could bankrupt us, I suppose. But who benefits, Colonel?"

"Indeed. Who benefits? Perhaps you will think about that, Mr. Carson, as I will, and then we can compare our thoughts."

EIGHT

City Hall, Yangon

Chris Carson led the way into Minister U Ba Thun's office, followed by Hyun Oh.

The greetings were affable, as always. Tea or coffee was offered, and Carson requested coffee. Hyun Oh opted for tea, and the three of them made small talk until they were all served.

In two years, Carson had watched Ba Thun grow into his job. In the early days, there had been frequent fumbles, back-pedaling on decisions, and delays while the minister sought the advice or support of his colleagues on the SLORC. Over the period he had known the man, Carson had noted the steady growth of self-confidence in his decisioning, his manners, and his appearance. He had become a true diplomat, and Carson wasn't certain whether or not that was good for GTI. Ba Thun would be more difficult to manipulate now, just when Carson needed to accomplish a little manipulation.

"Now, gentlemen, what can I do for you?" Ba Thun asked.

Hyun Oh was a salesman of the low-profile variety, and though their contract status with the government of Myanmar was equal, Oh tended to let Carson take the lead in multiparty conferences of this nature.

Carson said, "Minister, Mr. Oh and I have. been discussing the ramifications of the setback at Moulmein."

"A veritable coincidence!" the minister exclaimed. "I have been pondering that very question, myself."

"After an examination and determination of the facilities and equipment that can be salvaged, our analysts have calculated the total loss at six-point-four million dollars. With full crews devoted to the reconstruction, which has already begun, we estimate that it will require approximately twenty-six days to bring the Moulmein facility back on-line."

"In the meantime," Ba Thun said, "the entire region is without communications, except for radio. Perhaps we were premature in removing the old telephone exchange so quickly?"

"That will be corrected by this afternoon. As we talk, two of our emergency vans are being airlifted to the city, and temporary communications will be restored by midnight. At least, the city offices and the national governmental communications will be reconnected."

Ba Thun smiled. "That is a relief. If Mr. Pot in Moulmein could not call me to complain once a week, my life would be in shambles."

Carson grinned at Ba Thun's humor. The man appeared to be in a good mood, and Carson needed a good mood.

"In our discussion, Mr. Oh and I attempted to consider what was best for both the government and our respective companies."

"I am certain that you did."

"It seems to us," Oh put in, "that the State Law and Order Restoration Committee would be well served if Hypai Industries and General Technologies assumed the cost of restoring the facility at Moulmein."

Ba Thun raised his eyebrows, waiting for the quid pro quo.

"In exchange," Carson said, "we would like to see the primary schedule of project completion extended by twenty-six days, the estimated length of our rebuild time."

Ba Thun cocked his head to one side. "You are speaking of the master schedules for Hypai and for General Technologies?"

"Yes."

The commerce minister slid his chair back and opened the center drawer of his desk, extracting several sheets of paper.

He laid them on the desk and carefully read them, flipping the pages over one by one.

From his upside-down view, Carson saw that they were the monthly reports each contractor submitted to the ministry. The fact that he had them so readily to hand suggested that Ba Thun had indeed been considering the effects of the Moulmein sabotage on the schedule. At first, Carson looked upon that as a hopeful sign.

Then the minister spoke and dashed the hope.

"It appears to me," Ba Thun said, "that all of the contractors are doing well. Mr. Oh, you are almost eight days ahead of schedule, is that not correct?"

"That is correct, Minister."

"And Mr. Carson, your major projects are performing almost as well. Our major concerns, naturally, are the UltraTrain and the microwave communications. The UltraTrain will complete its inaugural run from Mandalay on July fifteenth, will it not?"

"It will," Carson told him.

"As you knew from the beginning of the contract, the committee was extremely concerned with its ability to keep its promises to the people of Myanmar. With another five years to run on the major projects, it seems possible to me that you could make up the twenty-six days."

"It would be very difficult, Minister. This schedule was extremely tight to begin with."

Carson didn't mention his other, very real concern. As native workers steadily replaced the imported personnel over the period of the contract, his costs would go down—planned in the budget, but the built-in inefficiencies of an unexperienced workforce would have a negative effect on the schedule. Some of that had been anticipated when drawing up the original plan, though as it turned out, Carson and his planning team had not been pessimistic enough.

"Nonetheless," Ba Thun said, "to extend the schedule at this point in time would be quite damaging from a public-relations standpoint, as well as setting a precedent for further delays that

I am certain the committee could not tolerate. No, I think we must adhere to the established agenda."

U Ba Thun's denial would have been a credit to any ancient King of Burma, Carson thought. The least he had hoped for was that Ba Thun would take the proposal to the entire committee for consideration. Now, he had to get back the 6.4 million.

"In that event, Minister, you will understand that we have to submit change orders for the additional costs?"

"I understand completely, Mr. Carson, and I anticipate no difficulty in approving them."

As they left Ba Thun's office, Carson puzzled over the man's apparent willingness to part with six million dollars. Normally, he was as tightfisted as Scrooge.

And Oh's face wasn't very inscrutable; it appeared as if he was taking the decision as a personal affront.

They had walked from the compound to their appointment, and as they walked back on Anawrahta Street, east toward Chinatown, Carson asked, "What do you make of the minister's position, Hyun?"

"I am somewhat surprised, Chris. I would not have expected an obstinate stance on a date that is five years in the future. There would have been ample time to prepare a palatable explanation for the delay."

"In fact, though it's not palatable, we do have a logical explanation. It's hard to argue that terrorist activity *wouldn't* affect the timetable."

"Exactly!" Oh said. "Perhaps another audience with the minister would result in a changed mind."

Carson thought about his conversation with Colonel Mauk and the question raised: Who benefits?

Say GTI and a couple of the subcontractors went over by a month. The fifteen million wouldn't actually be paid to the SLORC; it would simply be deducted from the final billings to the government. The deduction would lower the GTI Myanmar Project profit picture in that year—shared by management, by InstaStructure, by the PC division, and by others—but not by enough to really hurt. The project was only one of GTI's activities. The stockholder wouldn't even notice, as they might if the loss was assigned to one division.

On the Myanmar side, he wasn't sure of how the accounting was accomplished. Did someone have a hand in the till? And would the penalty aid in covering a shortage?

He didn't think he would raise that debate with Oh.

"I don't know, Hyun, but I'd guess we won't get Ba Thun to reverse his decision. To do so would now affect his pride."

Oh's face again showed his disenchantment. "Still," he said, "we could ask."

In his mind, Carson was already revising the Plan B that he and Gilbert had come up with, which Gilbert called Burma Road. If he put it into effect immediately, it could possibly serve two purposes.

"I'd argue against making any more requests of Ba Thun, Hyun. Let's wait a bit and see if he changes his mind on his own."

"That is not likely to happen."

"Unless you buy into my suggestion," Carson said.

As they walked along the crowded street, Oh listened intently to his suggestion, then immediately agreed.

Carson almost thought that Oh had a personal profit motive.

Mandalay

The Mandalay Yards of the Myanmar National Railway, south of the city and the airport on Seventy-eighth Street, were all but complete, and Stephanie Branigan was rather proud of the accomplishment. Maglev trains had been demonstrated innumerable times over the years, usually on short oval tracks, but nothing of this scale had ever achieved fruition.

She and the design staff had set simplicity as their guiding light for the maintenance and storage requirements. For one thing, every switchable section of the pedestal track—to shunt a train onto a siding or another main line—required expensive movable sections, massive motors, safety interlocks, and uncountable man-hours in developing the software for the computer control.

One third of the Mandalay Yards had been stripped of the original double-tracked sidings. The pedestal tracking that replaced them was over three miles long, located as six parallel lines. Both main lines fronted Central Station in Mandalay, but when they reached the yards, sidings allowed trains into the massive maintenance facilities. Because of the long rainy seasons, maintenance on electrical components was judged to be safer under cover. Two dead-ended sidings were used for storage, train makeup, and additional access to the maintenance buildings constructed by InstaStructure. The last siding would eventually service new cargo-transfer facilities to be constructed after the rest of the old yard was demolished.

The maglev freight cars were somewhat restricted in the weight they could manage. The cars looked exactly like the passenger cars, but without the windows. Each car was aerodynamically shaped for high speed, and there were no flat cars, gondolas, or tank cars. The cars could handle timber, crated goods, and bulk grains, though the grain loads were less than carried in conventional gondolas. The high speed of the trains, however, made up for the loss of capacity.

In the last three years of GTI's contract, as other subcontracts were completed and the country's cash flow freed up, a subcontractor would be installing pipelines throughout the country for the transfer of liquids which would no longer be transported by rail.

The overall design of the UltraTrain system carried forward the simplicity goal. Very few towns would have more than one freight siding. The major maintenance facilities were located in Yangon and Mandalay.

This morning, she had been playing guide, taking the managers and midlevel managers of the Mandalay Division on a detailed tour of the yards. There were sixteen of them, and all were currently enrolled in twice-a-week classes conducted by her education department. By the time they assumed control of the UltraTrain in their division, she hoped they were experts.

The tour ended at the control tower located in the center of the yard and elevated sixty feet above it. Though the structure was five stories high, there were only two floors resting on columns placed between sidings. The lower floor contained the computers and monitor stations for twenty operators. The upper floor was completely glassed-in by outward canted, bronze-tinted windows. Below the windows were control consoles for the technicians controlling trains as far south as Pyinmana—when that last hundred kilometers of track were completed—and north to the terminus at Myitkyina. Eastward, Mandalay Control would operate trains over the Burma Road Extension to the China border.

At the moment, the Mandalay Yards were all but barren. There were only two three-car trains and a pair of work shuttles in the yards. They had been freighted to Mandalay from the Yangon port on the conventional railroad, and they were used for testing track and training the technicians.

Branigan moved to the window and looked down on the two trains parked on the siding below the tower. Her charges followed her example, and she examined them closely yet again. The training school had told her that most of them were grasping the concepts well; a couple of the senior managers weren't going to successfully make the transition from steel wheels to maglev. Soon, she was going to have to develop a diplomatic process for culling out the inept managers, demoting them, or reassigning them. That process would have to be approved by Minister Ba Thun.

"Gentlemen, we have two trains in the yard. The closest is P-4, and next to it is F-103."

Passenger trains carried the "P" prefix and up to a two-digit number. The "F" prefix and a three-digit number were reserved for freight trains. Except for the lack of windows on the cargo version, these two trains appeared to be exact copies of each other. The end cars had steeply sloped noses for aerodynamic purposes, and both ends were identical since the trains could move in either direction, precluding the necessity of turning trains around. The lines were perfectly smooth, and the lower half of the train was finished in stainless steel. The upper half was painted a pale shade of blue, and down the full length of the train was a two-foot-high band of yellow dividing the stainless steel from the blue polymer paint. The yellow stripe was broken up in the center of each car, leaving a stylized logo of MNR for the Myanmar National Railway.

All of the vehicles assigned to UltraTrain were painted in the same colors since they would eventually be transferred to the railroad company.

She pointed to the west and said, "Over there, by kilometer marker one-point-five on Siding Four, will be the bulk grain-transfer point. Let's make believe it's there now."

Most of them nodded as they imagined the future facility. A few frowned. Those were the ones who didn't think much of a woman in a position of power and had let her know as much in subtle ways.

She turned to the technician seated at the console next to her and said, "I'd like to have F-103 at the grain-transfer building."

The technician grinned up at her, his smile missing an upper front tooth. He had already learned to ask for detailed instructions, and he said, "Which car would you like, Miss Branigan?"

She smiled. "Number two, please."

Turning to his keyboard, he touched the pressure sensitive keypad for Control, then tapped in F, 1, 0, 3. On the screen over the console were displayed two lines—P-04 and F-103, both in gray numerals and digits. If either were orange, he would know that the particular train was under the control of another console. When F-103 turned green, he knew he had control. He selected Destination and keyed in the commands for Siding Four, the grain facility, and the car number. Then he hit the Execute pad.

Branigan returned her attention to the trains below. Almost

immediately, the freight train noiselessly slid away, gathering speed quickly, and headed for the south. Ahead of it, the switches automatically aligned themselves. The train was doing fifty miles an hour by the time it reached the end of the yard, slid through a switch, and eased to a stop. The switches realigned, and the train shot backward, racing down Siding Four and decelerating to a stop exactly at Marker 1.5.

"Open up Car Two, please," she told the technician.

"For grain?" he asked.

"Yes."

He entered the commands, and as they watched, the top half of the car pivoted upward, prepared to accept grain from movable spigots. If cased goods had been the planned load, the right side of the car could also have been retracted.

The movement of trains to exact positions in the yard was accomplished so effortlessly only because her staff of software engineers had accomplished their tasks so well. The computers took the load off decisioning and made the training of the console operators that much simpler.

For the next hour, she had each of the managers sit at consoles, two at a time, and move trains to selected points in the yard. It didn't matter what commands they entered, or when. If the two trains were in danger of crossing each other's paths, the computers acknowledged the priority of passenger trains over freight trains and automatically stopped the freight train while the passenger train proceeded first to its destination.

Branigan and the training supervisor watched them carefully and made mental notes of the people who couldn't accept the power of the computer. They sat with fingers poised over the manual override switches or the Emergency Stop buttons. She and the instructor would compare notes later.

The group was breaking up for lunch when a stateside call was patched through to the control tower for her.

She waved goodbye to the Mandalay Division of managers and picked up a phone.

"Branigan."

"Branigan, I understand you're actually working."

"Of course I am, Steve. Tell me, what are you doing up in the middle of the night?"

Steve Pruett was a vice president of UltraTrain and her boss.

"I'm finishing up my standard day. You know that."

"I'm glad to know you don't finish your day without thinking about me."

"I do, you know. This company is a one-shot wonder, with one contract. Either you do the job that gets us more jobs, or we spiral our way out of existence. You'll understand if my mind is on you most of the time."

Branigan hoped it was simply professional. She and Pruett had almost been an item one time. The fact that he had a wife had deterred her, if not him.

When she did not respond, he asked, "Any recent train crashes?"

"Nary a one, Steve."

"That's the only good news I've had all day. But what I'm calling about, I want you to go ahead and test the Hypai magnets."

"And if they're any good?"

"We'll probably go with them for the balance of the project."

"That'll mean the loss of California jobs."

"I know how you feel about that, Stephanie, but it's a tough economic picture. If we can pad the profit line a bit, we'll have to do it."

"That's why I bucked it up to you," she said.

"Yeah, and you have my thanks, too. Just, well . . ."

"Just, what?"

"Nothing."

"You want to be sure my evaluation of the magnets isn't biased?"

"I know I don't have to worry about that. But the CEO wanted me to mention it to you."

Branigan had seriously considered finding the Hypai superconducting magnets inferior, but knew that, in the end, she'd let the test results speak for themselves. She was too much of an engineer to do otherwise.

Even if it meant a few thousand California jobs disappeared.

Mandalay Steamer Jetty, Yangon

Colonel Lon Mauk drove down to the riverfront after midnight. There weren't many people on the streets, and only a few trucks hauling produce and fish to the markets seemed to be on the move.

He parked his Land Rover on Strand Road and walked the rest of the way to the jetty. There were a few lights on, and one of the passenger steamers was secured to the jetty, but only a single security man lolled near the entrance gate. Farther north along the river, the Hydrofoil Marine operations were better lit, and he saw the movement of people.

Mauk stayed clear of this man, turning east to walk into the darkened area of wharves and warehouses. He disturbed a trio of beggars sleeping in ragged blankets beneath a loading dock, but he did not disturb them very much. They looked at him, sensed no hostility, and turned over to go back to sleep. He was wearing civilian clothing, a typical light-colored tropical suit; they would have been alarmed had he been in uniform.

Thirty meters farther along, where the shadows were blackest, he heard a low whistle and stopped.

The whistle came again, and he turned toward the sound, then walked toward the narrow alley between two warehouses. The ground was littered with paper, splintered remnants of crating, and old bottles and tin cans. He stepped carefully, but still made more noise than he wished.

The alley was simply a darker shade of blackness between the two structures. The lights of the jetty did not reach this far, but glancing back at them, Mauk thought they appeared inviting. The weight of his Browning automatic in the holster under his armpit was reassuring.

When he reached the entrance to the alley, his toe tapped a bottle. It went rolling away, clinking.

In a voice barely above a whisper, Mauk said, "Dove?"

The responding code name came back to him from the inkiness. "Mackerel."

A few seconds later, he heard the footsteps of two men. They approached him from the alley, stopping short of leaving it. He did not strain to identify their faces, for he knew them. One was a Karen tribesman and the other a Shan, related to the Karen through marriage.

Neither of the men would ever be seen with Mauk in public, and, in fact, detested him vehemently. Both of them, however, enjoyed his money, and both of them knew that Mauk held their arrest warrants in his desk. If they did not perform as asked, or if they lied to him, there would be no more money, and the warrants would be issued.

Without directing his question, he said, "Well?"

The Karen answered, identifying his position to Mauk's right. "The attack on the telephone exchange was not the work of anyone in Karen or Mon States."

"You are certain of this?"

"Absolutely."

If true, which he suspected was the case, it confirmed his earlier thoughts that the air force's intelligence section had accepted erroneous information from someone intending to mislead them. Mauk did not hold the air force or its intelligence-gathering ability in high esteem.

"Then, who?" he asked.

The Shan, on his left, shuffled his feet.

"What have you heard?" He spoke softly, but let a tone of menace ride his question.

"Only that," the Shan replied, "Daw Tan has sent his lieutenants to places where they do not normally go."

The Shan was not subject to Tan's control, being from the southern part of the state, but he would still feel he was betraying a clan member.

"What places?"

"I do not know. They say Meiktila, Myingyan, Pegu. Who knows?"

"They" inferred the grapevine, of course. Mauk would not press him on that. It was enough to know that Daw Tan's men were active outside their normal territory. If it were up to Mauk, he would order air-force planes to bomb Tan's compound outside of Man Na-su to encourage the man to retract his claws, but Mauk did not know the extent of Tan's payoffs. They were bound to be extensive in the air force, and an aerial strike would likely never take place, or if it did, the bombs would fall short of the target.

"What else?"

"That is all that we have learned," the Karen said.

From his left pocket, where he had placed the bills swaddled with rubber bands, Mauk withdrew two bundles. He passed one bundle of five thousand *kyat* to each man.

"That is much more than you normally receive," he told them. "You will earn it by intensifying your efforts. Go to where you have heard that Daw Tan's men are. I want to know what they are doing."

"If Daw Tan learns of our treachery, we will die, and slowly," the Shan told him with true conviction in his voice.

"You need not fear Daw Tan. You do not belong to him."

"But I should fear Nito Kaing, and I do."

Palo Alto, California

Dennis Larkin, the head of auditing, and Dexter Abrams went to lunch together at Milligan's, an Irish-style pub reeking of plastic reproductions of authentic Dublin artifacts.

The ale was good, though, and they each ordered a stein while they waited for their corned-beef sandwiches.

The place was crowded with Silicon Valley whiz kids, with an incessant buzz of technical conversation that would mystify the general American but would also blanket any sensitive information Larkin wanted to discuss.

Abrams was afraid the news wasn't going to be good. Larkin didn't often want to get away from his office for a conversation. His face was as sober as Abrams had ever seen it.

After the waitress left with their order, Abrams said, "All right, Dennis. What's with the cloak-and-dagger bit?"

Larkin looked around them at the densely packed tables, then leaned across the candle shielded in red glass and said, "We've been running the quarterly audit on computer systems."

Not many in the company knew that computer usage was audited. Every employee who used a computer logged on to the personal computer network or the mainframe machine with a distinctive password. In a number of instances, as with defense contracts, the project code had to be entered also. The codes for the classified projects were tightly held and monitored. And in the case of the mainframe IBM computer, each department or division was charged for computer time against their budgets. It helped to allocate costs against particular projects.

Every three months, Larkin's auditing office performed a random audit of usage, primarily to ascertain that everyone was following the rules and that actual project costs could be billed, for example, to the Defense Department. Even the executive offices were audited. It was no big deal.

"Somebody playing games? Or wasting time chatting on the Internet?" Abrams asked.

"A couple of those, and they've been warned. But no. My concern is with someone with an unrecognizable ID who spent forty-four seconds in the Ruby Star file."

"Shit!"

"That was my thought."

"Unrecognizable ID? What do you mean?"

"The password was P-I-C-K-8-8-6-4-1. It was never authorized for anyone, but when I checked the master password file, it was there, and it was unassigned. We don't know who managed to enter it in the file, or how. We don't know who's using it."

"Damn it!"

"I killed it, of course. But we went back and checked the whole history of the major defense and in-house classified projects. Seventeen months ago, that same password was used to access Ruby Star."

"For how long?" Abrams asked, feeling his stress level rising and wishing he hadn't ordered the corned beef.

"Twenty-seven minutes," Larkin said. His face told the story; his expression was one of total anguish.

"Oh, Christ! That's long enough, isn't it?"

"Yeah, boss. I think someone's ripped off the plans."

THE RAINY SEASON

NINE

City Hall, Yangon

By June 3, the rainy season had begun in earnest. In the six months of the southwest monsoon, when the wind shifted to bring rain from the Bay of Bengal, the regions facing the dominant winds received some of the greatest amounts of precipitation in the world. Sittwe in Arakan State on the western coast would receive over five thousand millimeters of rain in the year. In contrast, the dry zone around Pagan remained arid, and the Shan Plateau was pleasant and cool.

It rained almost daily, once a day, and it came down in torrents for short periods. After the insipid heat of the hot season, the first rains were a relief. Then they began to wear on the mind and body. Fabrics frequently felt damp and smelled of mildew. The humidity was high. Occasionally tempers were also high.

"Tell this to me again," the premier said.

The two of them were in Ba Thun's office. The windows had been closed because of the downpour, and the fans stirred only humid air.

"The foreign contractors have decreased the number of Myanmar citizens they are hiring. That is to say, they have decreased the rate of hiring. Furthermore, they have decreased substantially the number of people they are inducting into their training schools."

"How can you tell this?"

"The numbers are quite apparent in the monthly reports, Premier. Beginning in the second year of the contract, the contractors were to begin educating and hiring our citizens to replace their employees. This was so that, near the end of the contract, approximately ten percent of the project employees would be foreigners and the balance our own citizens. Up until the May report, they were, in fact, replacing about one to two percent a month. In May, they hired only two hundred Burmese, and they sent none of their employees home. For June, they project employing no new employees, nor do they plan to reduce their own force of foreign personnel."

"Do you have a reason for the change in the trend, Minister?"

To state the true rationale involved, Ba Thun would have to explain his decision to deny Carson and Oh an extension of the project schedule. He did not wish to do that at this time, and besides, the premier was not good with detail. He preferred to leave contracts and clauses and payments to Ba Thun.

Instead, he said, "If I asked Carson, he would likely blame it on the advent of the monsoons."

"I do not understand that."

"In their two years of experience, the contractors have learned that with the rain comes inefficiency. They lose time, construction is shut down for long periods, equipment becomes mired. They fall behind their schedules. They also have learned that, until they become experienced, new Burmese workers are less skilled and therefore less efficient. I suspect they are maintaining the level of foreign workers in order to stay on schedule, or to gain on it, during the rainy season."

"What are the ramifications?"

"For the contractors, increased costs since they are not replacing their highly paid employees with Burmese workers who will work for far less. For us, as more and more peasants come from the hills to the cities in search of work, they find none and the roster of our unemployed grows. Idle hands mean more crime. The police and the army become strained in attempting to cope. Worse, I believe, is the discontent that festers. It could be troublesome."

"Can we not force Carson to live up to the contract?"

"Unfortunately, Premier, the contract states only that the ratio of foreign to domestic employees will be one to ten in the seventh year. It does not specify a percentage in any given year."

This was Carson's work, Ba Thun knew. The man was taking his revenge against Ba Thun over the unsuccessful negotiations for an extension of the deadline. It was a conspiracy, in fact. There had been no overt orders issued as far as Ba Thun knew, but all of a sudden, Hypai Industries and General Technologies—and its subcontractors—had stopped new hiring. It could be one of two things. Carson was determined to make up lost time on the schedule—his increased labor costs would still be less than the fifteen million dollars a month in penalties. Or secondly, he was sending a message to Ba Thun that a contract was a two-edged sword. Both parties handling it could be cut. If Carson remained steadfast, the consequences could be deadly. A hungry populace might well rise up in anger.

"Perhaps," said the premier, "you could reason with Carson. Explain the possible results if he does not continue to train and employ domestic workers."

"I can do that," Ba Thun said, "but I cannot predict the outcome."

In fact, Ba Thun would not beg Carson to deviate from the course he had set. He was certain the price would be a deadline extension, and Ba Thun was not about to capitulate on that.

He could be stubborn, too.

Meiktila

When she saw the helicopter approaching at a little after four o'clock, just as promised, Branigan climbed out of the truck and told her driver he could go on back to the railhead which was about eleven miles east of the town.

With a population of twenty thousand people, Meiktila didn't rate a full-fledged airport, but it was on a secondary loop of rail line which left the main line at Thazi, meandered along the western side of the Irrawaddy valley, passed through Myingsam, then terminated in Mandalay. The loop was scheduled for replacement with the UltraTrain in the fourth year.

Since the town was on the rail line, and since it did have a few abandoned buildings available, Branigan had designated it as a supply depot. The designation provided a few local jobs and injected some currency into the economy. She had just pulled a surprise inspection of the depot, but hadn't found much to kick about. They were a couple days behind on paperwork, but a random inspection of the inventory had not revealed any significant shortages.

The helicopter, one of GTI's Gazelles, flared and settled to the center of the white X spray painted on the ground. Two men from the shed that watched over the field got in a pickup with a fuel tank mounted in the back and drove over to refuel the chopper.

Under leaden skies, which threatened to dump at any minute, Branigan walked across the damp field.

Carson slid out of the pilot's seat as she approached. He carried a thermos bottle.

He had agreed to meet her here so that she could give him a quick tour of the unfinished stretch of the line between Pyinmana and Mandalay. Carson was becoming a bit insistent that the Mandalay-Yangon corridor be finished on time for the July 15 inaugural festivities.

She had no intention of missing that date. The worldwide publicity would benefit her and UltraTrain more than it did GTI.

As the two men refueled the helicopter and checked behind the access hatches, she and Carson drank coffee from his thermos.

"It is kind of a coffee day, isn't it?" she said.

He scanned the skies. "I think we'll be all right. The Yangon meteorologist didn't expect anything heavy this far north today."

"You actually believe weathermen?"

"This was a weatherlady," he grinned.

"And you believed her?"

"She was a pretty weatherlady. How could I *not* believe her?"

Branigan shook her head.

The ground crew finished up, and they climbed into the helicopter, Carson in the right seat. Branigan buckled herself in, then pulled the headset on. It allowed them to communicate over the intercom, and hushed most of the sound from the turbine engine.

Carson started the turbine, let it warm for a minute, then lifted off. He dipped the nose, and the helicopter raced away to the east. She could feel the vibration in her seat. A few minutes later, and a thousand feet above the ground, they picked up the north-south main lines. Carson turned right to follow them south.

A few minutes later, they passed the railhead. A conventional train was parked on the main line next to the pedestal rail while a crane lifted sections of track from flat cars. Carson slowed the forward speed and decreased the altitude.

The railhead passed behind them, and soon she spotted the yellow bulldozers and landscrapers that were working two miles ahead of the track-laying.

"This is the second largest fill, Chris. The old roadbed was too narrow and lay on top of some bad geology. We've dug it out and backfilled, and in two days, we'll start pouring concrete for retaining walls."

"The second largest?"

"You'll see the largest one just before we reach Pyinmana. I've already got the backfill started there."

"But nothing else of a major nature?"

"No. There's the typical soft spots, but the rest of it's going to be straightforward construction."

"And the two railheads are ninety-five miles apart now?"

"By tonight, we'll call it ninety-one."

They continued to follow the roadbed, seeing small parties of construction workers from time to time. They were testing soil, tamping it, spreading layers of sand and ballast in preparation for receiving the pedestal track sections. A large drill punched holes in the earth in anticipation of the concrete trucks, which would pour the footings. Surveyors and engineers ran around, double-checking every aspect of the construction.

Branigan got excited watching it. On July 15, when P-01 pulled out of Mandalay on the longest straight run ever for a maglev train, history was going to be made. She would be on that train when it transited the 380 miles to Yangon in 1.77 hours.

Transportation history.

And she was part of it. A catalyst, even.

Carson increased altitude as they passed over Yamehin, then dropped back to inspection heights on the other side of the town.

A few minutes later, some kind of airplane appeared on their left.

"That's a T-37 trainer," Carson said. "No markings."

"That good or bad?"

"I don't think it's good, Steph."

Abruptly, the small jet turned toward them.

It dived from its higher altitude.

Right at them.

"Chris!"

"I'm watching it."

Seconds later, it flashed past, a few hundred yards ahead of them, passing from left to right, then slowly gaining altitude.

Carson had reduced speed, but now he swung the nose of the Gazelle after the departing aircraft and increased speed.

"What are you doing?"

"I want to stay behind this joker if I can. Keep him from turning back on us."

"Who is it?"

"I don't know. He was probably just buzzing us for the fun of it."

The T-37 kept gaining altitude, turning now to the south. It got farther away.

She looked at the altimeter. They were 6,500 feet above sea level.

"They're not coming back," she said.

"Good damned thing," he said. "I might have had to do something about it."

"Like what?"

"Damned if I know. Something would surely have come to mind."

Carson turned back toward the railroad line.

Over the dull *thrum* of the turbine, overcoming the mute of her headphones, Branigan heard a loud bang, then a horrendous grinding.

Carson's hands were flying everywhere.

"Chris! What's that?"

"We've lost the tail rotor drive."

The Gazelle started rotating.

Taunggyi

The capital of Shan State was sleepy in the late-afternoon sun. Though there were a few angry cloud banks in the west, it did not appear as if this city on the western edge of the plateau would receive any precipitation.

Hyun Oh waited by walking around the town like a tourist. Despite the rumored wealth of the drug lords, he could not see that any of the wealth had filtered down to the common people of the state. For the most part, Taunggyi looked poverty-stricken. Most of the buildings were in poor repair. The people he met seemed guarded and suspicious of him. He refrained from trying to start any conversations with them.

At the inn and at two restaurants, he had left word that he would very much appreciate meeting with Daw Tan. He didn't know how else to contact the man, and he assumed that his messages would eventually reach the warlord.

He had nothing else to do but wait. In the morning, he was to meet with two men—he had brought with him "envelopes" in the event of their need—who could possibly underwrite a local telephone company. He thought of that meeting simply as cover for the more important mission of meeting Tan.

If the man ever responded to his messages.

The Shanghai Hotel, Mandalay

Daw Tan kept a permanent suite at the Shanghai Hotel on Eighty-fourth Street midway down the block between Thirty-first Road and Thirty-second Road. Over the years, the hotel staff had come to know him, or at least to know his desires and his appearance. No one flinched at the sight of him when he entered the lobby.

Most of the tourists, not knowing who he was, would look away from him or, infrequently, take a second surreptitious look. If he glared at them, they melted away, finding themselves late for an appointment. Usually, he took no notice. He had more important tasks to accomplish than scaring away the tourists.

He dismissed his driver and bodyguards at the front entrance. He would not need them.

Entering the hotel, he headed directly for the stairs, walked the three flights to his floor, and unlocked the right of the paired and ornately carved doors. The suite was spacious, with a large sitting room and two bedrooms. Most of the furnishings were antique, but Tan had never cared enough to examine them closely.

In his bedroom, he turned on the lights and fan, then placed his valise on the bed. He kept several changes of clothing at the hotel and rarely brought luggage with him, but this trip was unique.

Unzipping the valise, he unpacked the silenced Uzi, the Russian-made Stechkin automatic pistol, and the ivory-handled razor, placing them in a drawer of the armoire.

Then he sent for a barber, had his ponytail clipped off and his hair cut short.

When the man was done, he tipped him lavishly, then ordered dinner from room service and sat on the sofa in the sitting room while he waited for it to be delivered. He did not completely relax, particularly because he had never known how to relax.

When he thought about it, Daw Tan decided he was pleased with the course of events. Initially he had been offended by Khim Nol's order for Tan to personally assume the operation. He had minions who performed those tasks. The more he considered it, however, the more intrigued he became. Many years had passed since he had tasted the sharp tang of danger.

His life had become one of indolence, with little to do except exercise harsh control, when it was necessary, over his subordinates, and count the riches he had acquired. No, this would be good for him. He would endear himself further with Khim Nol; he would demonstrate to others that he was undaunted by perilous activity; and he would prove himself capable of the same performances he had accomplished as a younger man.

He was certain that his skills were as finely honed as ever. And then, too, he had a wide range of resources available to him. Should he need them, well, Khim Nol would not have to know.

Daw Tan found himself looking forward to the immediate future with an anticipation he had not known for a long time.

He would enjoy himself.

Twelve miles southwest of Yamethin

When the tail rotor failed, Carson had felt it in the controls a split second before the warning lights blossomed. The Gazelle whipped around on her vertical axis a couple times before he got the autorotation started. He had plenty of altitude, but sick helicopters required a steep glide, and he didn't think he would make more than a mile of distance.

And everything below him was thickly forested. Ahead was Highway 1, but it was far out of reach. Four or five miles behind was a secondary road, but it was out of the question, too.

"Tighten your straps, Steph. Look for a soft spot."

He could hear the beginnings of hysteria in her voice, though she tried to keep her response light. "How do you tell if it's soft?"

He didn't answer as he tried the radio. "Mingaladon Air Control, GTI zero-six with a Mayday."

No response.

"Mingaladon Air, Mayday."

Again, no response.

He tried once more on UHF 243.0, the international distress frequency, known as Guard in the military, but without apparent success. He'd probably lost his antenna. Still, maybe they could hear him, though he couldn't hear them. Rapidly he repeated the Mayday and gave his approximate location.

Then he had to tend to more immediate matters.

He was in a forty-degree glide and had lost altitude to 2,100 feet AGL. Nothing had opened up in the forest yet.

"There!" Branigan yelled.

He followed her pointing finger, saw a lighter slash of green in the dark green of the rain forest.

"Looks soft to you?" he asked. He could feel the loss of lift, and while he had some control over his altitude, there was no directional control.

"Everything looks hard," she said.

The clearing came up fast, and there wasn't much room. He judged it at a couple hundred feet long by maybe fifty feet wide, barely enough to clear the rotors. There was a lot of stubble and weeds in it, but nothing around it looked any better to him.

Giant blobs of rain began to splatter the Plexiglas.

"Looks like rain," he said.

"Watch what you're doing!"

The tall peaks of teak and conifer reached up for him.

He was falling short of the clearing, and he tried to flatten the glide. Immediately he lost lift, but the skids smashed through the tops of several teak trees, and he was over the clearing.

He killed all electrical and ignition power.

The Gazelle slammed into the ground hard enough to collapse the skid on the right side.

It bounced back, rolled.

The spinning rotors slapped the ground, breaking up, and the fuselage leaped in counterargument.

When it came to rest, the Gazelle was on her right side, her crushed nose buried in the soft, wet ground. Carson heard fluids gurgling and dripping. Hot metal pinged as it began to cool.

He looked up to see Branigan hanging from her straps above him. Her head lolled over against her shoulder. She was shaking it groggily.

He began unbuckling his straps. "Steph?"

"Uhh, Chris?"

"You okay?"

"Yes. No. I don't know."

"Hold on."

The rain had increased in intensity. Raindrops smacked the cracked and starred windshield like emphatic gunshots.

Carson pulled himself around, out of his seat, until he was kneeling on the broken Plexiglas window of the right door. He got his shoulder under Branigan's side, then reached up, found her stomach, then her harness, and snapped it open. She dropped onto him, and he pulled her feet down so she could stand.

Pushing himself to his feet, he faced her in the cramped cockpit. She sagged against him, as if her knees weren't going

to stay locked. Her eyes looked a little dazed, the pupils enlarged.

"Mind if I check you over?"

"Uh-huh."

He quickly ran his hands over her arms and legs, up along
her back, against her ribs.

"Nothing broken, I don't think."

"Can we get out of here?"

Her words were slightly slurred, and he suspected she had a
concussion. A mild one, he hoped.

"You want to get wet?"

"I smell gas."

Carson did, too. The fuel cell had probably ruptured. He
didn't think he'd have enough hot metal, what with the downpour, to ignite flames, but the aroma wasn't all that enticing.

Bending over, he searched the fuselage side in the rear compartment, where a bunch of debris had landed. He found Branigan's purse and a small toolbox, neither of which was going to
help him much, but he also located a poncho and a plastic tarp.
Working quickly, he pulled the poncho over Branigan's head and
straightened the folds.

"Okay, Steph. Grab the instrument panel and try to stay on
your feet."

"You find my purse?"

"I've got it."

Women.

Carson worked his left foot into the hanging harness of the
left seat, reached up and unlocked the door, then shoved upward. It was warped and didn't want to move, but after he
stepped up into the harness and got his shoulder against it, it
popped loose.

The rain drenched him almost immediately.

Holding himself in place with his left elbow hooked over
the seat, he reached back for Branigan.

"Come on, Steph!"

She tried to grip him around the neck, but her arms didn't

have much strength. Carson got a hand under her right arm and tugged. She was lighter than he'd thought. Struggling, with his assistance, she crawled over him and out onto the fuselage side. He got a knee in the face.

He stepped back down, got the tarp and her purse, then pulled himself out alongside her. Moving slowly, he backed off the fuselage, grabbed the intact left skid, and lowered himself to the ground. The rain pelted his back. His shirt and pants were soaked through.

Talking to Branigan, he encouraged her to slide over the fuselage toward him, grabbed her legs, and pulled her down. She almost collapsed as soon as her feet touched the ground.

"Let's take a walk, dear."

With an arm around her waist so that he could carry most of her weight, Carson walked them away from the wreckage and into the forest. The undergrowth was thick and nearly impenetrable. Twenty feet from the clearing, where the canopy of tree boughs took the sting out of the rain, he stopped at the base of a grandfather teak, unfolded the tarp, and spread half of it on the ground. Easing Branigan to a sitting position with her back against the tree, Carson sat down beside her and then pulled the other half of the tarp over them.

Under the tarp and in the forest, it was dark. And it was cold.

He could feel Branigan shivering, so he put his arm around her shoulders. The slick, wet poncho she wore and his sodden shirt wouldn't create much warmth.

"C-Chris?"

"Yeah?"

"Thanks."

"For what?"

"For getting us down."

"All part of the service," he said.

Her teeth chattered as she spoke. "Wh-what next?"

"Best to wait. Someone will notice we're down and get a

search party out. The Emergency Locator Beacon will be transmitting."

The search would not materialize right away, he was afraid. He'd been flying Visual Flight Rules, and Mingaladon Air Control may not have been watching him. And they were slightly off the beaten path of air traffic; it might be a while before an aircraft ran into the signal from the locator beacon.

"It—it's freezing."

Working awkwardly under the tarp, Carson helped her slip out of the poncho, then shed his wet shirt and used it to wipe his face and hair. He shoved the shirt and poncho to one side, shifted to get his back against the tree trunk, then pulled Branigan's back and head against his chest. Her hair was wet. He wrapped both of his arms around her.

Within a few minutes, their combined body heat took the chill off. She laid her arms on top of his, gripping his hands with her own.

It was quiet in the forest, except for the occasional sickly plop of raindrops on the tarp.

"Better," she said.

"Good."

"I could maybe go to sleep."

"I wish you wouldn't."

"Not a good idea, you think?"

"You may have a slight concussion, Steph. Let's keep you awake until the docs have looked you over."

After a moment's hesitation while she thought that over, she said, "I didn't ask about you."

"I'm all right. Few bruises."

She felt good in his arms. Carson hadn't had a woman this close to him in a long time. Her damp hair smelled of jasmine.

"I'm really sleepy," she said. "Keep me awake."

"Without becoming overly familiar?"

"Preferably."

"Tell me about the principles of magnetic levitation."

"Boring. Tell me about you, Chris. How did you end up in Myanmar?"

So he told her, and he found himself spilling his guts about Marian and Merilee, subjects he had previously kept to himself.

By eight o'clock, the rain stopped, and by ten o'clock, he knew a lot about Stephanie Branigan, Richard Branigan, Seattle, and UltraTrain politics. He even learned something about magnetic levitation.

By eleven o'clock, when it was pitch-dark outside the tarp and the wind whispered in the tops of the pines, they hadn't moved much, and Carson was warm and comfortable.

They talked to each other like a couple of teenagers who hadn't seen each other in two days.

TEN

Mingaladon Airport, Yangon

Jack Gilbert had spent the night in the GTI operations office with an open line to the airport's chief air controller. Tracy Hampton and Don Evans—who had first alerted Gilbert to the overdue helicopter at seven o'clock last night—had shared the vigil. Other GTI employees had been in and out. Colonel Mauk had stopped by once to say the air force had fixed-wing aircraft flying search patterns.

It wasn't raining then, at six A.M., but the day was muggy. Hampton's red hair hung heavy and was matted with humidity. She sat at a desk behind the counter, monitoring the open line to air control and talking on another phone to various of her surface-fleet subordinates. Half-listening to her conversations, Gilbert knew she had a flatbed semitruck with a landscraper loaded on it mired in mud somewhere near Pyuntaxa and was trying to get wreckers to it. Somewhere else—Tugyi?—a D-8 Caterpillar bulldozer had slid down a hill and overturned. No one was injured. That was the first question she always asked: Anyone hurt?

Evans was outside on the tarmac, talking to the pilots of a Sikorsky S-65, which he had placed on standby. Half-a-dozen others lolled around the office, waiting for word, making coffee, consuming it by the gallon.

Gilbert poured his umpteenth cup of the dark brew, then leaned his elbows on the counter.

Hampton's voice raised an octave. She had a phone pressed against each ear, and she said into one, "Diego, just take care of it! Get what you need out of the Henzada Motor Pool."

She slammed the phone down and spoke into the other, "What was that? Where?"

Gilbert straightened up.

She looked up at him, her green eyes sparkling in the overhead fluorescent light. "A passenger liner spotted chopper wreckage in the forest southwest of Yamethin, Jack."

"We're gone," Gilbert said, heading for the door.

On the tarmac, Gilbert yelled at Evans, rotating his hand in large circles above his head as he ran. The pilots pulled open the doors and clambered into their seats, and by the time Gilbert reached the Stallion, the first of the GE turboshafts was already whining.

He pulled himself through the access door into the cargo compartment behind Evans and waited impatiently for the massive seven-bladed rotor to begin rotating. By his watch, they were off the ground at seven minutes after six.

The pilot zipped across the runway and headed north, following directions from the air controller.

Evans handed him a headset and they listened to the radio conversations, hanging onto the doorjambs of the access doors left open on each side of the fuselage.

Gilbert watched the damp landscape fly past below and noted the important passages in the radio dialogue: no apparent fire; fuselage intact, on its side; no sign of movement. The passenger liner, a Fokker Friendship, was circling the site, waiting for an air-force aircraft to assume the surveillance.

The Sikorsky topped out at 193 miles per hour, and they were 225 miles from the crash site. Evans had other helicopters closer to the crash, but they were all loaded and en route to construction sites.

They were twenty minutes out when a Myanmar Air Force Pilatus Turbo-Porter relieved the Friendship and got closer to the ground. They reported by radio that they had spotted a man waving at them.

Evans looked across the cabin at him and grinned. Gilbert gave him a thumbs-up. He was elated. Without a great many *close* friends in his life, Gilbert certainly didn't want to lose the best one he had.

As they got closer, Gilbert noted how dense the forest was, and he was thankful to the Burmese pilots who had spotted the wreckage. He leaned out into the downwash of the rotors and looked forward, spotting the ungainly, long-nosed Turbo Porter circling over the forest.

He pulled his head back in and ran his hand through his rumpled hair.

On the intercom, the pilot said, "Don, I've got a seventy-nine-foot rotor span, and that's a fifty-foot clearing."

"I'll go down," Evans told him, then motioned to Gilbert. "Jack, you run the hoist."

"Can do," Gilbert said and crossed the cabin to the right side. He helped Evans into the horse-collar sling, then used the control buttons to lower the weighted cable from its cantilevered perch outside the door. Fighting the wind, he hauled the end of it inside and clamped the snap fastener to the sling.

The S-65 lost altitude steadily, and Gilbert and Evans stood in the doorway and watched the clearing appear in the thick greenery below.

There was the Gazelle, its fuselage shining in the morning sun. It looked particularly forlorn, its back broken but still intact.

And there was Carson, waving at them as if they were an arriving train, holding Branigan next to him. They were both on their feet, and Gilbert felt a deep sense of relief rush through him.

"Bye-bye," Evans said and stepped through the doorway, letting the cable take his weight. The sun reflected off of his bald head just as it did off of the Gazelle. The downblast of the rotors frizzed out his big mustache.

The wind was not strong, and the pilot had no trouble bringing the big cargo helo to a hover eighty feet above the forest floor, the rotors clearing the tops of the trees by a scant ten feet.

Gilbert clutched the hoist control box in his left hand, braced his left shoulder against the door frame, and pressed the Lower button with his right thumb. Evans began to descend.

Watching intently, Gilbert stopped the cable as Evans's feet touched the ground. Carson rushed over to meet him, and the two of them quickly transferred the collar from Evans to Branigan, getting her arms through it and her elbows locked down over the sling.

Looking down at her, Gilbert thought unexpectedly of Pamela Steele. On impulse, he pulled the miniature camera from his pants pocket and shot five frames of the accident site. He had already snapped a dozen pictures of pagodas and street scenes on that roll of film.

Evans signaled, and Gilbert pressed the Raise button.

Branigan started up, looking upward at him, grinning. If she was hurt, it didn't show on her face.

Evans ran across the clearing to examine his broken helicopter. He had a great deal of affection for the toys in his inventory.

When Branigan reached his level, Gilbert stopped the hoist, dropped the control box, and reached out to pull her inside. He held her tightly in his arm as he worked her out of the sling.

"Damn, I'm glad to see you!" he shouted above the roar of the turbines.

"Ditto!" she yelled back. "Have you got anything to eat?"

"MREs," he said, pointing to a crate in the back. The surplus military Meals Ready to Eat were carried on most of the aircraft.

"Ugh!"

He helped her to one of the pull-down canvas seats against the side of the fuselage, then went back to lower the cable again.

Six minutes later, Carson and Evans were aboard, and the chopper was headed south. The four of them sat in the canvas seats and talked over the intercom. Gilbert thought Carson looked all right, if a bit damp. Branigan seemed to be slightly dizzy. She swayed more with the motion of the helicopter than did the others.

Carson gave them a précis of the accident, singling out the failure of the tail rotor drive.

Don Evans said, "I don't know what the Myanmar accident team is going to report, but that sumbitch was rigged."

"Rigged?" Carson asked.

"Plastic explosive, probably. Took out the ELB, the radio antennas, and the tail rotor drive shaft. They didn't want anyone to find you for a long time."

"Damn it!" Carson said. "It had to have been done at Meiktila, when the Gazelle was fueled and serviced."

"Who did it?" Gilbert asked.

"Two guys. I didn't know them."

"They won't be there now," Evans said.

Dr. Scott Remington, the General Technologies physician in residence, was waiting for them at the Mingaladon hangar when they got back. He overruled Carson's and Branigan's protests and took each of them into an office for an examination. Carson had some bruises, and Branigan was black and blue from her seat-harness straps in a few places. They both had suffered some exposure as a result of the cold and rain, and Branigan had a mild concussion. Remington ordered Branigan to bed for two days.

"I'm going to eat first," she told him. "I'm starved."

Palo Alto, California

Dexter Abrams, Dennis Larkin, and Troy Baskin—GTI's chief of security—had invaded the second-floor laboratory of the Ruby Star Project in Building Three at eight o'clock in the evening. Using Baskin's passcard with its magnetic strip coded for all locks, they had passed through two sets of locked doors. The last door also required all of their thumbprints, which were readily accepted by the computer. The three of them, plus a few vice presidents and selected security personnel, were able to access every space on the GTI campus. There were only two scientists on duty, and Abrams had unceremoniously given them the night off. They stood around, waiting, while the two scientists shut down the projects they were working on with pointed reluctance and signed out of the lab.

By tomorrow morning, the raid by company execs would be page-one news on the grapevine.

Baskin was a hard-faced, stoic man, who had put in twenty years with the Federal Bureau of Investigation. He immediately started going through the first desk in the first glassed-in office of the row of offices along one wall of the laboratory. Larkin, who also thought he knew what he was looking for, started in the eighth and last office.

Abrams, who wasn't certain just what they were looking for, wandered around the lab.

The seven prototype lasers were spaced around the lab and were each mounted on a heavy metal chassis bolted to the floor. Each one was slightly different in design as various courses in the design development were discovered and followed. These were not the miniaturized variety of lasers found in compact disc recordings or medical technology. Each of the machines was at least fifteen feet long. Heavy power cables hanging from the ceiling fed them. There were no sleek housings; skeletons of polished alloy struts supported the various components. Electrical and fiber-optic cables snaked within the skeletons like shiny entrails. All in all, they appeared quite arcane, and Abrams wished he were more of an engineer so that he could understand exactly what they did.

At the far end of the lab, toward which all of the lasers pointed, was a wall of concrete and steel, just in case a laser beam in testing accidentally passed beyond a target placed on an aluminum cart. It was a fallacy, of course. If mistakes were made, the beam would cut right through the wall.

A bank of seven minicomputers was placed along the wall opposite the offices, these controlled the lasers. There were workbenches and machine tools on the door end of the laboratory, and as Abrams walked by them, he saw a stack of boxes. He opened one and found a single mirror about three inches in diameter. These were the offending mirrors, ground to the wrong specifications, and now removed from the lasers. They looked perfect to him.

He turned and leaned back against the workbench, surveying this expensive part of his domain. General Technologies' domain. Dexter Abrams knew perfectly well that he was expendable, and if Ruby Star didn't start showing results soon, he would be expended in the twelve blinks of his board of directors' eyes.

It didn't seem like seven machines should be worth a third of a billion dollars. But when the research and development costs and the extremely high salaries of the brilliant scientists working the project over four years were added up, they added up high.

He looked at the machines and tried to make them fit what he understood of the principles, which were basically simple. They utilized an active medium that could be atoms in a gas, a liquid, and a crystal. When activated, the electrons in an atom changed energy levels from a high state to a low state, emitting light of a specific frequency when they were altered. Though he had been told by the quantum-mechanics people, Abrams never remembered the formulas. While three kinds of interaction were available in the process (absorption, stimulated emission, and spontaneous emission), the stimulated emission had to dominate. In effect, an electron in an upper level of energy was stimulated by light to jump down to a lower level, emitting additional light while making the transformation. The additional light was supposed to have the same frequency and directional traits as the light stimulating it.

To work properly, there was supposed to be more atoms in the upper level than in the lower level, a feature achieved by "pumping" the laser. In essence, each of these lasers was a series of lasers. Small lasers supplied light to larger lasers, then to yet larger lasers, continuously building light energy for continuous operation, which was a great deal more difficult than pulsed operation.

The pumping was also used to raise the atoms in a lower level to the higher level, continuing the process. Some of the emitted light was reflected directly back by the mirror to keep the action going, and some of it was rechanneled into the laser beam.

Abrams could picture it in his mind, but he certainly couldn't apply the diagram in his head to the skeletons sitting on the tables. Maybe it was all a hoax? These guys were building magic Legos kits so they could take home 333 million dollars.

Three hours after they started going through drawers, Larkin and Baskin completed their searches of the desks, the computer terminals, and the cabinets and drawers in the laboratory.

Baskin said, "Nothing."

"Nothing here, either," Larkin admitted.

"Damn," Abrams said. "You suppose whoever it is, is that careful?"

"No," the security chief said. "If it were someone from the inside, he'd have left me a clue of some kind. A note or number taped under a drawer. A drawing in the wrong place. Something."

"You said, Dennis, that the data bank was accessed through a terminal in the lab?"

"Yeah, boss, it was. Terminal L224-06954. That's the machine in the third office. Schneider's office. But there's a very big but involved. During the time the data bank was accessed, there was also an open telephone line to the outside. On the sign-in logs, which are automatic and controlled by the thumbprint reader, Schneider was out of the lab at the time."

"I'd put up a hundred bucks," Baskin said, "that an outside computer simply went through Schneider's machine."

"But we can't say anyone here wasn't involved?" Abrams asked.

"No, except maybe for Schneider. The guy would have to be damned dumb to use his own machine," Baskin said.

"What about blueprints? Did you count them?"

"I did," Larkin said. "Seven sets, one for each laser. Each was numbered as number one."

There was supposed to be only one hard copy of the plans for each model of the laser. All the backup diagrams were on the mainframe computer's database, supposedly protected by complex coding.

"I ran a test," Larkin said, "with Troy watching me. After accessing the database, which took about two minutes, I copied off one set of plans to my own hard disk. It took fourteen minutes. To put it all on floppy disks would require thirty-two floppy disks."

When he noted Abrams's raised eyebrows, Larkin said, "I destroyed my copy, naturally."

"So this guy could have copied more than one set of plans?"

"Probably two," Larkin said. "We don't know which two, though."

"Or maybe he didn't get any. Just looked through the data files."

"That's wishful thinking, chief. He was on-line too long not to copy."

"Shit. What do we do now, Troy?"

"I'd like to have Dennis load that fictitious code name back in the main code library. We'll put a constant monitor on the system and see if it's used again. If I'm ready for it, I can trace the call."

"He's only used it twice, right?"

"That's correct," Larkin said. "But maybe three will be our charm."

"Do it."

GTI compound, Yangon

Carson picked up a covered tray at the cafeteria and carried it the length of the compound to the north stairs. He climbed the stairs and walked down the veranda to Branigan's door.

He considered knocking, but didn't want to get her out of bed. Instead, he tried the knob, found it unlocked, and pushed the door open far enough to stick his head inside.

"Steph?"

"What? Who? Is that you, Chris?" Her voice came from the bedroom.

"Me. You want some lunch?"

"Desperately."

"Can I come in?"

"I'm decent enough."

He shut the door behind him and carried the tray into the bedroom. She was just repositioning herself in the bed, sitting up against fluffed-up pillows. Carson saw that she had washed her hair, and she was wearing a flannel nightgown with a rose-petal motif. She didn't attempt any false modesty, pulling up the sheet or blanket.

An opened copy of a Hillerman novel was resting facedown on the bed beside her.

"I was just dreaming about food and wondering if I was going to cook or send out."

"You weren't even asleep," he told her. "Remington said you were supposed to sleep."

"He said to stay in bed. Didn't mention a word about sleep."

"He inferred it," Carson insisted.

He hooked a toe around a chair and towed it over to the bed, placing the tray on the mattress next to her.

"You don't mind company?"

"I especially didn't mind it last night. Thanks, by the way."

"For what?"

"For being so good with helicopters. I really thought it was the end."

"Nonsense," he said, sitting in the chair and lifting the cover off the tray. "Most of the time, they're pretty tame beasts."

She leaned forward to pick up a bowl, removing its metal cover. Her face was scrubbed clean, the girl-next-door image.

"Ah. Chicken noodle."

"And toast. We're intent on getting you recuperated."

"You're having the same thing?"

"I didn't think you'd want me to gorge myself on pizza and spaghetti in front of you."

"And I appreciate that."

After a few spoonfuls of the soup, she asked, "Have you heard anything?"

"Talked to Mauk. The two men at the Meiktila air-service facility have disappeared, but Mauk thinks he'll find them."

"Were they ours?"

"They were both on GTI's Air Fleet payroll, but I suspect they belonged to someone else."

"And the Gazelle?"

"The preliminary investigation, which I also got from Mauk, confirms what Evans said."

She shuddered, which did some nice things for her nightgown, and for Carson. He brought his eyes back to hers. He didn't tell her that Evans had grounded all of his aircraft until they could be inspected. Evans was working with some of Mauk's men in reexamining the credentials of the indigenous personnel.

"I'm going to be scared to leave town," she said. "Or even the Zoo."

"I don't think so. I've noticed that you're pretty composed under fire."

"Not like you."

"My problem is I act without thinking much, then I get scared later."

They ate in silence for a few minutes. Branigan spooned a big glop of strawberry jam on a slice of toast.

She chewed for a minute, then said, "I'm glad I got to know you better, Chris. Even if it took a crash to do it."

"Not much to know," he said, but he remembered the damp, cool, uncomfortable hours of the night with some fondness. Branigan had felt good in his arms.

They finished lunch with easy talk of some month-end discrepancies in GTI's payment to UltraTrain, which Carson promised to correct. He loaded the empty plates on the tray, put the cover back on, and stood up.

"Try to sleep now."

"I'm confused, you know. You kept me awake all night, then Scott Remington wants me to sleep all day."

"He's the doctor. I'm not. I just remember parts of some class I took in the reserves, but you can count on the Army being wrong."

She grabbed his right wrist with her left hand and tugged him toward her, down, then put her right hand behind his neck. She didn't say anything, but she kept her deep-green eyes locked on his. There were flecks of gold radiating from the irises. He hadn't noticed that before.

Carson shuffled his feet and pressed his knees against the mattress to keep from falling on top of her.

"This is a wonderful idea, Steph, but probably not a good one."

"This is thanks," she said.

He leaned forward, felt her lips touch his own, firm and cool at first, then quickly building heat. He couldn't help but respond.

When she released her grip on his neck, he pulled his head back.

"Thanks."

"Go to sleep."

"As soon as Chee and Leaphorn get the bad guy." She patted the dust jacket of her book.

He locked the front door of her apartment as he left.

As he crossed the compound, taking the tray back to the cafeteria, he saw Gilbert watching him through the window of his office.

Gilbert grinned at him.

He couldn't get the taste and the feel of her lips out of his mind.

What the hell would Merilee say?

Ahlone Road, Yangon

At nine o'clock, Chin Li ushered Hyun Oh into U Ba Thun's study, poured cognac for the two of them, then disappeared.

"I am amazed, Minister Ba Thun, that you wanted to see me so late in the evening."

"Ah, it is not late yet, Mr. Oh. I often work into the hours beyond midnight." It never hurt to have others aware of how hard he worked.

The South Korean sat on the small couch in front of the wall grouping, and the back of his head was reflected in some of the mirrors. He took a quick look around the paneled room. "This is very nice. I have been in your home before, but not in this room."

"Thank you. I find it comfortable. Tell me, Mr. Oh, how was your trip to Taunggyi?"

If he was surprised by the question, Oh did not show it. Perhaps he knew that Colonel Mauk's security unit kept Ba Thun apprised of the movements of the principal foreigners when they left Yangon.

"Not all that successful, Minister. The two men I talked to showed little interest in creating a local telephone company."

"Give them a few days," Ba Thun said. "After they have had time in which to consider your proposal, I suspect they will call you back."

He also suspected that the two men in question would have long discussions with Khim Nol, who would eventually underwrite the company. Nol often needed legitimate places in which to store his wealth.

"I sincerely hope so. Most of the other small companies are showing promise of developing well."

"That is what I understood from your reports, though I note that no finalized contracts have been secured. I hope you understand that, in Myanmar, these things take time. The principals feel a need to ruminate over details."

"I do understand, Minister."

"Tell me also, Mr. Oh, why you wanted to speak with Daw Tan."

Now the eyes shifted, became darker, more guarded. "Daw Tan?"

"It is my understanding that you left messages for him to contact you."

"I did not see Daw Tan," Oh insisted.

He would not have, of course. Daw Tan was ensconced in the Shanghai Hotel in Mandalay.

"Why did you want to talk with him?"

Oh sipped from his snifter to give himself time to think, then offered what Ba Thun took to be a deceptive smile. "I am concerned about this business in Moulmein, Minister. I thought that, with some incentive, Daw Tan and his colleagues could be induced to leave the telephone exchanges alone."

"You seem certain that Daw Tan is behind the bombing."

"If not he, then someone he knows," Oh said.

"I recommend firmly that you do not attempt to contact Daw Tan. Or his colleagues."

"Of course, Minister, if that is your wish."

"That is my advice," Ba Thun said.

Ahlone Road, Yangon

Lon Mauk stood just inside one of the northern entrance gates to the estate, staying back in the shadows of a lemon tree. He had been there for half an hour, nearly caught when the headlights of a car suddenly turned in from the road and followed the crushed gravel of the circular drive to park in front of the columned house.

He had recognized the green Toyota Celica sports car immediately and had his identification confirmed when Hyun Oh left the driver's seat and climbed the steps to the porch.

After the servant let the South Korean in, Mauk circled the house to the back, staying on the grass and away from the gravel. He had to tiptoe across the drive where it departed the circle and went back to the garage in the rear. The grass was still damp from the afternoon shower, and he knew he would leave footprints, but he did not think anyone from the house would notice them.

On the back side of the house, he found the lit window of the study and moved close to it. With his back to the wall of the house, he slid sideways until he had an oblique view through the window. Ba Thun was sitting at his desk, and the South Korean was on the sofa.

He could not hear what they were saying.

Still, he thought it interesting that the commerce minister was having discussions with a major contractor after business hours. Mauk had stopped here, just to see if Ba Thun was entertaining anyone of interest, but he had not expected it to be Hyun Oh.

He retraced his steps across the yard, through the gate, and down to the side street where he had parked his Land Rover.

After some consideration, he thought it might be worthwhile to place an electronic ear in the minister's study. He would have tapped the telephone also, but after the new Yangon telephone system had been installed, Christopher Carson had presented each of the members of the State Law and Order Restoration Committee with new telephones for their residences. The state-of-the-art telephones notified the user if any kind of interference was detected on the line.

For that reason, Mauk did not think much of the new telephones. But there were ways around them, and he would talk to his specialist about them.

ELEVEN

YWCA, Yangon

When Pamela Steele came to town, she was required by the terms of her visa to stay at the YWCA on Merchant Street, a long block up from Strand Road. Jack Gilbert met her there in the lobby. Since it was midmorning, and since the sun was shining, and since the concierge was conscientious about who went to which room, they left to walk downtown and have coffee at an open-air cafe.

She looked radiant in a pale-aqua dress, and Gilbert told her so. Her curious blue eyes sparkled; the ruby ring on her right hand also sparkled.

"How busy are you going to be?" he asked.

"Very. They let me in for three days this trip, and I already have interviews lined up with the ministers of commerce, interior, and treasury. I'm trying now to reach a Colonel Mauk who is supposed to be involved with security for the Modernization Proclamation."

Gilbert thought the wiser course would be for him not to admit that he knew Mauk. If he did, she would urge him to line up the interview.

"Why would you want to see Mauk?"

"There's been nothing in the press, especially the international press, but rumors are flying all over Bangkok about rebel attacks against the government that are supposedly related to the modernization program. I'm hoping he can enlighten me."

He didn't respond, and she peered at him over the rim of her coffee cup. The curious blue eyes bored into him.

"Or maybe you can enlighten me? You're a honcho in the program."

"Not as honcho as you might think." Was he contradicting the level of his importance? The level that he had used to meet her on the airliner? Hadn't he called himself a wheel, as in big wheel? When he considered the information he was privy to, and didn't want to share with the world, he was less impressed with his braggadocio.

"Rumors are grist for the mill in Southeast Asia," he told her, avoiding the reply.

She put her cup down and leaned forward. "You know what else I heard?"

"What's that?"

"There's a bandit named Daw Tan?"

"I've heard the name."

"He's got a contract out on your boss."

"My boss?"

"Chris Carson *is* your boss?"

"Yes. Where'd you hear this?" Gilbert was intently interested now.

"I was talking to some Thais in the Cowboy Bar. It's probably third- or fourthhand."

"Or more. Sounds like something right out of an opium smoker's dream."

"Still. Where there's smoke . . . you know?"

Gilbert dawdled over his next statement, sipping his coffee while he considered the wisdom of what he might say. There was always the chance, he finally decided, that a little pressure on the government from the media might push Ba Thun and Mauk into action against whoever was behind the attacks on GTI.

"Carson just survived a helicopter crash."

"What!"

She grabbed her big purse from the floor beside her chair

and dug through it frantically, finally coming up with a pad and pen.

"I'm not going to talk to you about this at all if you quote me, or even refer to me as a 'high-placed source.' "

The downturn of her mouth showed her disappointment.

"I'm a spy, remember? You can't give away your spies."

"Okay, just background."

He gave her the basics of the story. "I don't know where you'll get your confirmations or quotes, love. But keep me out of it."

"Agreed. Bloody damn! I wish I had photos."

He gave her the roll of film.

"Oh, Jack!"

"I don't know if they're any good, and I halfway hope they're not. I sure as hell don't want them traced back to me."

"Can they be?"

"There was an airliner that first spotted the wreckage—you'll have to find out what flight it was, and I suppose any passenger could have snapped the shots. Maybe with a telephoto lens. I'm sure you'll disguise the source somehow."

She smiled her delight.

"Now, let's discuss our schedules and how we're going to make them interact."

"I'm to see Minister Ba Thun at one and the treasury minister at three."

"Then, after that, I'll introduce you to the Zoo."

"The Zoo?"

"The GTI compound. That's where I live as one of the animals. I do rate a private apartment."

That made her smile, also.

Yangon zoo

After U Ba Thun's warning to stay away from Daw Tan, Hyun Oh had been nearly petrified when he got a call from the man himself. He had taken it on an open line in his office at the GTI compound, and in his rush to get the warlord off the line, had agreed to a secret meeting at the zoo, the real zoo.

The zoo was located two kilometers north of the compound, between King Edward Avenue and Upper Pansodan Street. It was next to Royal Lake, and he had been near it once before, when he visited the history museum.

Oh had taken his Celica for a long and aimless drive through the crowded downtown area, hoping to shake off anyone who might be following him. After forty-five minutes, he decided that no one was, and he turned north on Theinbyu Road and crossed the railroad tracks. Above the street, elevated on piers, was the double main line of the new train, which made a loop through the center of the city. Rangoon Station was immediately on his left.

He parked a block from the main entrance to the zoo and entered as if he were a man bent on wasting his time. He bought approved tidbits for feeding some of the animals from a vendor with a cart, then wandered slowly toward the section reserved for big cats. Near the Bengal tigers, he found the park bench he had been told about, but he had to wait ten minutes before an old man got up and left him a seat.

Twenty minutes went by before a woman with a child left an opening on the bench and an old, old man with a pronounced stoop sat down beside him. His hair was white, and he wore a wispy white beard. Incongruously, he also wore Western-style dark glasses.

Oh was beginning to think that Daw Tan would not appear.

"Mr. Oh," the old man said, "you wished to speak to me?"

Startled, Oh looked around him at the swirling masses of people, and saw no one who was particularly interested in him.

"Mr. Daw Tan?"

"The same."

"But . . . that is, I understood that you were in Mandalay."

"That is where many people think that I am. I prefer that they think so."

"Yes, I can understand."

"What is it that you wanted, Mr. Oh?"

"I, ah, I wanted to . . . offer you a proposal." Oh knew that he was demonstrating his nervousness. He had never before conversed with a man who killed people. The mere thought of it chilled him.

"A proposal. I see."

"It would be, I think, mutually beneficial. Perhaps we could go somewhere private to talk."

"We have privacy here. Tell me your proposal."

Oh told him.

GTI compound, Yangon

Carson had the cafeteria send him over a bacon, lettuce, and tomato sandwich and a glass of milk while he worked through the dinner hour. Becky Johnson stayed late to help with keyboarding, but he ran her off at seven o'clock, complaining about her overtime.

His office was nicely free of interference and people barging in with complaints. The window was open to an evening that smelled of rain, but which hadn't yet delivered. His single desk lamp cast a pool of light on the blotter. The stereo in the corner had a couple hours of easy-listening CDs racked in their slots. Martina McBride sang, "Always." Carson enjoyed the solitude; he always accomplished more of his routine tasks at night.

He finished signing some thirty letters and tossed them in the KAPUT basket, then read the employment reports.

It appeared as if they had effectively put the brakes on local hiring. Though he didn't know what Hypai was doing, Hyun Oh had responded well to his suggestion, and he supposed that the telephone company was also slowing the induction rate into training classes and the subsequent hiring of new employees. Charles Washington had done the same thing at Hydrofoil Marine. Each of the GTI subdivisions and the subcontractors had abruptly cut off new hires.

He wondered if Ba Thun had gotten the message yet. He and the committee should be feeling the pressure since the demonstrations in the streets were increasing. And if he had read the message, would he ask to reopen negotiations on the schedule extension? Carson was afraid the man might be too stubborn.

Carson would hold out for a while longer before he made his own approach. Under Plan B—the Burma Road, Carson's and Gilbert's strategy called for a sharp detour in the logic. He didn't give a damn about the schedule extension, which should surprise Ba Thun. Carson would trade the reopening of training classes and hiring programs for a different prize.

He heaved the employment reports in the direction of the basket and pulled a tall stack of financial reports to the center of the desk.

He didn't really want to do this. All day long, his mind had interfered with his concentration, drifting unexpectedly into memories of Branigan's kiss. She had said "thanks," but there was the promise of a future in that kiss.

His mind was schizophrenic on the subject. On one side—the left side?—it kept telling him to take a good, hard look at that future. He had been single for so long it might have become a habit. He hadn't involved himself in any relationship with a woman since the accident, and the lack was probably obvious to others. He suspected that he was grossly independent and had lost some of his sensitivity to others. Marian had always kept him on track in matters of social awareness. His private life was compartmentalized and neat. And pretty damned boring. For family, he concentrated on Merilee, and that had been enough.

The other side of his mind made him feel guilty and reassured him that Stephanie Branigan was truly expressing only appreciation. If he thought more about it, and tried to pursue it, Branigan would cut him off at the pass. Carson's problem, he assumed, was that he had never really experienced the ritual of dating as a teenager. He wasn't certain how women reacted to him. It had always been Marian, and the rules of his road said that it would always be Marian. He had killed her, and therefore, he could never abandon her.

And what would Merilee think if she learned he was catting around?

On top of which, with his fourteen- and fifteen-hour days, he didn't need any further complications. Some people who engaged in affairs within the same organization got away with it easily enough, and some didn't. Workplace relationships could turn ugly.

Not that he couldn't handle it. He was accustomed to adversity, right? He was a macho, go-get-'em kind of guy, right?

Why not go get 'em?

Hell, yes!

So the first thing he'd done was to avoid Branigan all day. He didn't take her breakfast, lunch, or dinner. She had called in midafternoon and left a message. He hadn't yet responded.

Was he scared of her?

Hell, yes!

The way to handle it, he told himself, was to be brutally frank. Sure, he'd like to crawl in the sack with her, but that's all it could be. Christopher Carson couldn't be expected to . . .

RAP! RAP!

He looked up to see Jack Gilbert standing in the doorway.

"I've got to tell you, right off, boss, that this isn't my idea."

"Come on in, Jack."

Gilbert stepped back and let a tall blonde with the brightest blue eyes Carson could remember seeing enter the office ahead of him. Though she was tall, she'd never be described as skinny. The curves were lush and demanding.

"Chris, Pamela Steele. And vice versa."

Carson stood up and reached across the desk to shake her hand. It was cool and dry. "Now I know why Jack talks about you so much."

"He's talked about me, has he?"

Gilbert pulled up one of the bamboo chairs for her, saying, "Don't believe anything he says."

Carson sat back down, and Gilbert got a chair for himself.

Pointing to the stack of paper on the desk, Gilbert said, "See there, Pamela? I told you he was busy as hell. We won't stay, Chris."

"I can take a break."

"You don't want to," Gilbert insisted.

"Mr. Carson . . . ," Steele began.

"Chris."

"Chris. Thank you. Look, would you mind talking to me a little bit? For publication?"

Now, he was reading Gilbert.

"About what?" he asked. "I'd be happy to discuss the progress of the modernization program in Myanmar."

"Well," she said, "I was thinking more along the lines of your recent helicopter crash."

"That's easy." He grinned. "It didn't want to fly anymore, so I landed it. A little hard."

"But why didn't it want to fly?"

"Boy, you'd have to check with the Air Force accident investigation team. I haven't yet spoken to them."

Steele had retrieved a steno pad and a ballpoint pen from her purse, but she hadn't yet written anything.

"I can tell," she said, "that you're going to be a difficult subject."

"I don't try to be."

"Sure you do."

"Let's go off the record."

"Bloody hell! You're as bad as Jack."

"Off the record?"

She slapped the steno book down on her knee. "Very well."

"I know you've got a job to do, Pamela, but then so have I. And despite the public's right to know, I've got to maintain a public-relations persona. I can't do my job if I'm asked to leave the country because I've offended someone. And I suspect that you know as well as any of us that there are some delicate balances to be maintained in Myanmar. Now, if you want to keep all of that in mind when you ask your questions, I'd be pleased to tell you what General Technologies is doing. I'll even tell you about autorotating a damaged chopper and spending a night in the woods. I won't give you any speculations."

She studied him for a moment, then said, "Back on the record?"

"Right."

"Chris, what were you thinking about when your helicopter malfunctioned?"

She spent the next forty minutes conducting a straightforward interview, going after only the facts. Carson responded directly, and he even got in a few plaudits for the microwave team, InstaStructure, and Branigan's UltraTrain. He hoped that it came out in print as well as he was imagining that it would.

When she was finished, Gilbert said, "We're going up to my apartment for a drink, Chris. Can I buy you one?"

Carson slapped his hand on the financial reports. "I've still got to wade through this, Jack, but thanks."

After they'd left, Carson mentally reviewed his responses and decided he hadn't done too badly. He also thought that Gilbert wasn't doing too badly, and he could understand if his assistant was a bit goo-goo. The two of them together made Carson think of Branigan, but before he devoted more time to her, he had to follow up another idea.

He dialed the army barracks and was surprised to find that Mauk was still in his office.

"Yes, Mr. Carson?"

"Colonel, I was just interviewed by a newspaper correspondent. Part of it involved the crash."

"I see. What did you tell her?"

Her? Mauk knew everything.

"Just the facts, Colonel. I didn't get into the causes because

I haven't seen any reports. She'll probably be checking with your air-force people."

"That is very good, Mr. Carson."

"The thing I wanted to talk to you about, though, is this: There was another aircraft involved in some way."

"Involved with your helicopter crash?"

Carson told him about the T-37 Cessna jet trainer that had appeared out of the east and buzzed him just before the crash.

"This airplane drew you off course?"

"Correct."

"And it had no identification markings at all?"

"None, Colonel. It was painted black or dark blue, but I didn't see a number or a symbol on it."

"Did you tell the reporter of this airplane?"

"No. I had completely forgotten about it, probably because of the crash. I suddenly had more important things on my mind."

"Have you been interviewed by the accident-investigation team yet?" Mauk asked.

"That's supposed to be at nine in the morning."

"Let me look into this other airplane. I will call you before the time of your interview."

Mauk hung up abruptly, leaving Carson wondering whether or not Mauk was going to want him to tell the accident team about the Cessna. If that airplane had been spotted on someone's radar, and the team already knew about it, he was going to look damned silly ignoring it.

He looked at the stack of financial reports, then carefully lifted it and put it back in his In basket. Tomorrow.

Tonight, just after nine o'clock, if it wasn't too late for Branigan, he was going to be brave.

He shut off the stereo and lights, locked the doors, and walked across the parking lot to the northern stairs. Climbing them to the veranda, he walked down to Branigan's door. A number of people were outside, sitting and talking and drinking. He said hello to all of them, and he felt their eyes on his back as he stopped and knocked on the door.

No answer.

"She left about an hour ago, Mr. Carson," someone said from the dark. He thought it was one of the UltraTrain people.

"She say where she was going? The doctor told her to rest."

"Didn't say."

Carson walked on around the veranda to his apartment above the GTI offices. As usual, he hadn't locked the door, and he walked right in.

The fan was on; the windows were open.

Branigan was sitting in his easy chair in the dark, her face lit softly by the muted light of neon bulbs coming through the dining-area window. The red and green and blue pulsed over the smooth contours of her cheeks.

"You work too late," she said.

"I know," he told her, trying to shake off his surprise. "Sorry I walked right in."

"It's all right with me." He crossed the room and sat down on the couch next to the chair. "How are you feeling?"

"Hungry, actually." She smiled. "I had to cook for myself today."

Carson was trying to recall the speech he was going to give her, but he couldn't remember which side of his brain he was on. From his position on the couch, the light was behind her, and he saw that she was in a soft velour top of some kind, with white slacks. The way she sat, the neon behind her emphasized the curves of her silhouette.

His willpower eroded quickly.

"Steph. . . ."

"Chris, I know I came on a little strong yesterday. Let's blame it on the condition of my mind at the time and let it go at that."

Now she was backing off? The kiss was really born of appreciation?

"I had something a bit different in mind," he said, as one half of his brain ceased to function.

She tilted her head up, and the light shimmered on the side of her throat. "What's that?"

"I thought we might go to bed and worry about all the damned consequences later."

"Okay." She smiled. "Let's."

TWELVE

Rangoon Railway Station, Yangon

Branigan reached the station before seven o'clock in the morning, suffering from a rosy glow of contentment. Despite her best intention of keeping the tongues from wagging, she had spent the entire night in Carson's bed. It was after five before she crawled out from under the covers, trying not to awaken him, but did, then crawled back in to make love one more time.

"I think we passed our tests," he had said.

"If I were writing an employee evaluation," she had told him, "I'd have to write that the gentleman is considerate and tender and certainly devotes a great deal of attention to detail."

"Steph, we're going to have to figure out what this does to our relationship. The professional one."

"Later, lover. I've got to go change and meet Craig Wilson."

"Throwing me over, already?"

"Craig has a wonderful wife and five kids."

"Good. I'm glad to hear it."

She parked her blue-and-silver Pontiac behind the railroad station in the area reserved for construction vehicles and walked through the grand set of bronze-and-glass doors into the ground floor. The station was over a century old, constructed in the grand tradition. Granite floors worn with age were topped with ancient pew-type bench seats of walnut polished to a high gloss by the fabrics of several million passengers. Through the glass doors to the platform, Branigan saw a passenger train embarking passengers. Like its brethren, the train was in poor repair, its paint faded and dull. None of the conventional trains were receiving maintenance in hopes of their lasting until the UltraTrains assumed their roles.

The patterned plaster ceiling was twenty feet high, giving the waiting area an echo and the feeling of an ornate cavern. The walls were divided by massive pilasters, and she supposed that the spaces between them had once displayed the portraits of colonial leaders. Now, they were filled with posters showing landscapes. They were poorly enough done that she didn't recognize one scene.

The new escalators were not yet in operation, and she ducked under the flagged rope blocking them from the public and climbed the long stretch to the second floor.

This level had once contained dozens of administrative offices. The dividing walls were now razed and a new granite floor laid. The aroma of adhesive was pervasive. The walls were not yet finished, and ten or eleven men were fitting plasterboard, working on ladders placed on top of canvas tarps protecting the floor. When it was done, the new waiting room would match the original decor of the building.

The windows in the southern wall, which had once overlooked the ground-level tracks, had been enlarged into a series of doors which exited upon the new, second-level and glass-enclosed, passenger-train platform. The UltraTrain's passage through the city was elevated, and eventually, the ground-level trackage and platforms would be taken up. Pedestrian and auto traffic would be unimpeded by tracks and crossings through the center of the city, and some valuable downtown acreage—under the superquiet trains—would become available for development.

Branigan was proud of her design for the station—retaining the historical significance of the structure while adding the twenty-first century aspect of the UltraTrain, and some members of the SLORC—particularly the minister of the treasury—

had been enchanted by it. When they sold off or leased that reclaimed property, which was owned by the state, they would recoup some of their outlay for the Modernization Proclamation.

She went right out to the platform and found it bare but for one of the shuttles, small people movers with seats for ten and space for equipment. Controlled by either a central control tower or an onboard operator, they were used for shuffling maintenance and repair crews along the tracks. The shuttles also contained diagnostic instruments for gauging the level of tracking or measuring the power characteristics of electrical and magnetic loads.

The platform served only two tracks. The inbound trains from the west, on the outer track, would be accessed by corridors and escalators that went under the tracks, but which would not be installed until the conventional rail line was removed. The two main lines would service Yangon's population of one and three-quarter million more than adequately. The trains moved so rapidly, and were so accurately on time, that half of the rolling passenger car stock that was now in use by the conventional railroad was required.

As she walked down the platform to the shuttle, a door in its side opened, and Craig Wilson stepped out to meet her. She approached the waist-high barrier finished in pale blue, and because there was a train car on the track in that location, the sensors and computers approved opening a barrier. It slid aside and she passed through.

"Good morning, Craig!"

"God. How come you're so chipper this morning?" the chief of motive power asked.

"It's just a typical, beautiful morning."

"Yeah, typical. Heavy rains expected around ten o'clock. I worked until after ten last night. A beautiful day. You're supposed to be wounded or something, aren't you?"

"Just a headache, and it's gone now."

Wilson ushered her into the car and pressed a button which

slid the door closed. He headed toward the west-facing end of the car, and Branigan followed, taking a seat behind the windshield on the left side.

Unlocking a panel with a key, Wilson shoved the panel to the side to reveal the onboard controls. He tapped a couple commands into the keyboard, and the shuttle accelerated away from the platform smoothly, passing through the portal into the sun-drenched morning a few seconds later. The readout climbed rapidly to 75 kilometers per hour.

Looking forward and down, between the two pedestal tracks, Branigan saw a conventional freight rumbling along below them, making maybe 20 miles per hour.

The morning *was* beautiful. The sun shone on the verdant growth of trees and shrubs that blanketed the city. Even the shabbiest of buildings appeared freshly whitewashed by the days of rain. Yangon glistened.

The track paralleled Bogyoke Aung San Street for over a mile, then began a gradual curve to the right, eventually heading north through the Kemendine section. In minutes, they passed the automated-transfer facility at Hume Road. It was there that cargo from the wharves of the Rangoon River would be transferred to UltraTrain freights from the conventional rail cars servicing the docks.

The shuttle automatically slowed to 50 kilometers per hour as it passed through Kemendine Railway Station, another classic example of colonial architecture that was under the same kind of renovation as Rangoon Station. The train speed didn't really have to be restricted since the computers and sensors detected it, as well as pedestrian traffic, and closed the proper barriers. Still, it made some people less anxious if the trains went through stations more sedately. And if an onboard operator had to override the computers and utilize an emergency stop, the rate of deceleration was much quicker.

Several miles beyond Kemendine, with the track back at ground level, Wilson slowed the shuttle as they neared the Yangon Yards, which were twice as large as the service facilities at Mandalay. Beyond these yards, a single main line was being extended northward, up the Irrawaddy River valley to Prome. It would pass through Prome, then circle back to the south, following the valley down the western side of the river to Bassein in Irrawaddy State.

Much of the conventional trackage had already been ripped up in this yard. Two conventional freights, with doubleheaded diesel-electrics towing a string of flat cars, were parked next to the outermost pedestal track. Several cranes were in operation, transferring UltraTrain cars from the flat cars to the pedestal track. The stateside assembly plants were in full production, and UT cars were arriving by sea quickly now. They were assembled into trains and stored in the Yangon Yards. The first two sidings were impressively occupied with complete stainless-steel, blue and yellow trains. On the third siding were an additional three shuttles.

"What have we got now, Craig?"

"I can put together fifteen six-car trains now, Stephanie. Two of them passenger trains."

"Those are the ones I want to see."

They passed under the control tower. It controlled the Yangon traffic and the two approaches to Yangon—the Irrawaddy River valley and the Sittang River valley.

Four miles down the siding, Wilson brought the shuttle to a stop, then opened the side door. The two of them exited, crossed the space between tracks, and boarded a passenger train. The stainless-steel and blue-painted sides gleamed. The yellow stripe down the side was bold and bright.

"This is P-01, Stephanie."

As she stood in the end car, Branigan saw a train on the next track begin to move. There would be a class of operators in the tower practicing moves. She didn't worry about inexpert hands at the controls. It was virtually impossible to force a collision between two UltraTrains. The computers sensed the proximity and directions of trains, and reacted accordingly.

The interiors of the cars were spacious and airy. Paired seating ran down each side of the car on either side of a wide aisle. With the flick of a control switch, all of the seats in the train rotated to face the other way when the train was programmed to run in the opposite direction. The seats were cushioned and covered in a space-age fabric that would resist wear for years. These trains were expected to be heavily utilized for a great many years, and only materials and fabrics that were enduring were used.

The trains were also intelligent. Onboard computers controlled lighting, according to the light of day. They also counted heads, or rather, feet. Sensors embedded in the entrance and exit flooring kept track of the number of passengers aboard, closing the doors when a full load was achieved. Next to entrance doors on the exterior were digital readouts inviting approaching passengers to either PLEASE BOARD, or SORRY, TRAIN FULL. The messages were displayed in both English and Burmese. Corresponding chimes also warned passengers of a door that was about to close.

Branigan would have been quite confident to allow the full schedule of trains to run without operators. The government, however, thought the railworkers' union would be happier, as well as keeping jobs in the economy, if at least a single operator was assigned to each train. So they would be. The easiest job in the economy, what with nothing to do.

She and Wilson inspected each of the cars in the six-unit train.

"Looks damned good to me, Craig."

"I thought so, too. We're getting them off the ships, with relatively little damage."

"Okay, here's what we need to do. In the next few days, move this train into Rangoon Station. Put P-02 on the platform at Kemendine. In a couple weeks, after the station interiors are finished, we'll start opening on the weekends for tours of the trains. I want people to start getting used to the sight of them and even eager to ride."

"Good idea, Stephanie."

"When's the last time you were home?" she asked.

"L.A.? Eight months ago."

"Plan on taking ten days. Make your airline reservations."

"Oh, now, Stephanie! My desk is so full—"

"Just do it, Craig. You need to see Georgia and the kids more often."

"Well, hell. That's great!"

Branigan thought that if she spent much more time with Carson, she'd be attempting to make all of her subordinates feel good.

GTI operations, Mingaladon Airport, Yangon

Lon Mauk entered the building and was met at the high counter by a young Western woman. She quickly identified his uniform and rank.

"May I help you, Colonel?"

"I was told that Mr. Carson was here."

"I'll get him for you."

She went to a door that led into the hangar proper and was back a minute later with Carson.

"Come on back, Colonel, and we'll use this office," Carson said.

Mauk went around the end of the counter and followed Carson into the manager's office. Carson shut the door.

"You haven't met with the accident team yet?" he asked.

"They're in the back, looking over the chopper. We brought it in with a Skycrane and spread it out in the hangar. But no, I haven't made a statement to the team yet."

"Very well. The unmarked jet trainer cannot be traced to a specific organization. Khim Nol, Daw Tan, and Nito Kaing each own several. At least, they are reported to own several. Chieftain Shwe may have one, as well."

"Jesus!" Carson said. "These people have their own air forces?"

"They own a number of aircraft, yes."

Carson jammed an extended thumb over his shoulder toward the back of the hangar. "So what do I tell them?"

"The airplane was noted by Mingaladon Air Control; the controller saw it on his radar, though it did not respond to requests for identification. I should think you would tell the investigators what you saw, but draw no conclusions."

"What conclusions might I draw, Colonel?"

"It depends. If the device on the helicopter was detonated by a timer, the interception by the jet would be, or could be, coincidental. If the device was detonated by remote control, perhaps the jet intended to draw you away from the railroad and highway over more inaccessible terrain, then set off the charge by a radio signal."

Carson screwed up his face. "I hadn't thought of that."

Mauk shrugged. "Anything is possible."

Leaning back to sit on the corner of the desk and crossing his arms, Carson asked, "Does any of this make sense to you?"

"Have you considered that which we last discussed?"

"About who benefits? Yes, but I don't see any winners, Colonel. Say we went over the schedule by two months. The penalties would be allocated among GTI and any of the subcontractors involved in the delay. For two months, the total would run around thirty million. But it's not like we'd be making a cash payment. Instead, we'd deduct that amount from our final billings to the government. And in a twenty-one-billion-dollar deal, thirty million is peanuts."

"Peanuts to the government, perhaps," Mauk said. "To a single person, or to a group of persons, it is a large amount of money."

"You think one man might be involved?"

Mauk shrugged for the second time. "I do not know how the accounting is managed."

"Our books are examined regularly, and I'll stand by my accountants all the way, Colonel."

"I was not thinking of your books."

"The government's? There, I can't help you."

Minister Ba Thun was in charge of the government's accounting, and Mauk had no reason to suspect that he would be altering the books. Ba Thun's standing within the SLORC was quite high, in fact, and that stature had caused him to reevaluate his earlier thought to place electronic listening devices in the minister's residence. It would not be seemly to be discovered eavesdropping on his superior.

"Yes. What do you know of Hyun Oh?"

"Oh? What about him?"

"You know, Mr. Carson, that I am full of hypotheses. This is but another one."

"Well, Hypai Industries was a bidder for the master contract. I don't know how they bid on the request for proposals, but they lost out to General Technologies. As a consolation prize of sorts, they received the direct contract for the local telephone exchanges. I'm sure they were disappointed. Hyun Oh could have been doing what I'm doing."

"And the men involved?"

"I don't know much about Pai, except that he was one of the founders of the company. Hyun Oh strikes me as ambitious and a hard worker. He is not only managing the installation of the telephone centers but, as I understand it, is involved in creating local telephone companies."

"You said he is ambitious."

"In the sense of trying to get ahead," Carson clarified.

"And what if General Technologies was suddenly unable to fulfill its contract with the government?"

Carson grinned, but sadly. "I see where you're going, Colonel. Yes, Hypai might be considered a lead contender, since they're already on-site, for completing the master contract."

"Again, Mr. Carson, it is only a theory."

"You keep coming up with these theories that have me in the leading role of the deceased."

"You are already dead in someone's eyes, Mr. Carson. I only try to fit a scenario to that purpose."

"I hope to hell you find one that works soon, Colonel. Before the play gets into the third act."

Mauk hoped the same thing, but he was not all that confident of a quick solution.

Chinatown, Yangon

If one stepped into an alley off Lanmadaw Road, walked a hundred meters through the litter and refuse which cluttered it, then climbed the frail stairway hung on the back of a building, then crossed the narrow bridge to a landing on the back of the adjacent building, one could open the door and find a long hallway on the third floor. The second door on the left appeared as battered as any door off the corridor, but it was made of steel and had a new lock on it.

Behind the door was a simply furnished room that Daw Tan rented on a permanent basis. It was utilized primarily by his agents, and this was only the second time that he had personally been in it.

Old and tattered draperies were drawn across the single window. Had they been parted, the view was only of the bricks and windows of the building across a narrow air shaft. The room directly across the shaft was vacant. Tan knew this since he also rented that room.

As in the hills, one did well to have more than one path of escape. The secondary path might never be required, but if it was, one did not want to negotiate its use at the time of need.

Daw Tan sat in the single chair in the room and ignored the dilapidated dresser drawers and the narrow cot with its lone blanket. A pitcher of water and a shallow basin rested on the dresser. There was also a telephone, a rarity in rooms like this. Forty years earlier, the whole room would have been a luxury to him.

Daw Tan had two considerations and a problem, though he did not think it would prove to be a large problem.

On the one side, Khim Nol expected him to fulfill the mission left incomplete by the death of the Razor. Now, after his meeting with the South Korean, he had another scheme to explore. On the side of advantage, the two plans were not entirely incompatible. The problem could be resolved merely by enlarging the number of planned executions, thereby accomplishing the goals of both designs.

The Korean's concept was, naturally, self-serving, but there was much to be said for its ramifications. Under Khim Nol's operation, Daw Tan benefited far less; his own objective had been but to ingratiate himself with his superior. With Hyun Oh's approach, Daw Tan faced far greater risk, but the rewards certainly justified the added peril.

It was as if Fate had intervened late in his life. As Daw Tan had embraced the concept of once again handling his tasks with a personal touch, opportunity had rapped on his door frame in the personage of the South Korean.

He felt fully revitalized, the juices flowing.

It meant an additional murder or two.

But he was an expert at that.

Kemendine Railway Station, Yangon

Carson arrived at the station on the west side of the city in midafternoon. He parked his GMC Jimmy in the crowded lot, then went inside and climbed the inoperative escalator to the second floor. From there, he rode the keyed elevator to the third floor.

The director of microwave systems was waiting for him in the tiny new room enclosing the elevator entrance. It was painted white and was brightly lit by overhead fluorescent lights.

"Hello, Sam."

Enders grinned. "This is as far as you go, boss."

"Think so?"

"Try it."

Carson crossed to the screen inset next to the door and placed his palm against it.

Nothing happened.

Enders reached around him and pressed his own palm to the screen.

The door lock buzzed and Enders pulled it open.

"This was a quick installation, Sam."

"After what the assholes did to my place at Moulmein, I'm not wasting time, Chris. You said increase the security, and that's what I'm doing."

"Everywhere?"

"Everywhere. This is the primary center, so it's first, but all twenty-two facilities will be finished within the next couple weeks."

"I'll get a bill, no doubt?"

"You'll get a bill," Enders said in his deep, rumbling voice, "but my initial calculations say it'll be within the allowable cost overrun tolerance. Besides, they're getting a security system they'll probably need long after we're gone."

"We should have done it in the first place, you mean?" Carson asked.

"Hindsight talking," Enders admitted.

Had they proposed the security consideration in the initial proposal, it would probably have been lined out, anyway. The SLORC had redlined a number of proposed alternatives as being too costly.

They stopped in the computer center, and Carson had his palm read for storage in the data files. Now, he could enter the place on his own.

The Myanmar Telephone Company's Kemendine Microwave Complex was the largest and most complicated installation in the country. It was the hub of the whole system, and a maze of antennas were mounted on the roof, hidden from eyesight and the possibility of being an eyesore by fiberglass panels aligned with the edge of the flat roof. The panels matched the architectural decor of the structure and appeared to give the building an extra floor.

Not only were there microwave antennas for relay of voice and data from other in-country stations, but six massive dish antennas provided the linkage between Kemendine and the General Electric constellation of satellites on which Myanmar was now paying a subscription fee.

Myanmar was now connected to the world community, but according to the usage-monitoring computer, was not yet entirely involved in the global village. Carson had analyzed some of the reports and found that it was mostly the foreign residents in Myanmar who were using the satellite channels. There was some, and growing, usage by governmental officials. A few of the prominent Burmese businessmen were beginning to accustom themselves to the new systems. As they computerized their operations with Kiki Olson's personal computer networks, and hooked into the telephonic system, they were accomplishing more and more data transfers in relation to finance, ordering, inventory, and sales. Those who became the most acclimated to the new systems also became its most ardent supporters. When Kiki Olson made a presentation to a potential customer, she had only to take along a few converted Burmese businessmen to drive her points home.

Myanmar was an emerging market, and to GTI's advantage, it was still a restricted market as long as the SLORC enforced its strict definition of acceptable foreign visitors. IBM was here as a subcontractor for mainframe computers, but the only purchaser of mainframes was the government. Kiki Olson, on the other hand, had mounted an aggressive campaign of touring local businessmen through the personal computer networks her division had installed for the telephone company, the sanitary management system, and even GTI's own air-fleet and surface-fleet administration. Most of them were suitably impressed by what they saw, and Kiki's division was making a lot of side deals. She had five people dedicated to selling and installing GTI personal computers for businessmen in Yangon and Mandalay. She had already told Carson she was bringing in another ten salespeople in the next two months.

A year from now, those businesses wouldn't know how they had gotten along without GTI computers.

It was an exciting time, and Carson was happy to be part of it. He was, however, somewhat distracted as he followed Sam Enders on an inspection of the Kemendine Microwave Complex, trying to pay attention to the new security precautions.

He kept thinking about Stephanie Branigan.

Carson had never imagined himself ever becoming romantically involved again. Especially now, when he needed his concentration, and especially with Branigan, since their altered status would be readily recognized by anyone resident in the Zoo. It wasn't good for either of their professional lives.

He should be thinking of a way out of it, but he found himself checking his watch frequently, looking forward to getting back to the compound and seeing her. He found himself recalling the aromas of freshly washed hair and heated woman. His fingertips had memorized silky smooth flesh. He liked the feel of her in his arms. He liked talking to her.

Jesus, what was Merilee going to think?

He was acting like a teenager.

He'd be making mistakes and trying to explain them to Dex Abrams.

"You hear me, Chris?"

"Tell me again, Sam."

They were in the satellite-communications room, a fifty-foot-long space occupied by two rows of consoles.

"We brought the second bank of consoles on-line, and we now have access to five hundred channels on the satellite system. With digitalization, that effectively gives us a half-million circuits. It'll be ten years before Myanmar even gets close to that capacity."

"And by then, Sam, someone will figure out a way to compress the existing circuits even further."

"No doubt. I hope it's me since I can use the billion dollars."

Carson finished his inspection without really retaining any of the information, then went back down to find his Jimmy in the parking lot. All of GTI's road vehicles were painted white, with the simple G-T-I logo on the doors, and there were several in the lot. He had to double-check the vehicle number on the one assigned to him to be sure he had the right one.

Pulling out onto Lower Kemendine Road which, after it curved eastward, became Bogyoke Aung San Street, he found a niche in the late-afternoon traffic and concentrated on not being run over by forty-year-old two-ton trucks or ancient Citroëns and Renaults making a living as taxis.

He knew Branigan had been at Kemendine Station that morning. She was scheduled to visit Kanbe and Mahlwagon Stations, on the eastern side of the railway loop in the afternoon. He hoped she was finished and already back at the compound. They were planning on dinner somewhere in town. Anywhere but in the Zoo's cafeteria.

Passing Hume Road, with a glance toward the cargo-transfer facility under construction in a joint effort of InstaStructure and Cable Engineering, Carson glanced in the rearview mirror, then back to the front, and whipped the wheel to the right as a tuk-tuk slammed on its brakes directly ahead of him.

He managed to maintain his speed, then get back in his original lane after passing the tuk-tuk and the stalled Ford Anglia ahead of it.

He also managed to abandon the wheel and hit the floor within an instant of realizing that bullets were flying through the Jimmy.

THIRTEEN

Lower Kemendine Road, Yangon

The Jimmy slammed into the back of a produce truck. Cabbages flew everywhere.

Carson heard an engine roar, racing past him on the right. Shards of glass filled the air inside the truck. He could feel the Jimmy trying to move and reached up to turn off the ignition.

People yelled.

Another car engine screamed past on his right, a siren yelping.

But no more bullets.

Carson sat up and looked around. The street was in chaos, cars and trucks halted at odd angles. People crouched behind them, staring at him.

He pushed open the passenger door, and careful to avoid the small pieces of glass, crawled out onto the street. He looked the Jimmy over and counted at least twenty bullet holes in the sheet metal of the fenders and door. The windshield was starred and the right side glass had disappeared.

He checked himself over, found a few cuts on his hands. Blood dripped from the side of his jaw on his shirt, and he pressed his fingers against another cut on his right cheek.

A Burmese policeman approached him cautiously, and after a minute of trying to converse with him, Carson found that he didn't speak English.

It was going to be a long evening, he thought.

Then another car squealed to a stop, and two men got out. They were in civilian clothes, but they were unmistakably military in their bearing. They also appeared mildly menacing.

Carson didn't know whether or not to be relieved.

Ahlone Road, Yangon

Mauk's driver let the tires squeal as they slid around the corner, off Kemendine onto Ahlone Road.

The siren whooped and the blue lights behind the Land Rover's grille pulsed. Few of the other drivers cared much about the warning from the otherwise unmarked utility vehicle, and his driver was forced to saw the wheel back and forth as he fought his way through the traffic.

The green Anglia was nearly a block ahead of them, also fighting the traffic, but not attempting to avoid collisions. In its wake, three or four damaged cars had pulled to the side of the street.

Lon Mauk gripped the armrest at his side as the truck whipped back and forth. Major Lin Po, the railroad security commander sitting next to him, cursed aloud as the Anglia increased the distance between them.

"Do you suppose he was killed?" Po asked.

"I do not know. I hope not."

It was all happenstance. Mauk had been having Carson, Branigan, Gilbert, and several others of the contractors followed, unobtrusively surveilled. He and Po were examining the quality of the surveillance, checking on the two men assigned to Carson, when the driver of the Ford Anglia faked engine trouble, then accelerated quickly after Carson passed him.

The two-way radio was a confused mass of chatter from both police and military units. Mauk could not hear one intelligible report.

The driver swerved around a bus as they passed Minister Ba

Thun's house. The Anglia was all but out of sight, merely a flash of green roof that appeared infrequently.

"Do not lose him!" Po shouted to the driver.

"I am trying not to, Major."

"He went straight. Across Prome Road," Mauk noted.

The fugitive had crossed Prome against the traffic signal, causing a three-car collision, and when they reached the intersection, they were slowed, trying to get around the wreck. The driver accelerated hard, once they were past the blockage, but the road ahead no longer contained a green roof.

Schwedagon Pagoda, Yangon

Daw Tan strolled the grounds of the pagoda as would a man without a care in the world. He wore his white suit, dark glasses, and hat, and he ate peanuts from a bag he had bought from a vendor.

Sitting atop Singuttara Hill, the pagoda was the central feature of the city and of the country. Thousands of pilgrims trekked to the site annually, seeking spiritual guidance at the place that was built twenty-five centuries before to shelter eight sacred hairs of the Buddha. Situated on a terraced base, the bell-shaped structure was a treasure trove. Sixty tons of gold leaf coated the building. Gold and silver bells were suspended in the *hti,* at the pinnacle of the building, which was also embedded with rubies, topaz, and sapphire. The weather vane was of gold and silver, encrusted with 1,100 diamonds. The orb at the very top was the base for 1,800 carats of diamonds, including a single 76-carat stone.

Over the centuries, various monarchs had ordered restorations or additions to the pagoda. King Byinnya-U increased the height from nine meters to twenty-two meters in the fourteenth century; its current height of 107 meters was reached in 1774; King Mindon of Mandalay contributed the current seven-tiered *hti* in 1871. There were four entrances, the primary being on the south and east sides where the licensed stallholders offered their goods to the visiting pilgrims. The terrace surrounding the pagoda encompassed nearly 14,000 acres and contained sixty-four miniature pagodas, including four larger pagodas on each side. The eight planetary posts were located at the eight compass points, and Daw Tan stopped at his birthpost to leave a 100-*kyat* note as an offering to his guardian spirit. Since his religion was that of Islam, he did not think it would help forge his fate, but then, it might not hurt, either.

He was not certain what tomorrow might hold, but today had gone very well. After following Carson from the contractor's housing and office block to Kemendine Station, Tan had waited an hour for him to emerge from the station, then managed to place himself ahead of the GTI vehicle in traffic. The subterfuge of the stalled car allowed him to get into a firing position, and the resulting confusion assisted in his escape.

Daw Tan appreciated the bold move. In daylight, the attack was less expected, more shocking, and inadequately defended. He had been surprised at the immediacy of the pursuit, but it had been quickly outrun in the traffic, and the stolen car and the assault rifle were now abandoned in the People's Park, across U Wisara Road from Singuttara Hill.

After Carson's amazing deliverance from the bomb on the helicopter, Tan had elected to take direct action. Additionally, he thought, Khim Nol might have been displeased were he to learn that Tan had enlisted underlings in the helicopter venture after Nol's specific order for Tan to assume the task personally.

He was now happy that he had done so. The adrenaline high was one that he had forgotten, and it was good to experience it once again.

He could not help smiling to himself as he descended from the terrace in search of a taxi. He would go back to his room in Chinatown and relax.

The first of his objectives had now been met, and he could devote a considerable amount of time—the planning must be perfect—toward what he must do about Khim Nol and Hyun Oh.

Myanmar army barracks, Yangon

U Ba Thun flowed through the main entrance of the administration building like a raging river, carrying the newspaper in his hand. He yelled his question at the sergeant on duty and followed the cringing man down the long corridor to Colonel Mauk's office.

The sergeant melted away in fear as Ba Thun shoved open the door and barged into the commander's office. Colonel Mauk was at his desk and immediately came to his feet. Major Tawn Yin May spilled liquid from his cup as he scrambled to a position of attention.

"Good afternoon, Minister," Mauk said, his voice unruffled. The overhead lights reflected from his shaven skull.

"First of all, Colonel Mauk, why do you allow attacks against foreigners in broad daylight? In the middle of the city?"

"Please have a seat, Minister."

"I do not feel like sitting. Answer me!"

"I should leave," Yin May said.

"Stay where you are, Major."

Mauk stepped from behind his desk. "It is not, Minister, as if we had not anticipated the attempt. There were two men accompanying Carson at the time, but the assassin slipped by them."

"Incompetence!"

"It is extremely difficult to watch everyone on a street as crowded as Kemendine Road."

"And this!" Ba Thun tossed the folded newspaper on the desk.

Mauk reached for it and unfolded it. Ba Thun watched as he noted the banner, the international edition of the *London Times*. Then the headline: MYANMAR REBELS OUT OF CON-

TROL. Then the huge picture above the fold, a shot of the broken GTI helicopter lying in the forest clearing.

"I had not seen this," Mauk said.

"The publicity is damning."

"Where did they get the picture?"

"The Steele woman suggests it came from a passenger on the airliner."

"I do not believe it," Mauk said.

"It is possible," Ba Thun countered.

"Does she have evidence that rebels are responsible, Minister?"

"It seems to be mostly supposition to me. What is worse is that, in the time of our need to present a positive image to the world, we allow information like this to reach the international press. How did that happen, Colonel?"

"I did not even know the Steele woman was in the country," Mauk said.

"She will not be for long. The premier has ordered her to be deported immediately."

"Is that wise?"

"Wise? Why would it not be? With innuendo, she attempts to kill us. Saying that we cannot control the bandits!"

"If she is deported, what will her next story be?"

"Tell me."

"I suggest, Minister, that she will rally her fellow correspondents by saying that the government attempts to hide the truth by denying her access. It could be even more damaging in a public relations sense. Not that I am an expert at public relations, I hasten to add."

Ba Thun recalled the furor raised when the Nobel laureates gathered in Bangkok. He let his temper subside.

"What else do you suggest, Colonel?"

"Perhaps you could reason with the premier. I assume she is here on a limited visa. Extend it for thirty days. Invite her to pursue the story. Give her additional access to the countryside."

"This is ridiculous, Colonel! The premier will have you back as a lieutenant," Ba Thun said.

"Please, if you would look beyond the obvious, Minister."

Ba Thun forced himself to think about a raving, lying correspondent, and a woman at that, running anywhere she wanted to run.

"You would have her lead you to the perpetrators, Colonel?"

"She is as good a bait as any I might propose," Mauk said.

"Stop these attacks in the city," Ba Thun said as he turned on his heel and strode from the room.

The minister was quite sincere about his order. Atrocities in the jungle were one thing; in the city, another.

Palo Alto, California

"What we've got here is a master computer hacker, Mr. Abrams," Troy Baskin said.

The security chief didn't look happy, which reflected Abrams's own mood. He wasn't generally happy at six in the morning facing piles of paperwork, anyway, and his contemplation of his unemployed future was only relieved by the cheerful thoughts of the people he could fire before he packed his desk. Baskin was at the top of that list, and no doubt, he knew it.

"Give it to me," he ordered, sipping from his coffee.

He hadn't offered Baskin coffee, a clue to Abrams's frame of mind.

"One. After a thorough review of anyone with access to the lab, I'm ninety-nine percent certain that none of them were involved. Two, someone tried to access the file again."

"What!"

"Yes, sir. Mack Little says he was after the fourth version of the blueprints, so we're assuming he's already got the first three."

"Goddamn it!"

Number two was the model showing the most promise, and if that was gone, so was his job.

"Did he get it?"

"No," Baskin said. "Something—maybe his access program—tipped him to the fact that he was being monitored, and he shut down almost as soon as he got into the file."

"But you got it traced?"

"Only as far as an area code—two-one-three in Los Angeles—and a three-digit prefix. It's still a big unknown."

"Shit."

"While the access was being made, I had all of the lab personnel under surveillance. It wasn't one of them making the call, and no one from the company, as far as I now know, was in L.A. at the time."

"So what are you doing now?"

"Mr. Little and I both agree that he won't make another attempt. Today, Mr. Little and the computer people are completely changing the computer access security."

"That's all?"

"I've sent two of my people to L.A. They're going to track down every phone number on that prefix."

"Okay, Troy. Get out of here."

"Sir? Two things."

"What?"

"You should probably let DOD know, and you should probably alert the legal staff. If I find that phone number, and who might have been using it, we can zap them with an industrial-espionage lawsuit."

"Yeah, sure."

Baskin went out, closing the double doors behind him, and Abrams made a note to call the procurement office at the Pentagon. GTI didn't have a defense contract on the Ruby Star project yet, but the defense people were highly interested in it and following the development closely. If they were just a little more interested, GTI might have had some development money out of the defense budget. Times being what they were, though, the Department of Defense preferred having private enterprise put up the research and development costs on technology with a weapons-system potential.

He didn't think he'd say anything to the lawyers yet. He didn't have enough faith in Baskin being able to find a damned phone number.

His secretary wasn't in yet, so he called Yangon himself. Carson wasn't in the office, but the woman said she'd track him down.

It was after seven before Carson called back.

"Where the hell have you been?" he demanded.

"Police station."

"Jesus! What now?"

"Somebody shot up my truck."

"Oh, for Christ's sake! You all right?"

"Yes. A few cuts. Damn it, Dex, it's starting to get serious over here. We're going to go way off the schedule if we spend half our time looking over our shoulders."

Abrams had already read Carson's report on the schedule problems coming out of the Moulmein disaster.

"Go to Ba Thun and demand more protection," he said.

"I won't get it. You know the political concerns."

"Maybe Ba Thun would set up a separate unit for personnel security, so it doesn't look like Mauk's building himself his own army."

"I can try it, Dex, but I think it's a lost cause."

"I have my own lost causes."

"Which are?"

"The primary program has been compromised."

After a long pause, Carson said, "In what way?"

"The plans are gone. Been copied, anyway."

"Ah, damn. Any idea who?"

"Not yet, but Baskin's working on it. I don't hold out much hope that he's going to find anything, and we probably won't know until some company announces their hot new product."

"Which means you want me to produce?"

"Damned right. And right away. I'm going to tell Little to build five prototypes of the best design. All I need from you is five copies of the main component."

"You've got one."

"Four, then. You get them to me by the fifteenth of the month."

"No damned way," Carson said.

"The first of July, then," Abrams said and hung up.

Szechuan Palace, Chinatown, Yangon

As luck would have it, Carson didn't find a restaurant free of people they knew. Charles Washington and three of his associates from Hydrofoil Marine were in a booth at the back of the Chinese restaurant. As soon as he spotted them, Washington rose from his seat and crossed the floor. Despite his bulk and the way he towered over the Chinese and Burmese in the restaurant, he threaded his way through the tables like a linebacker intent on seriously maiming the quarterback. It was not a surprising accomplishment for the man, of course.

"Hey, Chris, Stephanie. Come on and join us."

"Hi, handsome," Branigan said.

"Love this woman."

"Thanks, Charles," Carson said, "but you're already into your dinner, and we've got some business to talk about."

"Another time, then? Saturday, we're having a little party to initiate the Prome-Yangon run."

"Saturday, it is," Carson promised.

The two of them were finally seated at a small table in the corner and ordered rice wine, wonton, spiced *szechuan* beef, and sweet-and-sour shrimp. The overhead fans turned lazily, but they didn't keep away the flies. Carson swatted at them aimlessly. He couldn't quite reach the state, as several of the people at neighboring tables had, where he could allow the flies to crawl unmolested over his arms and hands as he ate.

Branigan's face still registered the sober, reflective look it had taken on when he told her of his encounter with the machine gun. He waited for her to come back from wherever she was and openly studied her. She was wearing a linen dress of hushed green that set off her eyes and the dark red of her hair. The table candle flickered a reflection in the heavy darkness of her hair. He realized that, prior to a couple days earlier, he couldn't recall one outfit she had ever worn. A week ago, if he had been asked, he would have had to guess at the color of her eyes.

Now, he was acutely aware of the way she bent her wrist when she drank from her wineglass, the subtle curve of her upper arm beneath the short sleeve of the dress, the small birthmark at the side of her throat, all but hidden by her collar, and the tiny scar under her jaw. She wouldn't be described as voluptuous, but she was sleek in her own way. He didn't know how he had missed all of this for two years.

Her eyes suddenly focused on his face.

"I've got a question," he said.

"Shoot," she said, then added, "Sorry! Wrong choice of words."

He grinned. "What did you do to your jaw?"

She tilted her head up and pointed to the scar with a forefinger. "Here?"

"There."

"I used to be Wonder Woman."

"Did you now?"

"Uh-huh. When I was about nine. One day, when I was out practicing my flying abilities, I fell off the garage roof. Into a giant golden elder."

"Did that stop your flying?"

"Only the realistic part of it. Couldn't interfere with the dreams, though."

"I can understand that."

"How did you break your nose?" she asked.

"Would you believe crashing a helicopter?"

"I see. You've made a habit of this?"

"Just twice. Not my fault either time."

"When was the first time?"

"Iraq. We were extracting a squad of Saudi Arabian troops when we caught a missile."

"You're entirely too accustomed to being shot at."

"I never get used to it, Steph. I had thought those days were behind me."

"I'm thinking of sending the dependents home," she said in an abrupt change of topic.

While the companies paid the expenses of relocating their employees for the Myanmar Modernization Project, they had not supported the transfer of families. About ten percent of the American personnel had brought their families to Myanmar at their own expense.

"That's going to be tough without some statement by the U.S. State Department. Or without picking up the cost."

"I'd pick up the cost, Chris. It wouldn't be extremely high, and it might be enough to induce them to get their wives and kids back to safety."

"Washington and Chicago and L.A. aren't all that safe."

"That's true. Can you get some bodyguards?"

"Me?"

"I've just found you, Chris. I don't want to lose you." She reached across the table and laid her hand on his.

He turned his hand over, palm up, and gripped her hand. All afternoon and evening, until she returned from Kanbe Station with Craig Wilson, he had worried about her.

"You're not going to lose me."

"Surely, Ba Thun would approve a bodyguard."

"We've got them already. See the two burly Burmese guys in beige suits next to the door?"

Branigan turned her head to look.

"Who are they?"

"Compliments of Colonel Mauk. One's yours, and one's mine."

"Oh, God! I don't think I can stand being followed around."

"They've been doing it for a couple days, and you didn't notice them."

"I don't think anyone's after me," she said.

"Mauk doesn't want to take any chances," he said.

She squeezed his hand and smiled. "This makes our little secret even less of a secret, doesn't it?"

"I think it stopped being a secret about midnight, last night. Becky Johnson told me I was looking less peaked this morning. She asked me if I'd found a new vitamin."

"And you said?"

"What else could I say? I said 'yes.' Becky knows me too well."

"So we ignore the talk?"

"I'm going to."

She turned the corners of her mouth down. "Is this going to last, Chris? Are we going to last?"

"Let's not push it. We'll see where it goes."

"I haven't done anything so impulsive in all my life, you know. Positively brazen."

"To my vast good fortune," he told her.

Their plates and covered dishes arrived, and Carson spooned steaming white rice onto the plates for both of them. The shrimp count never came out even, of course, and she gave him the extra shrimp. He traded it back for more of the beef, which was hot enough to bring tears to his eyes.

Despite being shot at, shot down, and subjected to unattainable demands by his boss, Carson realized he was happy. He didn't even know that he'd been unhappy for so long.

He hoped it lasted.

FOURTEEN

GTI compound, Yangon

The downpour on Saturday morning was torrential. Jack Gilbert stayed under the overhead veranda as he walked down to the UltraTrain offices. The tin roof above the veranda took the beating of the rain with as much resistance as it could muster. The steady *thrum* could get on the nerves after a while, but fortunately, most of the rains were short-lived.

Stepping through the open doorway into the tiny entry vestibule, Gilbert turned to the right and stuck his head inside Branigan's office. Only Janice Cooper was present.

"Hello, Jack!"

"Morning, Janice. The boss lady around?"

"In the back."

"Thanks."

He went through the door at the back of the foyer, passed several cubicles with five-foot-high walls, turned left, and walked down a corridor to the room the inmates called the engineering center. Given the size of the building, it was a fair-size space, ringed with computer terminals. A large table in the middle contained a relief map of the entire Union of Myanmar railway system. The existing trackage for the conventional railroad was depicted with yellow thread lightly glued to the surface of the map. The UltraTrain pedestal rail was represented by mauve thread, the color chosen by Branigan, no doubt. Every time he looked at it, Gilbert was amazed by how rapidly the mauve thread was spreading. And even now, some sections of the yellow were disappearing.

He was always bothered by the lack of drafting tables in the center. Engineers should have drafting tables. But no. The computer-aided design, or CAD, software made such things as tables, protractors, and T squares obsolete. Now, a draftsman could lay out his design, say for a trestle, in a third of the time, then lift it, turn it around, turn it over, look at it head-on, in plan form, in elevation, or in perspective. If he could figure out how he liked looking at it, he zipped it off to one of the giant printers. The technology was one of the reasons the track-laying was proceeding so smoothly.

Branigan and Dick Statler, the roadbed engineer, were leaning over the table, talking. Eight more men and women dressed in Myanmar casual were working at the computers at the side of the room.

Everyone looked up when he entered, making him feel guilty of entering the stage too soon.

"Hello, Jack," Branigan said.

"How's the empire coming?" he asked, leaning over the table to look.

There was only a short gap now in the mauve line between Yangon and Mandalay. The line west out of Yangon was moving steadily from the Yangon Yards toward Prome. He was surprised to see, on the map, about an inch of mauve thread starting out of Thazi, an intersection of the Mandalay-Yangon main line, on the route toward Taunggyi. That section of the railway system was called the Taunggyi Division.

But then, on reflection, he decided he was less surprised.

"I see you're hell-bent for the Chinese border."

Statler grinned at him.

"What are you getting at?" Branigan asked.

"I don't think that—whatever you're calling it? The Taunggyi Division?—is a priority for the SLORC."

"We happen to have had crews available and in the area,

Jack. We're on schedule everywhere else, and we've got to build it sometime."

"That's b.s., beautiful."

"You think so?"

"Sure. Deep in my black heart, I know that UltraTrain sees this project as only a foothold on Asia. That's why your bid came in so low, sacrificing large profits in favor of a showpiece. One of your internal priorities is to complete that line through Keng Tung to the border so that the masters in Beijing can see how well it works. And how easy it would be to hook into it and carry the line to Kumming, Guiyang, Hengyang. Maybe a spur down to Canton and Hong Kong. Today, Keng Tung; tomorrow, Beijing."

Now Branigan grinned at him. "You're not going to tell anyone?"

"Of course not. As long as I get a piece of the action. Should I buy UltraTrain stock?"

"By all means," Statler told him. "The only way it's going is up."

"Other than to harass us, did you come all the way over here for a reason?" Branigan asked.

"Yup. You know that anyone with an 'assistant' in his title gets all the dirty jobs, right? Well, this assistant got handed the chore of putting people on your prize train."

"You're calling it the prize train?"

"That's more of your promotional effort, isn't it? All these bigwigs from the neighboring nations are going end up with a hankering for their own toy train. They'll be digging deep into their treasury pockets."

"You call it a toy train again," she said, "and I'll bop you on the head."

The perfectly good mood she was in supported Gilbert's theory about developments on the Carson-Branigan front. He was happy for both of his friends.

Gilbert grinned. "Anyway, on the inaugural run from Mandalay to Yangon on July fifteenth, the premier has decided he wants to invite more people than you've got planned, and he spoke to the minister, who spoke to the director, who spoke to me. I'm speaking to you."

"What do you want to know?"

"Basic stuff, like how many people fit in one of those things that really wants to be an airplane?"

"Twenty rows of seats per car. Eighty passengers."

"How many cars?"

"The normal configuration is six," Statler said. "We could add a couple of cars if you need them."

"So if the premier wants to invite six or seven hundred of his close friends, it isn't a problem?"

"Better keep it at six-forty," Branigan said. "The platforms at the stations are limited to eight cars. We don't want anyone walking in the rain. Especially at the elevated stations."

"Okay. See how easy it is to satisfy me?"

As he turned to leave, Branigan asked him, "Are you going to Washington's party?"

"Pamela got her visa extended, so I hadn't planned on it."

"Why don't you bring her along? Charles won't care. And besides, I haven't met her yet."

"The problem is," Gilbert said, "I don't want anyone to meet her. Especially guys like Dick."

"I'm married," Statler said.

"After tonight, you'll think of that as a rash decision."

University of Rangoon, Yangon

The problem with Saturdays at the university, Mauk had often thought, was that the students did not have enough to do. To fill the time, they complained. Their complaints often took a political bent because that drew the attention of the media, and if there was one thing the students desired, more than a resolution to their complaints, it was attention.

These overgrown children did not realize how fortunate they

were, just being in residence at the university. Myanmar, and before that, Burma, could boast of its high literacy rate, greater perhaps than that of any nation in Southeast Asia. More than seventy percent of the population was literate, a result of free primary education and only minimal charges for secondary and higher education. In the last thirty years, enrollments at all levels had expanded greatly. Westerners liked to assume that, because of its geography and its tribal demographics, Myanmar was a backward state, but that was simply untrue.

Still, the university frequently seemed to be the locale for organized unrest. Newly imbued with minimal levels of knowledge and massive doses of idealism, the students took it upon themselves to point out society's ills and the government's shortcomings. Mauk had yet to see any student dissident group arrive at workable solutions for the problems they enjoyed identifying, the operative word being "workable."

Dressed in a civilian suit and tie, Mauk strolled the campus, following a meandering route across it. He was in no hurry, and without appearing to be interested, he watched the small groups of students gathered on the lawns. Many seemed to be involved only in intellectual discussions of literature, art, psychology. A few were political in nature, young firebrands exhorting their fellow firebrands to some kind of action—any kind.

Lon Mauk did not interfere, but he listened with deep interest as he passed them.

When he neared the administration building, Mauk veered off the sidewalk and crossed the grass to sit on a bench under a hundred-year-old conifer. He sat for nearly an hour, absorbing the cool breeze and contemplating the overcast skies. It might well rain again. The respite gave him time to consider the last few days. He was worried about the foreigners with whom he was charged with protecting. They were an unpredictable group, flitting here and there about the country, and as far as he could tell, not overly concerned with their own safety. It made for difficulties. Then, too, incidents like the attack on

Kemendine Road raised the ire of members of the SLORC, which was not helpful. Mauk was relatively comfortable with his ability to handle Ba Thun, but if the violence escalated, the minister might be provoked into taking actions that Mauk would regret, such as removing him from his position of command of the security unit. Mauk could think of no other field-grade officer more capable of directing the specialized unit than himself.

He wondered, also, if the warlords had more ears in his orderly room than those of Corporal Syi. It seemed as if Daw Tan or someone knew things they should not know. The flight of Carson's helicopter came immediately to mind. Whoever was flying that Cessna jet trainer knew approximately the vicinity and approximately the time in which Carson could be intercepted. It would not take much of a forewarning. The Cessna, if it were based at Man Na-su, could have reached the railway in thirty to forty minutes.

Mauk was less certain of Daw Tan's involvement, especially in the escapade in Yangon. The reports from Mandalay indicated that Daw Tan was still secluded in his suite in the Shanghai Hotel. The reports did not coincide with his instincts, but Mauk sometimes was required to yield his spirit to the power of fact. There was another point of fact which he never forgot: Daw Tan was in the position of having his wishes carried out for him. He need not participate.

Just before eleven o'clock, a thin lanky-haired boy wearing white slacks and a colorful pink-and-blue shirt with the tails flapping in the wind crossed the grass and sat beside him.

"Good morning, Lu Tsong."

The boy may have thought less of the morning, for he did not respond. The sneer on his face suggested his distaste for this meeting. He was a self-proclaimed intellectual with a desire to participate in the political system. He would, of course, change the system to meet his own needs. At the moment, he was a campus representative of the National League for Democracy, and his professed idol was the political leader Aung

San Suu Kyi. He was also, however, destitute, and his desire for the finer things in student life—music, parties, transport, travel—frequently overcame his idealism. He had not fully considered how short-lived his political aspirations could be should it ever be revealed that he had cooperated with Col. Lon Mauk. And Mauk would not enlighten him.

"How do your studies go?" Mauk asked.

"Very well, as expected."

Mauk smiled. "And the movement?"

"The enrollment has nearly doubled in the last year."

There was always safety in numbers. The rash acts of a few were disguised by the masses surrounding them.

"And what is their concern currently?"

The boy hated giving these answers, but he always did.

"Have you seen the beggars on the streets? There is a committee studying the sudden rise in unemployment."

Mauk did not feel compelled to explain economics to the boy. Unemployment rates were not necessarily up if one based the numbers on a stable population; the influx of people from the hills had swelled the urban population. This fact, of course, weighed heavily on the SLORC, and as the pressure mounted, they would apply pressure on the foreigners to create jobs. Mauk knew that there was some tension between Ba Thun and Carson as a result of GTI's decline in hiring. He did not know specifically what was behind it, but he thought that the problem would soon come to a boil.

"Committees take so much time, do they not?" Mauk observed.

"I think this committee will recommend a demonstration."

Mauk always took recommendations as facts accomplished.

"When will the demonstration take place?"

The boy considered a lie, but said, "On the fourth of July."

Two weeks away. More than enough time to prepare, but Mauk would consider carefully how to handle it. He did not want to suppress the students, but to temper their exuberance. Suppression always backfired, especially when the media got hold of it. Investigative reporters were as tenacious as tigers with antelopes in sight.

"Is there anything else of importance?" he asked.

"Nothing."

Taking the envelope from his pocket, Mauk hesitated before handing it over.

The boy looked at it hungrily.

"What," he asked, "do your fellow students think of the foreigners?"

The boy looked him directly in the eyes for the first time. "They represent the hope for the future."

He gave the boy the envelope.

And continued sitting on the bench in the protection of the big pine tree for some time after the young man scampered away.

Myanmar Telephone Company, Windsor Road Facility, Yangon

Hyun Oh wore the new suit he had just picked up from his tailor on Phonegyi Street. It fit impeccably, and the luster of the silver-blue fabric gave him a feeling of importance.

He had been feeling more important every day since his secret meeting with Daw Tan.

For the first time, Oh had taken an initiative that would benefit him as well as Mr. Pai, and he was impressed with the sense of his own bravery. He was taking a risk, though a comparatively small one, he thought. The results could be quite satisfactory.

Leaving his Celica in the lot, Oh passed through the new security procedures to enter the building. This was the largest component of the Hypai Industries' project, controlling all telephone traffic in the capital city and connected by a fiber-optic backbone to the microwave center at Kemendine Station.

He went directly to the control room where the Burmese

manager and the Hypai director of training were waiting for him.

"Before we begin our meeting," the manager said, "I should mention that two boxes arrived today, Mr. Oh, directed to your attention."

"Ah, yes." He handed his keys to the manager. "Would you have someone put them in my car?"

"Certainly."

The boxes would contain several sizes of the Hypai superconducting magnets. If all went well with that undertaking, Oh felt he would be in a position to negotiate an increase in his salary, or, at the least, a bonus. He had already decided that his best approach with Stephanie Branigan would be low-key, low-profile. He would not press her unduly, for he was certain that the price differential between the Hypai and the UltraTrain products was substantially in his favor.

Lower Hledan Street Jetty, Yangon

Two blocks of ancient warehouses to the west of the ferry slips had been razed to make way for the boatyard and docks supporting what would be known as the Myanmar National Ferry Service. The new name would not apply until the operation was turned over to the government after the final shipments of marine craft and the final graduation of new pilots and crews from their training courses.

The new buildings fronting the river carried the distinctive concrete finish of the InstaStructure design. The vertical ribs on the exterior walls reinforced the poured concrete walls and immediately identified the contractor. They might as well have been a logo.

These buildings were four stories tall—but comprised only two floors—and almost four hundred feet deep. The top floor was segmented into administrative and storage spaces, and the bottom floor had thirty-five-foot ceilings so that the hydrofoils and hovercraft could be towed inside for maintenance and repair.

The new concrete docks currently had seven vessels in attendance, two of them the sixty-foot, light passenger-load hydrofoils like the one Carson had taken to Moulmein. Three of them were the larger, 140-foot model. All of the vessels, in following the color scheme of the UltraTrain, were finished with silver lower sides and pale-blue decks and superstructures. A broad yellow band divided the colors along the hull and incorporated the M-N-F-S logo.

The hydrofoils were sleek machines with smooth lines and a nearly full-length superstructure. A higher section of the superstructure near the bow contained the pilothouse, and the full main deckhouse was devoted to either passengers or cargo. On the passenger version, bench seating was utilized for the most part, with a few lounge areas. There was a cafeteria-style food service. Below the main deck was another and smaller passenger area, as well as crew and storage quarters. The total passenger capacity of the larger vessel was 250.

At rest by the docks, the vessels appeared to be standard marine craft. Under way, however, with the two aft and one forward hydrofoils extended from the hull, they rode the seas smoothly at over 48 knots, powered by one General Electric 18,000-shaft horsepower gas turbine.

Hydrofoil Marine Corporation also had a larger version of the boat for heavy cargo, but the SLORC had not yet decided whether or not to opt for the second half of the package.

The other two craft at the docks were hovercraft, which rode on a cushion of air produced by huge propellers driven by four gas turbine engines. They looked like oversize rubber Zodiak boats with a flat deck and a deckhouse on top. The fleet of hovercraft would be smaller, twelve boats in all, and used for higher-priced express service. The eighty-foot-long hovercraft carried only forty-eight passengers, but they carried them at over 100 miles per hour.

It was dark, still threatening rain, when Carson parked his

newly requisitioned GMC Jimmy utility vehicle in the lit parking lot. He noted, without mentioning it to the others, that the gray Subaru sedan carrying Mauk's undercover guards parked nearby.

The four of them—Carson, Branigan, Gilbert, and Steele—crawled out of the truck, crossed the lot, and entered an open back door.

On the far side, the big hangarlike door was open to the night and the river. Floodlights down on the docks lit up the vessels, two of which were festooned with multicolored pennants and balloons. Due to the threat of rain, the party had been located inside, and long folding tables were covered with blue and yellow tablecloths. Caterers hovered over a roast pig, and the tables were laden with side dishes and hors d'oeuvres from a mix of Burmese, American, and Continental recipes.

A four-piece Burmese band was set up in the far corner, playing a variety of American rock and country music.

At the moment, there were maybe sixty people, but Carson figured that, with Washington in charge, there'd be a couple hundred by the time it got into full swing. So far it was a fair blend: Myanmar government people and those who would be associated with the new ferry service, managers from Tourist Myanmar, Hydrofoil employees, and a sprinkling of personnel from GTI and its subcontractors.

As they entered, Carson felt a few appraising eyes. They may have been surveying Gilbert's latest flame, who was certainly worth surveying. Or they may have been analyzing Carson and Branigan. How many times had the two of them been together at business and social events in the past two years? Several dozen, anyway, but suddenly he felt as if everyone in Yangon knew there had been a change in the way the UltraTrain and GTI directors worked with each other.

And notwithstanding the sex appeal of Pamela Steele—dressed in a clinging aqua cocktail dress, Carson was rather proud to be escorting Branigan. She wore a white dress with a low-cut bodice that revealed the hint of cleavage and a sprinkling of freckles that all but disappeared in the tan of her flesh. There was just a dusting of makeup on the smooth flesh of her cheeks. Her eyes sparkled like he had never seen, or noticed, before. She had a bright smile for everyone.

Gilbert took Pamela Steele off for introductions, and Branigan whispered to him, "That woman's designed to make every other woman feel like a frump."

Carson smiled at her. "You're hardly a frump, Steph."

"I just realized I don't have any chest or hips."

"I'll be the judge of that."

She grinned at him.

Washington approached them, carrying a glass in a hand big enough to make it look like a thimble.

"I wasn't jealous of Chris until just now, Stephanie. May I say you're breathtaking tonight?"

"Thank you, kind sir."

"Why don't you ditch him, and we'll slip out early?"

"You're the host," she told him.

"Damn. Forgot."

"You have any more of that, host?" Carson asked, indicating Washington's glass.

"A little."

Washington led them over to the bar and had the Burmese bartender mix them Chivas and water. No plastic glasses for Washington; the tumblers were of heavy leaded crystal.

"Most of the SLORC are supposed to be here sooner or later," Washington said. "Be nice to them, will you, Chris?"

"I'm always nice to them, Charles."

"The word is that you and Ba Thun are feuding."

"Is it? Over what?"

"The hiring freeze, I'd assume."

"You haven't written down that freeze on a little old memo anywhere, have you?"

Branigan listened to them with a wry smile on her face. She had agreed to go along with Carson's slowdown on hiring, based solely on his statement that he wanted to apply pressure on Ba Thun. She hadn't asked why he needed the pressure, but as curious as she could be, he didn't know how long he could hold her off.

"Of course not," Washington said.

"I imagine that will be resolved soon," Carson said. "It's Ba Thun's move, at the moment."

"I've heard another thing you and Stephanie might be interested in."

"What's that?"

"You know my boats have multinational crews? Burmese, Indians, Thais, Chinese?"

"It doesn't surprise me."

"Well, as we get them integrated, they're turning out to be pretty cohesive. I mean, the crews develop a loyalty to their vessels, and they stick up for each other. They talk."

"About?"

"Buddy Baker, who's training officer on HF-4, says that his Burmese have been telling people that the UltraTrains will never run in the country."

Branigan looked up at him, startled. "What!"

"That's just what he hears."

"They say anything about who might be behind it?" Carson asked.

"Did you ever pin down a rumor?" Washington asked.

"Not recently. Especially not recently."

"The only thing Buddy got was that something's supposed to happen in July."

"The inaugural run," Branigan said.

"That would be logical," Washington said. "I got Mauk to put a couple armed men on the hydrofoils scheduled for their first runs tomorrow. Just as a precaution."

"Wise move, pal," Carson said. "Let me know if you hear anything else, Charles."

Carson and Branigan left him to move about the cavernous room, stopping to talk to almost everyone, but concentrating their attention on the Burmese government officials and businessmen. Though they didn't touch each other, Carson got the impression that most of the GTI people considered him and Branigan as a unit.

At one point, Branigan told him, "I think you and I are an item."

·"That's a gossipy description. I was thinking, 'unit.' "

"That's grossly engineerese."

"Engineerese?"

"For want of a better term."

Branigan went off on her own for a while, while Carson talked to the premier and the cultural minister.

He filled a large plate with slices of the roast pig, which was garnished with pineapple and was delicious. He listened to the band re-creating Brooks and Dunn and Alan Jackson. They did a nice rendition of George Jones's Corvette song.

He and Bob Mickeljohn of IBM were talking to the head of the Myanmar tourist bureau when Branigan and Oh approached him. Branigan waved him aside.

"Hyun and I are going to run back to the Zoo for a few minutes, Chris."

He raised an eyebrow.

Oh said, "I received a shipment today for Miss Branigan."

"Couldn't you take care of it in the morning?"

"In the morning, I must leave to meet some men in Myit-kyina in regard to a local telephone company."

"Don't be gone too long," he said.

"You wouldn't worry about me, would you?"

"Not in Hyun's care."

Lower Hledan Street Jetty, Yangon

"Would you mind if we left early?"

Gilbert grinned.

Pamela Steele said, "Don't get any radical ideas, just yet, Mr. Gilbert. I've met so many people that I've been trying to get appointments with that I've got to get some notes written while the subjects are still fresh in my mind."

"How long is this going to take?"

"Perhaps an hour."

"Let's go." He looked down at her high heels and decided they weren't going to walk back to the compound. "I'll see if Chris will give up the keys to the truck."

He turned to search for Carson in the crowd and saw Branigan and Oh headed their way.

"Have you seen Chris, Stephanie? I want to borrow his truck."

Branigan smiled at the two of them and said, "Are you headed for the Zoo?"

At Steele's puzzled look, Gilbert said, "That's the GTI compound, my dear. Yeah, we are."

"We're on our way there. Would you have room, Hyun?"

"Of course."

Gilbert introduced Steele to the South Korean, then they all went out and got into his car. The backseat was a little cramped, but Gilbert didn't mind.

Oh started the car, pulled out of the lot, and turned right on Strand Road. Gilbert glanced out the back window and saw a gray sedan follow them. It was nice to know that Mauk's civilian-suited soldiers were sticking close by.

Oh accelerated smoothly, went through second gear, and slapped it into third passing the intersection with Latha Street.

Just as a two-ton truck barreled out of the cross street.

And slammed broadside into the sports car Oh was so proud of.

FIFTEEN

Lower Hledan Street Jetty, Yangon

It was getting close to midnight, and Carson found himself taking frequent glances in the direction of the back door. No matter how hard he tried, he couldn't seem to make Branigan appear.

He had thought several times of calling her office, but he didn't want to appear too anxious, checking up on her. Hyun Oh wasn't much of a threat. He was about to give up on his self-image and call anyway, when he saw Washington waving at him from the side of the room. Excusing himself from his current conversational grouping—Marty Prather and two like-minded accountants for the blossoming National Ferry Service, he dodged several clusters of people to make his way to Washington.

"Jack's on the phone for you, Chris. In that office."

"Thanks."

He stepped inside, closing the door against the roar of multiple conversations, and picked up the phone.

"Jack?"

"Yeah, Chris. Look, we're at General Hospital. . . ."

"Goddamn it! What happened?"

"Pamela and I caught a ride with Hyun and Stephanie, and . . ."

"Steph? Where's Stephanie?"

"We got creamed by a truck. They've still got her in emergency. . . ."

Ah, shit! Not again!

Carson forced himself to keep his volume down and his voice level. "How is she?"

"I don't know, Chris. I . . ."

"How about you?"

"All right. Hyun and Pamela are okay. A few bruises."

"I'm on my way."

He slammed the phone down and pulled open the door. Washington was still standing outside.

"You okay, Chris?"

"There's been an auto accident of some kind, Charles. Stephanie's in the emergency room."

"Oh, Jesus! You—"

"I'll let you know."

The streets were fairly clear, and it only took him ten minutes to reach the hospital on Bogyoke Aung San. As he crossed Strand, he saw a melange of red and blue emergency lights down the street to his right. Some kind of freight truck was crossways in the street, and a car—Oh's Celica?—was on its side near the right sidewalk.

He didn't stop to gawk.

As with most of the architecture of the prominent buildings in Yangon, the British influence was evident in the hospital. He had never been in it before, and so he used the main entrance. Inside, the lobby and corridors seemed narrow and old, though the paint was fresh and the floors were waxed to a high sheen.

Gilbert was waiting for him. He had a large swelling on his left forehead that was going to be black and blue for some time.

"Damn, Jack. You sure you're okay?"

"Just a bump, daddy. I was on the left side in the backseat, and the truck hit us on the left front end. I slapped my head against the window."

"Where's . . . ?"

"Back this way." Gilbert headed him down a linoleum-floored hallway. "I called Scott Remington, and he got here a couple minutes ago. He's talking with the Burmese doctors."

"I'm glad you thought of that."

When they reached the trauma section, with a nurse who didn't look like she'd be able to speak English standing behind a window in one wall, he found Oh and Steele sitting in orange plastic chairs. The Korean had a large bandage on his left cheek, another over his nose, and his left arm in a sling. Except for a split and puffy lip, the British journalist appeared to be intact. She was busy writing in a steno book. Carson asked about their conditions.

Oh had a broken nose, a cracked cheekbone, and a large cut on his cheek. His left wrist was strained.

Steele touched her lip tenderly and said, "I managed to cushion myself against Jack. But his jaw is harder than my mouth."

"No one's heard anything about Stephanie?"

Gilbert looked at his watch. "She's only been in there twenty minutes, Chris. The ambulance guys were being gentle."

"Ambulance?"

"She was unconscious."

"Damn it."

Carson couldn't sit down, and he went to stand by a window and look out on a courtyard that held two ambulances. Gilbert came to stand beside him.

"This wasn't an accident, Chris."

He turned to look at his assistant.

"The driver of the truck disappeared, real quick. When we left in the ambulance, the cops were still looking all over hell for him."

"He was waiting for you, you think?"

"He was sitting on Latha Street, which is right on the route any of us would normally take back to the compound, waiting for someone. Why he picked Oh's car, I couldn't tell you."

"Unless he had a spotter watching the parking lot."

"That's possible, I guess."

Carson said, "I'm getting damned tired of sitting back, being a target, not knowing where the next shot is coming from, Jack."

"I'd buy that."

"And we're getting diddly shit out of Mauk. I think it's time to take a proactive stance."

"Guns, and all that?"

"I don't know that I'd go that far, but I might. No, the first thing you learn in the military is that accurate intelligence is paramount to any successful operation. Our problem is that Mauk keeps everything to himself."

"So we need an intelligence-gathering arm," Gilbert said.

"We need something like that. Hell, we've got a whole damned air force, even a navy, and we're in control of the latest electronic technology. It seems like we could do something to eavesdrop on the bad guys."

"I'll think about that, Chris."

"So will I, and we'll get together on it in the morning."

Carson heard footsteps on the linoleum, and he turned to see Scott Remington emerging from a pair of swinging doors.

They gathered around him in the middle of the waiting room.

"Not as bad as it could have been, I think," Remington said. "I don't think the truck got up enough speed to cause much damage."

"My car is a complete loss," Oh said.

"Sorry about that," Remington told him. "Stephanie has a broken right forearm. They've put it in a cast here, but when I get her back to the clinic, I'll give her a fiberglass model. She hit her head rather hard on the windshield. There's a couple cuts high on her forehead but nothing that required stitches. Her earlier concussion has been aggravated."

"She's conscious?" Carson asked.

"She was, yes. She has a headache and some pain. I approved the Burmese doctor's prescription for a painkiller and a sedative. Right now, they're moving her to a room, but she should be asleep by now. I'm going to stick around here and keep a watch on her."

Remington didn't say so, but Carson thought he didn't think too highly of the health care.

"I'll stay, too," he said, handing his keys to Gilbert. "The truck's parked out front, Jack."

"No need to stay, Chris," Remington said. "She's going to be out of it for a while."

"I'll wait."

Ahlone Road, Yangon

U Ba Thun had barely walked in the door of his home when the telephone rang. Chin Li answered it, then stepped into the foyer and said, "It is Colonel Mauk, Minister."

"Very well. I'll take it in the study."

He took his time, stopping to pour himself a small cognac, then settling into his chair and picking up the receiver.

"Yes."

Mauk told him about the accident on Strand Road.

"There were no fatalities?"

"Fortunately, Minister, no. I have just talked to the doctors."

"And the truck driver was not apprehended?"

"No."

Ba Thun told the security chief what he expected to hear. "Colonel Mauk, perhaps it is time to assign someone else to your post."

Unexpectedly, Mauk did not protest. "As you wish, Minister."

He did not respond for a moment, sipping his cognac while rapidly considering his options. Ba Thun did not like having his bluffs called. He knew that Mauk was the most qualified army man for the diverse position. He also knew he could not trust any of the air-force field-grade officers—Ba Thun had been army. The air-force intelligence chief, Col. Chit Nyunt, would leap for joy if handed the post. And quickly turn the entire operation into chaos, if Ba Thun relied on the man's previous experience. On the army side, he could probably not induce any intelligent officer to accept the position. They would all understand how easily they could fail in it and therefore terminate their careers.

"Let us consider the need for fresh blood," he said, "if this civil unrest cannot be quelled in the next thirty days."

"Thirty days, Minister?"

"Call it July fifteenth." Ba Thun almost forgot the festivities planned for the fifteenth. He could not afford a changeover in leadership a few days prior to that event. "Is that not satisfactory?"

"Of course," Mauk said.

Ba Thun hung up the telephone.

He sat and stared through the window at the shadows in the side yard. The street lights on Ahlone Road created strange shapes in the fruit trees. If he watched too long in one spot, it seemed as if he saw moving images, but he knew that it was his imagination.

Yes, he thought, he had made the correct decision. Almost everything would come to a head by the middle of July, and shortly after the celebration of the train, it would be the optimum time to remove Mauk. Like the interior minister, Ba Thun was somewhat fearful of Mauk accruing too much power, too many troops, to himself.

The man would have to go.

But not before his usefulness had ended.

Camp Roberts, California

The generator trucks were two forty-foot van bodies behind semitractors. Parked side by side with the eight diesel-powered generators idling through exhausts exiting the van roofs, they produced an ungodly bass rumble. When throttled up to full power, they would create a thunder that would echo off the low, pinion-covered hills and roll down the arroyos like the coming of, at least, another earthquake.

The Camp Roberts military reservation—generally used for field exercises and war games—was located off Highway 101 north of Paso Robles and was deserted but for several military policemen tending the main gate. That was four miles away. The landscape, with a few meandering dirt roads, reminded Dexter Abrams of some place he had camped with his parents once. He couldn't recall exactly where it was, but he remembered that he had hated every day of it.

It was dry, and the pine trees and scrub brush appeared undernourished even in the weak light of dawn. The two generator trucks were parked several hundred yards away, with two technicians tending them. Beyond them, pulled off the road into a weed-choked field, were a half-dozen cars and vans. The military observers had come in the vans.

Here, on the brow of a small hill, Mack Little had parked the two GTI trucks. From one, his technicians had extracted the skeletal frame of Ruby Star II. It was now mounted on a tripod base with a gimbal arrangement that allowed the laser to be aimed, and the techs were running cables along the ground from it to the second truck in which Little had installed his console. Two more men were running heavy cables down the slope to the generator trucks.

On the lowered tailgate of the truck was a large urn of coffee and five boxes of doughnuts. Abrams turned the spigot and ran another stream of coffee into his Styrofoam cup.

"Sorry about the quality of breakfast, General," he said. "We'd have catered it, but I don't have that many people cleared to watch the demonstration."

General Cartwright, an army four-star from the Pentagon's weapons-development section, shrugged it off. "No need to apologize, Mr. Abrams. This is more than we expected, I assure you."

Cartwright was the senior officer present. The air force and the navy were represented by flag-rank officers, also, and there were several colonels and a navy captain in attendance, too.

A dozen canvas director's chairs had been arranged in a row sixty feet behind the laser, and Abrams led Cartwright over to them. They sat down to wait.

"Keep in mind, General, that our computerized targeting system is rudimentary. We haven't taken the time to develop anything sophisticated as of yet."

"If it even hits the tank, I'll be satisfied."

A half-mile away, up on the slope of the next hill, a discarded M60 Main Battle Tank was parked. Its hardened steel armor was five inches thick.

"I guarantee we'll hit the tank."

"The question is, Mr. Abrams, what will you do to it?"

"Practically anything you want, General."

Most military laser applications were restricted to targeting, where a laser beam was used to pinpoint the target and align the weapons system for range and direction. Even small weapons, like rifles, utilized laser targeting, a small red dot identifying the target.

The problem with using a laser itself as the weapon was the immense amount of power required. Some experimental designs for the Space Defense Initiative project were cumbersome in size, and in order to generate enough power to do real damage, required the equivalent of a nuclear reactor for their energy sources. Along the same line, lasers used in the industrial sector, as for mining, were rare because of the huge initial cost and the cost of operation. For large projects, the power consumption was enormous.

"What are you generating with the trucks, Mr. Abrams?"

"We can get seventy thousand kilowatts out of them."

"That's all?"

"It'll be more than enough," Abrams said, hoping Mack Little was right. But Little had made a few independent tests.

Forty minutes later, Little stuck his head out of the back of the truck and called to Abrams, "We're set, Dex."

"How about a surgical strike first, General?"

"It's your show, Mr. Abrams. Let us remember, too, that this is an unofficial test. The Department of Defense is not as yet committing funds, nor promising to do so."

"That's understood," Abrams said, then told Little, "Slice it up a little, Mack."

Cartwright motioned to a couple of colonels, and they started tripod-mounted video cameras with telephoto lenses. The cameras would not only record the event, but as a by-product, the images they captured were relayed to two monitors parked on low tables in front of the chairs.

Both monitors bloomed with the image of the tank. In the magnified view, the tank, first produced in 1960, looked as decrepit as its true age. The paint was peeling, the insignia faded. It had been stripped of its armament, including the 105-millimeter cannon.

A tiny red dot appeared on the side of the hull.

"There's the targeting laser," Abrams said.

The dot moved forward and upward, found a starting point near the base of the turret, and steadied.

Abrams looked up at the Ruby Star II. It had tracked with the targeting laser, adjusting itself on top of its heavy tripod. Only the increased roar of the generators heralded the event.

Without warning, a thin ruby beam emitted from the nozzle end of the laser, instantly snapping across the half-mile of distance to the tank. The computers established the range, and when Abrams glanced down at the monitor, he saw that the beam passed inches above the turret.

"Dr. Little is showing off, I'm afraid," he told the general.

"Nice control, though."

As Abrams watched, the beam lowered, touched the turret, then moved to the right.

It left a thin, clean-edged slice behind it as it moved.

"I'll be damned!" Cartwright said.

Little cut a five-foot-long swath along the bottom edge of the turret, then shut down the laser. The generators went back to a rumbling idle. Cartwright sent a couple of his officers over to take a closer look. They came back to report that the full depth of the five-inch armor had been penetrated.

"We could go on and cut the entire top of the turret off, if you like, General Cartwright."

"I think you've made your point, sir. Now, part two?"

Abrams called out to Little, "Boost it to seventy percent, Mack! One pulse!"

"Coming up."

Again the targeting laser found the side of the tank, this time picking out the center of the hull. The generators started screaming.

It was so quick, it was almost unnoticeable. A flash of bright ruby red at the tip of the laser.

Silent.

Then the tank nearly vaporized.

"Jesus Christ!" the navy captain yelped.

Cartwright had been leaning forward to watch the monitor. Now he sagged back in the director's chair.

"That's a small unit, Mr. Abrams."

"Just under sixteen feet. It does weigh close to four hundred pounds."

"And you said seventy thousand kilowatts?"

"We didn't use it all."

"How many have you got?"

"Just the one, at present."

Get your butt in gear, Carson.

"What's the unit price look like?" the general asked.

"We've got a hell of a lot of R and D invested. All documented, of course."

"A rough estimate?"

"On the first hundred units, I think we'll have to get around six million each. Then, we can start tapering it off a tad."

"Is anyone else even close to you on this laser technology?"

"Not as far as I know, General."

Find those damned blueprints, Baskin.

258   *William H. Lovejoy*

"We'll be in touch with you," the general said as he stood up.

The military people collected their cameras and monitors and walked down the hill to their vans. Little came out of the truck, jetted some coffee into a cup, and came over to sit next to Abrams.

"They're impressed as hell, Mack."

"They should be."

"Didn't show it, of course."

"Any reaction to the price?"

"I saw a little tic in Cartwright's cheek. But I think he wants it bad enough."

"We've got to get those plans back, Dex."

"I know. Say someone got a lock on the material sources and had enough engineering to build the basic component, Mack. What do you think they could market it for?"

"With all of the development and research done? Jesus, Dex. They could sell the damned thing at two million a pop, and be clearing a million profit."

"Yeah, that's what I was afraid of."

Myitkyina

Hyun Oh missed his morning train out of Yangon. He had to call and delay his meeting, then recover the boxes from the wrecked Celica, then talk Don Evans into chartering one of his Gazelles for the flight. The problem with that, of course, was the cost. GTI didn't bill them for catching a space-available seat on flights already scheduled, but when one of the subcontractors wanted a helicopter for a special purpose, at the end of the month, the cost was charged to the contractor.

He arrived in the capital of Kachin State shortly after noon on Sunday and spent five hours giving his prepared presentation to the six potential investors. He used his prepared CD-

ROM, with its colorful pictures and statistical graphs, to provide the background and the solidity of Hypai Industries on an oversize monitor. Then, using a moderately postured approach, he explained the duties and fiscal requirements of investors in a local telephone company. Finally, he explained the profit structure and expected rewards. He gave them all abundant amounts of literature and sample profit-and-loss statements to study. He also gave them each a Hypai Industries Model 1021 multiline, speaker function, answering machine telephone set and a Model 12C cellular telephone. The cellular units would not be operable for a year, until the first of the cells was set up in Myitkyina.

Fortunately, he had brought extra sets with him, for Oh had expected to meet with five men. When the meeting was over, the unidentified man waited until the others had left the room, then motioned Oh to a seat near him.

"I enjoyed your presentation, Mr. Oh. The proposal seems to offer a solid investment, even if a slow return of investment."

"Thank you, sir. I think the investment will be recovered much more quickly than I presented. I tend to take a conservative approach."

The man nodded, his bald head shiny. His face was very pitted, and Oh tried to keep his eyes on the man's dark eyes.

"I'm afraid I do not know your name, sir."

"It is Khim Nol. I live in Shan State, but I do have business interests in Kachin."

Hyun Oh felt his palms begin to perspire. He was suddenly deathly afraid.

"You are not returning to the capital until morning?" Nol asked.

"No, sir, I am not."

"Wonderful. We will have dinner together."

Oh smiled his appreciation while wondering how he would be able to bolt his food down.

Just a few days ago, he had foolishly suggested this man's execution.

General Hospital, Yangon

Until noon, Branigan's awareness of what was real and what
was imagined was intertwined. She thought that Carson had
been in her room when it was dark, but she wasn't certain.
Scott Remington came by three times, and she remembered the
last visit. He spent a lot of time looking into her eyes and
checking the cumbersome cast on her right arm.

After a luncheon of which she managed to eat only a slice
of bread, she had called for a telephone. The nurse, who had
a limited command of English, didn't want to give her one.

Branigan yelled.

She got the phone.

And called Janice Cooper, but Cooper only told her that
everything was going smooth as silk. Besides, the office was
closed today. Rest. Recuperate. We're all pulling for you.

She called both Carson's apartment and office, but only got
the answering machines.

For most of the afternoon, she tried to get used to the damned
cast. It weighed a ton, and she couldn't find a comfortable way
to sit or lay. Only Remington's promise to change it for a lightweight fiberglass cast gave her any hope of surviving the near
future.

She tried to remember the accident, but could only recall the
headlights of the truck coming at them. She was pretty sure
Carson had been there when she woke up once in the dark. He
held her hand. Didn't he?

The television provided only one English-language channel,
and reruns of British sitcoms with their dry humor didn't hold
her interest. Several plants and bouquets were delivered to her
room. The cards were signed by the people at Hydrofoil, GTI,
IBM, Hygienic Systems, InstaStructures, and her own Ultra-
Train.

At six o'clock, an orderly brought her a tray for dinner. She
lifted the top off of one plate, couldn't identify the mush that
was on it, and set the tray aside.

For half an hour, her hunger continued to build, and she kept looking with second thoughts at the tray.

She had almost decided to at least give it a taste when her door pushed open.

"Hi, love."

"Oh, Chris! God, am I glad to see you!"

His arms were full of paper bags and packages.

And flowers.

Orchids. Purple and lavender. Two dozen of them in a huge bouquet.

"Chris, they're beautiful!"

Dropping the sacks on the chair, he held the bouquet for her to smell, then found a space for them on a side table.

"This place looks like a florist's shop," he said.

"Keeps the room from looking so dreary, which it is," she told him. "Come here."

He bent over to kiss her, and she got her left arm around his neck and held him in place.

His proximity made her feel much better. His mouth was sweet. She tried to tug him into the bed.

Pulling away, he grinned and said, "I don't think you're ready for that."

"Who are you to tell me what I'm ready for? All I've got to do is figure out how to maneuver the damned cast."

"Scott says you're in good shape."

"What does he know?"

"How's the head?"

"A little bit of an ache. Nurse Cratchett gives me aspirin regularly."

Carson went back to the chair and got one of the sacks. "Feel like a taco?"

"A taco? That's heaven!"

"Care package from the cafeteria. Eat what you want."

Moving the castered hospital table over to her, Carson removed the hospital tray and spread out a feast of tacos, burritos, enchiladas, refried beans, and Coca-Cola. He sat on the edge of the bed and ate with her.

"How'd you know what a mangled girl needs?" she asked around a mouthful of beans.

"I've been there."

"What have you been doing all day? I tried to call you."

"I've been hard at work, woman. Evans and Gilbert and I had to place an order for materials from the States. It took longer than I thought it would, and I had to argue with some Palo Alto people who didn't like getting out of bed in the middle of the night to take orders. I suspect I'm building a reputation as a dictator."

Branigan thought there was something different about him, a subtle change. For as long as she'd known him, Carson had demonstrated a confident leadership, but one that was low-key. People did what he wanted them to do because he asked them, made suggestions, inquired about opinions. Now, there was a new glint in his eyes and more rigidity in his back. Maybe she'd noticed it before when he was flying. Some kind of intense concentration. He never said so, but she was certain he loved flying, and when he was in the cockpit, different aspects of his personality rose to the surface.

"What are you up to?" she asked.

"There's plenty of time. I'll tell you later."

After they had eaten, Carson unpacked his other sacks.

"I broke into your apartment," he said.

"Ah, clothes!"

He hung a pant suit in the tiny closet and laid out her toiletries and makeup on the lavatory. She sat up in the bed, and he helped her into a print robe she had bought, hated, and hung in the back of her closet. She didn't know how he'd found it.

Then he stacked a few magazines and her unfinished Tony Hillerman novel on the bedstand.

"And finally, the latest newspapers."

"Anything earthshaking?"

"You made the front page of the *Times*."

Myanmar army barracks, Yangon

Hyun Oh's green Toyota Celica made the international editions of the *Washington Post* and the *London Times,* the front page of the latter. Lon Mauk thought the composition of the photograph was well done; it captured the truck, the car on its side, and one of the police vehicles that had responded. Someone unidentified, but probably Stephanie Branigan, was on a gurney, being attended by paramedics.

The byline belonged to Pamela Steele, naturally. He thought that she must have great presence of mind to crawl out of the damaged automobile, shoot the picture, then compose the story.

Though Ba Thun had told him to keep a close watch on her, Mauk had not really tried. He saw no way in which he was going to preapprove the stories she wrote, and anyway, the new telephone system made interception of her articles difficult. The YWCA where she was staying had been one of the first to convert to the new system, and it had fax machines available for its guests.

The minister was not going to appreciate this headline, either: TERRORIST ATTACK IN YANGON. She had made that supposition based on the disappearance of the driver and an interview with one of the policemen. The policeman did not know enough to keep his mouth shut, or perhaps he had become enamored of a beautiful Western woman, especially one who climbs out of a wrecked automobile and begins shooting photographs.

He glanced at the clock—after eleven—and wondered if Ba Thun would call him tonight. Mauk thought that he had better prepare his strategy for dealing with the demands Ba Thun was likely to have.

He would want the correspondent evicted from the country. That would not serve Mauk's purpose. After some in-depth thought, Mauk had determined that additional pressure on Ba Thun and the SLORC from international sources was beneficial. It might well drive them to provide him with added manpower. Though he was sensitive to concerns about his amassing too much military control, if he was to protect the expanding networks of communications, rail, and watercraft, he needed the personnel with which to accomplish it.

He picked up his phone and dialed Carson's apartment.

"Carson."

"This is Colonel Mauk. I apologize if I awakened you, Mr. Carson."

"No. I just got in. How can I help you, Colonel?"

"First, I am happy that your Miss Branigan is going to be all right. I called her earlier."

"Yes, I am, too. Did you find that truck driver?"

"No."

"Did you find his lookout? The one who notified him from the parking lot?"

"You are very quick, Mr. Carson. As a matter of fact, I have a suspect in custody."

Carson did not ask him who the suspect was, and Mauk was not certain he would have told him, anyway. It could be embarrassing to admit that one of the bodyguards assigned to Branigan had very likely made the radio call to the truck driver. He would know more after the interrogation was complete.

"I wonder, Mr. Carson, if you might help me with a . . . delicate matter?"

Mauk did not like asking the favor. If Carson followed through, he would be in the man's debt, a situation that was always better in the reverse.

"Let's hear it."

"You have seen the articles by Miss Steele?"

"I have."

"I am afraid that there are . . . some in government who might press for her deportation."

"And you don't favor that?" Carson asked.

"Mr. Carson, I am aware that there are many in the international community who consider my country backward in some respects, particularly in regard to human and civil rights. I personally believe that shedding some light on those flaws will eventually eliminate them. I am not, you will understand, in a position to make that statement in public."

"I appreciate your position, Colonel. Also your enlightened stance."

"Yes, well, I cannot approach Miss Steele. But I believe you know her?"

"Barely."

"Would you pass a message to her?"

"What's the message?"

"I would not tell her what or how she should write her stories. If, however, she chose to, let us say, balance her articles, I might be able to stop any deportation proceedings. I would need to have her assurance, through you."

"Balance. You're asking her to write a positive article for every negative one?"

"Precisely."

"I'll see what I can do, Colonel."

SIXTEEN

GTI compound, Yangon

Carson didn't run into Pamela Steele until Tuesday morning, when he saw her leaving the cafeteria with Gilbert. He intercepted the two of them in the middle of the compound.

"How's the lip?" he asked.

"Tender," she said, touching it with the tip of her finger, "but I guess I'll survive."

"When are you leaving?"

"Leaving? I'm not planning to . . . oh, you've heard something?"

"I've heard that some people are not happy."

She sighed. "Well, it doesn't surprise me. Bloody bastards!"

Gilbert looked, if not stricken, then close to it. "They're going to kick her out again?"

On impulse, Carson decided not to mention Mauk's name. The colonel would probably prefer it that way, and if she wasn't ejected from the country, Carson would prefer having her in his debt, rather than Mauk's.

"I've a suggestion for you, Pamela," he said. "Why don't you write something laudatory about the country?"

"What? You're as bad as Ba Thun, Chris. You can't dictate what the news is. If these bastards think——"

He held up a hand to stop her. "Are you telling me your readers, or even your editors, wouldn't be interested in the Shwedagon Pagoda? You haven't written one thing about what

the UltraTrain or the hydrofoils or the television system will
do for the country. Sure, I've got a self-serving interest here;
we could all use that publicity. But if you look around, it's a
beautiful country."

"What are you really telling me?" she asked.

"Not what to write, Pamela. But . . . If you'd promise me
that you'd even out your coverage, I might be able to head off
an attempt to boot you out."

She was instantly suspicious. "How do I know Ba Thun is
even thinking about deportation? Maybe you just want some
free PR?"

"You don't know. However, I'll bet you a hundred bucks
you're on a plane by tomorrow."

"Ah, hell, Chris," Gilbert said.

"Besides, you've got all those street scenes and landscape
shots that Jack took for you."

"You think you could intervene with Ba Thun?"

"All I can do is try. I can't guarantee a thing, but I'll have
to have your promise before I even attempt it."

Reluctantly, she said, "Very well."

"Come on, Pamela. The words."

"I promise."

"Good. We don't want to lose you. Jack, we got a shipment
in from the United States last night. We've got to go to work."

Steele went off to do whatever she was going to do, and
Gilbert went to get a truck. Carson stopped in his outer office
and placed a call to Mauk.

Becky Johnson was watching him, so he kept it cryptic.

"I've got a word of honor."

"Is it good, do you think, Mr. Carson?"

"I believe so."

"All right. I've stalled the minister for today. Now, I'll see
if I can extend her visa."

Carson told Johnson he'd be at the airport, then went out
and crawled into the truck with Gilbert. In the heavy morning

traffic, it took them nearly an hour to reach the GTI hangar. It was raining steadily by the time they did.

Dashing across the lot through the downpour, the two of them were half-soaked before they reached the shelter of the office. Carson stamped his feet on the mat in front of the counter, then walked around it.

Don Evans, Sam Enders, Kiki Olson, and half-a-dozen others were already there. Evans's office off the main room had been cleared of furniture, and several folding tables were placed against the walls. Olson and a couple of her technicians were setting up computers, network servers, and tape decks on the tables and the floor. An electrician was installing additional pulse-protected outlets. A heavy-duty air conditioner sat on the floor, ready to be installed in the window. The equipment they would be using required a more stable temperature and humidity environment than nature provided.

Evans pointed to his black plastic nameplate on the door. "I've got to change that to G-T-I-I-C, Chris."

"I don't think we want to advertise our intelligence center, Don."

"I don't know why not. It's going to be a classy operation."

Carson turned to Enders, whose white hair was uncombed and pointing in ten different directions. "Sam, how's your end coming?"

The head of the microwave division said, "We installed the microwave antenna on the roof yesterday, and we'll be hooked into Kiki's operation by afternoon. Hey, Carlos!"

A short, olive-skinned Hispanic detached himself from the group in the smaller office and came over.

"Carlos, this is Mr. Carson. Carlos Montoya, Chris."

Carson shook hands with the man.

"Carlos is one of my sharpest electronics and software engineers," Enders said in his deep voice. "I've put him in charge of this place, which we've been calling the information center. Maybe we'll change that to data-processing center, just to put anyone off the scent."

"I like that," Carson said. "That's what you can do with your sign, Don."

"Anyway, Carlos will have a team of nine people on three shifts. Tell him what we've got, Carlos."

In a soft voice, Montoya said, "We've locked up, that is, secured six microwave channels for our own use. The automatic switching has been reprogrammed to keep others off those channels. The action is transparent; no one will know that we have done this. From this room, working through the Kemendine facility, I will be able to tap into any telephone circuit in the country."

"Even those that haven't been converted?" Gilbert asked.

"Yes, though that is slower since I must go through the temporary Hypai conversion systems."

"How about phone numbers? Do we know what we're going after?"

Montoya grinned. "At the Kemendine center, I entered the Myanmar telephone system and downloaded the indexes for the people and offices you are interested in, Mr. Carson. From the list Sam gave me. The government numbers were not a problem. In the northern areas, there are a great many unlisted numbers, and we will set up a filter system to screen them until we know what or who they are. That will require some time."

"If you run into any scrambled circuits, that'll be a tip-off," Carson said.

"Yes. And among the equipment shipped in from Palo Alto are telephonic and radio-wave encoding and decoding devices, like those we produce under Defense Department contracts. With some trial and error, I believe I will be able to convert scrambled conversations into the clear."

"That's great, Carlos!" Carson told him.

"Also, once we have identified particular lines, we will put them on automatic recording. Any time the line is used, the conversation will be recorded."

After he and Gilbert had talked about it, Carson had decided not to go halfway. They were going to tap government lines, too: Ba Thun, Mauk, the chief military commanders, their offices. Carson wanted to know what the colonel was not telling him.

"Okay, then, Carlos. At your discretion, if you find an interesting call to a number we're not monitoring, add the new number to your system."

"Of course."

"Let's go out back," Enders said.

Carson and Gilbert followed him back into the hangar. A Skycrane was being serviced just outside the partially opened doors. Various-size cardboard boxes were stacked in one corner, and Enders stopped in front of them.

"I don't know how you talked the Palo Alto boys out of these, Chris."

"Let's just say they're not very happy, Sam. How did it go with the customs inspection?"

"One very sleepy guy showed up to check the plane. He saw electronics, like he always sees with our shipments, but this guy couldn't tell the difference between a tape recorder and a bicycle."

"Good."

"What we've got is six encrypted receivers and their antennas. We'll place those around the country at microwave installations and channel them through to us here. We've got three dozen GTI Listening Posts."

The Listening Posts were designed for use by the intelligence services. Disguised as anything from shrubs to old tires, they were frequently dropped by aircraft into areas where it was handy to have an extra set of ears. Extremely sensitive, they could pick up sounds for several hundred yards around the positions and transmit them digitally to the receivers, which would forward them to the control room. Special software programs helped interpret the sounds, from footsteps to trucks shifting gears. If they were discovered, the target knew only that he was under surveillance; he didn't know where the signals were being sent, or to whom. In Myanmar, Carson thought that any bandit would automatically assume the government was behind it.

"Okay," Carson said. "We want to place a few of those along the Mandalay-Yangon rail line at any place that looks vulnerable to attack. Also near the primary microwave stations. Those are defensive, and they may give us an early warning of attack.

"We want to be a little offensive, too. According to Mauk, Daw Tan has a compound somewhere near Man Na-su. Nol works out of a compound a few klicks south of Keng Tung, Nito Kaing is near Me-kin, and Shwe's got a place close to Wan Ta-pao. I'm going to have Evans send the King Air out for some recon photos in those areas. If we can pinpoint the sites, we'll drop a few Listening Posts on them during the night.

"The rest of them we'll keep in reserve. Anyone else have any other suggestions?"

"No suggestions," Enders said, "but I hope we're going to get something out of this. It's a hell of a lot of work just to listen in on someone's bedroom conversations."

"It's better than being completely in the dark, Sam," Gilbert told him.

"We also want to make damned sure Mauk doesn't get wind of what we're doing," Carson said. "Our contract could turn out to be five years shorter than we planned."

He knew the risks, but Carson was relieved to be taking some kind of action. Sitting around, waiting for lightning to strike unannounced, was frustrating.

"Did we get the rest of it?" he asked.

"Yeah. Over here."

Sam Enders went to a storage room at the side of the hangar and unlocked the door. The three of them stepped inside, and Enders closed the door and turned on the light.

Metal shelving in five short rows supported a wide array of aircraft replacement parts. One row against the wall contained plastic containers of various lubricants. The opposite wall had boxes stacked seven feet high.

Enders pulled a few cardboard boxes off the top, then opened an elongated box.

"These scare me, Chris. If Mauk finds them, we're history."

He pulled an M-16 assault rifle from the box. It was wrapped in clear plastic and coated in Cosmoline.

"We have thirty of the M-16s and six Browning nine-millimeter automatics. Two thousand rounds of ammo. One hundred fragmentation grenades."

"We've never had a chopper inspected by Myanmar officials, have we?" Carson asked.

"I asked Don, and the answer is no. But if a helo goes down, like yours did, and they find one of these, there'll be hell to pay."

"I'm not going to send our crews out anymore, without some firepower, Sam. We'll put one rifle on each chopper. Keep the grenades here."

Enders went back to the front office, and Carson dug out a cleaning kit, then showed Gilbert how to disassemble and clean two of the automatic pistols. He loaded four magazines and rammed two of them home in the pistols. They strapped ankle holsters under their pants legs and slipped the automatics into place.

"I don't see me ever using this," Gilbert said.

"You never know, Jack."

Koe Htat Gyi Pagoda, Yangon

The Shan obviously did not like being seen with Mauk in broad daylight. The crowds swirled around them, and Mauk leaned against a tree, looking to the west, away from the pagoda behind him. Several hundred meters away, one of the UltraTrain shuttles whispered along its track, going toward Kemendine Station. Mauk assumed it was testing the track.

The Shan stood next to him, but facing the other way, examining the gold leaf of the pagoda walls.

"So. Tell me where you have been."

"I went to Meiktila. I went to Myitkyina in the north."

"And what did you learn?"

"I heard from one of Daw Tan's lieutenants, a man with loose lips and a desire to impress, that Daw Tan is in Mandalay."

"We knew that," Mauk said. "Tell me something new."

"He is not in Mandalay."

"That contradicts what I know to be true."

"He often uses the Shanghai Hotel to disguise his true movements. The room service delivers meals to his suite, but the dishes remain uneaten."

Mauk wondered if his observer in the hotel was watching an empty room. It was possible. The man only reported indirect activities—the room service, telephone calls. All of that could be faked, with payments in the right places.

"If he is not in Mandalay, where is he?"

"That, I do not know."

"What else?"

"In Myitkyina, I saw with my own eyes Khim Nol."

The Kachin capital was not normal territory for Nol.

"What was he doing?"

"He ate a dinner with a *farang*."

"Who was the foreigner?"

"I do not know."

"A caucasian?"

"No. Korean, I think."

Mauk found this information very interesting. It was worth an additional one thousand *kyat*, and he passed the currency to the Shan, then watched him disappear into the crowd.

He checked his watch. He still had time before his appointment with Carson, so he wandered back to his Land Rover, with little show of haste. It was parked near an open-air cafe, so he stopped for a leisurely lunch.

In his truck, headed down Lower Kemendine Road, he radioed the barracks, but there were no messages for him. He issued an order for Tawn Yin May to have Daw Tan's suite at the Shanghai Hotel searched.

At a few minutes before one o'clock—Mauk detested people who were habitually late for appointments—he parked in the middle of the General Technologies compound and entered Carson's office. The secretary ushered him into the private office immediately.

Carson got up from behind his desk and came around it to shake hands. He seemed to be favoring one leg.

They sat in the two chairs before the desk, and Mauk declined Carson's offer of coffee.

He was conscious of the slight bend in Carson's nose as he held the blue eyes with his own. That small flaw of the broken nose made him seem more human and less of the educated and all-knowing American.

"Mr. Carson, let us, as the poker players say, place our cards on the table."

"I'm certainly in favor of that, Colonel."

"What do you wish to know?"

Carson grinned. "We're not going to volunteer, are we? Okay. Why do you want Pamela Steele free to do what she does so well?"

Mauk offered a small smile. "Minister Ba Thun agreed to a ten-day probationary period, to see how she performs. I have tried to convince him that, in the real world, governments are subject to criticism as well as praise, and more often the former. But you wish to know my rationale. It is simple. I anticipate that added pressure on the committee from international sources might result in additional manpower for my security operations. As your program progresses, my forces become strained by the need to secure more area.

"Also, there is an unwritten, but fully understood, policy of, what would you call it?, being a good neighbor with the chieftains of the north. I would hope that, if I find evidence that

Daw Tan, for example, was behind our troubles, the committee might allow me to increase the level of retaliation."

Carson seemed to understand the last part of his explanation, and went right to his next question. "Do you have any idea who's behind the attacks?"

"My first reaction is to say that it is Daw Tan. I cannot prove that, and while I thought I knew where he was located, I now find that my knowledge may be in error. I am now attempting to prove or disprove his currently reported residence."

"More important," Carson said, "why?"

"Yes. As you know, I am pursuing many theories. The primary one was that the chieftains resented the intrusion of foreigners and progress in their strongholds. I now think that, while that may be a consideration, there are other motives at work."

"Such as?"

"I have learned that Hyun Oh may have met with Khim Nol. That is a strange pairing, is it not, Mr. Carson?"

Mauk waited while Carson thought that over.

"It may well be," the American said, "that Nol wants to invest in one of the local phone companies Oh is trying to set up. I'm sure Nol has bunches of money to invest."

"That is true. I will keep it in mind."

Mauk wondered if he were becoming paranoid about the South Korean. He was an ambitious man, and his meetings with Ba Thun and Nol might simply be attempts to further Hypai's business interests. Certainly, if Mauk were a businessman, he would expect to go where the money was, and Tan and Nol controlled large amounts of money.

"Is there anything," Carson asked, "that I should know about? As the director of the modernization program?"

"There are two items. One, the night before last, there was an attempt to enter the microwave station at Sandoway."

"That one's not even finished."

"Yes, but there were two men who breached the fence, but who were run off by fire from the guards. They were not captured. Then, on June sixth, another man attempted to place an explosive at the new sewage plant in Prome. He was killed by the guard."

"So the frequency of the attacks is increasing?"

"Yes, though we are not advertising them. I would prefer that Miss Steele not know of these."

"All right," Carson said. "I'm not feeding her anything. She's a bit perturbed with me, anyway, for attempting to form her stories for her."

"And not me?"

"I left your name out of it, Colonel."

Mauk smiled. "Thank you. What it comes to, Mr. Carson, is this: I think Daw Tan is involved in the attempts to sabotage your operations. Daw Tan, however, could be receiving his orders from elsewhere."

"Khim Nol?"

"That would be my thought, though Khim Nol has been very good about observing our unwritten treaty. There may be others, and I will continue to look for them."

"You have something of a balancing act to perform, don't you, Colonel? Keeping me, the committee, and the bandits happy?"

Mauk shrugged, then said, "I assume you are taking precautions. Could you outline them for me?"

Carson told him about the memos Gilbert had sent out. GTI and subcontractor employees were being especially alert on the roads, inspecting automobiles and trucks before driving them, not wandering off alone.

"Miss Branigan has offered the dependents of her employees transportation back to their homes, and some of them are accepting that arrangement. I intend to do the same for GTI families, and I look for some of the other subcontractors to make the same offer."

"It is the safest course," Mauk agreed, "though I would not like for it to be publicized."

"We will try to avoid that, Colonel."

"Are you taking any other precautions?"

"Nothing overt."

Mauk pointed his forefinger at Carson's leg. "What of the pistol?"

Carson grinned ruefully. "Damn, Colonel. You've got eyes like a hawk."

"The committee frowns on armed civilians."

"And I'm tired of getting shot at."

"Who else has a weapon?"

"Jack Gilbert."

"I will issue permits for the two of you, but let us not have this become widespread, Mr. Carson."

Carson ran his tongue across his upper lip. "I won't tell you about the others, then."

Mauk shook his head as if in defeat. "Tell me, please."

"I've put M-16 assault rifles in the cockpits of the helicopters. I think my people should be allowed to return fire if they're attacked."

"Are there more?"

"That's it."

"I will also issue permits for those, but they must remain in the helicopters."

"Done."

"There is one thing more I would ask, Mr. Carson, though I would understand if you do not wish to respond."

"Let's try it."

"I have noted an increasing . . . tension with Minister Ba Thun in regard to, I am not certain, the contract, General Technologies, or perhaps yourself. Do you have the same perception?"

Carson took his time. Mauk looked down at his hands, found his thumbs battling each other, and pulled his hands apart and placed them on the arms of the chair.

"There is a bit of a tug-of-war going on," Carson said, then explained the schedule and cost problems with the Moulmein loss. "The minister appears unreceptive to a negotiated settlement."

"I confess that I do not understand that. I am not a financial person. But it does explain the unease I have felt with the minister. He can be stubborn, I think. And you? Are you as adamant?"

"Well," Carson said, "it could mean some major losses for my company. They don't like that, nor do I."

"But is there anything you can do about it?"

Again, Carson hesitated before saying, "Between you and me, Colonel?"

"Absolutely."

"I stopped hiring local workers and shut down the training schools."

Mauk could not help grinning. "Ah! That explains even more. Minister Ba Thun will be under pressure from the premier and the interior minister as the unemployment figures rise. I am glad that I do not play such high-stakes poker, Mr. Carson."

"I wish I didn't have to."

When Mauk left the compound, he felt even more confident about Carson. The man could have tried to hide his possession of the weapons, after all. He did not have to explain his strategies for negotiation with Ba Thun.

Mauk would not let himself be misled by the apparent candor, however. Carson was an intelligent man, and one who was becoming frustrated. He was probably planning activities that he left undetailed and that Mauk should know about, and therefore Mauk would intensify his surveillance of the prominent personnel residing in the compound.

General Hospital, Yangon

Branigan was antsy by four o'clock. She had never been comfortable with leisure hours, and a forced hospital stay wasn't going to change that. For most of the day, she had been on the telephone, tracking Statler's and Wilson's progress and dictating letters to Janice Cooper. Steve Pruett, her boss in L.A., had called to console her and to offer her a transfer back to California.

She had called him a few bad names.

Her arm itched.

She did finish the Hillerman book.

The nurse came by, finally, with her paperwork and Scott Remington's release order. She got up, surprised at how dizzy she felt, and got her clothes from the small closet. She was half-dressed, trying to get her pant suit top over the cast, when Carson rapped on the door.

"Steph?"

"Come on in, Chris. I need help."

He pushed the door open and came in, grinned when he saw her.

"Don't laugh at me."

Pursing his lips, he moved over behind her.

"I can't hook the bra."

He did it for her.

"And the cast is too large for the sleeve."

He found a small penknife in his pocket, turned the sleeve inside out, and cut a few threads. With both hands, he pulled the bottom seam of the sleeve apart, then helped her into the top.

"That *was* a good jacket."

"I'll buy you a new one," he said.

There was a skimpy sling arrangement, and he helped her get it around her neck and under the cast. After packing her personal items in the paper sacks, he placed her left hand on his forearm and led her into the hall.

"I don't even get a wheelchair ride?"

"You want one?"

"No."

"Then, be happy they don't force you into it."

After checking her out of the hospital, Carson helped her into his truck for the short ride to the Zoo. A dozen people stopped to say hello as he got her up the stairs to her apartment and into the big chair in front of the TV. By the time all of that was accomplished, which didn't seem like a lot, she had a splitting headache.

Carson poured a glass of water for her, from the bottle in the refrigerator, and found a couple aspirin in one of the cabinets.

She gulped them down.

"I feel like an invalid."

"I don't mind."

"I do."

"At eight in the morning, Scott's going to change your cast. You'll feel better after that."

She pulled back her sleeve and eyed the heavy chunk of plaster encasing her arm from the palm of her hand to above her elbow. "Making love is not going to be the easiest thing I ever did."

Carson sat down on the couch next to her chair. "We can wait."

"Not on your life!"

"Then, we'll make do." He grinned. "I'm just glad it was only your arm."

She had a sudden mental image of herself in a full body cast.

"This is getting seriously dangerous, isn't it, Chris?"

"Keep a secret?"

She wrinkled her nose at him, and he told her about his talk with Mauk and what he and Gilbert had set up at the airport.

"Are guns a good idea?" she asked.

"Probably not, but Mauk approved them. We've got a few extra if you want some of your work crews to have them."

"I don't think so. I've been thinking about it, and except for two instances, where you were involved, the attacks have not been frontal. They sneak around at night with explosives. These guys are pretty cowardly, Chris."

"I thought about that, too," he said.

"They're really after you."

"Maybe."

"God, Chris! You've got to be more careful."

"I'm keeping my eyes open. Mauk has a man watching my back."

"Tell me again about these . . . Listening Posts."

He explained how they were going to be spaced along the main line of the Mandalay-Yangon corridor so they could hear if anyone approached the track.

"With those," he said, "and the electrified access doors you've installed, the main line should be relatively safe."

"Thanks for thinking about us."

"Hey, you're my main contractor. You lose, and I lose."

"Are you this solicitous about all of your contractors?"

"Just the main one."

"What else are you going to do for me?"

"I thought about ordering up something to eat."

"Did you think about helping me shower?"

"As a matter of fact, I did."

"Let's start with that," she told him.

Chinatown, Yangon

Daw Tan could not believe the abominable luck that served him. He sat in the gloom of his tiny room, resting his eye, and considered the manner in which the fates conspired against him. Carson had survived the attack on Lower Kemendine Road. The idiot he had paid to alert him when Carson or Branigan left the party at the Hydrofoil docks had only told him, "The green car." Tan had not known until it was reported in the newspaper that the car belonged to Oh.

He had nearly killed the man he needed to accomplish his

goals. And simultaneously, he had failed to rid himself of the woman. Reluctantly, Tan attributed the misjudgment to his singular eye. Since losing the right eye so many years before, his depth perception had disappeared and he had never been able to overcome it. He had gravely miscalculated the speed of the stolen truck and the impact point with the car.

Or perhaps his age had deteriorated his skills. Was he overestimating his ability?

But no. He had always overcome his adversaries by adapting to the requirements. Despite Khim Nol's wishes, Daw Tan decided he would have to enlist the aid of his subordinates. He would put aside his pride and set out to accomplish the task, no matter what it took to do so.

That was, after all, the reason he had constructed his organization in the first place. He would . . .

The telephone rang.

It startled him, for the telephone in this room had never had an incoming call before.

There were only three who knew the number, so he was not surprised when he picked it up and the voice on the other end told him, "Thamaing."

The man was one of his trusted lieutenants, currently managing the operation in Mandalay.

"Yes?"

"Chieftain, I report that soldiers have entered your room in the hotel."

So. That ruse was at an end.

"Very well," he said and hung up the telephone.

After a moment's thought, he picked it up again and dialed the number in Man Na-su.

His wife answered, and after reassuring her of his good health, told her to transfer his call to the house of Kanbe.

"Yes, Chieftain?"

"Get four good men and bring them to the apartment in Yangon."

"At once, Chieftain."

Daw Tan replaced the receiver and went back to sit in his chair. Now, he would dedicate himself entirely toward the end of the foreigners' reign in Myanmar. There would be no mercy shown, and he could now, despite his singular eye, see the result very clearly.

It was days away, just over a month.

He looked at his watch. The next event was but hours away, and he looked to the satchel resting on the floor near the door.

It appeared to be innocent enough.

The Strand Hotel, Yangon

Hyun Oh ate a solitary, late dinner at his favorite restaurant, but the quality of the meal did not cheer him.

His mind was laden with thoughts of his proximity to his afterlife. The enforced meal with Khim Nol had not buoyed his spirits, though the time had been spent with small talk and discussions of the local telephone companies. Nol seemed genuinely interested in an investment. If rumor were fact, the man was worth billions, and if a way could be found to circumvent the policy of no cross-ownership between the fourteen local telephone companies, Nol might be induced to invest, say, forty percent in each of the companies. That would preclude the need for Hypai to set up either a venture capital company or an insurance company. Surely, if Khim Nol were a major player, there would be no requirement for insurance against terrorist activities.

It was an exciting prospect, and surely one worth pursuing.

If only he hadn't suggested to Daw Tan that Khim Nol was a blockage to Tan's future.

He had many things to think about, but concentration was difficult.

The accident on Strand Road had shaken him severely, once he learned that it was not truly an accident. It made him think constantly of the stories he had heard of Daw Tan's treacherous ways. If Tan were truly the adversary, then Oh had negotiated with the Devil himself. If this was what he could expect for his future, then he sincerely regretted having ever met with the man.

His stomach ached.

He could not focus on his expensive Beef Wellington, and he finally gave up, paid the bill, and exited the hotel through the lobby.

On the street, he walked to the west, avoiding contact with the many people sharing the sidewalk. He continually looked over his shoulder, but saw no one with an inordinate interest in him. When he reached Shwedagon Pagoda Road, he turned the corner to the north, toward the compound. He glanced westward first, at the site of the accident a block away. It made his stomach churn all the more.

The walk, too, caused him to lament the loss of his car. It had been a beautiful car, and he was not certain how he would replace it. The problem was the insurance.

After climbing the stairs to his apartment and unlocking the door, the first thing to catch his eye was the blinking red light on the message machine. He dreaded listening to it, but did.

Mr. Pai wanted him to call immediately. The time of day or night was inconsequential.

With a shaking forefinger, he pressed the Speed Dial button.

"It is I, Mr. Pai."

"Why did you not report your automobile accident, Mr. Oh?"

"I was not seriously injured, sir. It seemed of little importance."

"I did not realize that you owned an automobile," Pai said. "Not until I saw the newspaper picture and read the account. And a sports car, yet?"

How best to soften the blow?

"It was, of course, a company car, Mr. Pai."

"Hypai Industries does not buy sports cars."

"The availability of automobiles here is limited," he defended.

"Kim Sung-Young tells me that you charged the contingency fund for the amount."

The damned accountants!

"He also tells me that the automobile was registered in your name."

"A formality only, Mr. Pai."

"It was insured, naturally?"

"Of course."

"And in whose name?"

"Ah, my own. Because of the registration."

"When you receive the check, Mr. Oh, it is to be deposited to the contingency fund. Should there be a difference, you will make it up."

"Certainly, Mr. Pai."

"And we will be buying no more sports cars. No more cars at all, in fact."

"Yes, sir."

"You will provide me with a full report of the incident."

"Yes, sir."

"And Mr. Sung-Young is providing me with a full disclosure of expenses charged to the contingency fund. You will assist him if it is necessary."

"Immediately, sir."

Pai hung up abruptly, leaving Oh in a state of anxiety. Kim Sung-Young was his assistant, but tomorrow the man would become an inquisitor.

By morning, Hyun Oh felt he would be nearly incapacitated by his stomach.

GTI compound, Yangon

After returning Pamela Steele to the YWCA, Jack Gilbert got back to the Zoo at eleven o'clock. He was in a good mood, and he wasn't tired, and he had six or seven memos to write, so he went directly to his office and unlocked the door.

He turned on the overhead lights, flipped the power switch for the computer, then slipped a Dire Straits tape in his cassette player. Flopping in the chair, he called up a memo form to the computer screen, then leaned back and studied the grouping of pictures on the wall above the computer credenza. They were candid shots taken along his life's road. The road had taken some sudden turns: Saudi Arabia, Spain, the Philippines, Arizona, California. He'd had some good times, but sometimes felt like one of the hockey pucks he played with as a student at Denver University. There was a snapshot of his senior hockey team at DU.

He didn't have a picture of Pamela Steele, and he thought he ought to correct that oversight. As he surveyed the snapshots, he thought that maybe he wasn't getting as much out of his nomad life as he once had. Maybe it was time to consider, well, settling down. Just a little. The problem, he saw right off, was that the one he wanted to settle down with had no intention of doing so. Steele loved her running around, seeing everything, knowing new mornings in new places.

It was a puzzle, and he was going to have to devote some time to solving it. For the present, he sat up in his chair and started typing:

```
TO:      All Personnel, GTI and
         Subcontractors
FROM:    Gilbert, Assistant Director
SUBJECT: Communications Security
         As of June 11, GTI and sub-
sidiary units assigned to the Myanmar
Modernization Project will begin to ob-
serve certain precautions relative to
interunit comm
```

The blast knocked him completely out of his chair and slammed him against the wall. The plaster ceiling came down in huge chunks.

The music kept playing.

THE DEAD SEASON

SEVENTEEN

GTI compound, Yangon

By the twenty-fifth of June, a Tuesday, hostilities around the country had increased to levels Carson didn't like in the least. Once, the unmarked Cessna, or one like it, had tried to force down a Sikorsky S-65 and had broken off the attack when the copilot blasted the slow-flying trainer with a full magazine from an M-16. The jet hadn't been damaged, but the pilot had probably undergone a shock. Carson felt justified in arming the choppers in his minimal fashion, and Colonel Mauk had even agreed with him.

Seven times, Mauk's men had repelled attacks against GTI and UltraTrain operations. Twice, company vehicles had been fired on while on the highway. The fatality count was rising: two unknowns dead, one wounded and captured. Three Myanmar soldiers killed and seven wounded, one InstaStructure truck driver seriously wounded and evacuated to the States.

The property damage was comparatively light. InstaStructure lost a semitractor and a flatbed trailer. GTI lost some office equipment and office space in the explosion of June 11. Carson lost his apartment in the same blast.

The sapper had placed his shaped charge against the outside wall of the compound, and when it went off, it took out most of the rabbit warren of cubicles in back of Carson's office, along with a bearing wall. His second-floor apartment, as well as the one occupied by Marty Prather, crumpled into the collapsed void of the first floor.

Fortunately, at the time, Prather had been playing pool in the cafeteria's recreation room, and Carson had been in Branigan's apartment. And also fortunate, the only one in the offices, Jack Gilbert, had been protected by a bearing wall when the upper floor caved in. He crawled out of the wreckage with a couple bruises and his ears ringing from the concussion. Carson had offered him a couple days of rest and recuperation in Bangkok, and Gilbert had grabbed Steele and left on the morning plane.

About half of the incidents had made the international press, courtesy of Pamela Steele. True to her word, however, she had written some positive items about the country: a pictorial layout on the Shwedagon Pagoda, a future-is-now article about the UltraTrain, and an upbeat three-piece series about the new communications systems reaching out to the nation's citizens. Gilbert told Carson that Steele had halfway surprised herself by becoming immersed in the research for those articles. Her efforts had kept Ba Thun at bay, though he was now, according to Mauk, incensed about a three-column, front-page exposé of police brutality in Moulmein. Two political dissidents had reportedly been tortured to death. As a result, the Moulmein police department was under investigation by the minister of the interior. Carson had complimented Steele on her work, and she seemed satisfied that some good was coming from it.

The hostile environment wasn't helped by the demonstrations taking place in the streets and on the university campus. The students were threatening a strike over the alleged atrocities in Moulmein, and they were supporting the thousands of people marching through the downtown streets complaining that the government had not produced promised jobs.

Carson felt some guilt on that score, and both Washington and Branigan were urging him to relent. He was about ready to give in and open up the training schools again, conceding that Ba Thun had outlasted him and that Plan B hadn't worked. Gilbert encouraged him to remain steadfast.

And he was glad that he had when Ba Thun called him at the airport just before he was about to take off.

He took the call leaning on the counter in the operations room. Kiki Olson and one of her techs were performing some software maintenance in the back office now identified as the Data Processing Center.

"Mr. Carson," Ba Thun said, "I wonder if we could meet today?"

"I'd be happy to, Minister Ba Thun. It'll have to be late, though, since I'm just leaving for Myitkyina."

"Over dinner, perhaps?"

"I'm afraid I won't be back by then. How about nine o'clock?"

"That will be fine. In my office."

"I'll see you then."

He grinned at Gilbert on the other side of the counter as he hung up.

"Breakthrough?"

"I sincerely hope so, Jack."

"Good. Don't get shot down before you get this settled, huh?"

"No one's going to shoot at us."

"That's what they say in the brochures," Gilbert said.

He and Gilbert walked through the hangar and out to the tarmac where the King Air was prepped and ready to go. Don Evans was waiting with one of his ground crewmen.

"Now, boss," Evans said, "I've got a basic ground rule."

"The hell you do?"

"Gary's the pilot," he said, dipping his head toward the curly-headed man standing in the doorway of the plane. "You can sit in the copilot's seat, but let's keep in mind that your fixed-wing certificate has lapsed, and I only have one fixed-wing airplane."

"Would I hurt your airplane, Don?"

"You didn't intend to hurt my Gazelle. Gary's flying."

"Promise," Carson yielded.

An airframe technician named Fritz Bolter, who had volunteered for the mission, climbed into the King Air, and Carson followed him. The door on this aircraft wasn't the folding airstair type. There was a short length of steps that swung up and in to lie flat on the floor, and the doorway was wide, with a pair of hinged doors, to accommodate cargo loads. Inside, all but one of the passenger seats had been removed.

Gary Foster went forward and settled into the left seat in the cockpit, and Carson took the right seat. They strapped in, pulled on headsets, and went through the engine-start checklist. The 750-shaft horsepower Pratt and Whitney engines fired easily.

Carson handled the radio and obtained the clearances identified in the flight plan filed earlier. During the rainy season, and because of the threat from hostile forces, most of their flights were now recorded prior to takeoff. And most flights went IFR (Instrument Flight Rules). By eight-thirty, they were a thousand feet off the ground, pulling gear and flaps.

Foster headed north, following the railroad, as if they were actually going directly to Myitkyina.

A hundred miles later, shortly after they passed over the town of Pyuntaxa, Carson notified Mingaladon Air Control that they were going to survey the rail line from less than a thousand feet above ground level and would be lost to the air controller's radars.

The notice was a familiar one to the air controller, and he readily acknowledged it.

Then forgot them, Carson hoped.

"Let's get down in the weeds, Gary."

"Going."

Foster took the plane down, and at 500 feet AGL, turned to the northeast.

They were soon into plateau country, their altitude increasing as they followed the rising terrain. At a cruise speed of 275 miles per hour, it took them fifty minutes to cover the next 210 miles to Me-Kin. Carson studied the reconnaissance photos while they were en route. They had been taken with a shaky camera from fifteen thousand feet, but they were good enough for his purposes.

Nito Kaing's home was a cluster of buildings about three miles south of the small village and a half-mile east of the paved Highway 45. The structures were difficult to pick out of the thick forest, but the airstrip was not. A straight line had been cleared through the woods, and on the photos, seven aircraft could be seen clearly, parked back in the semiprotection of overhanging branches. There were two beat-up Douglas DC-3s, three Cessna light twins, a Piper Aztec, and a Piper Cherokee sitting on Kaing's private airport at the time the photo was taken.

Carson could only assume that they all belonged to Kaing. It spoke for the amount of money she commanded.

He had decided against a nighttime delivery since, with the instrumentation available to them, the accuracy of their bombing would be questionable. Instead, he hoped to surprise them enough that no one on the ground realized what was really taking place.

Checking the photos against the chart, Carson said on the intercom, "Ten miles out, Gary."

"Roger. I'm coming off a couple points."

Foster banked the plane to the right, taking up a course that would pass south of the target.

"You ready back there, Bolter?" Carson asked.

"All I need is a minute's notice," Bolter said.

At their altitude, with the density of the forest, Carson couldn't pick out the clearing that was the airfield. Instead, he watched for the highway.

It came up quickly, and they passed over it south of the village of Mong Hang.

"Any time now, Gary."

Foster lost more altitude as he turned the King Air onto a heading of 0 degrees, due north.

Carson scanned the green forests ahead, telling Bolter on the intercom, "Go ahead and open up."

Bolter pushed one of the double doors open into the airstream, and the wind noise filled the cabin, muffled by their headsets.

Carson first saw a shack in the trees.

Then, the clearing.

"Your one o'clock, Gary. Come right."

Foster corrected his heading.

The dirt strip popped into view.

Several men working around the parked aircraft looked up in shock as the roar of the big Pratt and Whitneys hit them.

Foster took the King Air directly down the side of the clearing, between the airstrip and the buildings, which were mostly hidden in the trees. Carson only saw a few of them, there, then gone, at their speed.

Three quarters of the way down the strip, he called, "Now, Bolter!"

Looking back into the cabin, he saw Bolter kick a dried shrub out the door.

It was one of the best-looking tumbleweeds Carson had ever seen. Made of carbon-impregnated plastic, the tangled yellowish tendrils of the shrub were designed to soften the impact when it hit the ground. The thickened center of the shrub disguised the sensor and its radio transmitter. The antenna was one of the yellow branches.

Bolter pulled the door shut and secured the latch.

"Good show, Gary," Carson said. "Let's try the next one."

Foster rolled out onto an easterly heading and gained a little altitude.

Those on the ground behind them would have to figure they'd only been buzzed. Whether or not there was a message in the buzzing—that Carson was notifying Kaing that he knew how to find her—she would have to figure out on her own. He didn't think it likely that anyone at the compound would go hunting for a tumbleweed.

Their next target was Wan Ta-pao in the far eastern node of the country. Ten miles to the south was the Laotian border, and ten miles to the north was China. Then they would turn back to the northeast, make a pass on Khim Nol's compound near Keng Tung, then finally, drop a package on Daw Tan's home base at Man Na-su. By noon, they would put down in Myit-kyina and get back to the real work.

Carson waited ten minutes, then dialed the radio into the scrambled circuit and used the code words he had assigned.

"Chuckwagon, this is Posse."

"Go ahead, Posse."

The encryption circuit gave voices a metallic, hollow sound, but he thought that Kiki Olson had responded.

"Stage One is deployed."

"Roger that, Posse. We've got a clear signal."

"That's all we need. Out."

Bolter came up to lean into the cockpit. "This is kinda fun, actually."

Carson didn't think of it as fun, but he didn't put the kid down.

Bolter and Foster hadn't been in the Persian Gulf.

Pegu

Daw Tan drove a rented car the seventy kilometers to Pegu. He got there first and took a table in the cafe, ordering coffee. He was wearing his white suit, his hat, and his sunglasses, but the deference of the waiter indicated that he was known to the man.

He was accustomed to that servitude in his home territory, but it was nice to know that his fame was spreading. Very soon, he thought, his presence would be even more pervasive.

Nito Kaing arrived a half hour late, and Daw Tan would have been upset at the tardiness if he had not needed her support. He would not tell her, of course, that her support was necessary to his plan.

After the customary greetings, the two of them sat at a small table in the back corner of the cafe and talked of inconsequentials while their meals were served. Over coffee, Tan made his overture.

"Are you distressed at all by the path our country is following?" he asked.

With half-lowered eyelids, a mannerism she had taken up several years before in the assumption that it made her mysterious, or all-knowing, or something similar, she said, "You know that I am. Already, my product sources have become undependable as farmers seek to become city dwellers."

"They have been given hope."

"Perhaps."

"One could counter that migration by increasing the amount one pays to the producer."

"Causing an extreme deterioration in the profit margin," she countered. The white smile in her perfectly smooth complexion had always entranced him. At times such as this, he wondered why the courses of their lives had failed to completely entwine.

"That is exactly my thought," Tan said. "The delicate question, naturally, is who put us in this position?"

She did not hesitate to place the blame. "Khim Nol, with his agreement to cooperate with the government."

"And we are bound by it."

"Yes. Of course."

"Or are we?" Tan asked her. "Could we not suggest an amendment to the agreement? In one way or another?"

Her eyelids drooped even farther as she considered his question. Finally, they rose when she said, "It is possible."

Daw Tan thought that he had said enough. She would think about it for several days, or even several weeks, before informing him of her decision.

He was, however, relatively certain of what it would be. Behind those lowered lids, in the depths of her dark eyes, raged a fearless ambition. She might even be projecting beyond Daw Tan already.

He was prepared for that eventuality.

"Enough for now?" he asked.

"I will consider it."

"There is another matter," he said. From his pocket, he extracted the barber's razor and pushed it across the table to her.

She looked at the aged and carved ivory handle. Was that a tear in her eye? Was that possible?

"Thank you," she said.

GTI operations, Mingaladon Airport

Jack Gilbert spent the afternoon listening to some boring tapes selected by Carlos Montoya, who now had his Data Processing Center humming like a well-oiled sewing machine. Three technicians each on three shifts manned the center around the clock. Since the computers were programmed to monitor ever more phone numbers, the stack of tape recorders against one wall sprang into operation more frequently.

There were twenty recorders now, and Gilbert was half-amazed when the reels of one or another, without apparent command, suddenly began to turn. It was a silent operation, though the operators could tap into the conversations and listen over their headsets.

The center's monitoring operation hadn't picked up one conversation that was damning or incriminating in any way.

So far.

One computer was dedicated to monitoring the Listening Posts deployed along the railroad main line and scattered about by Carson. Whenever activity was noted, the machine sounded an alert and one of the operators determined the location of the Listening Post and called in a warning. To date, they had intercepted a few feral animals, some kids, and three curious people wanting a closer look at the pedestal track.

On the communications end, they had tracked down, identified, and were monitoring over four hundred telephone numbers. Some of them were used fifty times a day, some only a couple times a week.

One of the problems was that most of the conversations took place in Burmese, so Montoya had enlisted his Burmese-speaking techs for the review of those tapes. Of the recordings culled for further analysis, the original played first, followed by a translated version.

Gilbert and Montoya had been sitting at a table in front of the recorders for over three hours, listening to the wiretaps through headsets.

He thought that Montoya had taken to his new role of electronics spy with all too much excitement and dedication. Yet, he was glad that someone had. Gilbert would have hated being stuck with the job.

"This one, I've saved for last," Montoya said, "I think it may be the best, and it came from the lobby phone at the Shanghai Hotel. We didn't get everything traced and translated until yesterday."

"The Shanghai?"

"We hit their whole switchboard since this Daw Tan character is supposed to be staying there."

"Okay," Gilbert said, "roll it."

The Burmese part of the recording didn't mean much to him.

In the translation, the interpreter said, "The caller gives his name, 'Thamaing.' The other man says, 'Yes?' The caller says, 'Chieftain, I report that soldiers have entered your room in the hotel.' The man called Chieftain says 'very well,' and hangs up."

Montoya punched a button and stopped the machine.

"Okay," Gilbert said, "I get it. The first guy, Thamaing, calls the chieftain, who must be Daw Tan, to tell him the cops are onto his ruse."

"That's the way I read it, Jack."

"So what have we got?"

"The other phone number, what else?"

"And?"

"And an outgoing call from the new phone a few minutes later. It went right through to the number we're watching in Man Na-su."

Montoya tapped the Play key, and Gilbert waited through the Burmese.

The translator said, "There is dialogue with a woman about health and daily chores, then another man comes on the line, saying, 'Yes, Chieftain?' The caller says, 'Get four good men and bring them to the apartment in Yangon.' The unknown man says, 'At once, Chieftain.' The call ends."

Gilbert pulled his headset from his ears and looked at Montoya. "I don't suppose . . . ?"

"The address of the apartment? I've got it."

"Good man! Any other calls of note?"

"From this apartment? There was only one, directed to the number we think belongs to Nito Kaing. That occurred yesterday, but we didn't get it translated until this morning. They set up a meeting in Pegu, but it's over by now."

"Damn, Carlos. I'm going to put you in for a medal."

"I didn't know this outfit gave medals."

"We should."

Gilbert got up and went back into the operations room. There was only a receptionist at the desk, so he went back into the hangar and found Don Evans inspecting a Gazelle pulled inside for maintenance to the rotor head.

"Hey, Don. When's the boss due back?"

Evans looked at his watch. "Six o'clock now. Probably in the next hour, Jack."

He went back to the center and got the apartment's details from Montoya.

"It wasn't hard to track, Jack. There's only two phones in that whole building, and one belongs to the building's manager."

Stuffing the address in his shirt pocket, he went back to the operations room, found a copy of *Aviation Week,* and sat down to read and wait.

City Hall, Yangon

Carson was impatient. The information he'd gotten from Gilbert made it difficult to concentrate on what he had to accomplish with Ba Thun. He found himself anticipating the end of the meeting just as, a few years before, he had waited impatiently through preflight briefings for the chance to get his Blackhawk airborne and the adrenaline pumping.

He sat in the reception room for fifteen minutes so that the minister could impress him with the minister's industry and importance. It was an act he had come to understand, so he didn't worry about it.

The door finally opened and Ba Thun came out. "Please excuse the delay, Mr. Carson. Always, there is a crisis of one kind or another."

"I understand fully, Minister," Carson said, rising to shake his hand and follow him back into the inner office.

Ba Thun sat behind his desk—keeping that symbol of authority between them—and got right to the heart of the matter.

"Mr. Carson, when do you suppose you will resume the training and employment of Myanmar citizens?"

Carson didn't want to offer any hope, just yet. "It may be quite some time, Minister Ba Thun. So far, we've only recovered two days of the lost days on our schedule."

Ba Thun sat with his hands clasped on the polished surface of his desk. His eyes held Carson's in a steady gaze.

"You are not unaware of the demonstrations taking place?"

"No, sir. I run into them almost daily."

"Something must be done."

"I fear my hands are tied. If we are unable to negotiate a new schedule, I must do my best to protect my company's interests."

"Altering the schedule is out of the question. For matters of national interest, you understand."

He understood that Ba Thun could not afford to have his decision reversed as a matter of the man's pride.

But Ba Thun also feared the bad public-relations image. Carson could understand the problem. When the city government delayed the opening of the five-billion-dollar Denver International Airport four times because the 193-million-dollar baggage system didn't work, the results were ridicule, million-dollar-a-day interest costs, and the downgrading of airport bonds to junk status—which drove up the interest rates.

The SLORC was financing the Modernization Proclamation in part with bonds sold internationally, and delays meant increased costs.

Carson felt as if he had some leverage, however. The SLORC was feeling the pressure of the employment demonstrations, and they would be passing that pressure to Ba Thun. Whatever Ba Thun's personal objectives were, he had to do something about the people marching in the streets, screaming their heads off, as well as save face over his decision not to renegotiate the schedule.

"I have been thinking about your problem and mine," Carson said, "and I might just have a solution that could benefit both of us."

Ba Thun raised his head, looking down the side of his nose. "I would be most interested to hear it."

Carson put the Burma Road Plan into words. "If General Technologies were to secure another long-term contract that would offset its penalty losses, the company might be inclined to absorb the financial loss—and we're looking at fourteen million dollars at the moment—and put the training and hiring schedule back on schedule."

The carrot dangled in front of the minister, and he considered it for a long moment before asking what it would cost him. "What contract did you have in mind, Mr. Carson?"

"We would suggest that GTI be licensed to operate the government's mining operations."

"For how much, and for how long?"

That immediate response made Carson believe that Ba Thun had been thinking about this particular topic, and he wondered why.

"I think, off the top of my head, that our subsidiary, GTI Geologic Operations, would be able to operate the mines for twenty percent of the production. We would want a twenty-year license, though we would entertain clauses in the contract allowing for adjustment of the percentages at, say, five-year intervals."

"Explain the percentage, please."

"I haven't cleared this with my bosses, Minister, but I believe they'd go for an eighty-twenty split of the raw product, the gemstones. Based on carat weight, I suspect. I do think they would want a first right of refusal on the largest stones. This way, the SLORC would not have to put up any money. GTI would rely for its income on selling directly to the gem and industrial markets."

"We have one hundred percent of our production, right now," Ba Thun said. "I see no benefit in reducing our revenues to eighty percent."

Despite Colonel Mauk's efforts, Carson was virtually certain that the mines were losing at least ten percent of their production to pilferage. Put the brakes on that, and the production of record would climb right away.

"I've seen the mining operations, Minister, and the methodology hasn't changed in three centuries. I wouldn't hesitate to say that, with GTI's technology and efficiency, your eighty percent would be substantially higher than the one hundred percent you currently receive."

Ba Thun lowered his head again, stared at the desktop, and mused. Then he asked, "What is your interest in the large stones? Why would we compete with you in the gem market?"

"There are industrial applications for larger stones, which you do not now pursue, and I see no competition between us there. With the smaller stones, yes, we would be looking at the same gem dealers for sales. However, with some . . . cooperative efforts, I shouldn't think that either the government or GTI would miscalculate and drive prices down. It would serve neither of us to do so."

"I find this proposal most interesting, Mr. Carson. I have had a similar proposal just recently."

And that was why it was on his mind. It took Carson only a few seconds to realize that it must have come from Hypai Industries, through Hyun Oh. They were already involved in mining operations.

"How similar is it?" Carson asked.

"I should not divulge that at this time, I think. However, let me discuss this with other members of the committee, and then we will talk again. Do you . . . that is to say, could you have a formal written proposal prepared if asked?"

"It shouldn't take more than a few days to put something together."

Ba Thun made little circles on the desktop with his forefinger. "It is understood, is it not, that this proposal of yours also carries with it the resumption of the training and hiring programs."

"That is understood," Carson said.

Top that, Oh.

Hyun Oh could certainly resume his own hiring of locals without GTI's approval, but that would only affect fifteen percent of the employee pool.

Ba Thun stood up and offered his hand.

Carson shook it firmly. They were back on friendlier terms.

It was after ten o'clock when Carson parked his Jimmy in the GTI compound. His escort of Mauk's guards had left him at the entrance to the compound, though he saw one of them watching him until he let himself into Gilbert's apartment.

The two of them were sharing space until the bombed-out section of the compound was rebuilt. GTI's administrators were also sharing office space all over the compound—with Ultra-Train, with Hygienic Systems, with InstaStructure, with Bluebird, and with Cable Engineering.

The apartment was dark, and Carson turned on a lamp beside the couch, then went into the bedroom, crowded with the two double beds. He changed clothes quickly, donning jeans, a dark blue T-shirt, and black running shoes. He made certain the Velcro straps of the ankle holster were secure.

Traversing the veranda and stairway, he went back to ground level, walked along the porch, and entered the IBM offices, located next to Gilbert's destroyed cubicle. He passed through a back door into the section that was being reconstructed. The odor of fresh sawdust was pleasant.

Carson edged his way past some sawhorses to the back wall. There was a convenient exit to the outside of the compound created by someone's plastic explosive. He slipped through the opening and sidled along the outside wall under the black plastic that had been tacked into place, emerging into the alley that ran along this side of the compound.

Gilbert and three InstaStructure employees, including Billy Kasperik, were waiting for him. They were all volunteers, and they were all armed with the Browning automatics.

"How'd it go?" Gilbert asked.

"The bait's out, the fish has it, but the hook's not yet set."

He turned to the others. "You sure you want to be part of this party?"

"Damn right," Kasperik said.

"Let's go."

It was a short walk. They went south to Anawrahta Street and tried to blend in with the crowd surging along it. Two long blocks to the west, the five of them turned down Lanmadaw Road, and then into the alley opening from it. The alley was dark and cluttered with refuse.

"How in hell did you locate this place, Jack?"

"It wasn't easy, Chris. Kiki Olson had to hack her way into the city's computer and figure out how many times the building's been altered, along with changing addresses."

Gilbert led the way, then stopped next to a rickety set of stairs tacked onto the side of a building.

"This is it?"

"No. We go up here, though, then cross to the building on the east."

The stairs creaked and groaned as the five men climbed it. They reached a landing at the second-floor level, then Gilbert crossed a short catwalk to another landing on the side of the next building. The door was locked.

"Let me at it," Kasperik whispered.

He bent over, and working with his picks by feel in the dark, had the lock opened in three minutes. He pulled the door open, peered into a hallway lit by sixty watts at the far end, and said, "Looks clear."

They all stepped into a foul-smelling hallway, and Gilbert pulled the door shut behind them.

"Second door on the left," Gilbert said.

Carson might have laughed if he could have stood aside and watched the five big men moving on tiptoe down the corridor. Kasperik held up a hand, leaned forward to examine the door, then put his head close to Carson's and whispered, "It looks like the other doors, but it's steel in a steel jamb. New lock."

"Not going to bust it?"

"Don't think so."

"Bet they don't open up for a knock," Gilbert said.

"Shoot the son of a bitch," Carson said.

Kasperik didn't need more instruction. He pulled his Browning from his belt under his loose shirt, held the muzzle close to the lock, snapped the safety off, and pulled the trigger.

Pulled it twice.

The gunshots reverberated in the narrow hall. Cordite stink filled the air.

Kasperik kicked the door open, then fell back.

A Kalashnikov chattered from inside.

Bullets sprayed the opposite wall.

Carson dropped to his stomach on the filthy floor, fighting to pull the automatic from his ankle holster. Everyone around him was also on the floor.

Pulling himself forward, Carson slipped the safety, stuck the gun around the corner of the doorway, and squeezed off three shots, changing his firing angle slightly with each one.

The assault rifle fired another short burst. Splinters flew from the floor in front of him.

This was a damned dumb idea.

Along the hallway, he heard doors slamming open, people screaming.

From the other side of the doorway, Gilbert fired a couple shots. He was still a novice; the shots could have gone anywhere.

A scream from within.

Heartening.

His hearing was numbed by the shots. Down the length of the hallway, more people yelled.

He heard glass breaking.

One of Kasperik's men crawled up beside him. Carson, Gilbert, and the construction engineer emptied their automatics inside the room.

There was no return fire this time. Carson could hear heavy breathing, a man groaning.

Carson stood up, his back to the wall, and inched his head forward until he could see inside.

There was a single overhead bulb still lit.

A table. A chair. A single bed.

Two men flopped limply across the floor, another hanging over the side of the bed.

He stepped quickly through the doorway, looked to either side and saw no one, then stepped to the bed and pushed the AK-47 away from the man's hands, onto the floor.

Gilbert came in and checked the two on the floor, pulling an automatic pistol from one victim's hand.

"We've got one still breathing, Chris."

Carson pressed his fingertips against the carotid artery of the man on the bed. Nothing there.

Kasperik strode across the room and whipped the tattered curtains aside on the window.

"Check this, Chris."

Walking around the bed, Carson joined him at the window and noted the glass broken out of the frame. Across the narrow airshaft, perhaps three feet wide, was another window, and its glass was also broken.

"Damn it! We lost one or two."

"Looks that way to me," Kasperik said.

He turned around and looked at the room, at the men crowded into it, at the bodies. One of his volunteers appeared a bit stricken; his face was pasty and Carson thought he was on the verge of vomiting. Carson felt pretty much the same way, himself. This wasn't quite the same as having the door gunners blasting away at a faceless enemy from the anonymity of a Blackhawk.

"I think I screwed this one up," he said.

"I don't know, Chris," Gilbert said from the tiny closet he was examining. "The bastards were armed to the teeth. They weren't choirboys."

Inside the closet were several more assault rifles and a couple cardboard boxes. Gilbert held up a fragmentation grenade.

"There are some C-4 plastic explosive and detonators here, too."

The yelling outside had died away, and the hallway was now deathly quiet.

"The question," Kasperik said, "is what do we do now?"

If it weren't for the wounded man on the floor, Carson might have tried to slip away, but he was certain that any resident who might have seen them would remember five big Caucasian men.

He looked around, saw the telephone.

"I guess I'll call Mauk."

"He's going to love this," Gilbert said.

EIGHTEEN

Chinatown, Yangon

It was after midnight by the time the duty officer at Myanmar Army Barracks roused Mauk out of his bed, and the colonel arrived at the dingy apartment off Lanmadaw Road.

Carson and his crew, after thoroughly searching the apartment for something more incriminating than the weapons cache, and finding nothing, waited in the corridor outside the shot-up apartment.

Three soldiers had arrived within minutes of his call, and they had posted themselves in the now open doorway at the end of the hall, at the foot of the stairs in the alley, and in the room. Shortly afterward, an army doctor had arrived to tend to the wounded man.

Mauk crossed the catwalk to the landing and strode into the corridor. Three uniformed soldiers trailed after him. Carson noted that he was wearing a fresh set of khakis.

He was also wearing a frown of impressive proportions.

Without looking at Carson or his team, Mauk went directly inside the room, spent several minutes exploring it, then emerged. The frown had changed to a rage that suffused the skin of his face.

Carson could detect the repressed fury in the man's voice when Mauk ordered one of his men, "Collect their weapons."

Carson had shoved his Browning in his waistband, and he

pulled it free, checked that the safety was on, and handed it butt-first to the soldier. Gilbert and the others followed his example.

"Mr. Carson," Mauk said, "you are in this country for the express purpose of fulfilling construction contracts."

Carson thought it was a statement, so he didn't respond.

"Is that not correct?"

"That is correct, Colonel."

"In light of that objective, would you explain this fiasco?"

"I have reason to believe that the men in there were responsible for acts of sabotage against our operations."

"So you came in shooting, like your famous John Wayne."

"That wasn't the intention."

"How did you find this apartment?"

"An informant's tip." He wasn't about to reveal the existence of his Data Processing Center.

"The name of the informant?"

"None offered, none requested."

"Do you know who these men are?"

"Finding them here was a complete surprise, Colonel. I expected to find Daw Tan."

Mauk leaned around Carson to study the bullet holes in the opposite wall of the hallway. He turned back and looked over the door.

"They opened fire, first?" he asked.

"Ah, after we opened the door."

"Daw Tan was not here?"

"Unless he went across the airshaft. I think that he did."

"And what would you have done with Tan, had you detained him?"

"I'd planned on a long and intimate conversation."

"Which, in all probability, would have resulted in reprisals from his friends," Mauk said.

"Well, goddamn it, Colonel! I'm tired of people like Tan roaming around with apparent immunity, because of some unstated understanding, putting my people in danger. You asked what my job is. I want to do it without interference from bastards like Daw Tan."

Carson let the heat of his anger rise to the surface, then took a deep breath and held it in check.

"Daw Tan is my job, Mr. Carson. If you would let me do it, we might now have Daw Tan and live prisoners. You could have told me of this magical informant."

Carson acknowledged that possibility with a nod.

"I should take all of you to the barracks and charge you with murder."

"I'm not buying that. Look at the damned bullet holes in the wall. Charge us with self-defense."

"The next time you receive an informant's tip, you will notify me immediately."

He sighed. "All right, Colonel."

"Go back to your quarters," Mauk ordered.

"What about our weapons?"

"You offered to replace the Browning of mine that you scratched, Mr. Carson. I thank you for doing it so many times over."

Emigrant Peak, Nevada

The sun was merciless on this side of the Sierra Nevada mountains, on the edge of the desert. Although they were at five thousand feet of altitude, the mountains and foothills didn't offer much protection from the harsh glare and the heat. Abrams guessed the temperature at over ninety degrees, and though it was supposed to be dry heat, his handkerchief was sodden from wiping the perspiration from his face.

The back doors of the van-bodied truck were swung wide open, and Abrams sat on the back of the bed, swinging his legs aimlessly. Next to him sat Tim Grace, president of GTI's subsidiary, Geologic Operations, specialists in mining enterprises.

Mack Little and a couple of his scientists were at the console behind them, keying instructions into the computer's keyboard.

The Ruby Star laser on its tripod mount was sited a hundred yards away, aimed directly at the side of a granite cliff. Its power and control cables snaked over the ground to the control truck and to the generator trucks five hundred feet away. The small valley in which they were located felt desolate. Only a pair of twin ruts normally used by four-wheel-drive vehicles led out of the box canyon downslope toward some hint of civilization. Getting the larger trucks to the site had been a major endeavor involving winches and towing by the four-wheel-drive vehicles.

The sheer cliff climbed straight upward for eighty or ninety feet, and the granite rock appeared as solid as . . . granite.

"Like butter? That's what you said, Dex?" Grace asked.

"Just like butter, Tim. Compared to a tank, this is nothing."

Little called out, "I've got a range. How deep do you want to go, Dex?"

"We don't want to totally screw up the landscape, Mack. Make it five feet."

"Gotcha." Little adjusted the depth of the cut—the range of the laser beyond the rock face as measured by the secondary laser range finder—via the computer, then said, "Bringing up the generators."

The diesel engines groaned into high idle.

From where they sat, the ruby rod of light that jetted from the nozzle of the laser appeared to have the same diameter as a nickel. It lanced out, found the cliff face at its juncture with the ground, and as they watched, inexorably moved upward. It left a fissure behind, climbed about six feet in an ideally straight, computer-guided line, then abruptly turned ninety degrees and went sideways for six feet. Again, it turned ninety degrees, fell to ground level, then traversed back to the starting point. The ruby ray died away, leaving a perfectly aligned picture frame in the side of the cliff.

"That's five feet deep," Little said.

"Prove it," Grace told him.

"I will."

With sudden sharp bursts of the ruby beam, dozens of holes were punched into the granite inside the picture frame. A few X-shaped slices also fragmented the rock, but amazingly, left very little rubble behind. With the square of rock face punctured, allowing pressures and fragmentation to transfer inward, rather than outward into the rest of the cliff, the laser hesitated while the generators built up higher output, then suddenly erupted with one heavy jolt of energy.

The bolt of crimson slammed into the cliff, and the defined square simply caved in. A small pile of rubble rested on the floor of a new tunnel entrance.

The generators whined down.

"Want a tape measure, Tim?" Little asked. "It'll be exactly five feet deep."

"My eyes are that good," Grace said, slipping off the bed of the truck.

Abrams followed him, and the two of them walked past the Ruby Star, which had now aimed its muzzle at the sky. Crossing the uneven ground, climbing a little, they reached the tunnel entrance.

The walls and ceiling were perfectly smooth, almost shiny in their gloss.

Abrams judged the depth at exactly five feet.

"The computer," he said, "remembers the coordinates, of course. We can continue punching through the cliff, aligning each bore."

"What's the max depth of a cut?" Grace asked.

"We've gone eight feet. Beyond that, it gets a little ragged."

Grace looked at his watch. "Five feet every twenty minutes?"

"For a six-by-six bore."

"Absolutely amazing, Dex."

"How many do you want?"

"Start with ten. I'll find work for a couple hundred by the end of the year."

"At six mil a copy?"

"You guys own me, so I'll get a discount, right?"

"You could find enough work for two hundred machines?"

"In a minute. I'll have them paid off in two years."

"Damn!" Abrams said. "I wish I had more than one."

GTI compound, Yangon

Hyun Oh thought that Kim Sung-Young was not attempting very hard to keep the smirk from his face. The engineer and self-proclaimed accountant addressed him respectfully, but below the surface of his voice and his eyes, there was a self-satisfaction that was highly annoying.

"And this, Mr. Oh?" Sung-Young pushed a blank receipt across his desk.

To make a bad situation worse, they were meeting in the assistant director's office rather than Oh's. He felt his mantle of authority slipping badly.

He glanced at it. "The Maha Bandoola Street Tailor. It was for a shirt. Perhaps a tie, too."

"Ah." Sung-Young tapped at the keyboard of his computer, then picked up another receipt, gratefully the last in the pile. "Here is one that I cannot pin down, either, Mr. Oh. It is for a billing by the Strand Hotel. Another one."

Oh peered at it. May 26. The amount suggested at least three dinners.

"That is when I entertained two potential telephone company investors."

"And you have a corresponding entry on your calendar?"

Oh leafed through the calendar he held in his lap. Nothing. He was not good at recording *every* action he took, every meeting.

"I remember the meeting distinctly," he said.

"These men, have they agreed to invest in a company?"

"No."

"Without corroboration, Mr. Oh, I must bill you the difference between the cost of this meal and the per diem rate. . . . It will be one hundred and forty-seven dollars and sixty-seven cents."

"I am allowed to entertain clients," he insisted.

"But not at these rates. Mr. Pai specifically placed limits on the amount to be spent on meals."

Oh seethed, but said nothing. Sung-Young was taking advantage of what he considered an opportunity to charge him with every unsubstantiated billing to the contingency fund, legitimate or not.

"This is a large wardrobe," Sung-Young said as he sent the listing on his computer to the printer.

Oh devised tortures for the assistant director, Myanmar contract, but did so only in his mind.

Reaching behind him to take the listing from the laser printer, Sung-Young studied it, then bent over his desk and began filling in a form. When he was done, he turned it around to Oh.

"You must sign and date at the bottom."

"What is it?"

"A note of indebtedness to Hypai Industries. You will be required to pay it off through a payroll deduction."

"Of how much?"

"It amounts to nine hundred *won* each month."

"But that is ridiculous! It will leave me with less than two hundred dollars American to live on." After the deduction sent to his wife.

"Still," Sung-Young said.

He read the note. The total amount was 22,465 *won*.

"This cannot be correct."

"The interest is included."

"Interest! At what rate?"

"Mr. Pai said ten percent. Do you wish to calculate it yourself?"

Scribbling his name angrily on the signature line, Oh stood up and stormed from Sung-Young's office. He went into his own and slammed the door shut.

He knew, absolutely, that Mr. Pai had no intention of turning him over to the police over a measly fifteen thousand *won* worth of clothing. He was performing a valuable service for Hypai Industries, as well as services that would not bear intense scrutiny.

Pai did not want to reward him for this; he wanted Oh in the role of indentured servant.

It did not seem fair.

City Hall, Yangon

The premier asked, "Do you have written proposals?"

"As yet, no," Ba Thun said. "I have not requested them, for I did not know how far you or the other members wanted to proceed."

The premier scowled. "I do not like this. These people are intruding into areas where they have not been asked to go."

Ba Thun understood. There were certain perquisites associated with the mines. He himself had accepted a few baubles offered as gifts from time to time. Not that he needed them; every stone still rested in the vault in his house.

"Nothing has been formalized," he said.

"Yet, do you not find it interesting that both Hypai Industries and General Technologies approached you separately with the same proposition?"

"I have thought about this, Premier, and I am not totally surprised. Both Christopher Carson and Hyun Oh had requested permission to tour the mine sites earlier. Oh went to Mogok just last May. I suspect that both men are of a similar breed. Their business nature makes them seek out areas of profit."

The premier shifted uneasily in his chair. "I do not like it."

"As you wish," Ba Thun told him.

"But then, is it possible that we could derive more income from the mines?"

"I suppose that is more than probable," the minister said. "Despite our best efforts, there is possibly still some . . . wastage. Losses that we cannot control. And then, as both Carson and Oh pointed out to me, our methods are dated. New technology would undoubtedly improve the production."

"They would steal from us."

"Hyun Oh said that we would be expected to place our own monitors on the operations. I suspect that provision could be negotiated with General Technologies, too."

"But you said that Hypai Industries had the lower bid, at fifteen percent of production."

"That is true, Premier. However, Carson wields a larger prize, that of employment."

"Hah! It is blackmail."

Ba Thun thought it was blackmail, too. However, he had been surprised that the leverage of employment had not been applied against reopening negotiations in regard to an extension of the schedule. He was forced to appreciate Carson's subtlety; the man was allowing Ba Thun to protect his position on that issue, while using his club against Ba Thun on the mining contract. If the SLORC ever agreed to issue such a contract, Ba Thun knew now that Carson would get it. Hypai Industries could offer to operate the mines for no profit whatsoever, and they would still fail.

"You can hear them shouting in the street, if I open the window."

The premier sighed, the scowl again crossing his face, making his eyes appear maddened.

"Very well. Let us take it to the full membership."

It was what Ba Thun had expected. Like the premier, he was

not enamored of giving up yet more economic control to the foreigners, but he saw no way to avoid the necessity at the moment. And yet, the development could still play into his long-range plans.

Prome

Major Tawn Yin May led the way onto the wharf.

Mauk followed him, but slowly; his eyes scanning the ancient docks projecting into the river. Hundreds of boats were tied to the weathered pilings and to each other. Some of them were three and four generations old, and their smoothly worn decks and scarred hulls did not disguise the fact. Whole families had grown up on them: born, worked, married, begat more of themselves, died. Those on the closest boats eyed Yin May and himself with suspicion. Theirs was a closed and nearly self-sufficient culture, and they did not appreciate unannounced intrusions by the uniformed government.

At this time of late afternoon, the charcoal fires in steel hibachis on the boats issued a blue haze that hung over the river, and the aroma of cooking fish was overpowering.

Mauk thought with some dismay that any one of them could be disenchanted enough at the sight of the hydrofoil boats, an incursion on the livelihood of many, to have resorted to extreme measures.

At the end of the dock, the giant black man was waiting for them.

"Hello, Colonel Mauk, Major Yin May."

"Good afternoon, Mr. Washington," Mauk said.

"Sorry to bring you up here so late in the day."

"It is not a problem."

Washington looked over their heads toward the shore. "You brought your explosives people?"

"The demolitions squad has been notified and will be here shortly. Can you show us where it is?"

"This way."

Washington led the way up the short gangplank to the deck of the hydrofoil. It was such a sleek craft that it made the surrounding boats appear to be made of orange crates. Mauk thought that, if he were the owner of a fishing or cargo craft that had supported his family for a century, he, too, would feel threatened by the newcomer.

They entered the cabin through a wide door off the side deck, and Mauk saw that a section of the interior decking had been opened. Washington went first, turning to slide quickly down a short ladder into the bottom of the boat. Mauk followed him.

He found himself in a well-lit and immaculate engine room. The giant diesel engines dominated the space.

"Right over here, Colonel."

The bundle was fastened to the side of a large, plastic-appearing wall. It was not large; perhaps ten centimeters long by five wide.

"That's one of the fuel cells," Washington said. "If that hummer went off while the boat was en route, we'd have had a hell of a fire, not to mention a couple hundred dead people."

Yin May bent to examine the bundle. He used his fingernail to peel back the brown paper from one end, then peered beneath the paper.

"It is plastic explosive," the major said.

Mauk saw the two wires dangling from the package. "You cut the wires, Mr. Washington?"

"The boat captain did."

"Very dangerous. It could have been booby-trapped."

"He didn't think about it, Colonel. He was worried about the boat and the passengers who had already boarded."

Washington squatted next to the adjutant and pointed to the other end of the cut pair of wires, showing their route along the deck to a niche between fuel cells. They led to a black box.

Mauk had seen similar boxes.

"This is what I thought you'd be interested in, Colonel Mauk."

Mauk leaned over and read the legend stenciled in white on the top of the Bakelite box. In Burmese, it identified the box as the property of the Union of Myanmar Army.

"Yes. It is a self-contained timing and detonation device."

"Stolen, no doubt," Washington said.

"I should think so, yes," Mauk said.

But he could not be certain of that, and the uncertainty bothered him immensely.

GTI compound, Yangon

After his botched night in Chinatown, Carson had gotten to bed late, then slept in until nearly nine o'clock, something that hadn't happened to him in years. His day seemed to run the same way: appointments late, calls not returned, paperwork with more errors than expected. Skipping lunch hadn't made much difference in catching up.

The call from Charles Washington at six o'clock didn't help, either. More bombs. More danger for the Americans working in-country. He felt totally responsible for the peril. They were his people, in one way or another.

He didn't leave his temporary office in the IBM section until Washington called back to say that Mauk and his demolitions experts had arrived in Prome and that the bomb was defused.

Carson stood on the porch outside the office and looked across the compound at the cafeteria, then looked up at Branigan's apartment. She had been out all day, but there were lights on now. He was surprised she hadn't called to let him know she was back.

Crossing the compound, he climbed the stairs and walked down the veranda to knock on her door.

"C'mon in!"

Carson pushed open the door and stepped inside. Branigan was in the kitchen, zapping something in the microwave.

"I'm having a TV dinner. Want one?"

"Sure."

"Turkey or meat loaf?"

"The turkey's fine," he said, moving to the dinette and pulling out one of the chairs.

Digging in the freezer, she pulled out another dinner and set it on the counter. She poured from an open bottle of Chablis into two stemmed glasses, placed them on the table, and sat in the chair opposite him. She looked awfully good. Her face was scrubbed, as if she'd just gotten out of the shower, and she was wearing a pair of old cutoff jeans and scoop-necked tank top. And not much else, he judged. She was barefoot.

"I ought to run over to Jack's place and take a show—"

"You're a really, really, stupid son of a bitch," she said.

Her eyes grabbed his and wouldn't let go. The deep green was almost black. He thought she was deadly serious.

"You heard, huh?"

"Billy Kasperik was acting suspicious around me. I thought he was trying to hide something from me, and he was. To his credit, I damned nearly had to use pliers on his fingernails to get him to confess."

"It probably wasn't my best idea," he admitted, "but Mauk doesn't seem to be getting anywh—"

"I think we ought to back off from each other, Chris."

"What?"

"I need some time to think."

"About what?"

"About us. I don't want to fall in love with a man who thinks he's God's choice for the lead in a B movie."

"Now, Steph—"

"I mean it. Did you even think about me when you got your band of hooligans and their guns together?"

He hadn't thought about her, of course. He'd been so wrapped up in his scheme to bust open the conspiracy against GTI that he hadn't thought much beyond the next ten minutes.

He wasn't able to respond before she added, "One night in the forest may not be enough to kick off a new relationship,

Chris. I know we're both carrying around some emotional cargo, and maybe we need some time to make certain we've jettisoned it."

"Stephanie, can I say something?"

"Not now. We'll have dinner, and then you can go."

"I'll go now."

Carson was careful to not slam the door on his way out.

It hadn't been a good day, and it certainly wasn't ending on an upbeat.

NINETEEN

Myanmar army barracks, Yangon

U Ba Thun fully expected something drastic to occur today. It was the Fourth of July, a date of singular importance for the Americans, and a prime day for a symbolic gesture on the part of the chieftains.

Unfortunately, it was also a day on which the university students planned a massive demonstration in protest of the government's employment policies. If it were not so serious, he would be amused by the naivete of the students. They assumed the government could create jobs out of thin air and a bare treasury. For both of those reasons, the minister met with Col. Lon Mauk at nine o'clock, traveling out to the barracks, since he knew the man would be extremely busy.

He was. Officers and noncoms were in and out of the orderly room, racing about as if the farmer chased them with a cleaver.

Ba Thun's driver parked in front of the redbrick building, and he got out of the car and marched inside.

Mauk was standing at a desk, leaning over a duty roster with a sergeant. He looked up as the room quieted upon Ba Thun's entrance.

"Minister, good morning."

"Good morning, Colonel. If you would have a moment."

"Of course. Sergeant, take the second platoon of the two-fifty-first from the railway and have them downtown by twelve o'clock. They are to report to Captain Yi for administration and ordnance issue."

"Yes, sir."

Mauk ushered Ba Thun through the door and down the hallway to his office.

"You are taking men from the railway security?" Ba Thun asked.

"I have no choice, Minister. The general issues the orders, and I follow them. My men are disciplined enough to use only rubber bullets and tear gas if it is necessary. The general frequently calls upon us to provide troops when the students march."

"You are aware of the date?"

"The American Independence Day, yes."

"It would be like Daw Tan, if Daw Tan is involved, to select this day for a raid of significance."

"Oh, it is Daw Tan," Mauk said.

"You are certain?"

"He is not seen anywhere in the country. His subterfuge of hiding out at the Shanghai Hotel has fallen through. I am confident that it was he who retained the rooms in Chinatown. The landlord gave a skimpy description of the renter, hoping to not implicate himself should Tan seek revenge, but it was enough."

"And what of that fiasco?" Ba Thun demanded.

"The third man has died, but the three of them are known to be in Daw Tan's employ."

"How is it, Colonel, that Carson found them in the middle of Yangon and you did not?"

"I have pondered that very question, Minister, and I have come to one conclusion. There was a telephone in the room which is a rarity in that part of Chinatown."

"A telephone?"

"Do you understand the implication?" Mauk asked.

Neither of the men had taken a chair. Colonel Mauk leaned his hips against the front of his desk with his arms folded across his chest, and Ba Thun paced the small office.

He stopped his pacing to look at the officer. "You are saying that Carson is tapping the telephones?"

"I see no other answer. The Americans would be treated with suspicion if they attempted to approach any Burmese for information, despite their ability to pay large sums. And who but they are experts in the new communications systems? The new technologies may be greater than the SLORC anticipated."

Mauk's statement gave Ba Thun pause. He tried to recall all of the dozens of calls he had made lately, what had been said.

"What are you doing about it?" he asked.

"What would you have me do? There is no evidence that wiretapping is taking place. I conducted an unannounced security inspection of the Kemendine Microwave Facility, the most likely center for such activities, but I discovered nothing that appeared out of line."

Ba Thun settled heavily into one of the visitor chairs. "Are we to the point of suspecting our contractors?"

"I would welcome guidance on the subject," Mauk said. "However, I also try to understand Carson's point of view. I do not think he would direct activities against the government. His aim is to protect his employees, I think."

"True," Ba Thun agreed.

"In the meantime, I am treating Carson with some distance and disfavor. I do not want him repeating his adventures."

"Very well. But also, you are thinning the protection of the railway. It is not wise."

"Major Lin Po, the commander of railroad security, would agree with you wholeheartedly, Minister. If I am not provided additional manpower, and if I must continue to loan my forces to the Yangon police, though—"

"Or if the students were to study, instead of attempting to run the government."

Mauk nodded, but asked, "Is there no hope that General Technologies will resume hiring soon?"

Ba Thun wondered how much Mauk knew of the negotiations taking place between himself and Carson. The man always seemed to know much more than he revealed.

"At the moment, everything is static," Ba Thun told him.

Both he and the premier had been surprised that the other members of the SLORC had balked at their recommendations to enter into an operations agreement for the gem mines. The others complained that the foreigners were now running the communications, transportation, and sanitation sectors.

"What," the minister of the interior had asked, "do we give them after the mines? Will they not seek to take over my office?"

So, nothing had transpired as yet, and the students and the workless yelled all the louder. He was afraid that a repeat of the 1980s riots would lead to many deaths and much more condemnation by the world.

"I will speak to the general about reducing his demands on you," Ba Thun said.

"That would be appreciated, Minister. It is going to be a long day, and if something happens, I will need every man."

Two kilometers north of Pyu

Daw Tan, accompanied by his lieutenant Kanbe and a man known as the Rat (because of his scrawny, pinched, and pockmarked face), parked the truck in a copse of trees a few meters from the road.

A few cars and many trucks were utilizing Highway 1 at this time of day, and they went by with a steady drone of tires on hot asphalt. None appeared interested in the old Fiat that had left the road, probably for necessary repairs to a tire or radiator. Certainly, none stopped to offer assistance.

After a wait of twenty minutes, studying the clouds building up in the southwest, Tan was assured that they would be left alone, and the three of them got out of the car. Kanbe opened the trunk and lifted out two backpacks. With his two men carrying the packs, Tan took the lead and pushed his way into the thick growth of the forest.

The wooded area was not large, and they soon emerged onto a grassy slope leading down to the stream, a tributary of the Sittang River. Angling back toward the highway as they descended below its level, they followed its rising embankment. When they reached the stream, they turned westward, passing under the overpass of the highway.

Then it was a matter of a short walk along the uneven shore of the river to reach the railroad bridge. The old timbers of the original bridge had been replaced by concrete abutments and footings and new steel girders at the time the UltraTrain trackage had been emplaced. Tan looked upward to the top of the trestle. The pedestal sections of track appeared mildly obscene to him. They did not belong in his country.

He stopped short of the bridge, in a tangle of shrubbery, and surveyed the line north and south. Nothing moved. No trains, new or old, were in sight. The highway was over a kilometer away behind him, and he did not think that any driver would be looking this way.

"Let us move quickly," he told his assistants. "One bundle at each of the piers."

The three of them trotted the last two hundred meters to the base of the trestle, and Kanbe and the Rat split up, moving to the concrete foundations that supported the massive steel uprights on this side of the stream. Shrugging out of their packs, they climbed onto the concrete platforms, spilled the plastic explosive from the canvas packs, and began to tamp it into place against the gray-painted girders.

Daw Tan took a roll of braided wire from Kanbe and started unrolling it between the piers, giving one end to each of his helpers. Midway between the footings, he squatted and placed the timing device on the ground. It was a military unit and one of six that Corporal Syi, a man placed right within Lon Mauk's orderly room, had obtained for him. With wire cutters, he cut the wire to length, and then used his knife to strip the plastic from the copper wire. He wrapped the wire leads to each pier around the binding posts of the timer, then waited.

Kanbe called, "I am inserting the detonator."

"Hurry."

A few minutes later, both men joined him near the timer. Daw Tan used a small ohm meter to check that the circuits were complete, then slid aside a plastic door on the timer. The current time on the digital readout matched that of his watch: 1147. Pressing the small buttons, he advanced the timer readout until it read 1300 hours. That would give them over an hour to reach a safe haven. They could be halfway back to Yangon, which was 250 kilometers away.

"I would like to see this," Kanbe said.

"Yes. That would be foolhardy, however."

Jogging swiftly through the thick grass and weeds, they followed the stream back toward the highway bridge.

GTI compound, Yangon

"Seven o'clock, then?" Gilbert asked.

"Make it seven-thirty," Pamela Steele told him. "Correspondents don't often get access to Aung San Suu Kyi, and I want to spend as much time with her as I'm allowed."

His number-two telephone line was blinking, and Gilbert reluctantly agreed to the later time, then punched the button for line two.

"Gilbert."

"Jack, Carlos Montoya."

"What's up, Carlos?"

"We've got some kind of activity in sector four."

"I don't know sector four."

"It's a Listening Post north of Pyu, on the main line."

"What kind of activity?"

"The computer tells us that there were three different people.

The range from the sensor suggests they were moving around the bridge."

"For how long?"

"About six minutes."

"They still there?"

"Just leaving."

"Tell Evans to get a chopper ready. I'll try to find Carson."

Gilbert hit the first line again and called Becky Johnson.

"He went out to meet with Colonel Mauk, Jack."

"I'll try there."

Myanmar army barracks, Yangon

Mauk and Carson had barely settled in the two chairs in front of his desk when his telephone rang.

Irritated, Mauk reached over to the desk and picked it up. "I said no calls, Sergeant."

"It is an urgent call, Colonel. For Mr. Carson."

Mauk handed the phone to Carson.

"Yes . . . what have you got, Jack?"

As Carson listened, Mauk watched the line of his mouth become tense. The skin of his upper lip paled a little.

He stood up from his chair and replaced the receiver in the cradle. "Colonel, I've got a small crisis to attend to."

"Tell me about it, Mr. Carson."

"Let me check on it, then I'll brief you."

"Brief me now, Mr. Carson."

Mauk's disenchantment with Carson's personal paramilitary tactics hadn't gone away. The set of his shoulders and the tone of his voice should have told Carson that he was on thin ice.

In something of a rush, Carson told him a story of audio sensors placed along the railway line and of a concern for something that had been heard near the Pyu bridge.

"I believe I will look into this," Mauk said, standing and reaching for his cap on the desk.

"All right. I'll go with you."

"No, Mr. Carson. I will do my job, and you will do yours."

Mauk left his office, and passing through the orderly room, told the sergeant to order a helicopter for him. He did not wait for his driver, but ran down the steps and got into his Land Rover. The wheels spun on the gravel drive as he headed for the gate and the airport.

GTI operations, Mingaladon Airport, Yangon

By the time Carson reached the airport, he had seen four military helicopters take off and streak away toward the north. By the time he received his clearance and got the Gazelle airborne, it was twelve minutes after noon.

He had three volunteers with him. Don Evans was in the copilot's left-hand seat; Carlos Montoya, who had begged to ride along, was in the back; and next to him was Charles Washington. The Hydrofoil Marine boss had been in the operations office, just back from Mandalay after catching a ride on a GTI S-65 Super Stallion and wouldn't accept "no" as an English word. Evans had an M-16 resting muzzle down between his knees. It was their only armament.

Maintaining an altitude of a thousand feet above the ground, Carson increased his speed until he was holding 210 knots, close to the maximum-weight sea-level top speed.

"How long will it take to reach Pyu?" Montoya asked over the intercom.

"About forty-five minutes," Carson told him.

"I just came from this way," Washington said. "I should have gotten off at the second bus stop."

"You should probably just stay out of it, Charles," Carson said.

"Bullshit! These guys put a bomb on my boat. I don't like it."

Far ahead, Carson could see the four black dots of the Myanmar helicopters. They, too, were keeping their altitude low and their speed high.

"I wish we could listen in on the military frequencies," Evans said.

"It would all be in Burmese, anyway," Montoya reminded him.

He soon found the railway and swung in above it. The new pedestal track shone whitely in the sun alongside the gray ballast and steel ribbons of the old trackage. Near Penwegon, he saw a conventional freight train headed south, passing a northbound freight that waited on a siding.

"Kanyutkwin," Evans identified the next town. "Another twelve miles to the bridge."

Minutes later, they passed over Pyu. The military helicopters ahead were already circling the bridge. As he watched, one of them settled to the ground, dropping out of sight behind a slope.

Carson angled off to the right, to avoid interference with the military craft, passing over the highway, then circling back toward the railroad trestle. He came back over the highway from the east. A few cars and trucks had slowed, and some had come to a stop at the edge of the road, as their drivers gawked at all of the helicopters.

"GTI helicopter, this is Tiger One."

It was Mauk's voice.

Carson depressed the Transmit stud. "Tiger One, GTI Four."

"You will please stay back."

"Roger, Tiger One."

Carson went into a hover a half-mile from the bridge.

"They've got some guys out down there," Evans said.

Carson saw two men approaching the base of the bridge, coming from an Aerospatiale Alouette, which had landed on the bank of the stream. They were close to the vertical steel bridge members, and one of them started waving frantically.

And as he watched, two bright red flowers blossomed at the bottom of the trestle.

The concussions came seconds later, barely heard over the roar of the turbine.

"Son of a bitch!" Washington yelped.

The main vertical girders buckled, and the south end of the trestle sagged into the gorge.

Both of the men on the ground had disappeared in the fire and smoke which enveloped the southern shore of the river.

TWENTY

Two kilometers north of Pyu

Mauk ordered the copilot to switch frequencies so that he could talk to the helicopters in his flight.

"Tiger Three, land and assist Tiger Two. Tiger Four, follow the highway north. Look for a suspicious vehicle. Take care to examine the side roads." On the intercom, he told his own pilot, "We will go to the south."

As his Alouette dipped and banked to the left, he saw Carson's helicopter streaking in low to land on the southern bank of the river below the destroyed bridge. Christopher Carson always seemed to be exactly in the place where Mauk did not want him to be.

Lately, however, Carson was frequently a step ahead of him, and Mauk did not care for that either. The American had located the apartment in Chinatown. Now, it seemed that he had some kind of sophisticated alarm system surrounding the railway, sophisticated enough to pinpoint *three* men walking to the bridge and doing *something* near it. It was not much in which to place one's faith, and yet, Mauk had ordered four helicopters into the air. That was costly.

And he had done it without once questioning Carson's facts. Could he be relying on the engineer too much?

Perhaps.

On the intercom, he told the copilot, "Tell the others we are looking for three men in a vehicle. Alert the police and the military patrols along the highway."

City Hall, Yangon

U Ba Thun was reading a *London Times* general-interest piece about the new sanitation systems appearing in Myanmar's principal cities. It was not, he thought, a topic that would have aroused his curiosity, but Pamela Steele had interviewed health-department officials, cited statistics on disease, and quoted many citizens. All in all, it painted an optimistic future, and he was pleased with it. Colonel Mauk had been correct in arguing against her eviction. Reports such as this pointed out to the international community that the SLORC was pursuing a policy of assistance to the citizens. It tempered the strident voices in the United Nations.

His intercom buzzed and he picked up the telephone. The secretary said, "Minister Ba Thun, we have just received notification from the army that the railroad bridge at Pyu was destroyed by an explosion."

"When was this?"

"About forty minutes ago, Minister. At one o'clock."

"Were there casualties?"

"One man is dead, another seriously injured."

"Civilians?"

"They were army security personnel."

"Call the security section and tell them to keep me aware of developments."

He replaced the telephone and leaned back in his chair, the brilliant piece of journalism spread on his desk forgotten.

Well, he thought, this is Khim Nol at work.

Pegu

As soon as they reached the town, they abandoned the Fiat in an alley, and after he gave them instructions, Kanbe and the Rat disappeared into the throngs of people milling about the market.

Daw Tan stopped in a nearly deserted, open-air cafe and had

an early dinner before locating his rented car on a side street. He drove carefully through the town and took Highway 1 toward Yangon.

Traffic between Pegu and the capital was heavy in both directions, but Tan was content to stay with the flow at about 50 kilometers per hour and not draw attention to himself. He was ever careful with his driving since his depth perception was nonexistent. He gave himself large gaps between the cars front and rear. Before he reached Intagaw, he noted an increase in the number of military vehicles, the drivers intently scanning the occupants of automobiles and trucks coming from the north. Two helicopters passed over, flying low beneath the spreading overcast and also watching the activity on the road.

The manhunt was on, but he was not worried.

In fact, he was quite pleased with himself.

The destruction of the railway bridge had been entirely satisfying. More important, it met the objectives of three people: Khim Nol, Hyun Oh, and himself. All of the plans were falling into place, and Daw Tan took a great deal of self-satisfaction in knowing that he was the only one fully aware of all three schemes. Chieftain Nol was in the dark about the South Korean, and Oh had no inkling of Nol's designs.

And neither of them was cognizant of the final chapter outlined by Daw Tan.

GTI compound, Yangon

Stephanie Branigan reached Dick Statler at the bridge using the railroad's integrated telephone system. Statler had only to plug his portable phone into a jack located behind one of the access panels in the pedestal.

Janice Cooper and a few of the people from the engineering center were crowded into her office, waiting for word on the damage.

"I damned near shocked myself, Stephanie. Almost forgot this was one of the booby-trapped doors."

"How bad is it, Dick?"

"It's not good. Segments AA546 through AA559 will have to be replaced. We lost the two southern piers, and not many of the girders can be salvaged. I'm going to have to borrow steel for the piers from some other site. About half of the decking is totaled."

"The conventional trackage?"

"Same story. My counterpart from the Myanmar Railway is here, and he's crying, too. He's not going to be moving freight or passengers between Mandalay and Yangon for a while."

"How long?"

"If I take crews off the Taunggyi Division, and knowing that the engineering is already done, maybe a week."

"Try for less, Dick."

"Always do."

She replaced the receiver and scratched at her cast unconsciously. Her arm itched with an intensity that she tried to keep banished from her mind. She wasn't always successful.

"Let's go back to the center," she told the others.

They trooped ahead of her into the engineering center, crowded with her full complement of personnel. She had given half the staff the day off for the Fourth, but they all turned out as soon as they learned of the sabotage. Everyone gathered around one of the consoles, and a senior engineer out of MIT named Mitch Cole took the seat in front of it.

"Call up AA546, Mitch."

A few seconds later, the drawing appeared on the seventeen-inch screen. Its specifications and the settings for the molding jig were listed below it.

"Has a slight curve in it—radius six hundred feet, Stephanie."

"AA547."

They went through each of the segments, and found that most of them were straight, which made the casting easier.

"All right," she said, "dig out the drawings and prepare orders for the casting plant. We want these units as soon as we can get them."

"Do we interrupt production of the Tatkon segments?" someone asked.

They were within four miles of completing the Mandalay-Yangon route. The railheads were approaching each other at a fast clip.

Until now.

"What do we have up there, now?"

Another console sprang to life and the shipping schedule appeared. The junior engineer, a woman out of Stanford named Connie Marshall, said, "Seventeen segments arrived on site this morning, Stephanie."

"That will have to hold them for a while," Branigan said. "Until we get the trestle repaired, we can't get more through to them, anyway."

"How about Skycranes?" Mitch asked her.

"I'll talk to Carson, but I don't think it's going to be feasible, not for that distance. Put the bridge segments on priority and interrupt the production schedule. Can we see the trestle?"

Cole called up the drawings, and she studied the structure.

"The damned thing would be sixty feet tall."

"It's one of the bigger ones that we've replaced," Cole agreed.

"Where do we steal the components?" she asked.

Connie Marshall had another drawing up on her screen. "TB11. That's on the Taunggyi Division, near Aungban. The girders are on site, but construction hasn't started."

"Okay, grab them. Reorder steel out of the States to replace what we take. Mitch, talk to Don Evans about a heavy-lift chopper to move it. Connie, see what this does to the schedule. I'll need a revised date for the Mandalay-Yangon completion as soon as possible."

"I don't see us making the July fifteenth date," Cole said. "Not with production diverted."

"We *will* make that date," Branigan told him.

He nodded, but still looked skeptical. "Do you want those test results now?"

"Test?"

"The Hypai magnets."

She didn't want to deal with that now. "How did they perform?"

"They're not any better than our own, Stephanie. Just as good, though, and I guess cost will be the determining factor."

They had a four-month supply of the superconducting magnets on hand, ready for installation in the track pedestals after they were cast. That was ample time for Steve Pruett, back in the States, to cut off American production and switch to the Hypai units. Over the balance of the contract, with the trackage yet to complete, it could amount to a savings of fifteen or sixteen million dollars. If she had any more disasters like today's, she might need the money to cover the added costs.

"I'll let L.A. make that decision, Mitch," she said, but was afraid that she'd be recommending a Hypai contract.

She went back to her office, flopped in her chair, and tried to work her finger into the top of the cast, searching for an itch she couldn't quite reach. She gave up and picked up the telephone. Punching the number for Pruett in L.A., she remembered at the last second that it was still dark in Los Angeles.

She canceled the call and tapped in the phone number for Carson's temporary office in the IBM section. Becky Johnson answered.

"Any chance the boss is back, Becky?"

"None. I talked to someone at operations a few minutes ago, and he said the helicopter was at General Hospital."

"The hospital?"

"Chris brought the injured soldier back. He should be back at Mingaladon in half an hour or so."

It figured. Carson had to be in the thick of the action. She tempered her silent criticism with the fact that, at least, this was a humanitarian effort on his part. The raid on the apartment, with guns blazing, was less humanitarian. She was dismayed by the changes that had taken place in him in the last few weeks. For the first two years she had known him, he was a perfect leader—low-key, suggestive rather than directive, easygoing. That was the man she had found herself falling in love with, not the hotshot combat soldier intent on winning the war all by himself. Well, she wasn't going to be in love with a potential corpse.

Was she?

"Anything I can help with?" Johnson asked.

"I need about fifty Skycranes."

"Nope, nothing I can help with."

GTI operations, Mingaladon Airport, Yangon

Jack Gilbert was waiting on the ramp when Carson landed the Gazelle at ten minutes before five. An S-65 Stallion fifty yards away was just starting its turbines.

He walked out toward the helicopter as Carson, Washington, Evans, and Montoya crawled out of it.

"Bad, was it?"

"Not pretty, Jack," Carson told him. "Have you talked to Stephanie?"

"No, but when I left the compound, it looked like most of her people were on the job."

"Good. We've got to be ready for that inaugural train or Ba Thun loses face. And we lose more than face."

"I've got a bit of a problem, Chris," Gilbert said.

"Personal?"

"No. Recall my telling you about Mr. Chao?"

"Chao? Oh, yeah. In Bangkok."

"He's gotten hold of one of the articles we need."

Carson raised an eyebrow. "The hell he has."

"I've got to take a look yet tonight because he has another buyer lined up if I don't want it."

"And the problem?"

"No commercial flight until midnight."

Carson turned to Evans. "Where's the King Air, Don?"

"Mandalay. They took some computers up there."

"Refuel the Gazelle, then, and get Jack a pilot."

"For Bangkok? Air control will raise hell, Chris. We're not supposed to be crossing the borders."

"Tell them it's got something to do with the main-line sabotage."

"Like what?"

"Make it up."

Gilbert went back into the operations building with the others, got his carry-on, said goodbye, and went back out to the ramp. Forty minutes went by before the helicopter was refueled and preflighted. Don Evans got on the radio and argued with the air-control people for a while, but finally got permission for the helicopter flight to Thailand.

A young pilot named Jack MacGregor introduced himself to Gilbert, and the two of them climbed into the front seats. MacGregor fired the turbine, called for clearances, and lifted off. A spatter of raindrops bleated against the Plexiglas.

"We may just be able to stay ahead of the rain, Mr. Gilbert."

"I hope so. I'm getting tired of wet."

Gilbert pulled his harness tight and laid his head against the headrest. He wanted to take a nap, but Aerospatiale hadn't designed these seats for sleepers. He wanted to call Pamela Steele and explain his cancellation. She had been out, and he had been forced to leave a message at the YWCA desk.

This was the night when he had worked up the courage to talk to her about marriage. Just talk. He didn't want to be turned down right away.

He hoped that Mr. Chao had an excellent example of a ruby for him. A successful acquisition would be the only justification for a night flight by chopper to Bangkok.

MacGregor leveled out at 1,500 feet above the city as he took up a southwesterly course. The overcast had settled in well, making the city dark long before sundown. Quite a few lights were beginning to show along the streets to his right.

They crossed the outer boundaries of the airport while MacGregor was dialing in a local English-language station on his backup radio. Randy Travis filled Gilbert's earphones.

He hadn't yet been able to convince Steele that she liked American country music.

They shot over the Pazundaung Creek at cruise speed.

Gilbert idly watched the countryside.

Saw a blink near the creek bank.

Blink?

Elongating into a trail of white.

"What the hell's that?" he asked the pilot, pointing.

"What? Where? Oh, that's . . . shit!"

The helicopter lurched into a violent right bank, began diving.

"What is it, damn it!"

"Missile!"

It slammed into the underside of the Gazelle.

Gilbert heard a tremendous explosion.

And then he heard nothing.

Menlo Park, California

Alicia had made a big pot of coffee, set out some Danish, then discreetly left them alone in the breakfast room. It was six o'clock in the morning.

Abrams and Baskin sat at the table looking through the big window at the backyard. When he bought the house, Abrams had insisted on a large yard. He liked puttering around, running the garden tractor, trimming the shrubs. He wanted to put in a vegetable garden eventually.

In the time they'd lived there, Abrams got as much fun out

of the backyard as he got out of the ketch, *Alicia Mae*. He'd never had time to do any of it. Instead, he paid out big bucks for some guy to come over and ride his garden tractor.

Baskin commented on how good the yard looked as he bit into a prune Danish.

"So, what have you got, Troy?"

"I've got the telephone. Or rather, the telephone modem."

"Of the hacker?"

"That's the one."

Abrams was surprised. He hadn't thought there was a chance in hell of tracing it.

"It took a long time because we had to examine the whole six-eight-six prefix, but my old buddy in LAPD fixed me up with a Pacific Bell investigator, so we had an inside track. We went after the business listings, first, since it seemed the most logical, but that ran right into a dead end. Then we ran a comparative program against all the residential lines, looking for lines that were open at the same time as our machine was tapped. That got us fourteen hundred names, and it's taken this long to examine each one."

"And you found?"

"An apartment in Studio City. I think the guy bailed out the minute he knew we were onto him. He left everything behind—computer, groceries, some clothing."

"But not the Ruby Star plans?"

"The computer was a blank. Not even operating software left on it. If it means anything, there wasn't a printer in the place. There was a tape backup system on the machine, so the data's probably on a tape cartridge."

"Do you have a name?"

"George Bixbee, but that's bound to be false."

"You're sure?"

"According to the neighbors, he was an Asian, and he didn't live there full-time. Just showed up every now and then. They thought he was on the road for some pharmaceutical company."

"Can you find him?"

342   *William H. Lovejoy*

"Fifty-fifty. He'd had the apartment for fifteen months, and he made other phone calls from it. I've got his call listing and I'm checking out the numbers now. Our number for the Ruby Star lab is on the listing, by the way, for every time we got hit."

"This is damned good work, Troy."

"Be better work if I hadn't let him into our system in the first place."

"We won't sweat that crap right now."

"How far do we go, boss?"

"What do you mean, how far?"

"If I ID this guy, and he works for one of our competitors . . ."

"We run his ass, and theirs—whoever they are—right to jail. Do not collect two hundred dollars."

Abrams got up to refill their cups, and the phone rang. He grabbed the remote from the kitchen counter and sat down again.

"Abrams."

"Carson, Dex."

The voice was very tight.

"Something wrong, Chris?"

"Jack Gilbert was just killed."

"Ah, shit!"

"He was killed along with one of Evans's pilots. They took a Gazelle down with a missile."

Abrams felt sick to his stomach. "Goddamn it! This is getting—"

"I'm done being defensive, Dex."

"Look, Chris, take it easy."

"That's the way I've been taking it. Now, we've got some tables to turn, and I'm going to turn them. I want the Ruby Star."

"What! Not in this life!"

"I want the generators, also. Put 'em on a cargo flight by tomorrow."

"That is out of the goddamned question, Chris. Hell, you can't even operate the thing."

"I want Mack Little, too. Plus as many techs as he needs."

"Forget it. That's the only prototype we have."

"I'll trade you a stone for it. I'm on my way to get it now."

"I'm sorry, Chris. I just can't authorize it."

"Your choice, Dex. You can have it my way, or you can have my resignation."

"Chris—"

"By tomorrow," Carson said and hung up.

Troy Baskin gave him a funny look. "What's up, boss?"

"Carson is starting a war."

Bangkok, Thailand

Carson chartered a Piper Navajo twin flown by an expatriate Vietnam vet known only as Danang Doug. He flew all of Southeast Asia out of a base in Bangkok, and he probably flew cargoes best left undiscussed. He had happened to be in Yangon, and he was happy to pick up a fare for his return to Bangkok. Carson appreciated the man's smooth control over his airplane.

As soon as they landed at Don Muang Airport at eleven o'clock and were rolling down a taxiway, Carson asked, "Want to make the return trip?"

"Hadn't planned on it."

Danang Doug had stringy hair tied back in a ponytail, and he wore a headband fashioned from a piece of a North Vietnamese flag.

"Double the fare."

"How long you gonna be?"

"The rest of the night, probably."

"I'm supposed to be in Ventiane at noon."

"So you'll be a little late."

"You probably don't want to ride with me."

That meant the cargo was questionable.

"You probably don't want to fly me," Carson said.

Danang Doug looked over at him. "Big package?"

"Very small."

"Triple the fare."

"Done."

The trip into town from the airport was only fifteen miles, and during the day, it could take ninety minutes. At this time of night, the traffic was lighter, and his cabbie made it in fifty minutes.

It was just after midnight when the taxi parked in front of the address on Mahesak Road. Carson told the driver to wait, got out, and rang the buzzer at the street-level door.

On the intercom, Mr. Chao, he presumed, said, "Mr. Gilbert?"

"Mr. Gilbert couldn't make it. My name is Christopher Carson, and I have the same interest."

Chao didn't like the change, judging by the long time he took in making a decision. Finally, the door buzzed, and Carson went in and climbed the old wooden stairs to the top floor. He was checked out through a small window before the steel door was opened to him.

"Identification, please."

Carson produced his driver's license and his GTI identification.

"You work for the same company as Mr. Gilbert?"

"I do. I was his boss."

"Was?"

The man picked up the nuances quickly.

"Mr. Gilbert was killed tonight in an aircraft accident. That is why I have come in his place."

"I am sorry to hear that."

"Thank you. He was also a good friend."

"Come in, please."

Carson sat on the sofa and declined coffee. The Thai opened a huge old safe and removed a single briefke. He brought it across the room and sat next to Carson on the couch.

"It is not good to look without natural light, but I have promised another a chance at the gem in the morning, should it not meet your requirements."

Chao pulled the head of a lamp behind the sofa closer and offered Carson a loupe.

Carson took it and lodged it in his eye socket. He hadn't had as much practice as Gilbert, and he certainly wasn't as comfortable as Gilbert had been with the criteria for which he was looking.

He opened the briefke.

It was not what he expected to see.

It was in the rough, though a viewing window had been polished in one of the six sides.

"It is one hundred and fifteen millimeters in length," Chao said. "It would finish at better than one hundred."

Carson tilted his head near the light, arranged the gem for the best light, and louped the stone.

After a moment's peering, he felt as if he could get lost in the deep cherry color.

"The silk is magnificent, Mr. Chao."

"It is definitely a Burma stone."

Carson had studied the ruby now held in Palo Alto, and if anything, he thought this one better. He would like to have had a second opinion from Gilbert before he talked money, but that was not to be.

Just thinking about Gilbert aroused the rage he was bent on suppressing. He wanted to take one of Daw Tan's portable Stinger missiles and ram it down his throat just before pressing the trigger.

"This may be what I have been looking for, Mr. Chao."

"It is by far the finest stone I have seen in a long time, Mr. Carson."

"What is your price?"

"The rarity of the size alone drives the demand. My morning visitor could well top anything you might offer."

"Who is your visitor?"

"Mr. Carson."

"Sorry," he said. "I thought it might be helpful to know who I might be bidding against."

"I am certain that it would be helpful. However—"

"Three hundred and fifty thousand."

"American?"

"Of course. Mr. Gilbert had the letter of credit with him, but I can have a cashier's check, or cash, for you as soon as the bank opens."

"Cash would be preferable."

"Cash it is."

"But. Perhaps I should allow the other gentleman an opportunity to view the stone?"

"Four hundred thousand."

"Still . . ."

Carson hated negotiating against an unknown bidder—one who might be nonexistent. But Gilbert had felt good about Chao, had told Carson he thought the Thai was an honorable man. He was aware that Chao had not yet mentioned a figure, but the gemologist who had tutored Carson and Gilbert had given them an accurate picture of current world prices.

"Plus," Carson added, "I would still be interested in acquiring more rubies of the same caliber."

"Four hundred, then."

Finding a hotel room in Bangkok was a taxing proposition without advance reservations, but Carson managed to locate a suite—the only thing available—at the Oriental. For six hundred bucks, he thought, it had better be his best four-hour night ever.

He hadn't brought any clothing with him, so he sent his suit out to be pressed while he slept. It was ready for him in the morning, along with his highly polished shoes, and he was in the coffee shop by seven. At eight o'clock, he made a hefty withdrawal from GTI's local bank, the cash stacked in an attaché case supplied by the bank.

At eight-forty, his taxi made the turn onto Mahesak Road, and Carson told the driver, "Pull over here. Right now!"

The cab swung to the curb, and the driver stared him down in the rearview mirror.

Carson was looking up the street, however.

Where Hyun Oh was just getting into his own taxi.

In front of the door to Mr. Chao's place of business.

"Well, now."

"Sir?"

"Nothing."

He waited until Oh's cab pulled away, then said, "You can go ahead now, driver."

TWENTY-ONE

U Ohn Khaing Street, Yangon

A block north of the Rangoon Railway Station, Daw Tan had secured run-down quarters where he read the morning newspaper with dismay.

He had been so careful.

For nearly two hours, he had waited patiently in a shallow defile near Pazundaung Creek, watching the airport with binoculars. He had seen the General Technologies helicopter arrive from the south and had identified the shapes of four men in it. He had been unprepared at that time, the Stinger missile still in its canvas carrying pack.

Though the distance had been great from his position on the stream bank to the area of the General Technologies parking ramp on the east end of the airport, he had seen the feverish activity of refueling. He knew the helicopter would take off again soon.

And he had been ready.

And now to learn this morning that Carson had not been aboard. There were only two nonentities named Gilbert and MacGregor. He had heard of neither of them before today.

He would have been far ahead to shoot down the heavy-lift helicopter that had taken off a few minutes before the smaller one.

There was a tentative knock at the door, and Tan rose from the edge of the bed where he sat, picked up his Smith and

Wesson revolver, and moved to the side of the door. The plaster of the wall was so old and unprotected by paint that flakes of it fell to the floor when his elbow brushed it.

"Yes."

"It is Kanbe, Chieftain."

Reaching out, he turned the key in the lock, then the handle. Kanbe slid through the door and pushed it shut.

"Did you obtain the weapons?" Tan asked.

"I did. They are in the car. In the trunk."

"And the car?"

"I have parked it two blocks from here, and it will not be connected with this place."

Kanbe moved to the bed—there was no table in the room—and placed his canvas bag on it. Unstrapping the top, he lifted boxes of C rations from the inside. They were twenty-five years old or more and probably stockpiled from supplies stolen in Vietnam. Without cooking facilities, Daw Tan was forced to eat them.

The two of them sat on the floor and peeled open the cartons.

"There is word on the street, Chieftain."

"Yes?"

"Colonel Mauk wishes to speak with you."

Daw Tan did not wish to speak to the colonel. In less than ten days, Mauk and his soldiers would be superfluous.

"He will have to find me," Tan said.

Mingaladon Airport, Yangon

Danang Doug did not shut down his engines, but whipped the Navajo into a tight turn behind two Sikorsky Stallions. He had radioed ahead to let Mingaladon Operations know that he was dropping off a passenger and asked for a customs officer. When the operations officer learned that Carson was the passenger, he opted to skip a customs inspection. Carson was well-known to him and unlikely to smuggle anything *into* Myanmar.

"Hey, man! Maybe you and me could do a deal," an impressed Danang Doug suggested.

"If I had the time, it might be worth discussing," Carson told him.

"You need me again, just holler."

"Will do."

Carson crawled out of the right seat, ducked for the low overhead, and walked back to the airstair. Unlatching it, he shoved it open, skipped down the steps, then slammed the door shut and relocked it. He waved to Doug, and the Navajo moved away, headed back for the taxiway.

The ruby hurt his instep.

In Bangkok, Carson had purchased a pair of shoes two sizes too large for him and taped the gem into the right shoe, against the side of the leather. He hadn't expected to be passed through a customs inspection on the say-so of some tower-operations officer.

In the GTI operations office, Evans was on the phone at his desk, now banished from the data center, which had its door closed to preserve the air-conditioned environment.

One of Evans's assistants was tending the counter. Carson thought her name was Billie Jo, but he couldn't remember for sure. He asked her to place a call to Menlo Park and gave her the home number for Abrams.

With a mug of coffee from the ever-going fifty-five-cup pot, he pulled a chair next to Evans's desk and listened while he argued with someone at Moulmein.

"Your call's gone through, Mr. Carson."

"Thanks."

He grabbed a phone from the next desk.

"It's ten o'clock here," Abrams said. "I barely got home, and Alicia's got dinner on the table."

"I'll keep it short. You have my package ready to go?"

"Damn it, Chris. We have to talk about this some more."

"You'll need to charter a 707 cargo liner. On the return flight, it'll be carrying my shipment to you."

"Sheesh! You got it?"

"Done. Beautiful specimen, by the way."

"Mack Little's not going to like temporary duty."

"Little sun, little rest. He'll love it."

"I'll see what I can do, but damn it, Chris, it's a hell of a risk."

"It'll be worth it, Dex."

Carson hung up at the same time Evans put his phone down.

"How was Bangkok?"

"I mostly saw it at night, and not much of it, at that," Carson told him, unlacing his shoe and pulling it off.

He plucked the ruby out. It was still wrapped in its briefke, but was taped tightly. He tossed it on Evans's desktop.

"What's this?"

"Little bauble. Can you find a safe place for it?" He put his shoe back on. It felt loose.

"Probably. Is it valuable?"

"Close to half a mil."

Evans's eyes grew in size. He grabbed the stone and shoved it into his top desk drawer.

"You ain't kidding, Chris?"

"Nope. We're going to have a 707 in here in the next day or two with a special cargo. You need to find a cubbyhole on the plane for that. It's headed back stateside."

"The guys up in City Hall don't know about it?"

"That's right."

"There's only a couple thousand hiding places on a 707."

"Just so we don't lose it."

"Why in hell do you give me these things?"

"I want to send MacGregor's and Jack's bodies back on the same plane."

Evans nodded somberly. "Okay. Shit."

Carson felt as if he hadn't had time to grieve. And wouldn't have time for a while longer.

"Okay, the special cargo. There's going to be two semitrailers. They carry four diesel generators apiece. What do you suppose they weigh?"

"You know what model?"

"No. Big, though, I'd bet."

"As a round figure, I'd guess about a ton each."

"Eight generators, sixteen thousand pounds."

"That's probably pretty close, Chris."

"And the Skycrane's max lift?"

"We can get off the ground at forty-two thousand pounds gross. With a full fuel load, I can manage a payload of ten tons if I push it. One of those trailers isn't going to be a problem."

"How about both?"

"At the same time?"

"Yeah."

"The weight of the trailers themselves will put me way over the max," Evans said.

"So let's get Billy Kasperik involved. He can figure out some kind of platform with maybe a canvas cover. We pull the generators out of the trailers and mount them on the platform."

"That, we can probably do, Chris."

"Great. Pick out your best chopper and get the maintenance up to date. When you get those trailers, see what you can figure out."

"They have to go as one load?"

"With the generators running."

"Once again, you ain't kidding?"

"I ain't kidding, Don."

City Hall, Yangon

Colonel Mauk read the London newspaper in Ba Thun's reception room while he waited to be called.

Pamela Steele had written it, and it received the front-page headline: TERRORIST MISSILE DOWNS HELICOPTER. *The as-*

sistant director of General Technologies Inc. Myanmar Project
was killed last night when . . .

She also covered the destruction of the railway bridge, but
refrained from mentioning any Fourth of July symbolism. It
was, Mauk thought, a cold and calculating report, a bit short
of detail, striving very hard for objectivity. He found it strange,
considering how much time Gilbert and Steele had been spending together. Mauk's watchers had reported such, at any rate.

The secretary finally signaled to him with a fluttering hand,
and Mauk went into the minister's office.

U Ba Thun was behind his desk, its top barren of any paperwork. He indicated that Mauk should take a seat, so Mauk
assumed he was not to be chastised in the extreme for the latest
incidents. It could be, he thought, that Ba Thun had already
sought out a replacement for the security commander and had
found no takers. He was stuck with what he had.

Still, the man's voice was deadly cold when he asked, "What
have you to report?"

Mauk decided against revealing the detection system Carson
had installed along the main line of the railroad. Ba Thun had
not yet reacted to the hypothesis that Carson was eavesdropping
on the telephone systems, and he did not want to become involved in a debate over the American's supposed technological
intrusions into privacy. Perhaps in the back of his mind, he
feared that one or more members of the SLORC would like to
commandeer Carson's systems for their own use.

"Based on a tip from an informant, Minister, we had reason
to believe that there would be trouble for the railroad near Pyu.
We were not, unfortunately, able to get there in time. The explosive used was C-4 plastic, and it was timed. The timer, like
the one recovered from the hydrofoil boat at Prome, was military issue."

"So they are into our stores?"

"It would appear so."

"Go on. What of the missile?"

"It seems likely that a Stinger shoulder-fired unit was utilized. They are, of course, widely available from arms markets around the world, but I have still ordered an audit of our own inventories. The results of that are not yet ready."

"The premier has already received messages from the American State Department and the United Nations Security Council relative to our ability to protect foreigners. He is not pleased."

"Understandably," Mauk said. "I am not pleased myself."

"You are still convinced that Daw Tan is responsible?"

"I am. We have been unable to locate him anywhere, much less at his compound."

"This, I do not understand," Ba Thun said. "If Tan were as disenchanted with the Modernization Proclamation as you would lead me to believe, he has ample resources of men and arms to mount concerted attacks throughout the country. This piecemeal approach does not fit him. Especially, it does not fit if he is personally involved. That has not happened for many years."

"I confess, Minister, that I do not understand it. I agree with you fully. The motive is unclear."

"And what of Nol, Shwe, and Kaing?"

"They are where they are expected to be. Nito Kaing went to Pegu several days ago, but her trip was uneventful."

"Why did she go?"

"To shop. The report says she bought clothing."

"How often does she shop in Pegu?" the minister asked.

Interesting, Mauk thought. From time to time, Ba Thun surprised him.

"Not often," he admitted. "Once in the past three years."

"So you think the shopping was a cover for something else?"

"I think she met with Daw Tan. I could not prove that, of course. My man lost the trail for several hours."

"If it is true, I wonder if Khim Nol is aware that Tan and Kaing meet without his knowledge?" Ba Thun mused. He rested his round face in his hands, elbows braced on the desk.

The statement led to a theory Mauk had been developing, but he was not yet ready to share it with Ba Thun. Amazingly, he thought he would rather test it with Carson, first.

"Khim Nol has many ears," Mauk said. "If Tan and Kaing were to betray him, or to think of it, he would know of it soon."

"Yes. That is true." Ba Thun abruptly switched to another topic. "I talked with Miss Branigan on the telephone this morning. She tells me that she still expects the railway to be open for the July fifteenth ceremonies."

"But she will not guarantee it, Minister?"

"The purpose of her call was to entreat for additional security."

"I cannot provide it unless more soldiers are transferred to my command. Perhaps only for the next two weeks?"

"I will talk to the committee," Ba Thun said, "but as before, I expect you will be denied."

"There is an alternative," Mauk proposed. "Rather than attach them to the security command, an infantry company from, say, the First Division, could be detailed to patrol the Mandalay-Yangon railway. Also, the air force could be ordered to fly regular patrols over the main line."

Ba Thun scrutinized him for a minute, then asked, "Without formally assigning them to you?"

"Exactly."

"You understand the political concerns, then?"

"Of course, Minister. No one wants me to gain unseemly power. You, however, know me. I do not have aspirations of power."

Ba Thun dropped his hands and his moon face nodded imperceptibly. "I will make the suggestion."

Lon Mauk left the office wondering where he could find Carson.

GTI compound, Yangon

Mr. Pai called him at his office at four o'clock. Mr. Pai talked as if nothing at all had changed in their professional relationship. He talked exactly as if he owned Hyun Oh.

Which he did.

"I did not expect to talk to you on a Friday," Oh said. "I have not yet compiled my weekly report."

"Tell me about these two incidents that have been in the news."

Oh told him what he knew of the bridge explosion and the death of the GTI assistant director, Jack Gilbert.

"How do you interpret these events?"

"There may be some backlash relative to the American presence in Myanmar," Oh said cautiously.

"Explain that."

"General Technologies has ceased hiring indigenous workers. At least, they have for the time being. I believe Carson is attempting to place pressure on Minister Ba Thun for some reason."

"And you? Are you still hiring?"

"Yes, although at Carson's request, I slowed the rate of induction into the training programs."

"Why would you do this?"

"It is important, Mr. Pai, that we maintain our relationship with Carson. We rely, after all, on the General Technologies' microwave-relay stations for our connections between cities."

Pai was silent for a moment. The balances were delicate.

Then he said, "Without upsetting anyone, is there an advantage to be gained from these incidents?"

Oh smiled inwardly. What he had set in motion was taking another step forward. It was like a row of dominoes. Once the first one fell, the others would also fall. It was his job to make certain that they were aligned to fall where he wanted them.

"I believe there may be, Mr. Pai. Should Christopher Carson and General Technologies fall from favor, we are well positioned to assume the master contract and complete the contract."

"The profits would be enticing," Pai said.

"I may be able to arrange that outcome."

"You also have an urgent commitment to another task," the president reminded him.

"And I have not forgotten it, Mr. Pai. The mining contract has been proposed to the government."

"Why have I not seen a copy of it?"

"It is still in an oral form. Minister Ba Thun informs me that it is under consideration by the State Law and Order Restoration Committee. I fully expect a positive decision."

"Very well. Do what you can about both prospects."

Oh took a deep breath. "Mr. Pai, should I succeed with either, I believe it only fair that I receive additional compensation. Either the mining contract or the master contract would bring enormous benefits to the company."

"You already have a bonus arrangement in regard to the construction schedule, Mr. Oh."

"This is entirely different."

After a brief pause, Pai said, "We will tear up your note."

A pittance!

"Mr. Pai—"

"Good day to you." He hung up.

Oh slammed the phone down.

Slave labor. That's what he was. Mr. Pai expected to reap millions while Oh struggled to find food to sustain himself.

He would not do it!

Tomorrow, no, this afternoon, he would start composing a résumé for himself. He could send it out to many places where he would find appreciation for the work that he performed. Mr. Pai could forget the mining contract as well as the master contract.

The phone rang.

He picked it up, almost yelling, "Mr. Oh!"

It was Pai. "I have reconsidered. Should you finalize either contract, you will receive a fifty-thousand-*won* incentive."

"One hundred thousand."

"Each?"

"For either contract, Mr. Pai. Plus, the note is to be destroyed."

Pai's long exhalation of breath could be heard over the telephone. Reluctantly, he said, "It will be so."

Finally.

Hyun Oh felt at last as if there were a real reason for him to see Christopher Carson and Stephanie Branigan dead.

The American Cafe, Yangon

"I didn't love him, you know?"

Carson had never considered himself much of a counselor, and he didn't know how to respond to Steele.

He nodded.

"I liked him a great deal."

"We all did."

"But I used him, too."

"And now you're feeling guilty?"

"Yes, I suppose that I am."

Carson looked around the restaurant. Some enterprising Burmese had taken an old building on Lanthit Street, parked a rusty Harley-Davidson motorcycle out front, postered the walls with Elvis, James Dean, a young Elizabeth Taylor, and early Brando, and stuck a jukebox with a never-ending audio stream of Ricky Nelson, Fats Domino, Gene Vincent, and Little Richard in one corner. The diner-style food wasn't the best, but the American workers kept the place profitable. At seven o'clock, it was packed.

The few times that Carson had been in the cafe, he had been struck by the fact that most of the patrons hadn't been born when Fats Domino came out with "I'm Walkin' " and "Hello, Josephine." The Americans liked the familiar touch of home, though.

Just then, it also struck him that the American Cafe would be a perfect target for a bomber. He suddenly felt uneasy.

He took a bite out of his cheeseburger, then chased the grease with a swig of Budweiser. Carson certainly didn't feel like being there in the smoke and noise, but Steele had called and asked to meet him. She'd promised that everything said was off the record.

"If I'd been able to talk to him, to insist that he not go to Bangkok, he'd have stayed for me."

"Jack was pretty dedicated to his job, Pamela. Just as you are to yours."

"Still."

There was a tear in the corner of her left eye. She dabbed at it with her napkin. Most of her hamburger was still in the plastic basket in front of her. She hadn't touched her fries, and Carson didn't blame her for that.

They were drawing some attention from a few people who might, or might not, know who they were. Steele was worth the appreciation, dressed in a safari-style outfit, with a cinched belt that emphasized her tiny waist and full bustline. Her blond hair glistened under the lights, and her water-filled eyes seemed even deeper and bluer than they were.

Carson felt a little sorry for her, but he felt sorry for himself, too. Losing Jack was like losing a brother, and he was very aware of it. Gilbert had been his closest confidant for a long time.

He also knew he was going to avenge Gilbert's murder, and he would use every weapon he could find to do it.

Pamela Steele was a weapon.

He didn't want to scare her off. Not until he'd made use of her, if he needed to. It was a cynical outlook, he knew, but one he was quite willing to take.

"If you want to do something for Jack, you can support what he was doing."

"What do you mean?"

"Beyond all the hype and the technology, Jack felt that what he was doing was going to benefit a lot of people. Raise the standard of living, create hope."

"Do you believe that, also?"

"That's why I'm here, Pamela."

"And what would you have me do?"

"Just what you've been doing. The piece on Creighton's Hygienic Systems was good. So was the article about the Ultra-Train's impact on the country. That's what it's all about, making life better in this part of the world."

"Yes, I can do that. Do more of it."

Carson hoped her sense of guilt, if that's what it really was, would push her into a whole series of positive articles. It would be good, not only for GTI, but for the Myanmar Project. Maybe it would get the SLORC into action.

He was feeling fairly good about this conversation when Branigan came into the cafe accompanied by Dick Statler, Craig Wilson, and a couple other UltraTrain people.

She stood at the entrance, looking around the smoky room for a table, and saw Carson.

She also saw Pamela Steele.

Carson waved at her.

She acted as if she missed his gesture in the crowd, then ushered her party toward a vacant booth on the far side of the room.

Carson felt as if he were back in high school.

He was the football quarterback.

And he had just been snubbed by the cheerleader.

TWENTY-TWO

GTI compound, Yangon

Stephanie Branigan didn't sleep well. First of all, the cast always gave her fits, even though Scott Remington had replaced it with much lighter fiberglass. She was accustomed to sleeping on her stomach, but the cast, angled at the elbow, prevented her from finding that position comfortable. She tried sleeping on her back, with the cast resting on her stomach, but that left her staring at the dark ceiling, her eyes wide open, thinking. She drifted in and out of a dozing state all night. It rained sporadically through the night, and while she normally found that soothing, on early Saturday morning, it was only irritating.

Secondly, in those moments of near wakefulness, when she wasn't certain of what was real and what was imagined, fleeting images of Chris Carson came to her, caressing, whispering, loving. She would feel herself reacting to his touch only to be suddenly repulsed by a knife suddenly in his hand, twisting. Pamela Steele held his arm possessively, smiling with devilish control. She might have called out several times in the night; she couldn't recall.

She was wide awake, and fatigued, at six in the morning, and she got up and showered, then dressed. She checked the cuts on her head, above the hairline, and they seemed to be healing all right. She took two aspirin.

Opening the shades in the living room, she saw a light on in Gilbert's apartment. The door was wide open, and the warm glow spilled out onto the balcony in the shadow of dawn. She went out and walked the veranda to the apartment and stood in the doorway.

Three cardboard boxes were stacked in the living room, and an open box rested on the kitchen table. Carson stood over it, wrapping a ceramic Buddha in a towel.

He was dressed in jeans and a plaid sport shirt, and she figured he'd been up for a couple hours.

She found the scene somehow touching. He could have delegated the packing to workmen, but here he was by himself, carefully stowing Gilbert's possessions into shipping boxes.

"Do you want some help?" she asked.

He looked up, startled.

"Uh, good morning, Steph."

"Help?"

"I can get it."

"That's one of your problems, you know. You always have to do it yourself. You want to be the chief, as well as the Indians."

She stepped inside and walked to the kitchen.

"Not always," he insisted.

He watched her closely, maybe not sure of her mood.

She wasn't sure of it herself.

"Do you have coff—"

The phone rang.

Carson crossed to the coffee table and picked it up.

"Carson."

His tone changed, elevated, as soon as he heard his caller.

"Hi, Merilee!"

She tried not to listen to his half of the conversation. It was difficult to imagine him with a college-age daughter. It was another, and possibly disturbing, element to weigh in the equation of their relationship.

Looking around the kitchen, she found the empty percolator and, working awkwardly with her good left hand, devoted her time to finding the coffee and getting a pot started.

She leaned against the counter and waited. There was a bit of an argument taking place on the phone, she thought. Rummaging through the cabinets, she found two mugs.

Leaned against the counter.

More arguing.

He was trying to be firm and yet be a daddy.

A daddy.

Was she ever going to be a mommy? The prospects weren't favorable.

The sun cleared the buildings on the other side of the alley, and hot rays splashed through the slats of the shade over the dining-area window. Rows of light coated the floor, the table, and the half-packed box.

The coffee gurgled to a stop, and she poured the mugs full, then carried his into him and returned for her own.

"Love you, hon, but you understand?"

There was no response from Merilee, apparently. Carson stared at the phone for a moment, then put it down.

"My daughter," he said, taking the mug she offered. "Thanks."

"I gathered."

"She just read the news story about Jack. Wanted me to drop everything and come home."

"That's understandable. Why don't you?"

Branigan sat in the chair opposite the couch where Carson was seated.

He gave her a queer look, as if she had just suggested the unsuggestable.

"Then she wanted to drop out of her summer classes and come here. She and I don't agree on that, either."

"It's safe for you, but not for her, right?"

Carson sipped his coffee and studied her. "Everyone wants to argue with me."

She didn't want to pursue that line, so she said, "I came to help you pack."

"It's almost done. Another couple of boxes. And the pictures and stuff from his office. Jack didn't carry a lot of baggage around with him."

"This is it?"

"He's got a condo in Menlo Park that's rented out. I don't know what he might have had there."

"Where do you send them? The boxes?"

"To his parents, I guess. They're listed as his beneficiaries on his insurance policy."

He leaned forward to hold her eyes. "Steph, about you and me . . ."

"I don't want to talk about it."

"We've got to, sometime."

"Have you talked to Merilee about me?"

His silence answered that question.

Ignoring that line of thought, she said, "I want to know what you've got planned."

"Planned?"

"I'm beginning to know you well enough to know that you won't let Jack's death go by without some response."

"Steph—"

"Something stupid like shooting up a building?"

"No."

"What, then?"

"Stephanie, it wouldn't be good for you to—"

Branigan placed her mug on the table, stood up, and started for the door.

He came after her, reaching out to tentatively take her arm. The touch of his hand created a tingle on her skin.

She turned to him.

"I feel guilty as hell that you got hurt, Stephanie."

"You shouldn't."

"But I do. I don't want it to happen again."

"Tell me what you're up to."

"You'd just worry."

"I'm going to give up worrying about you, Chris. This is precisely why we have nothing to discuss. If you're going to continue doing foolish things—and keep them from me—I don't want to have anything to do with you."

She shrugged her arm from his grasp, but his blue eyes held her own. They appeared somehow anguished.

"I love you, you know," he said.

"I don't want to hear it. Take it to Pamela."

She hadn't meant to say it, and she regretted it immediately.

"What the hell?"

"It didn't take you long to console the girlfriend, did it?"

She hadn't meant to say that, either.

Carson dropped his hands to his sides. "You're putting the wrong spin on this, Steph."

"Sorry. It's the same spin everyone else got."

She turned and walked out of the apartment.

San Francisco International Airport, California

The Boeing 707 freighter, with the AirFreightCharter logo on its tail, sat on the tarmac behind the warehouse. The semitrailers and the large crate housing the Ruby Star had already been loaded. They had waited until dark to accomplish the loading even though the cargo was innocuous enough. The customs official had taken a quick look at the diesel generators and at the crate labeled Electronic Stimulated Emission Amplifier, signed off on it, and went back to his coffee.

"I have strong reservations about this," Dexter Abrams said. He stood on the warm asphalt beneath the wing of the airplane.

"You do?" Mack Little asked. "You're staying here. I'm the one going where they have bullets in the atmosphere."

The director of laser technology did look a little pale, but that may have been the result of the glare of floodlights from the back wall of the warehouse.

The four technicians he was taking with him were less subdued. In fact, as they hauled out the luggage and loaded it aboard the airplane, they joked with each other and horsed around. For them, it was a lark, which included some temporary duty pay.

Abrams couldn't believe he was doing this. That machine, figuring some R&D cost, was worth fifty million bucks. But his relationship with Carson was screwy, too. He had even fired Carson once, back at GM, then ended up hiring him back. Carson had always been loyal and supportive, so he figured he owed him one. Besides, in their last phone conversation, Carson had suggested calling it a field test, and he would send the machine and Little back as soon as he could. Maybe even before Abrams had to report anything to the board.

"After you get in and talk to Chris, you give me a call," Abrams said. "I want to know what state of mind he's in."

"What do you expect, Dex? Jack was killed. He's not happy."

"Yeah, but Jesus, if he's going to run around the country, vaporizing it, he'll be jeopardizing a hell of a lot, not just himself."

"If you didn't trust him, the machine wouldn't be on that airplane."

"It's an expensive machine."

"How many would you give away to get Jack back?"

"Yeah, okay. You're right. But I want to know what he's going to do, before he does it. You tell him that."

"I'll tell him."

Little went out to board the aircraft, and Abrams moved back to where he had parked his Lincoln. He sat in it and waited while the freighter started its engines, warmed up, then taxied out to the southern end of the runway.

He watched the takeoff roll and rotation, the navigation lights climbing and disappearing into the dark sky over the blur of lights from San Francisco.

And hoped this wasn't the worst decision he'd ever made.

His gut instinct said that it was.

City Hall, Yangon

"Did you see that seventeen people were injured in the Bogyoke Aung San Street riot?" the interior minister asked.

"Not to mention the three policemen, one of whom may die," the premier said. "Personally, I have more concern for the policemen. These radicals are getting out of hand once again, and it is time we did something about it."

"Closing the university for sixty days might urge the students to appreciate what they have," the minister for the treasury suggested.

"If you recall, we have done that before, with less than spectacular results," Ba Thun said.

"Out-and-out lawlessness cannot be tolerated by this administration," the cultural minister professed.

U Ba Thun listened patiently to the debate. He assumed that nothing would come of it. The State Law and Order Restoration Committee had lost much of its sting when it began listening to world opinion. Where once decisions were reached unanimously and quickly, and consequences ignored, now the seven powerful men around this table bickered endlessly, worried about the tiniest negative reaction to a manifesto of the SLORC. Their power as a group, as well as individually, had deteriorated, and Ba Thun lamented the fact. Lately, the treasury minister had been siding with the ministers of the interior and culture in delaying decisions and backpedaling. Ba Thun frequently thought of how quickly he himself could react to crises and achieve peaceful resolutions if he were not hampered by the committee process.

"A public-works program?" the interior minister asked. "If we could put a few people to work, say ten thousand, it would relieve the pressure. The students and the radicals could not say we were doing nothing."

"And where do you suggest the money come from?" the treasury minister responded. "The balance is painfully thin, as it is. Our immediate resources are committed to the ongoing operations of the government and to the Modernization Proclamation."

This dialogue would not be taking place had not the demonstration of Thursday night gotten so far out of control. Ba Thun had dreaded reading the Friday papers, but the student rebellion had disappeared under the more spectacular headlines surrounding the railroad and helicopter incidents. He had been so relieved by that outcome that he had failed to reproach Col. Lon Mauk sufficiently.

The premier banged his hand lightly on the table, and when the babble died away, spoke to Ba Thun.

"The commerce ministry must have some recommendation."

"It is the same as it was at the last meeting," Ba Thun told them. At least he and the premier were of a single mind on this topic. "The mining contract. It is one way to increase revenues, and probably within six months."

"And we let the foreigners control yet more of our destiny," the minister of the interior said. He led the opposition to the mining proposal.

The treasurer was less opposed than before. "We might at least request written proposals, so that we know the amounts involved."

"Right away," the premier said, "we know that the Hypai proposal will generate the higher income."

"But," countered Ba Thun, "the General Technologies concept includes reopening the training schools and the entry-level jobs. This is an understood condition, and it could occur very quickly, relieving a great deal of anxiety in the streets."

"If we wait, what?, five years, they have to provide those jobs, anyway," the interior minister said.

"Can we wait five years?"

After a few moments of group silence, the premier asked, "Would Carson commit to restoring the jobs program on the basis of our requesting a written proposal?"

"Without a commitment on our part?" Ba Thun asked.

"No commitment, but a willingness to review the proposal."

"He might go partway," Ba Thun said.

"And we throw out the Hypai proposal?" the cultural minister asked. "I do not see that as beneficial in the least."

"No," the premier said. "We ask the same of each. But we do not tell each about the other. Or of the conditions."

"That is risky," Ba Thun said.

"We will take the risk. Minister Ba Thun, ask Mr. Oh and Mr. Carson for written proposals from their companies. Obtain from Carson a commitment to restore the jobs program."

Ba Thun saw the successive nods go around the table and said, "I will do what I can."

"Now, the next item," the premier said. "The July festivities."

The inaugural journey of the UltraTrain was originally intended to be a somewhat subdued, if not a minor, event, something like the joining of the Central Pacific and Union Pacific railroads at Promontory Point, Utah. Originally, there were to be about sixty people present. Over the last year, however, it had blossomed into something else entirely.

The premier himself had decided the occasion was ideal for demonstrating to the international community the progress the Union of Myanmar was making under the administration of the SLORC. He had invited a few heads of state from neighboring nations. Then a few more. And surprisingly, many had accepted and would be represented in person or through an agent.

Other members of the committee had also had suggestions, and the guest list grew.

Stephanie Branigan, unable to resist the opportunity to display her company's engineering skills and products, had offered recommendations, and so now there were industry and governmental specialists in railroading from Japan, Germany, France, and the United States also coming.

Some of the guests would begin to arrive in Yangon as early as July 12. Jack Gilbert, who had been managing the logistics, had devised a schedule of flights, utilizing Myanmar air-force aircraft and General Technologies helicopters, which would take the visitors to Mandalay. The stream of transport aircraft and helicopters between the two major cities would be formidable on the twelfth, thirteenth, and fourteenth of July. The hotel rooms in Mandalay had been requisitioned and assigned to the guests. Many of Ba Thun's assistants were already in Mandalay, seeing to the preparations.

On the fifteenth, the guests would board the UltraTrain at Mandalay's Central Station at noon. Less than two hours later, after traveling at two hundred miles per hour, the train would arrive at Rangoon Station, where a gigantic reception was planned.

Although construction on many projects would continue for many more years, this event had come to symbolize the Union of Myanmar's arrival in the world community, and as Branigan would have it, the nation's leading-edge step into the next century. The media coverage would be extensive.

Ba Thun thumbed through the typewritten notes on the table before him and waited.

The premier asked, "Where does the guest list stand now?"

"We had set six hundred and forty persons as the maximum," Ba Thun said. "Mr. Gilbert explained to me that the platforms at Central Station and Rangoon Station would accept that many cars. However, due to the requests from television and newspaper correspondents, we have added another car. There will be sixty-five correspondents accompanying us."

"Over seven hundred people," the cultural minister observed, "and many of them carrying famous names. With the events of the past few days, I begin to see this excursion less as a public-relations extravaganza and more as the ideal target."

"My thought, exactly," the premier said. "What do we do about it?"

"I would cancel it," the minister of culture said. "We talk of the worldview, and I cannot imagine anything more damaging to us than if that train is somehow destroyed."

"I concur," the interior minister said.

The treasury man was less resistant. "The celebration must take place. A successful inaugural train trip will do more for us in the long run, in terms of tourism dollars and a lessening of the reputation for human-rights abuses. My friends, we need the money."

"Then," the premier said, "the only course is to substantially increase our security."

"The air force will be flying close support on the train, with helicopters and combat aircraft," Ba Thun said.

"Unless it rains."

"Unless it rains," he agreed.

"As minister of defense, I will deploy two battalions of the First Division along the route," the premier decided.

"There is another aspect to consider," the treasury minister said. "If the railway line is cut again in the next six or seven days, we could have our seven hundred guests waiting in Mandalay with no train to ride. To say the least, the humiliation would be extreme."

"Tell Colonel Mauk to increase his surveillance," the premier ordered.

"Colonel Mauk demands additional troops in order to accomplish that," Ba Thun said. "He says he is spread too thinly as it stands. It is his weekly request, as you know."

"It is not acceptable," the minister of the interior said. "His troop strength is already far above prudence on our part."

Ba Thun did not mention Mauk's recommendation for support from an independent command.

But the premier may have been inside Mauk's mind. He said, "I will simply deploy the First Division battalions early. The orders will be drawn up this afternoon, and they will be en route in the morning. They will not report to Mauk. Would that be acceptable to everyone?"

Again, the succession of nods passed the resolution.

Ba Thun thought that the soldiers spread along the seven-hundred-kilometer route would be a deterrent to Daw Tan.

Though not a large one.

Pagoda Road, Yangon

Just under the new elevated track and across the old conventional track, north of the downtown area on Pagoda Road, was the State School of Music and Drama. Carson didn't know why he was going there, but the message taken by Becky Johnson was emphatic. The drama school was only a short distance from the compound, so he walked.

It had rained in the late afternoon, and the streets were freshly washed, the stale odors scrubbed away. The crowd was thinner here, a few groups strolling the street after the dinner hour. One of the strollers was his bodyguard; he picked him out a couple times when he looked back suddenly. Groups of students were gathered in outdoor cafes, engaged in animated discussions. He tried to remember a time when he worried about the state of the world without realizing the reality. It seemed like a long time ago.

He took his time and arrived at the school a few minutes after nine o'clock.

There were lights on in some of the rooms of the building, and he assumed the artistic students were involved in evening classes, which was better than staging protest marches in his view. From somewhere, he heard a choir singing. The alto voice was especially clear, though the language escaped him. Taking the steps two at a time, he climbed to the front door, pulled it open, and stepped inside.

Mauk was waiting for him.

"Good evening, Mr. Carson."

"Colonel."

"We can go in here. It will be private."

Mauk unlocked a door and led him into a darkened office. He turned on the lights, shut the door, and said, "It is an administrator's office. There are no listening devices."

They sat in two armchairs in front of the desk facing each other.

Mauk sat with his elbows on the arms of the chair, his hands locked together, his fingers twiddling. He said, "Before, you and I agreed that we would be candid with each other, is that not true?"

"That is true."

"And yet, we have not been entirely open."

To hell with it.

"That is also true," Carson said. It might be the time to find out just how trustworthy Mauk really was.

"I think that Jack Gilbert was your *confidant*. Perhaps Miss Branigan is, also."

"Jack and I were close. We could bounce ideas off each other."

"And he can no longer do that for you."

Carson shrugged a response.

"You have been lucky, Mr. Carson. I myself have had no one in the same role as your Mr. Gilbert. I am most often left to my own counsel, and I freely admit that my counsel is frequently lacking. At this moment, I propose that you and I share our innermost thoughts."

Carson found himself pursing his lips, doubtful.

Mauk read his expression correctly.

"To assure you of my good faith, I will, in your idiom, 'spill my guts' to you. Please take what I say in confidence."

Carson wasn't certain he wanted to know everything the colonel knew, but he said, "I will."

"First of all, we are meeting here since my orderly room has suspect ears in it. I know of one pair of them, which I make use of from time to time, but there may be more."

Carson shook his head affirmatively.

"I am sure you understand, in the broad perspective, some of the political elements present in Myanmar?"

"I think so."

"Let me summarize a few of the elements. The State Law and Order Restoration Committee, in response to international pressures, is attempting to align the nation according to worldly concerns, simultaneously improving its infrastructure. That is their primary agenda."

"Agreed."

"And yet, there are seven people on the committee, each of whom may have private, and perhaps dissimilar, goals. The premier has always been closemouthed, and he is difficult to read. Yet, I must remember that he came out of a strict discipline, and he prefers strict discipline. This business with the students and the dissatisfied—and unemployed—workers must weigh on him heavily. He would, I truly believe, prefer to take direct action to suppress the dissension. I give him high marks for restraint."

"I'll buy that interpretation," Carson said.

"The cultural minister, whom I have known for fifteen years, is a religious and conservative man. He does his utmost to support the arts, such as this school. I trust him, but I also know that he . . . accepts gratuities. It is a tradition."

"Yes."

"Both the treasury minister and the minister of the interior would like to be premier. For that reason, I am careful with both men. They seem to me to be capable of betrayal, though perhaps in small ways."

Carson didn't know either man well, so he kept his mouth shut.

"Minister Ba Thun is also difficult to discern," Mauk said. "He can be stubborn, and on the surface, I think he strives to improve conditions for all. He does, however, give me the . . . feeling that he has a hidden agenda."

"I don't know about that. I'll grant his stubbornness, but most of our dealings have proven to be mostly fair."

"As with the schedule extension?"

"That's a case of stubbornness, I grant."

"I am trying to be very open here, Mr. Carson."

"Okay. I don't know why he took the position he took. It doesn't seem to benefit the country or GTI."

"Yes. That is a puzzle, but let us leave it for a minute. That is my general picture of the government. Is it yours?"

"Pretty much."

"Now, there are the chieftains and the hill tribes. For many years, the posture between the government and the chieftains has been one of, shall we say, tolerance. If we do not interfere with them, they will not interfere with us. We allow them to maintain private armies, though it is understood that they will not be armed beyond hand-carried weapons. They have aircraft, even jet trainers, though they are not to be armed. Do you know the hierarchy?"

"I understand that Khim Nol is the big guy, and that Tan, Shwe, and Kaing have a great deal of autonomy, but essentially report to Nol."

"Correct. Now, within your own organization, that of the contractors, there are also some distinctions."

"That's right," Carson agreed.

"Most of your subcontractors do not create problems?"

"No."

"Hyun Oh?"

"Hypai Industries has a separate contract. They don't work through us, but with us."

"And Hypai Industries was one of the failed bidders for the master contract," Mauk said.

"True. One of the failed bidders."

"All right. Given that picture, let me share with you some facts. They are piecemeal; they may not be related; they may not even be pertinent. They are facts that I have accumulated."

Carson leaned forward, his elbows on his knees, concentrating on the colonel's monologue.

"The policy of the SLORC is that committee members or ministry chairs meeting with foreigners must keep notes of the meetings."

"I didn't know that."

"It is true. The notes are maintained in files in City Hall. I have reviewed them, though I was not supposed to. There is, for example, no record of a meeting that I witnessed between Hyun Oh and U Ba Thun. I do not know their topic.

"Additionally, Oh has met with Khim Nol. The subject of their discussion is unknown. I have reason to believe, though no evidence, that Oh has also met with Daw Tan.

"Those meetings mystify me."

"And me," Carson said.

"Nito Kaing met with Daw Tan in Pegu. Again, that is a supposition, but I think it likely."

"It's important?"

"Khim Nol does not care to have private meetings between the chieftains when he is not present."

"Ah."

"U Ba Thun has met several times with Khim Nol, most often in the company of the other chieftains. The notes of those meetings are on file, but they seem abbreviated for the length of time involved. I suspect that topics other than those reported took place."

Mauk looked at him as if the recital were over.

Carson said, "When you told me you were going to list facts for me, I expected you to talk about the attacks against facilities, against me."

"Those are certainly relevant facts, Mr. Carson, though obvious. I would, based on instinct and the current unavailability of Daw Tan, lay the incidents to him and his lieutenants. Whether he acts on his own, or at the instruction of others, is open to debate."

Carson thought about Mauk's comments for several minutes before he said, "I don't know the personalities of the chieftains well, but what I think you're telling me is that there is ample opportunity for treachery here."

Mauk smiled. "Such as?"

"You're not going to hold this against me?"

"My solemn promise."

"There may be some scheme involving a member, or maybe

a couple of members, of the State Law and Order Restoration Committee. It would, I assume, be aimed at acquiring power."

"It is possible."

"Hyun Oh, perhaps with Hypai's concurrence, would have a profit motive. He wouldn't do anything to jeopardize his relationship with the government, but he might make some deals on the side with the chieftains, which would eventually improve his bottom line."

"Against whom?"

"General Technologies. Any contract Hyun Oh can take away from us benefits him."

"Again, it is possible. What of the chieftains?"

"I'm at something of a disadvantage here, Colonel, not knowing them well enough. Offhand, there could be a power struggle of some sort taking place. Maybe Daw Tan is operating independently of Khim Nol, and Nol doesn't like it. Maybe Tan would like to assume Nol's throne. Or Kaing. I heard some story about her knocking off her husband in order to take his place."

"It is a popular anecdote, and possibly one based in truth. All of what you say, Mr. Carson, is not only likely, but even probable."

"Which one do you favor, Colonel?"

Mauk smiled enigmatically. "All of them. As you said, there is ample opportunity for treachery. I am certain Daw Tan has a plot in mind, perhaps with Nito Kaing's assistance, to take over Nol's position."

"And the committee?"

"It is difficult to assess. If pushed, I would say—between us—that the ministers of the interior and the treasury would like to see another form of administration."

The two of them were silent for a long time. Mauk continued to wage war with his left and right fingertips. The security chief was placing a lot of faith in Carson. Some of what he had revealed would be called betrayal on his own part by his superiors.

Carson finally replied. "Now, you want to know about me?"

"If you do not mind."

"All right. Along the political lines, first." Carson detailed the clauses in the master contract that allowed him to withhold jobs until the last year of the contract. "I stopped hiring in order to put pressure on Ba Thun to extend the schedule deadline. When he proved stubborn on that, I offered him a way out by proposing a mining contract."

"What is this mining contract?"

Carson explained how he thought new technologies applied to the mining industry would benefit both Myanmar and GTI. He did not mention why the contract was important to GTI.

"This is a dangerous game you play, Mr. Carson."

"I didn't know the students were going to get involved."

"The students *always* get involved."

"I had hoped for long lines at City Hall, the unemployed banging on government doors."

"There are other agitators, as well. You can be assured that the committee is feeling the pressure. Have you had a response yet?"

"No."

"I hope," Mauk said, "that Ba Thun will not be stubborn on this issue. A social explosion can be more difficult to deal with than one in a microwave station or under a railroad bridge. What else have you been doing?"

Carson told him about the additional Listening Posts sown near the chieftain's encampments. With some reluctance, he detailed the other activities of the Data Processing Center, tapping telephones all over the country.

"My own?"

"Yes."

"Go on."

"That's it. All we've been trying to do is gather information, hopefully in time to prevent further attacks against us. We were too late for the bridge."

"That is not all, Mr. Carson."

"Honestly, Colonel . . ."

Mauk smiled. "Historically, that is all, yes. I cannot imagine, however, that you will take Mr. Gilbert's murder serenely. What have you planned?"

Carson wouldn't have told Branigan, but after the past hour of listening to Mauk, he thought that a few things had changed. He didn't have Gilbert to trust, so he would trust Mauk.

"Oh, that."

"That," Mauk said, encouraging him with a nod.

"I'm going to blow the hell out of Daw Tan."

The colonel didn't seem surprised. He said, "That could upset some people."

"At this point, I don't give a damn, Colonel."

"Very well. I will help you."

TWENTY-THREE

Moulmein Airport

In the predawn hours of Sunday, Daw Tan waited off the side of the unlit airstrip. It was dark, and only a few lights were visible in buildings near the middle of the field. Moulmein was not a round-the-clock airport, so the landing lights were activated only when necessary.

A strong breeze blew in from the Gulf of Martaban, so he had taken his station on the western end of the strip, deposited there by Kanbe.

He did not have to wait long before he heard the subdued whine of the jet engines. It circled to the north of the city once, then headed back to the east, lining up for a landing into the prevailing wind.

Tan's pilots were experienced at night landings on terrible fields. The long, paved runway at Moulmein, even unlit, would present no problems.

And it did not. The Cessna T-37C, a jet trainer which had ended production in 1977, and which had become available on secondary aircraft markets, rolled to a stop, and Daw Tan trotted across the concrete to where it had stopped. Even this close, it was difficult to see because of its black paint.

The pilot had the canopy raised and the right turbojet engine stilled, and Tan carefully found the push-in step in front of the right engine intake. Shoving his foot into the step, he reached up and grabbed the coaming, then pulled himself up and into the tandem-seat cockpit. The pilot, who was a Thai named Kul Pot, restarted the right engine and turned the aircraft around as he was strapping into his seat and buckling the helmet on his head. The canopy came down, deadening some of the noise of the engines. With the power available to him, Pot did not return to the east end of the runway but took off downwind, climbing quickly and turning north to avoid Thai airspace.

Daw Tan did not understand airplanes very well. With his single eye, he could never have flown them, and so he had simply owned them. To his mind, they served two functions: transport for people and product, and a symbol of his power. There were nine aircraft in his fleet, two of them helicopters, two of them the Cessna trainer, and the rest transports of various description. Shwe and Kaing each had nine airplanes, too. Khim Nol owned twenty-two. It was yet another demonstration of the equality and the superiority of beings.

He would prefer to own the twenty-two.

At fourteen thousand feet, the dawn broke blindingly into his eye, and he pulled the helmet's tinted visor down. He watched Kul Pot working with the controls, adjusting trim, tuning in Vortac stations to guide his flight. The airspeed indicator reported that they were flying at 580 kilometers per hour.

Kul Pot loved what he did, and as a mercenary, he would have flown for anyone willing to provide him the airplane, much less a salary. Among the other pilots, he was fond of telling war stories, or rather, stories of his great escapes and great air battles with drug-enforcement craft of the Thai government. To hear him tell it, his foes were all ex-CIA Air America and ex-U.S. Air Force pilots qualified as aces, and Pot's exploits, therefore, proved him a greater aviator.

Perhaps it was true.

Perhaps Daw Tan would find out.

The T-37 in its earlier models had served only as a trainer. The T-37C was capable of carrying four Sidewinder missiles or two 250-pound bombs. Later models, known as the A-37 Dragonfly were much better armed and were used by many governments in counterinsurgency roles.

By way of the unspoken agreement with the government, Shwe, Kaing, and Tan were allowed to have their T-37s as long as they were not armed. The agreement had been satisfactory so far, though Daw Tan had prepared for contingencies. He had a cache of weapons for his airplanes, including two machine-gun pods with two hundred rounds of 12.7-millimeter ammunition, forty-eight bombs, and even six of the Sidewinder missiles.

He intended to press Nito Kaing for an agreement whereby he provided her two T-37s with missiles and bombs, and the four airplanes would be used to demolish Khim Nol's air force. He would still do that, but now he had a new mission for his jet airplanes.

The new operation was forced upon him since he had been unable to get close to Christopher Carson. Tan and Kanbe had tried for two nights to approach the foreigner's compound, but found it surrounded by government soldiers. They had driven Highway 1 and discovered that large numbers of walking patrols and armored cars were dispersed along the railway. The repair of the trestle at Pyu was all but complete.

Tan had attempted to lie in wait for either Carson or Branigan between the compound and the airport, but their paths had not crossed.

And the time was short. He had but eight days in which to cancel the government's plans.

The instructions Khim Nol had given him were to eliminate Carson and Branigan—and that action accomplished personally—and to disrupt the new communications and railway systems. The railway, especially, was to be severed before the celebratory journey on July 15. Khim Nol did not want thousands of foreigners flocking to Mandalay to ride the train.

Daw Tan, in light of the heavy protection provided for Carson and Branigan, had rethought the entire scheme. Daw Tan found Khim Nol to be decidedly shortsighted.

Rather than probe at all these things, he could, in one fell swoop, accomplish the entire job at once.

On the intercom, he asked the pilot, Kul Pot, "You have often flown in bad weather?"

"Often, Chieftain."

"It does not bother you? What of your colleague T-37 pilot?"

"Neither of us worries about a little rain."

"Let me add other factors," Tan said. "Perhaps a few government helicopters or airplanes. Armored cars with machine guns."

The pilot turned his attention from his instrument panel to Tan. There was a lively glint in his eyes. "It would be best if we were armed."

"With, let us say, the machine-gun pod and two bombs apiece."

"The Sidewinder missiles would be more effective against aircraft."

"But your assigned objective would not be aircraft. Your target would be a train."

The man's eyes positively glittered now. "A train."

"A very high-speed train."

"The new UltraTrain. It travels at over two hundred and thirty miles per hour, Chieftain."

"So, you could not hit it?"

"Of course I could hit it. The matter of detection . . ."

"Should be of little concern," Tan told him. "Shwe and Kaing both have similar airplanes. If the pursuit is heavy, you would simply land on Shwe's strip, abandon the airplane, and run. Let them bomb Shwe in retaliation."

"It is an interesting proposition, Chieftain."

"I do not mean it to be merely a proposition."

"Then I look forward to it. When?"

"On July fifteenth, shortly after midday."

GTI operations, Mingaladon Airport, Yangon

The Boeing 707 had been held over in Honolulu for hydraulic repairs, but Carson had been notified as soon as it put down at Mingaladon. He had been accompanied to the airport by two carloads of soldiers. Mauk had gone overboard with the protection game, he thought.

They were still unloading the semitrailers when he walked into the operations office, so he skirted the high counter and went back to the Data Processing Center. When he knocked, Carlos Montoya opened the door for him.

"Good morning, Carlos."

"Morning, Mr. Carson."

"Do you have the transcription for the item you called me about last night?"

"I do. Come on in."

Carson locked the door behind him, as if it mattered. He hadn't had the heart to tell Montoya that his secret operation had been compromised. By no one other than the boss.

Kiki Olson was sitting at one of the improvised consoles, and she looked up and smiled. "Hi, Chris!"

"Don't you have important things to be doing?"

"There's a teeny little software bug here, and I've about got him. I thought *this* was important."

"It is. But don't forget we want to sell your little toys, too."

"I haven't. I pitched the University on Friday afternoon, and I think they'll go for a whole lab of PCs."

"We discounting much?"

"Thirty-five percent. But we'll make it up with future sales."

Carlos came back with a printout. "We've got one machine set up now to read voice off any tape we want in hard copy and convert it to visual. Doesn't take long at all, Mr. Carson."

"Carlos, would you call me Chris, please? No reason for you to be any different from anyone else."

"Uh, yes, sir."

Carson read through the transcript, then moved to a table

and grabbed a phone. He called Mauk's number, he now had committed to memory.

Some sergeant put him right through.

"Yes, Mr. Carson?"

"Daw Tan has gone home."

"You are certain?"

"He called his home phone last night and asked for a plane to pick him up in Moulmein. The timing must have been pre-arranged, or in some kind of code, because no one talked about a time or date."

"I do not know whether or not we are fortunate."

"All these soldiers may have scared him off."

"Daw Tan does not frighten, I think," Mauk said.

"Anyway, the indication is that he's back in Man Na-su."

"Thank you," the colonel said and hung up.

Carson turned back to Montoya. "Have we gotten anything from those Listening Posts scattered around the bandit camps?"

"Nothing substantive. We have miles of tape recordings of feet tramping, trucks roaring, and airplanes taking off, but nothing that we can interpret as significant."

"Okay, thanks. The intelligence agencies we sell those things to must have better ears than we do."

"What I think they've got," Montoya said, "is comparative software programs. They've got sounds in storage, and the computer tells them if they're listening to a certain kind of tank or something similar."

"We don't want to spend our time developing that crap," Carson said.

"I didn't think so."

Carson went back through operations to the hangar. Looking through the wide open doors to the big AirFreightCharter plane, he saw a forklift trundling toward it, carrying the two crated caskets.

Goodbye, brother. Sleep well.

Don Evans left the cargo plane by a side hatch, spotted Carson, and came into the hangar.

"That little rock?"

"Yeah?"

"They'll never find it. Hell, I probably couldn't find it again."

"Well, get on a phone, Don, and call Abrams. Give him at least a clue since he's going to meet this bird on the other side."

The boss? Hell, I've never talked to him before."

"Then you need to. We want him to remember you the next time I make bonus recommendations."

"Oh, yeah! Good idea."

"What happened to Mack Little?"

"I gave him and his assistants my truck so they could go get something to eat. They'll be back in a bit."

"I hope they don't get lost."

"Billy Kasperik went with them."

Carson gave Evans the home phone number for Abrams, and the air fleet's manager went back into the operations office.

Carson walked around the two short, forty-foot semitrailers. They looked like semitrailers except for a few holes punched in their sides and tops for exhaust and other connectors. Behind them, at the back of the hangar, was a long wooden crate and a couple of smaller crates. They looked like crates, anyway.

Next to the two trailers, resting on a bunch of two by fours to lift it above the concrete floor, was a standard InstaStructure product. It was a honeycombed arrangement of carbon-reinforced fiberglass, about six inches thick. This piece appeared to be thirty feet long by twelve feet wide. Carson knew they were extremely light and extremely strong, often used as premanufactured floors in quick construction jobs.

He wandered out into the sunlight where a Skycrane was parked near the door. The ungainly thing looked like a giant praying mantis. The rotor had a seventy-two-foot diameter and stood twenty-five feet off the ground. When the rotor was turning, the whole aircraft was eighty-eight feet long. It consisted of one long fuselage, high off the ground, a pod hanging down from the fuselage in front for three crewmen and a couple of jump seats, a pair of 4,800-shaft horsepower turboshaft engines on top, and a widely spaced set of main landing gear. The idea was that it could lower itself to straddle a load or a military pod—surgical unit, command post, communications center, troop carrier—and lift it for transport to the field. It was a real workhorse and consistently carried heavy loads—railway sections, bridge components, even completed small buildings—into rugged terrain, where other forms of cargo haulers were hampered by inadequate access.

Carson had flown the S-64 Skycrane a few times, but was by no means proficient with it. Flying it felt akin to handling a sixty-foot motor coach dragging a twenty-two-foot boat on a trailer, when one was used to driving a Volkswagen Bug.

He turned back to the hangar when he heard new voices enter. Billy Kasperik, Mack Little, and a few other people he didn't know came through the door from operations.

Little saw him coming along the side of a trailer.

"You son of a bitch!"

"Hi, Mack. Glad to see you, too."

"It's hot here."

"If we'd planned better, we could have air-conditioned the place for you."

"You could get me killed."

"I knew you'd volunteer. Anything to get out of that stuffy lab."

"When Dex asked me if I'd volunteer for a quick jaunt to Myanmar, he didn't really say what we'd be doing."

"You want to go home? I'll do it."

"Hell, no! You'd break my machine."

The Boeing 707 on the tarmac fired its engines, drowning out conversation for a few minutes, until it pulled away.

Little turned somber, dipping his head in the direction of the airplane. "That was Jack?"

Carson nodded.

"The bastards. All right, let's put this thing together."

"You know what we want to do?"

"Don Evans talked it over with Billy, and Billy and the rest of us worked it out over breakfast."

"Had to show 'em where they could get a decent meal," Kasperik said. "You got to do everything for the new guys in-country."

"So, tell me."

"I've got to work with reduced power, what I can generate with six diesel generators."

"That going to affect the output?"

"Not that much, Chris. We're going to pull the generators out of the trailers and mount them on that slab of fiberglass. Billy says it'll hold up, but I've got my doubts."

"Bullshit!" Kasperik said. "That piece is stronger than the Space Shuttle. Hell, it's made of the same stuff used on the Shuttle. Problem is, Chris, I can only go twenty-seven feet long if I want to lift that slab up behind the cab on the Skycrane. The bird could handle the weight, no sweat, but dimensions are the problem, and I don't want to suspend a bigger unit fifty feet under the chopper. So, we're going to use six generators, but that'll still leave us space for the fuel cells we need to run them."

"You leaving it exposed?"

"Nah. Once we bolt those hummers down, I'll build a little framework of fiberglass struts and we'll cover it with canvas."

"What about operation?"

Little pointed to a sandy-haired guy of twenty-something years. "Jerry's my generator man. He's going to have his controls in the cab, back in the third crewmember's seat."

A clear Plexiglas pod on the back of the helicopter's cab allowed the third man to see to the rear and control lifting operations.

"How about you?"

"We'll pull one of the jump seats and somehow screw around and get my computer in its place. I sit in the other jump seat."

"And the laser?"

Kasperik laughed. "Evans like to come unglued when I told

him I was going to punch holes in his aircraft. But we're bolting the tripod through the skin to structural members on the left side of the cab."

"On the side?"

"Low down. It'll look like hell, but it'll work."

"I've got to do some reprogramming," Little said, "since I'm turning it on its side. My aiming system has to be adjusted by ninety degrees."

Carson noted that Little hadn't objected when Carson called it a laser. He didn't think anyone was going to call it the Ruby Star.

"I've never operated it from a mobile platform," Little went on. "It may be touchy, but I think the computer will be able to compensate for any movement in the chopper."

"It's not a true fire-control computer?"

"Oh, no. Just something we jury-rigged in the lab for our tests."

"What about sleep? You guys need it?"

"After the first three hours on that tin can they call a cargo plane, I was so exhausted I went into a coma for the rest of the trip. We can sleep later."

Carson was glad that Little didn't ask about the mission for the laser. He didn't want to talk about it in front of Kasperik's crews.

"Okay, then, I'll get out of your way and see if you can actually make it work."

As Carson turned away from the group, Little followed him and stopped him near the door to the operations office. He looked around to make certain no one could overhear him.

"Dex said you'd found another ruby?"

"It just took off. Dex will get it stateside."

"Damn. That's good, Chris."

"Mack, thanks for coming."

"I wouldn't have missed it. Jack was my friend, too."

Carson went to look for Evans, to make the other preparations.

GTI compound, Yangon

On Monday morning, Hyun Oh was in his office enjoying the fact that he had just dressed down Kim Sung-Young for being late with the weekly financial report. Sung-Young could not understand Oh's renewed confidence and was understandably confused. He might even call Mr. Pai, learn of Pai's faith in Oh, and become depressed about the odds of his assuming the director's position.

The prospect of Sung-Young's depression encouraged Oh.

At eight-thirty, Mr. Gyi called him.

"Hello, Mr. Gyi! How are you this fine morning?"

"I am well, Mr. Oh, and you?"

"Excellent, sir! How may I be of service to you?"

"After long consideration, my friends and I have agreed that an investment in the telephone company makes economic sense. We wish to proceed."

"Very good, Mr. Gyi. What I will do is prepare the legal papers, along with a memorandum of understanding. I will then send the papers to you, and if you would be so good, please sign the memorandum and send one copy back to me. That is simply to cement our joint intentions to negotiate. You may then have your attorneys peruse the legal documents. When that is done, we will all get together and discuss any alterations in the language or in the provisions that you might like to suggest. Will this be satisfactory?"

"Absolutely, Mr. Oh."

"Fine. I will look forward to hearing from you."

When he hung up, Oh was quite pleased with himself. This item on his Sunday report to Mr. Pai would further increase his stature.

The telephone rang again.

He picked it up and said, "Mr. Oh."

"This is Minister Ba Thun."

"Ah, Minister! I am happy to hear from you."

"Mr. Oh, I have tested your mining proposal with other members of the committee."

Ba Thun's tone did not give him hope, and Oh steeled himself for rejection.

"I am pleased," he said.

"The decision has been reached that we need to know much more about such a project. I would request from you a detailed, written description of the project, particularly in regard to forecasts for production and the division of profits."

Relief flooded through Oh's arteries.

"Absolutely! You shall have it within the week."

"That will be fine. Good day, Mr. Oh."

In his happiness, Oh released a long sigh that seemed to fill his office. He could not wait to make his weekly report to Mr. Pai.

Myanmar army barracks, Yangon

On Monday afternoon, Lon Mauk received a call on the private line that Carson's technicians had installed in his office that very morning. His calls no longer had to go through the switchboard in the orderly room.

He was a little uncertain about how to answer the second telephone on his desk. None in the government knew of it and would not be calling him, so he did not use his normally crisp and military opening.

"Yes?"

"Chris Carson, Colonel."

"Good afternoon. And thank you for the telephone."

"It's not a bribe, Colonel. We can be candid on this line."

"No one else is listening?"

"Just people I know."

"I am not certain that that makes me feel better."

"A couple more weeks, and we'll pull out the taps," Carson promised. "I called to tell you that tonight's the night."

"What time?"

"Eight o'clock. I wonder if you could call off the guards around seven? Give them a bit of a holiday until tomorrow morning."

"Which guards?"

"The guys who are watching me along with the detail at GTI operations."

"Yes, I will see to it."

"Do you want to come along, Colonel?"

"I would like that very much."

"I'll see you about seven-thirty."

Mauk hung up the telephone and went back to the duty roster he had been reviewing. Since the battalions of the First Division had been moved into place along the railway, he had been able to recall forty of his men. He did not think the premier—the defense minister—realized that the arrival of the First Division troops had freed up men for the Myanmar Modernization security detail. He luxuriated in the discrepancy, and he used his manpower wisely to reinforce the guard at the foreigners' compound and to provide other relief. For the first time in months, and by shifting duty assignments carefully, he was able to provide substitutes in order to give others two-day leaves of absence. Within a month, he would give each of his men a short respite. It did wonders for morale.

He wondered how he was to improve his own morale.

Perhaps tonight, he would find his answer.

Mingaladon Airport, Yangon

Carson, Little, Evans, and Kasperik had had dinner together in the cafeteria at the Zoo. Branigan, eating with a bunch of her own people, had given him several reproving looks from across the room. Evidently, his association with the stranger Mack Little—whom she did not know—convinced her that he was up to no good. Being with Kasperik, whom she did know, probably didn't help, either.

Though he was up to no good, Carson didn't want her to think so. He delayed their leaving the dining room until after the UltraTrain crowd had departed. He delayed leaving the compound until he had called Abrams—not getting him, but leaving a message into his voice mail, "We've now got a formal request for a proposal on the mining project. Would you mind getting the accountants, lawyers, and mining people hot on drawing up something? It looks like we're competing with Hypai on this."

He didn't report that his knowledge of the Hypai Industries submission had been obtained through Carlos Montoya's tap on Ba Thun's telephone. This was getting dangerously close to industrial espionage, and Carson didn't want to engage in any of that. Knowing that others were bidding, he thought, was all right. He had told Montoya, though, that if Oh or Ba Thun mentioned numbers on the phone, Carson didn't want to know about it.

He also didn't mention that he had reached a compromise of sorts with Ba Thun. Carson wouldn't agree to reopening the hiring process just yet, but he had ordered the training schools to begin inducting new and small classes of trainees. Washington, Branigan, and Oh were all relieved to see some progress on that end. The appearance of potential job openings would take some of the pressure off the SLORC and yet allow Carson to maintain some leverage. Plus, it would get all of those instructors who had been idled back into the production of graduates, and it would also create a pool of qualified entry-level employees for whenever he decided to begin hiring anew.

They arrived at the airport in two utility vehicles, nine members strong. There had been no trail of bodyguards on the trek up Prome Road. When they passed the army barracks, a single Land Rover pulled out and followed them.

There were a hell of a lot more men involved than Carson wanted to put at risk, but every one of them had volunteered

happily. The four pilots—two for the Skycrane and two for
the S-65 Stallion—had been handpicked by Evans. Evans was
going along, he said, because they were his helicopters and
he'd complain to someone, anyone, if he wasn't accommo-
dated. Kasperik was going along because it was his fiberglass
platform that mounted the generators. When Carson told him
the rationale wasn't good enough, Kasperik said, "The other
reason is that I'll kick your ass to hell and back if I don't
get a ride."

They parked in front of the building and got out. Colonel
Mauk pulled up and parked next to them. Carson took a couple
minutes to introduce the colonel to Little and his generator
operator, then the pilots.

He raised his hand and his voice, and got the attention of
the entire group. "Gentlemen, the colonel is not here. Is that
understood? By the same token, Colonel Mauk does not remember any of you."

Unlocking the door, Evans led them through the operations
room and the hangar to the tarmac. The Skycrane and the Stallion were parked in a row with other helicopters.

A single guard prowled among them, carrying an M-16.
Mauk did not make a comment about the weapon. Carson did
not tell him that the man was guarding a fifty-million-dollar
addition to the Skycrane.

Mauk and Carson walked up to the flying crane, and Mauk
looked over the clumsy and elongated attachment to the side
of the craft.

"What in the world is that?"

"Believe me, Colonel, when I say that I'd like to tell you,
but I can't. It truly is classified. You will, however, get to see
it in action, though I would ask that you not report your ob-
servations."

"You have my word," Mauk said. His face was still a map
of curiosity as he walked farther along and stopped to study
the canvas-covered load slung from the helicopter's hoist. Additional nylon lines had been wrapped around it and attached

to the overhead fuselage to steady the load. Under a full test, with the helicopter airborne and the generators running at full throttle, the vibration had been noticeable for the pilot, but was not distracting enough that it would interfere with his flight control.

The guard shoved his rifle inside a parked Gazelle and became a ground crewman, pulling chocks and releasing tie-downs. Evans and Kasperik went to help him.

"We'll go in the Stallion," Carson said, heading toward the lowered cargo ramp of the S-65.

The giant heavy-lift helicopter was known as the CH-53 Sea Stallion to the Navy and Marine Corps, who had first commissioned its development by Sikorsky. Powered by twin 3,925-shaft horsepower General Electric turboshaft engines, it was capable of lifting a ten-ton load from its external hoist. The rotor was comprised of six blades with a seventy-two-foot diameter. The model had seen use in Vietnam for search and rescue as well as transport. The Navy used them for mine-sweeping.

Carson climbed the cargo ramp, staying clear of the rollers set in the decking. Winches at the forward end of the cargo bay were used to draw heavy loads into the interior.

A heavy rubber fuel bladder was tied down in the middle of the cargo bay.

"What is this?" Mauk asked. "If the information is not classified."

"Fuel bladder, Colonel. We fill them up here and take them out to construction sites. In this case, we've loaded aviation fuel. We've got a five-hundred-mile flight ahead of us, and these choppers can make it barely, though they can't get back. We're going to the GTI airstrip outside Mandalay and refuel, which should see us through the operation. Still, we're carrying an extra thousand gallons, just in case."

"You prepare well, Mr. Carson."

"I hope well enough, Colonel."

Carson had the distinct impression that, lately, most of what he had been doing had turned out badly. The abortive raid on the Chinatown apartment. The too-late arrival at the Pyu bridge. The attempt to hide from Mauk his information gathering and armory.

And worst of all, his missteps with Branigan. If she had become wary of him, he couldn't blame her. Refer to the above listing.

Behind the flight deck, several extra seats had been fitted to the deck, and Carson settled into one. Mauk took the seat next to him.

"You are not going to fly the machine?"

"Believe me, I want to. And I might take a short stint somewhere along the way. I'm not rated for the S-65 though, so I'll leave it to the guys who fly it regularly."

"Do you always pick and choose among the regulations you will follow or not follow?" Mauk asked.

Carson grinned at him, "I guess I do."

After they had preflighted their helicopter, the pilots came aboard and closed the ramp. Evans and Kasperik entered through the port-side hatch and took seats. The copilot passed out headsets, and they plugged into the intercom system. Twelve minutes later, they were airborne and headed north.

Carson had a large window next to him, and he watched the landscape pass below at 120 miles per hour. The S-65 could do better than that—196 miles per hour at sea level—but was constrained by the Skycrane's maximum.

They put down at the GTI strip outside Mandalay just after eleven o'clock. There was a three-quarter moon, but it was partially obscured by cloud cover. The ceiling was seven thousand feet. The strip was deserted except for two guards who helped them refuel. They were airborne again by eleven-forty.

Carson had attempted to be prudent and to restrain himself, but with every mile closer to Man Na-su, the more agitated he became. Finally, he unstrapped his seat harness, pulled the headset off, and stood up.

Mauk grinned at him and said something Carson couldn't hear.

He leaned over and Mauk repeated in his ear, "You are going to change the regulations?"

Carson grinned back at him. "Just a little," he yelled over the roar of the turboshafts.

Slipping past Mauk, he stuck his head into the flight compartment and tapped the copilot on the shoulder.

The man looked back, and a shadow of disappointment washed over his face.

They exchanged seats, and Carson buckled into the left seat. The pilot smiled at him, his face a little grotesque in the red light from the instrument panel.

Steph is right. It's hard for me to take the backseat.

The pilot had a clipboard in his lap, and Carson took it. The chart for the area was folded and stuck under the clip along with two photographs from the earlier photo recon flight.

"Where've you got us?" Carson asked over the intercom.

"That's Highway four-four-two passing under right now. Two, three lights up ahead? That should be Man Hpai. Tiny village. The compound is about twenty-five miles beyond the village."

Carson found their position on the chart and oriented himself. He remembered the area from his flight in the Beechcraft.

Leaning to the left, he looked out the side window and back. The Skycrane was two hundred yards behind, and a quarter-mile off to the left.

The radar scope in the panel ahead of him was passive at the moment, showing nothing, and also not radiating a signal that might be detected by hostile radars. He knew that Daw Tan's airstrip had a radar antenna.

Carson kept track of their course on the chart, and ten miles out, went to the radio. "Jackhammer Two, Jackhammer One."

The code names had been suggested by Billy Kasperik.

"This is Two."

"Let's douse the nav lights."

"Roger."

Carson reached over and cut off the navigation lights.

"This could turn into a hot LZ," Carson told the pilot. "With our passengers, we don't want any heroics."

"Got it."

He looked at the chart, then checked the chronometer on the panel.

"Two minutes."

They had been flying low, a thousand feet above ground level, but the pilot began losing more altitude. The peak to the north of the encampment was shown on the chart at 2,060 feet of altitude, and they were currently moving along a valley at 1,900 feet above sea level.

He couldn't take it anymore.

"Ah, hell! Let me have it." He put his hands lightly on the stick and collective, eased his feet onto the rudder pedals.

"Mr. Carson . . . okay."

"I'll pay for whatever I break."

"My neck?"

"That too."

He felt the pilot release the controls, then tested the feel lightly.

On the intercom, Colonel Mauk said, "Mr. Evans, you owe me twenty dollars American."

"Damn," Evans said, "I really thought he could do it."

Carson ignored them and tried to recall the layout. The airstrip ran parallel to the road leading into Man Na-su, and was a quarter-mile south of it. Daw Tan's spread had about fifteen small houses and sheds in addition to the big house, and the cluster of buildings was another quarter-mile from the airstrip.

"Jackhammer Two, One's going in."

"Roger that."

He dipped the nose and started down. The dark forests surrounding them absorbed whatever light the moon offered. It was difficult to judge the distance to the earth. He kept glancing at the AGL readout.

Altitude AGL 400 feet.

Found the road, a lighter color slashing through the forest. Turned slightly to follow it.

"My heading is zero-eight-five, Two."

"Roger. I've got a visual on you."

Airspeed 80 knots, 320 feet AGL.

"There!" the pilot said. "Bear right five."

Carson went into the slight turn, then saw the airfield. It was hacked out of the forest, and was only a darker spot in the blackness of the trees. As he angled away from the road, the clearing came closer. He saw a light. A yard light next to a maintenance building.

Airspeed 50 knots.

Altitude 160.

"Some of these trees reach seventy, eighty feet," the pilot said.

"You damned well take care of my aircraft," Evans said.

And then they were over the airstrip, shooting down its length.

Carson continued to decelerate.

Airspeed 30 knots.

The aircraft were all parked off the strip to the right. He counted seven.

"What have we got?"

"Chopper, two T-37s, one light twin, three transports. Christ! One of 'em's an old DC-6, four-engine job."

"Okay, Jackhammer Two. You've got seven in the middle of the strip on the right. Burn 'em!"

Carson circled out to the left, away from the housing compound. He pulled around and slowed to a hover. He heard and felt movement in the back as the passengers all moved to the window on the right side. He turned the Stallion a little, to give them a better view.

Mauk stuck his head into the flight compartment, standing between the two pilots.

"Somebody just came out of that shed," the pilot said.

"He's heard us, wonders who it is," Carson said.

Through the right window, past the pilot, Carson saw the Skycrane come in, picking it out by the flare of its engine exhaust. It came down the strip, hovered, turned to face the parked aircraft.

A bright crimson jet flashed from its side, lashed toward the ground, found a T-37.

All in an instant.

Silently.

No noise, other than the turbines turning.

In the dark, it was difficult to tell what the results were.

The airplane on the ground glowed for a second.

And then the fuel cell ignited.

A burst of reddish-orange.

"Excellent!" Mauk cried out.

"Hot damn!" the pilot echoed.

Then flames climbing toward the sky.

Lighting the ground, improving the view.

One by one, the laser ray lanced out, found prey, and ignited it.

Carson figured Little wasn't using full power, just finding fuel tanks, slicing them open, and heating the vapors until they burst into flame.

"That's seven," Mauk said. "It is amazing."

"The guy by the shed took off running into the woods," the pilot reported. "He's going to remember this night for the rest of his life."

"Jackhammer Two, One's on the move."

"Roger."

Carson ran up the power and shot back across the runway, passing quickly from the carnage that was now lighting the sky.

"Two's behind you," the radio blurted.

Carson turned on his navigation lights. There would be no pursuit now, and no reason to either hide or to invite a midair collision with the Skycrane.

The buildings came up fast. Lights were coming on all over the compound. People were outside, running around. The explosions of the fuel tanks had brought them out of slumber.

A few trucks were on the move, their headlights aimed in the direction of the airfield.

"Take the trucks, Two."

"Wilco."

Carson sideslipped to the right, to give Little a clear field of fire.

The laser specialist used more power this time.

Crimson fire spit from the Skycrane.

A truck on the ground exploded in a white-and-red flash.

Seconds later, the next truck all but vaporized.

And two others immediately cut their lights and ground to a halt, the drivers spilling to run for cover.

Systematically, the two helicopters moved across the compound, Carson picking out targets, and Little destroying them. Most of the inhabitants ran in terror for the forests and canyons.

They hit a fuel supply, which was spectacular.

They found an ordnance dump, which was even more spectacular, spewing fountains of fire and shrapnel that threatened the airborne craft.

Finally, Carson swung around and headed back to the large house. He eased collective and settled the chopper to the ground directly in front of the porch, fifty yards from it.

The pilot switched on the floodlight, and the porch of the house brightened as if it were noon.

Switching to the PA system for the external loudspeaker, Carson said, "Daw Tan, come out of the house!"

His voice boomed and echoed across the ground.

No one appeared on the porch.

On the radio, he said, "Mack, you there?"

"Got me."

"Can you take off just the left wing of the house?"

"In how large a piece?"

"Your choice."

The Skycrane was behind them, hovering sixty feet above the ground. This time, the laser emitted a steady, fine beam of cerise light. It reached out like the tongue of an anteater, lightly touched the stone wall of the house, then climbed the wall, walked across the thatched roof, winked out.

The roof caught fire.

Another shot with the laser, two feet closer to the end of the house wing, crawling up the wall, over the roof.

Pieces of the wall and roof crumbled, fell in.

Daw Tan appeared in the doorway at the front, shielding his eye from the blinding beam of the floodlight.

With the PA, Carson said, "Come away from the house and get in the helicopter."

On the intercom, he said, "Colonel, you ready?"

"We are ready."

Tan had trouble making his decision. In the bright light, Carson could clearly see the conflicting emotions crossing his ugly face. He looked to the north, where his airfield was in flames. He looked to the south, where his outbuildings, fuel, and arms were also in flames. Behind him, his house was also falling apart.

Carson hoped that he knew his entire world was falling apart.

He stepped down from the porch.

Began walking toward the helicopter, shielding his face from the light with his right hand.

The pilot tracked him with the light, kept it full in his face.

And before he reached the chopper, Evans, Kasperik, and Mauk intercepted him, pulled a black bag over his head, and secured his wrists with handcuffs. The black bag was to keep Mauk's identity anonymous.

A minute later, they were off the ground, headed back toward Mandalay and fuel.

"It's all yours," Carson told the pilot.

"Ah, jeez, boss. Thanks for nothing."

Ahlone Road, Yangon

At six o'clock on Tuesday morning, Chin Li knocked softly on his bedroom door, and Ba Thun groaned and rolled onto his side to eye the clock on the bedside stand.

He cleared his throat and asked, "What is it?"

"Colonel Mauk is on the telephone, Minister. He says it is important."

When he picked up the telephone, Mauk said, "We have something of a startling development, Minister."

Ba Thun swung his feet to the floor and sat up on the edge of the bed.

"What is that, Colonel?"

"I have Daw Tan in custody."

Ba Thun's eyes widened, and he was wide awake.

"How could that happen?"

"Christopher Carson turned him over to me."

"What! You will release him immediately, Colonel. You know there is an understanding—"

"Therein lies the difficulty, Minister."

"I do not know what is difficult to understand, Colonel, and how did Carson capture him, anyway?"

"I am not aware of the details. Carson said something about a preemptive strike."

"A preemptive strike! We are now allowing Carson a paramilitary role?"

"I will have a long discussion with him, Minister."

"Tell me about this difficulty."

"Carson has identified Daw Tan as the man who attacked him on Lower Kemendine Road, and has demanded that the government charge Tan with attempted murder."

"Ridiculous!"

"Perhaps, Minister, but the story has already been given to Pamela Steele by Carson. I checked with the YWCA where she is staying, and the article has already been transmitted by fax machine. Should we release Chieftain Daw Tan, accused of attempted murder against a prominent American, there would be, I think, diplomatic problems."

"Deport Steele!"

"Again, the same problems arise, Minister."

"We cannot be forced to do Carson's bidding," Ba Thun claimed. "And Steele has ingratiated herself in such a way that we will never get her out of the country. It is insane! Who commands here?"

"There is more," Mauk told him. "Carson suggested that Daw Tan's fingerprints—we have never had them before, you understand—be compared with the fingerprints of the bomb timer found on the hydrofoil boat at Prome, as well as with those on timer fragments found at the Pyu trestle. That was done, and we found them to be perfect matches. By all rights, Minister, I imagine we should bring additional charges against Tan. Traitorous activities would be one, suggesting a death penalty."

Ba Thun sighed. Daw Tan was so *stupid.*

He said, "I will call you back."

Dialing the premier, Ba Thun got him out of bed to listen to the staggering news. The two of them made additional calls to other members of the committee, then the premier called him back.

"What did you learn from interior and culture?" the premier asked.

"They worry that Khim Nol will be displeased."

"Yes. All of us do. Or, as was suggested to me, that Daw Tan's lieutenants will attempt to either free him or avenge him."

"I think that our hands are tied," Ba Thun said.

"This can be turned to our advantage. How many times have we been chastised by international law-enforcement agencies for granting refuge to the drug lords? Wide publicity on this would serve us well, Ba Thun."

"I grant you that."

"Throw him to the sharks, then. There will be no media present at the trial, if it comes to a trial. I do not believe that Tan would make foolish statements in public, but we will not assume that risk."

As Ba Thun dialed Colonel Mauk's number at the barracks, he shuddered. In his quest to make a bargain, to save his life, just how stupid would Daw Tan turn out to be?

GTI compound, Yangon

The grapevine had spread the news of Daw Tan's imprisonment by midmorning, and Oh heard of it when he went to have coffee in the cafeteria at ten o'clock. Billy Kasperik of Insta-Structure, who would provide no details to his listeners, but who seemed to speak with confidence and authority, spoke of the bandit being charged with attempted murder, sabotage, and other crimes against the state.

Hyun Oh's stomach flip-flopped and he no longer wanted coffee. He went back to his office.

He sat at his desk, removed his wallet from his trousers, and dug around in it to find the telephone number he had been given over dinner in Myitkyina.

He punched it carefully into his desk set.

The man who answered spoke in a language and dialect he did not know.

Oh said in English, "My name is Hyun Oh. I wish to speak to the chieftain."

There was babble on the other end of the line, then another took the phone. "How may I help you?"

He repeated his request.

"The chieftain is not available."

"Tell him that we must meet. That is, tell him that I request a meeting. There has been a . . ."

What? What was he to say?

"Tell him that Daw Tan has been arrested, and that we might discuss options of a mutually beneficial nature."

"I will give him the message."

TWENTY-FOUR

Myanmar army barracks, Yangon

At eleven o'clock in the morning, Lon Mauk left his office, crossed the parade ground to the jail, walked around the exercise yard, and entered the military police office.

He told the captain in charge, "I want to see Daw Tan."

"Of course, Colonel."

The chieftain was being detained in a solitary cell, and a sergeant, unlocking corridor doors as they went, took Mauk down several hallways to the cell. He unlocked the steel-encased cell door, Mauk stepped inside, and the door closed behind him.

The only furnishings were a waste bucket and a cot with a bare mattress. The aroma left much to be desired, such as fresh air. Very little of that commodity entered through the glassless, barred window high in the wall, which was small enough that only two bars were necessary. The walls were of brick and mortar, filthy with accumulated mildew. Daw Tan sat on the cot, and when Mauk entered, looked up and smiled. His smiles, when viewed within the context of his face, were somewhat grotesque, but always arrogant.

"You are here to release me, Colonel?"

"I think not. This afternoon, you are to be charged with attempted murder. Later, there will be other charges."

"Nonsense! I wish to speak to the premier."

"The premier does not wish to speak to you."

It required some effort on Daw Tan's part to hold the insolent smile. "Then he will speak to Khim Nol."

"Perhaps, though such a discussion cannot benefit you. It was the Americans who captured you and who force the indictment. Neither Khim Nol nor the premier will challenge the international media." Mauk decided to play out his bluff. "Additionally, it is my understanding that Khim Nol suspects you and Nito Kaing of conspiring against him. He will not rally to your cause."

His guess apparently hit home. The smile went away. The single eye went opaque.

"You have no strength, Tan. Your airplanes are destroyed on the ground. Your armory went up in flames. Your organization is in disarray. Already, your lieutenants are seeking asylum elsewhere."

He had seen the physical destruction at the Man Na-su compound. If his mind was truly as simple as Mauk thought that it was, he would accept the extension from the compound destruction to his organization's destruction as logical.

He continued to stare past Mauk, over his left shoulder.

"I have money," Tan said finally, refocusing on Mauk. "You could have millions—ten million dollars American! Anywhere in the world."

Daw Tan was no stranger to bribery, but to offer such a sum to Mauk suggested that he was on the brink of despair. The chieftains had long known that Mauk was not to be purchased.

"What would I do with money? Nothing I cannot do now," he said.

Tan took a new tactic. "I should be in a government jail, not a military one. I demand to be transferred."

"That is not to be. I have determined that security, yours and mine, is best served with you here."

Mauk believed that to be the case. There were some in the government—in the bureaucracy as well as the political posts—who would be dismayed by the committee's decision to allow Tan to be tried. His possible revelations in a court, public or not, could be damaging. If he were not under Mauk's close supervision, his escape or death were certainties. Mauk had understood from U Ba Thun's tone of voice that the SLORC was not happy with the decision that Carson had forced them into. It meant that the committee had transgressed the agreement with the chieftains, and they would be worried about the consequences.

"I should tell you also," Mauk said, "that your friends in this command are thinning rapidly. Corporal Syi, for example, has been arrested. His fingerprints, like yours, were found on the detonation timers at Prome and Pyu.

"Circumstances have turned against you, Tan. I should imagine that the prosecutors will raise the charge of treason, so that at the conclusion of your trial, you will be hanged."

Tan rose from the cot and turned to face the wall.

"That charge might be avoided, should you decide to speak with me."

"We have nothing to discuss, Mauk."

"Well, you will let me know, if you change your mind." Mauk rapped on the door, and the sergeant opened it.

Daw Tan continued to stare at the wall.

As he followed the sergeant back down the corridors, Mauk thought that the possibility of Tan changing his mind was a good one. There was much that Mauk would like to know of Khim Nol's organization, even if the rest of the government did not.

Palo Alto, California

The board meeting had run late, and it was nearly midnight by the time Abrams returned to his office and unlocked his doors. He poured himself a scotch and water and sat in his desk chair, turned toward the windows. The darkened Bay was not discernible, but he saw the lights of three vessels moving steadily through the night. He couldn't tell how large they were, but probably freighters.

The meeting had not gone well, as he had expected. The nine members of the twelve-member board who had attended had been appalled at his decision to turn their only prototype of the Ruby Star over to Carson. A wave of rebellion began to rise when he also revealed that the Ruby Star plans and specifications might also have been spirited away by some unknown computer expert. He couldn't remember a time in his life when his job was so much in jeopardy. If the chairman of the board had called for a vote at that point, he'd be packing his desk now.

They were only slightly mollified when he showed them the ruby he had personally recovered from a conduit leading to an electrical junction box on the Boeing 707 cargo plane. That damned Don Evans had had a bad time explaining to him how to find it.

The majority of the board members relaxed a little when he told them that the gem cutter was being flown in from New York in the morning and would spend three days with the stone. Mack Little's laboratory team would have a second prototype completed within ten days. The near potential for a mining contract eased their minds a bit, too.

Then the San Francisco banker raised the specter of Carson creating a civil war in Myanmar if he got slaphappy with the Ruby Star. They could be ousted from their master contract even before they got near the real prize, access to the Myanmar mines.

The meeting had finally broken up without accomplishing much. The agenda had fallen apart early, and Abrams hadn't gotten approval on seven routine matters. Everything seemed muddled.

Except that he'd been told to get the Ruby Star out of Myanmar.

"Until Carson gets that train to Yangon on the fifteenth, he won't want to give it up," Abrams had told them.

"No problem," the banker said, "fire Carson."

Abrams sipped his scotch and thought that now would be a good time to call Carson.

He put it off.

His phone rang.

He picked it up.

"Dex, this is Troy. I see a light on in your office."

"Come on up."

Baskin arrived five minutes later, and Abrams pointed him toward the sideboard and the scotch bottle. The security chief mixed himself a drink and pulled a chair up to the desk.

"I just got back from L.A."

"I'm glad to hear it," Abrams said, not really caring.

"I found our man."

"Our man?"

"The guy who rented the apartment in Studio City. We tracked the serial numbers on the computer equipment he left behind."

"I'll be damned. He bought the stuff in his own name?"

"On a credit card. The guy's a genius with computers. On practical matters, he's less of a genius."

"So who is he?"

Baskin swallowed a healthy slug of his drink. "American-born Chinese named Donald Ming. He bills himself as a technology consultant and has an office near Century City. Hires himself out to a lot of outfits who are willing to pay big money to have him troubleshoot their problems."

"How do you know this?" Abrams asked.

"You don't want to know."

When Baskin told him that, Abrams figured something illegal had taken place. Baskin, or someone, had probably taken a midnight stroll through Ming's office.

"So don't tell me."

"There's nothing particularly incriminating in the office, but the guy has a nice copying machine."

Abrams frowned. "You've got copies of something?"

"Of most of his consulting contracts. No one will ever know how we got hold of them. They could be copies from someone else's file. As it turns out, though, we're only interested in one of his contracts, I think."

Baskin pulled a folded set of papers from his inside jacket pocket and tossed it to Abrams.

He unfolded them. There were eight pages stapled together. Lots of legalese, but the first page told him that Donald Ming had entered into a contract with Hypai Industries to provide:

> Technological assistance with the company's laser-development project for a period not to exceed eighteen (18) months. The fee shall be $100,000.00, plus reasonable expenses.

"Hypai Industries?"

"That's the one. I didn't even know they were working on a laser."

"I didn't either," Abrams said.

"Unless they're working on ours."

"Damn. I'm going to have to tell Carson he's shooting at the wrong target."

Abrams had forgotten his original intention for calling Carson.

GTI compound, Yangon

Pamela Steele's article had been picked up by the London, Paris, Washington, and New York papers. On the satellite feed for CNN, it was a lead news item. Branigan was certain that Carson had fed the details to her.

She read the *New York Times* international edition while eating a chicken-salad sandwich in the cafeteria. Most of the world's readers, not aware of the political realities of Myanmar, would not realize the manipulation created by this story, she supposed. The arrest of Daw Tan, an alleged billionaire drug lord, on a long string of potential criminal charges was reported factually, but the bombings, attempted shootings, and suspected connections to brutal assassinations in the past were presented in detail. Tan was not a nice man. If he were allowed to evade the courts, the Myanmar government would sink under a deluge of criticism. To cap it off, companion articles, written by other reporters, collected quotes from national leaders or their spokesmen from around the world. The United States, Canada, France, Britain, Germany, Russia, and dozens of other nations lauded the SLORC for their positive action in ridding the world of a villain like Tan. The SLORC was urged to go after Nol, Shwe, and Kaing, also named in Steele's story as alleged masterminds of drug production.

Under that onslaught of praise, the premier and his committee members could not very well let Tan slip out the back door. Branigan suspected that Carson had had a hand in the entire publicity scheme, and perhaps Colonel Mauk was involved, too. She was beginning to believe that Mauk was trustworthy.

Branigan had never met Nol, Tan, Shwe, or Kaing, and wouldn't have recognized any of them if she met them on the street, but she had heard the stories, rumors, and gossip. She assumed one or more of them were behind the assaults she had survived on the road to Banmo and aboard the helicopter with Carson.

She remembered that night in the forest, the pitch-black darkness, the rain dripping through the leaves, Carson's arm around her, the shared heat of their bodies, the . . .

"You ready, Stephanie?"

She looked up to see Dick Statler standing by her table.

"I'm ready. Do we have transport?"

"Evans found us a Gazelle. It'll be ready by the time we get to Mingaladon."

Branigan wasn't too fond of helicopters anymore. Whenever a tour by air was scheduled, she found herself a bit more anxious than usual.

Folding her newspaper and leaving it for the next diner, she settled her cast in its sling and took her tray to the kitchen window, then joined Statler and went out to the parking lot. He drove the blue-and-silver Pontiac, allowing her to indulge in her preoccupation with Carson.

She had just about decided that a Branigan-Carson liaison was not to be. When she had learned of the brazen attack he and his trigger-happy buddies had made on the Chinatown apartment, she had been shocked. In her engineering world, people did not run around shooting at other people, no matter how angry they were, or how felonious the other side might be. It was a side to Carson she had glimpsed on the Banmo Road and in the stricken helicopter, but she could never have imagined it would boil over as it did. Now, there was this— according to the rumors—kidnapping of Daw Tan. The chieftain might well be a vicious bastard, and she was certain that he was, but kidnapping was still an illegal activity where she came from. The harshness of the act was softened a few degrees by the fact that Carson had turned Daw Tan over to the authorities, but still . . .

And there was Pamela Steele, the gorgeous and relentless correspondent. Judging by today's front-page stories, Steele was doing Carson's bidding. There was something strange in that relationship. Steele seemed so independent. She wouldn't easily bend to Carson's will unless . . .

Carson had been very quick to chase her down as soon as Gilbert was killed.

No. He wouldn't . . .

If Steele weren't so damned pretty . . .

The rain dripped from the leaves, splattering on the hard plastic of the tarp. Her teeth chattered against the cold, and yet she was warm. And held.

It was just the abstinence since the divorce. A moment's infatuation. A sexual interlude.

Carson had them all the time, was her guess.

"You want a penny for your thoughts?" Statler asked, pulling to a stop in the lot next to the operations building.

"Sorry, Dick. I seem to be drifting today."

"You sure you want to make this trip? I mean, the arm and all."

"The arm is mending nicely. I'm fine."

After signing the manifest, they boarded the helicopter with its two pilots and headed north. Until they were airborne and north of the airport, she felt her anxiety trying to engulf her. After ten minutes, she relaxed a little.

The pilot landed the Gazelle near the Pyu trestle, and they spent twenty minutes surveying the progress. The bridge had been restored, and the conventional trains were again running, allowing for shipments of pedestal track segments to the railhead.

The replacement pedestal track for this damaged section was not yet on-site, but was scheduled to arrive on flat cars the next day.

Statler talked to several of the foremen, then rejoined her near the trestle.

"Are we going to make it, Dick?"

"Here? You bet. They'll be finished up by the twelfth. The last two sections were cast yesterday afternoon, and they'll be working all night to get them wired. We robbed magnets from the Taunggyi Division for the time being."

Which reminded her that she had not yet talked to Pruett about the Hypai magnets. Was she subconsciously putting off the decision to throw five or six hundred Americans out of work?

"How's the morale?"

"Much better, especially among the Burmese workers. There's less looking over their shoulders now that that SOB, Daw Tan, is in jail."

The helicopter next took them to the railhead, now twenty miles north of Pyinmana. From the air, the gap between the southern and northern railheads appeared to be infinitesimal. On the ground, it seemed longer, but was still less than a mile.

"We're two days behind schedule here," Statler said. "With the conventional track cut, we had to use Skycranes and trucks to transport the rail sections. Then, we got further behind when Evans took one of the Skycranes away from us."

"Why did he pull it off?"

"I don't know. I haven't seen it around."

"But we'll still link up on the thirteenth?"

"We'll do it. We're going around the clock with three crews. I've got the fourteenth set aside for test runs. We'll do that all day."

"Safety's the first priority," she said.

"It'll be safe. I'm riding that train."

They spent a half hour touring the main line. The roadbed had been augmented with additional fill in four spots, to make it wide enough to accept the new trackage. She paid particular attention to the core samples tested by the geologists. The last thing she needed was a roadbed that washed away in the daily rains.

It was beginning to rain heavily by the time she headed south in the Gazelle, leaving Statler behind to work with the field engineers on the details of the final linkup.

At six-ten in the afternoon, the helicopter landed at Mingaladon in a steady drizzle. She made a dash for the hangar, walked around an S-65, which was under maintenance, and opened the door to the operations room.

In the back office, which had its door standing open, she saw five or six people standing near a line of computers. Carson was with them, so she didn't bother stopping.

Digging the keys Statler had given her from her purse, she trotted across the lot and unlocked the driver's door of the Pontiac. She slid into the seat and fumbled the key into the ignition while looking through the rain-streaked windshield at the leaden sky.

"Miss Branigan!"

She turned her head to see a diminutive, but very pretty woman standing next to her. She wore a conical hat, which dripped raindrops. Her complexion was almost porcelain in its smooth texture.

The dark eyes bored into her own.

"Yes?"

"You will come with me."

"I'm sorry, I don't know who—"

The woman's right hand reached toward her. The muzzle of an ugly pistol pressed into her side.

"Now, Miss Branigan."

She looked helplessly toward the hangar. No one was out front.

Branigan dropped the keys on the floor and got out of the car.

Data Processing Center, Mingaladon Airport, Yangon

"I know the voice," Carson said. "The Hypai rep, Hyun Oh."

"So why's he calling Khim Nol?" Carlos Montoya asked.

They had just listened to the tape together. No translation had been necessary since both men spoke in English.

"Mauk told me that Oh had met with Khim Nol, but why he so urgently wants to meet with him now, I don't know," Carson said.

Don Evans, who had been listening in, said, "It's a damned strange pairing, the chieftain and the South Korean."

Perhaps not, Carson thought. After his early-afternoon discussion with Dex Abrams, he had decided that maybe some of the Korean's actions weren't illogical at all. If Hypai had ripped off a copy of Ruby Star, then their interest in obtaining the mining contract was understandable. And Oh could be involved in a lot of other under-the-table dealings around the country, too.

The man's motivations were becoming clearer.

"He warned Nol that Daw Tan had been arrested," Montoya said. "Why would he do that?"

"Nol is Tan's boss," Evans said.

"Big deal. There's still no reason for Oh to pass the information on."

"Unless," Carson said, "Oh and Tan had something going together. Look, Carlos, make a quick copy of that conversation and get it over to Colonel Mauk, will you?"

"Sure thing."

"Do it personally. Make sure he gets it, and not some sergeant. Tell him we were monitoring Nol's phone."

"Right."

Montoya went off to make the copy, and Carson went back into the operations room to find a telephone. The other topic of his conversation with Abrams had been more bothersome, and he had been thinking about it most of the day.

Abrams: The other thing, Chris, you have to send the Ruby Star back.

Carson: I'm not done with it.

Abrams: Doesn't matter. It's a board decision.

Carson: I don't have a plane here.

Abrams: I'll send you one.

Carson: Do it in a couple weeks.

Abrams: I'll get it out yet today.

Carson: I want the machine a while longer, Dex.

Abrams: Hey, Chris! I've got my orders.

Carson: And if I decide to hold onto it?

Abrams: I've got orders for that eventuality, too.

Abrams hadn't had to elaborate on that theme. The Ruby Star went back to Palo Alto or Carson started pounding the pavement. Carson said he'd send it back.

He didn't say when.

He called Branigan's office. Janice Cooper said she wasn't back yet.

"How about Craig Wilson? Where's he?"

"Let me check, Mr. Carson." A couple minutes later, she told him, "He's out at the Kemendine Yards."

Carson called out there, and someone said they'd have Wilson call him back. He waited ten minutes for the return call from the motive-power chief.

"Hello, Chris. I was out in the yards."

"Sorry to bother you, Craig. I've got a favor to ask."

"Name it."

"Do you have an UltraTrain cargo car I could borrow for a couple days? One in Mandalay, preferably."

"Oh, hell, yes. You want a head-end car or an interior car?"

"Head-end, if you've got it."

"I'm going to put you on hold a second." When he came back, Wilson gave him the car number. "We'll pull it off the train it's on and park it wherever you want."

They agreed on a parking spot in the Mandalay Yards, and Carson held the phone button down for a second, then called the transient quarters at the compound. The valet had to track Mack Little down for him.

While he waited, he asked Evans, "Don, you have a chopper available?"

"I've got a Gazelle just back."

"Sign it out to me and preflight it, would you?"

"Is your insurance up-to-date?"

"All that's behind me, Don."

"I hope to hell so."

Evans went out to check on the helicopter.

Little came on, "You got me out of a hot poker game, Chris."

"How would you like to get your team together and go for a little ride?"

"Tonight?"

"Yup."

"Like last night?"

"No. I'm putting you on the road to Mandalay."

"Like Bob Hope?"

"Not like that, either. You're not on vacation, you know, and I've got work for you."

"Ah, hell! Right now, I suppose?"

"That works for me."

Myanmar army barracks, Yangon

Just after eight o'clock, the phone rang. It sounded shrill in the solitude of his office.

Mauk picked it up.

"Captain Nu, sir. Daw Tan is dead!"

He slammed the phone down, grabbed his hat, and ran down the corridor, sliding on the waxed floor. He hit the front screen door hard enough to pull a hinge loose, skipped down the steps, and crossed the parade ground at a full run.

Skidding around the corner of the jail building, he yanked open the door, and stomped into the reception area.

Captain Nu was shaking with fright. A sergeant hid behind a desk.

"Take me back there!"

"Sir!"

The captain led the way, unlocking and locking doors as they went. Mauk counted them. Three doors to be gotten around, plus the cell door.

When they reached the cell, he found it open. Two enlisted military policemen and a military doctor were inside. Daw Tan was sprawled on the bare mattress of his cot, one leg draped over the edge, resting on the floor. His face appeared particularly peaceful.

"What happened?" he demanded.

The doctor turned both palms up. "I do not know, Colonel. I can find nothing traumatic. An autopsy will be required."

"Get to it, then! I want to know within the hour."

"But, Colonel—"

"Within the hour. You are wasting time."

He turned on the captain. "Who was in here, Nu?"

"The guards. Checking on him hourly, as ordered. His lawyer, as appointed by the general, visited in midafternoon."

"That's all? No more?" Mauk had left orders for no visitors except the attorney selected by the government. Daw Tan was not to have his own lawyer.

"That is all, sir. Except, of course, for his wife."

"His wife! Your orders were no visitors!" Mauk yelled.

"But, sir! His wife—"

"What did she look like?"

"A woman, sir. Quite beautiful."

"Come on!"

"Ah, short. She was very short. Her hair in a bun. Her . . ."

That was all Mauk needed to know. He grabbed the keys from the captain's hand and made his way back to the front office. There he called Ba Thun.

The minister seemed stunned by the news.

"The media correspondents will crucify us! They will say we killed him to avoid a trial."

Mauk was less worried about the media and what they might say. He was furious because he had not yet had the opportunity to interrogate Tan. He had been waiting for the hours of solitude and the morbid specter of his own hanging to weigh on the man.

Daw Tan now had all of the solitude he would ever need.

And Lon Mauk had nothing.

HARD RAIN

TWENTY-FIVE

GTI airfield, Mandalay

It was eleven o'clock when Carson landed the Gazelle, and the five men crawled out of it and stretched.

"How is it," Mack Little asked, "that you always do your work at night, Chris? It seems a bit like Dracula to me."

"You don't understand that I'm trying to accommodate you, Mack? It's daytime on your side of the world, remember?"

"Yeah, but during the night, I usually sleep."

"You had your chance today, but you'd rather play poker."

"I was winning, too!"

They crossed the field to the temporary steel hangar where they had left the Skycrane. Several floodlights under the eaves of the hangar were on, bathing the ground in bright light. Two men armed with M-16s watched them with suspicion as they approached.

Carson identified himself, but as they should have, the guards required all of them to produce ID cards.

Inside the hangar, they turned on the lights, and Little's men began searching through the rolling steel cabinets for the tools they needed. Little dug out a tape measure and measured the fiberglass platform secured under the helicopter.

"Okay, Chris, got it."

They went back outside.

Carson asked the first guard, "Do you have a company car here?"

"The Wagoneer around back, Mr. Carson."

He handed over the keys, and Carson and Little went to find the car.

Carson drove, bobbing over the bumpy field until he reached the road. It was only five miles to the Mandalay Yards south of the city, and the road turned to asphalt before he reached them. A long overpass took them across the top of the yard, and on the other side he turned south and drove alongside the lots planned for future development of industry and shipping facilities.

Four miles down the road, as Wilson had promised, they found the solitary cargo car. Carson turned off the road, crossed the lot, and parked as close to the car as he could get.

He had toured the UltraTrain vehicles a few times, but this was a first view for Little.

He whistled. "We really are in the twenty-first century."

"About as close as we can get, Mack."

"This sucker does two hundred miles an hour?"

"Faster than that, Stephanie tells me. And all by its lonesome."

They got out of the Jeep and walked up to the pedestal track. Carson found the side hatch near the front end—aerodynamically sloped on this car, which would be situated at the front or rear of a train, located recessed controls, and opened the hatch.

Once the door swung open, another control unfolded a set of steps in the side of the car, and they climbed aboard.

Carson turned on the lights. The interior was utilitarian. Rub rails along the perimeter prevented damage to the vertical beams supporting the exterior skin. The front end had two seats, one against each side, and in front of the right seat was a control panel. The seating took up about five feet of length, but the rest of the sixty-foot car was available for cargo.

"It's long enough, for damned sure," Little said.

He pulled his tape measure off his belt and slipped it across the floor.

"What have we got?" Carson asked.

"Eleven feet between the rub rails. The platform's twelve feet exactly, so I'm going to have to lose a foot and a couple inches for tolerance."

"Can you do it?"

"I think so. We have to shave eight inches off either side of the platform. We may have to shift some of the fuel and air plumbing for the diesels, but we'll get the clearance we need."

"Good."

"How does the damned top work?"

"I don't know."

Looking around, they found another control panel, and Little fiddled with it for a while, until they heard the *clack-clack* of bolts being drawn.

"That'll be the pins that align and secure the roof," Little said. "Neat stuff. Now, we hit this button, I think."

With a suction sound as the seal was broken, the top half of the car, aft of the control compartment, began to raise. With hydraulic smoothness, it rose several inches, then rotated, opening like a clam, until it stood upright, a few degrees past the vertical. The right side of the car was completely exposed for cargo loading.

"Leave it open?" Little asked.

"Might as well. I think it's done raining for the day."

"Morning, you mean."

It was midnight. They returned to the Jeep and drove back to the airfield.

The Ruby Star laser was already dismounted from the side of the aircraft, and the umbilical cord from the canvas-covered platform to the crewmember's seat in the flight cab had been disconnected. Little's computer, released from its mounts in the cab, rested on the concrete floor.

They stripped the canvas and canvas supports from the platform, released the cables connecting it to the helicopter's hoist, and then Little measured and marked a line down each side of the platform.

Two of the technicians, wearing goggles and forced-air masks, and wielding big circular saws, began cutting an eight-inch strip from each side of the platform. The cut took several hours and a dozen carbide-tipped saw blades. The honey-combed carbon-impregnated fiberglass was tough to cut. By the time they were done, fiberglass dust filled the air and coated everything inside the hangar.

They rerigged the platform cables to the Skycrane's hoist, and Carson climbed into the cab and used the electrically driven winch to lift the load several inches off the floor.

"You sure you can do this, Chris?" Little asked.

"I've flown one before. The flying's no sweat, Mack; it's running the hoist that's no fun."

"Well, I think I can figure that out."

Opening the hangar door, one of the techs cranked up a tow tractor and pulled the helicopter out into the night. They loaded the computer in the Wagoneer, wrapped the laser in old blankets, and then strapped it to the roof of the Jeep. The technicians, after getting directions from Carson, took off in the car.

Little climbed into the cab, belting himself into the aft-facing hoist operator's seat. Carson took the pilot's right-hand seat.

The guards watched them.

"As soon as I get back," he told them, "you guys can have the rest of the night off."

He didn't tell them that they'd have to walk back to their quarters, which were located in a compound two miles away. Their company Jeep had been drafted for the night.

Locating the aircraft checklists stuck behind a conduit, Carson rested them in his lap and pulled a flexible reading light over so that it shone down on the lists. He hadn't flown a Skycrane in years, and he took care to follow the checklist exactly as he went through the ignition sequence.

The engines came to life smoothly, reflecting the value of Don Evans's strict maintenance schedule.

He let them warm for three minutes, then eased in collective.

It was a hell of a lot heavier than he expected, and it took a good deal of power to lift off.

The helicopter dipped. Banked.

The two guards ran for the security of the hangar.

He steadied it.

Over the intercom, Little said, "You said you'd done this before."

"Well, not with a load, Mack."

"Shit. Can I get out now?"

"It's a ten-foot jump."

Carson made each of his movements slowly, becoming re-accustomed to the controls and the reaction of the aircraft. He gained altitude to a two-hundred-foot ground clearance, then circled away from the airfield.

By the time he reached the Mandalay Yards, he saw the head-lights of the Jeep just coming off the overpass on the other side, so he turned north toward the city to waste some time. There were few lights on in Mandalay at this time of the early morning. The streetlamps defined the neat grid in which some planner had laid out the central part of the city.

On the near side of the yards, there were lights near the huge maintenance buildings, and a night crew was working on train cars both inside and outside the structures. From his distance, Carson couldn't tell whether or not they were interested in him.

He came around and worked his way south along the western side of the yards until he found the opened cargo car. The Jeep was parked nearby.

He had been flying without navigation lights, and the light from the inside of the car was bright enough that he decided against using the landing lights or the floodlights on the heli-copter.

Slowing to a hover, he worked the chopper sideways until he was over the car, about fifty feet off the ground. He couldn't see directly down but when he leaned over and peered through the side window, he saw one of the techs climbing into the car.

"Up to you, Mack."

"I'll give it a shot. Whoops!"

"What?"

"Too fast. There, that's better."

Carson wanted to look back over his shoulder, maybe give Little a bit of encouragement or instruction, but he forced himself to concentrate on holding the helicopter steady. Branigan's comments were striking home; he had to learn to delegate a little better than he was doing lately.

"Okay, Chris. I'm down about twenty feet, but we've got to get lined up better. Come back about seven feet."

"Seven."

"Right."

He eased the stick and focused on a signpost near the track, trying to estimate his position and the change in it by the way the post moved.

"Easy now . . . little more . . . right on!"

They had twenty-five-foot tolerance, to the front and rear, so Carson wasn't exactly elated by Little's satisfaction.

"Now, we've got to go left, your left, about four feet."

He focused on the signpost, and leaned the chopper left.

"That's it . . . that's it . . . hold there. I'm lowering some more . . . more to the left. Keep coming. Ten feet more."

"Ten feet!"

"I mean ten feet down. The guys are there to guide us in. Back to the right . . . easy, now. Going down."

Carson felt the Skycrane try for heaven as the weight of the cargo touched down. He eased off on the power.

"Shit! This is great. We're damned good, Chris."

"We knew that to start with, Mack."

"Hold now! George is releasing the cable."

As soon as Little had winched the cable back onto its spool, Carson moved over near the Jeep and settled the monster to the ground.

Little unstrapped himself and climbed out of the seat.

"How much time are you going to need?" Carson called over the whine of the idling engines.

"I want to do it right. Give us twelve hours."

"I'll have someone bring some food over later. Then we'll send you some guards around noon."

"Good show, old boy!"

Little slipped out of the cab, and when he was clear, Carson lifted off. He made it back to the airfield, circling clear of the railway maintenance activity, and landed without damaging much of anything, he thought. He also thought Evans would kill him if he found out he'd been flying the man's Skycrane.

He was happy to trade the heavy-lift helicopter for the fleet Gazelle.

Ahlone Road, Yangon

By midmorning, the telephone was still ringing steadily. U Ba Thun hadn't been free of it long enough to drive down to his office. Most of the calls were from newspaper and broadcast media, and most of those originated from outside the country. He had been forced to tell them "no comment," which he hated to do, or to suggest that, later in the day, he would have more information.

Finally, Lon Mauk returned the calls Ba Thun had been placing to him all morning.

"It was not until now, Minister, that I obtained information relative to the autopsy of Daw Tan."

"Give it to me now, Colonel Mauk! You have no idea what I have been through this morning."

"I do, Minister. The reporters have besieged me."

"You did not speak to them?"

"I referred them to you."

Which increased the volume of telephone calls to his residence, but Ba Thun preferred that to having Mauk giving interviews.

"Very well. And Daw Tan?"

"Do you want the clinical detail?"

"Of course not!"

"Then, it appears that he was injected with a strong sedative, perhaps to calm him or to cause him to lose consciousness. When that was accomplished, he was given a massive overdose of heroin. If he was alert, we could assume he died a deliriously happy man." Mauk said this with a tone of voice that suggested he was not attempting humor.

"I do not care what frame of mind he was in. This is disastrous! We will be accused of executing the man."

"He was worthy of execution, Minister."

"The world expects a trial."

"You may, of course, tell the reporters that we have identified Daw Tan's murderer."

"You have!" Ba Thun felt the first dribbles of relief easing his mind.

"There are positive identifications from three people: the captain of the guard, a sergeant, and the guard at the barracks entrance."

"Is he in custody?"

"Not as yet, Minister. I will need your guidance."

"In what way?"

"The murderer is Nito Kaing."

The web constricts!

Ba Thun's pulse rate increased dramatically. He could hear his blood pounding in his ears. Mauk was doing this to force a heart attack upon him.

"That cannot be."

"There is no doubt, Minister."

"She committed this murder personally?"

"Yes, posing as Tan's wife. The guards did not know, though they should not have let her in."

"But this places us in the same . . . no, a worse position,"

Ba Thun complained. "The chieftains are running amuck. They do not understand the pressures we are under."

"If we identify her to the press," Mauk said, "we will be compelled to mount a manhunt for her. Have you spoken to Khim Nol?"

Ba Thun heard the doorbell ring. Chin Li moved to answer it.

"I have not."

"Well," Mauk said, "I await your decision."

"I will call you back."

Ba Thun tried to call Khim Nol, but was told that he was away, and no one knew when he would return. He replaced the telephone and stared out the window. Under the concrete skies, the yard appeared lushly green and wet. The steady rain streaked the window. Long rivulets worked their way lazily down the glass.

"Minister?"

He turned to find Chin Li standing in the doorway.

"Miss Steele is here to see you."

"I must go to the office. Tell her to see me there."

"She is most insistent, Minister."

Ba Thun sighed. "Very well."

Steele came into his study smiling radiantly. She was wearing a yellow pant suit of a Western style. The jacket was loose-fitting, open in front to reveal a white silk blouse. Ba Thun could not accustom himself to women in trousers, much less a woman taller than himself. In the several times he had met with her, she seemed to intimidate him. Worse, her power had grown proportionately to the number of articles about Myanmar that she had written. His leverage of ordering her deportation dwindled with each day that passed.

"Good morning, Minister Ba Thun!" She held out her hand to be shaken.

He shook it, noting the smooth dry softness of it.

"Please sit, Miss Steele. What can I do for you?"

She sat gingerly on the edge of the couch, retrieving a tape recorder and a stenographer's pad from her purse. She checked the tape on the recorder and turned it on.

He hated the ritual.

"I'm interested in your reaction to the murder of Daw Tan, Minister."

"It is lamentable that he was killed while in our custody. The committee had hoped that the crimes with which he was to be charged would have been revealed in a public trial."

"Yes. I can understand your concern. How did he die?"

"I have not yet read the autopsy report, Miss Steele. Unofficially, I have been told it was an overdose of heroin."

"He was an addict?"

"Not that I know."

"You said that he was killed. That implies that the overdose was not self-administered."

"That is correct."

"As he was in custody," Steele said, "his killer must have been apprehended?"

"No."

She raised an eyebrow.

"We have a suspect."

"The suspect's name?"

"I cannot reveal that at this time."

She smiled with such all-knowing condescension that Ba Thun considered throwing the vase on his desk at her.

"How was the suspect able to get into the prison?"

"By posing as a visiting relative."

"His wife?"

"A relative," Ba Thun insisted.

"And the visit was unobserved?"

"That is true."

When she raised her eyebrow again, he added, "Our military prisons may not be operated like the ones with which you are familiar."

"I'm sure that's true, Minister. When do you expect to have the suspect under arrest?"

"I have no details on the current whereabouts of that person. It will be up to the police and the military."

"How will this affect the celebration planned for July fifteenth?"

"It should not affect it at all, Miss Steele. This incident has no bearing on the inaugural train journey."

"How would you respond to the positive comments of world leaders in regard to the arrest of Daw Tan?"

"I was pleased."

"Pleased that the international community was supporting the SLORC for a change?"

"I was pleased."

"Do you expect that the death of Daw Tan before his trial will alter those comments?"

"I have no way of knowing," Ba Thun said.

"Would you think that some will believe that the government eliminated Tan so as to prevent possible incrimination of others?"

"My thoughts would only be conjecture. I will say that Chieftain Tan's death came as a shock to everyone on the committee. We were eager to let him have his day in court."

"And, once again, the suspect's name?"

Ba Thun smiled.

Steele smiled, too, shut off her recorder, and stood up.

"Thank you, Minister Ba Thun. You have been most gracious."

"Any time, Miss Steele."

As soon as she was gone, Ba Thun tried to think of some way in which he could have her visa revoked. Unfortunately, nothing came to mind.

Moulmein

Hyun Oh took the six o'clock hydrofoil to Moulmein. The passage across the Gulf of Martaban was smooth despite a choppy sea, overcast skies, and several squalls. It seemed much darker than it should have when the boat tied up at the dock in Moulmein.

He rented a car, an aged Renault, drove through the crowded streets of the city until he found Highway 8, then started south. He was to go almost sixty-five kilometers, but the streets, then the highway, were so crowded that he could not manage a decent average speed. He passed through Mudon, then later saw the small village of Kada off to the right.

The paved highway became narrower and in worse repair when he reached Paungsein. There were large potholes, which appeared in his headlights, and he was forced to slow down even more to avoid them.

Several kilometers past Paungsein, he found the 2nd World War Cemetery. He turned into the drive, stopped in front of the gate, and shut off the headlights. It was quite dark by now, and he did not want to leave the car. Khim Nol was entirely too morbid.

As his eyes became acclimated to the dark, the tombstones and crosses glowed eerily in the darkness. They would be the graves of Englishmen, Americans, and Burmese, he supposed. He did not know the history well, and he . . .

There was suddenly a darker shadow standing next to the passenger window.

The door pulled open, the courtesy light came on, and Khim Nol got in and shut the door. For only a brief moment did Oh see the malevolent eyes and smallpox-scarred face.

"Good evening, Hyun Oh."

"It is good to see you again, Chieftain." His mouth felt dry, and he tripped over his words. He hoped that Nol did not notice.

He wondered how many of Nol's men were out there in the night. There were bound to be some.

"You thought that our meeting was imperative," Nol said.

Too frequently, Oh had moments of inspiration in which he grabbed the telephone. Afterward, he regretted his impulsiveness, as he did now. He had called Nol when Daw Tan was merely under arrest. Now that he was reported dead, circumstances had changed once again.

"I wished to discuss our arrangement, in view of the fact that Tan is now dead."

"Our arrangement, yes." Nol spoke as though he were aware of it.

Oh had determined that his safest course was to approach the chieftain as if Oh had been dealing with Daw Tan in full light of Khim Nol's knowledge. The man would either deny it or remain silent in the hope to learn as much as he could.

"Daw Tan told me that the scheme had your blessing, though you were not aware of the details."

"That is true."

Ah. The man was hooked.

"Tan was to . . . eliminate Christopher Carson and Stephanie Branigan, as well as destroy the UltraTrain prior to its inaugural run."

"Yes."

"As a result of the railway loss, the government would be in disarray. The administration of the master contract would be in confusion also. Since I am familiar with the entire modernization project, and am a close personal friend of Minister Ba Thun, it is likely that Hypai Industries would be awarded the completion of the master contract. I would serve as the director. Hypai Industries would also be awarded a contract to operate the mines."

Nol seemed unprepared, as well he might be, to react to this. He simply said, "Yes."

"In exchange for your services in this regard, I would instruct your designated representatives in little-known methods for controlling the communications network and the new railway."

Nol did not seem to grasp the import.

"Naturally," Oh went on, "I knew that you understood the importance of that control, for those who manage the communications and transportation have the power to own the country."

"Of course."

Though it was dark in the car, Oh could imagine the light dawning on Nol's face.

"With Daw Tan's demise, I simply need to know if this arrangement is still satisfactory to you."

Nol took a long time to consider before responding. Oh knew that he was fumbling with ideas that had never before occurred to him. When Oh had first presented the concept to Daw Tan, Tan had also had trouble understanding the long-range implications. Of course, Tan had also been dealing with the necessity for eliminating Khim Nol in order to assume all power to himself. Oh did not know for certain, but he thought that Tan was going to come to an agreement with Kaing and Shwe in regard to the takeover of Nol's empire.

"I think," Nol said, "that I do not recall Daw Tan telling me how long this arrangement was to remain in place."

"Oh, yes! Until the end of the master contract, which has about five years to run. After that, there would simply be the mining contract administered by Hypai Industries."

Again the man ruminated, then said, "I see no reason to alter the agreement at this point."

"Wonderful, Chieftain! Now, there is the small matter of the train. From what I hear, it will achieve operation in time for the celebration."

"I can arrange for it to be inoperative."

"What would be most spectacular, and bring the world's criticism to the SLORC, is if the train were to be destroyed during its celebratory journey."

Oh felt very much a commander of world events. He could develop and manipulate strategies. A Napoleon. Of smaller stature, naturally, he told himself with modesty.

"Yes. That would be advantageous," Nol agreed. "We will see what can be done."

"Then, Carson and Branigan . . . ?"

"The Branigan woman has already been taken care of," Nol said.

For some reason, Oh's stomach suddenly felt queasy.

Moulmein

Colonel Lon Mauk was certain that the man who had entered Oh's rented automobile was Khim Nol. He had only a glimpse when the interior light came on, and the sudden light had come as a surprise to him. He was not prepared for it, and he missed his chance.

When it came on again, and the man got out of the car, Mauk was ready. In his binoculars, he saw that it was indeed Khim Nol.

The sighting verified what he had learned from Carlos Montoya's wiretaps. Someone calling Oh from Nol's telephone had arranged this meeting spot with Hyun Oh. Mauk and two of his sergeants had been resting on their stomachs in the cemetery for nearly two hours prior to Oh's arrival in the car. He did not know how Nol had arrived.

But what did he know?

Only that Oh and Nol knew each other and met under the cover of darkness. What plots were afoot, if any, were a mystery.

He had a decision to make.

And he made it.

He let them both leave the memorial cemetery unmolested. He leaned over and whispered to the sergeant nearest to him.

"Follow Nol for as far as you can. Try to determine where he goes."

GTI compound, Yangon

Carson had slept for most of the day, after getting back to Yangon at eight in the morning. He had been awakened by

Mack Little's call at one o'clock, telling him that all was in readiness in Mandalay.

For the balance of the afternoon, he and a few others helped Becky Johnson get the office moved back into the reconstructed building. Since they had had to rebuild the section from the foundation up, with crews from InstaStructure, they had revamped the floor plan, and it was a much nicer suite of offices. Johnson now had her own space, not having to share the reception area. Marty Prather and his auditors were grouped together, and the accounting section was no longer scattered down a hallway. The construction-management team was relocated on the second floor, in what had been Carson's old apartment.

When they were done, Carson took Johnson, Larkin, and Prather to dinner at the American cafe, then went back to his office to catch up on paperwork and update the master contract tracking board. A few things were beginning to reach completion. By the end of the month, the bus transport system would have received its last shipment of buses, most of them bound for Mandalay. Kiki Olson had the computer systems in place for the bus system's scheduling, personnel, finance, and payroll. The last training classes for drivers and mechanics were enrolled. When they were graduated, Phillip Draft and the Bluebird Bus people would leave the country, their subcontract completed.

The Hydrofoil Marine project was only a few days off schedule, and Washington's report projected that they would be leaving Myanmar by the end of next April, provided their full training and hiring programs were soon revived. Carson made a note to himself to allow Washington to begin hiring native replacements as soon as they completed their training programs. To hell with U Ba Thun and the contract standoff. He didn't want his feud with the commerce minister to stand in the way of Hydrofoil meeting its obligations.

His last project for the evening was the proposal for a contract to operate the Myanmar mines. It was in three copies, each thirty-five pages long, prepared by the geologists and legal experts in Palo Alto, and it had been printed off on Becky Johnson's laser printer after transfer by satellite links from California. He read it carefully, then signed off at the bottom of the last page and dated it. In the morning, he would deliver it to Ba Thun.

Carson was beginning to think that his chief adversary was no longer the commerce minister. With Daw Tan out of the way—and Carson could care less about the manner of the man's exit from the stage—some of the tension had gone out of his life. He wouldn't yet relax the vigilance of the field teams since Tan could have a few lieutenants around seeking revenge, but he thought the bandit activity might be on the ebb. Mack Little's preparations in Mandalay could well be for naught, and Carson hoped that they were.

The fact that Dex Abrams might have to fire him, at the board's direction, was something he would have to deal with next week.

At the moment, though, Carson was beginning to think that the mild-mannered Hyun Oh was emerging as a foe he should have been watching more carefully.

If Hypai Industries had indeed lifted a copy of the Ruby Star's electronic and physical schematics, it would explain Carson's sighting of Hyun Oh in Bangkok's gem district. Oh was the invisible suitor for Mr. Chao's big ruby. It also explained Hypai Industries' interest in securing the Myanmar mining contract.

The Myanmar mines, which had been producing the most spectacular and brilliant rubies for over five hundred years, were essential to the Ruby Star laser. The Ruby Star was so named because it used the ruby as its active medium. The pseudoruby rod did not allow this particular laser to develop its tremendous power.

Auguste Verneuil had developed the flame-fusion process in 1902, allowing artificial rubies to be produced from ammonia alum and chrome alum. In 1960, an artificial ruby created from

that process was used in the first working laser. While the Ruby
Star had been operated on artificial ruby rods in some of its
variants, it was the model sitting in the Mandalay Yards, using
the real gem as its active medium, that developed the most
power while utilizing the least amount of input power. Some
of the Space Defense Initiative experimental laser models—intended to knock down incoming ballistic missiles—required
power equivalent to the full output of a nuclear reactor. As a
result, the Ruby Star had the most potential for large-scale industrial use. And military use. Carson had already conducted
the experiment on the military end, though he didn't think he'd
write it up for Abrams.

And to match the scale of the Ruby Star laser, the gemstones
had to be over one hundred millimeters in length, in order to
be cut to their finished length of ninety-six millimeters. The
interior structure of silk—the densely woven needles—contributed something to the refraction of light, and the Burmese rubies were specified for this laser.

What it came down to, Carson's and Gilbert's primary objectives in Myanmar had been to secure the mining contract.
The Modernization Project was only mildly profitable to General Technologies. The company had shaved its profit margins
to the bone to land the master contract for two reasons: to get
a foothold in the country, which might lead to the mines, and
to create favorable publicity for the company in its humanitarian pursuit of improving the standard of living for Myanmar
citizens.

The benefits for the Burmese people through the Modernization Project were secondary to the tremendous profits GTI
could realize from a monopoly of the Ruby Star laser. The
scarcity of the ruby active medium alone would drive the per
unit cost sky-high. It was better than selling rubies to the socially elite to sport around New York and London and Paris on
their fingers or pendants.

By subjugating himself to the duplicitous corporate goal,
Carson had often thought that he was becoming a very real

bastard. In many ways, GTI was no better than Saddam; they both were greedy. GTI chose to invade Myanmar economically while Saddam picked on Kuwait. As a rationale for retaining his moral balance, Carson kept reminding himself that, despite the eventual objective, his role in Myanmar would actually benefit the people.

Still, he could recall vividly his discussion with Lon Mauk about the ample opportunities for treachery. He couldn't help but feel that he was in some way betraying his overt posture in the country, pushing the modernization project as a cover for getting his hands on the mines.

It didn't make him feel very good about himself.

At times, like tonight, he felt as if he couldn't boast of better personal motives than Hyun Oh.

He took another look at the contract. At his suggestion, the lawyers had written it up with a twenty percent split to GTI, though Abrams had given him permission to negotiate down to seventeen-point-five. The South Koreans always worked cheaper. Their version of a Ruby Star would likely undercut the American price significantly, since they didn't have to recover a third of a billion dollars in research costs. By the same token, Carson suspected that the Hypai mining proposal would come in at less than twenty percent. Probably around fifteen. Hypai could absorb that level in order to achieve access to the rubies.

Carson had the leverage of jobs to offer. The SLORC could spend a couple weeks debating the differences in the contract. Was the committee to be swayed by higher profits to itself, or by reducing the tension in the streets?

Spinning around in his chair to his computer credenza, Carson turned on his computer. A few minutes later, he had dipped into Becky Johnson's files and called up the contract. He found page two and changed the percentage rates from twenty to fifteen. He sent the page into the print queue, then went out to Johnson's office and turned on the printer. As soon as it warmed up, it spit out three copies of the new page.

Walking back to his office, he read the page, almost threw it out.

Then replaced the original pages in the three copies of the contract with the new ones.

To hell with it.

GTI would get the mining contract without the SLORC having to pore over the differences between economic and political decisions. Hypai would be out, GTI would make less money on the mines, but billions on the laser.

To hell with Abrams.

Carson would be out, too, but that conclusion had been reached the moment he decided to defy Abrams's order.

He wished he could have tested his reasoning with Jack Gilbert. It was at a time like this that he truly missed his friend.

It was eleven-thirty. Carson shut off the computer, the lights in his office, and the printer in Johnson's office. He was about to kill the lights in there when he heard someone banging on the front door.

He went into the reception room and saw Janice Cooper standing outside the glass door.

He unlocked it.

"Is Stephanie here?" she asked.

"No."

"We all thought she'd stayed up at the railhead, but Dick Statler just got back from there and said she'd flown back last night. No one's seen her, Chris!"

Carson felt his pulse rate increase. He'd been so damned busy, he hadn't had time to figure out how he was going to handle Stephanie Branigan. He knew he had to; there was something special there, and it hadn't yet had time to blossom. But if something happened to her, he'd blame himself forever.

"Who have you talked to?"

"I've called all the construction sites. I talked to Don Evans. Her Gazelle did come back last night, and the pilot saw her headed for the parking lot. But, Chris, the car's still in the lot. Her purse and keys were on the floor."

"Damn it! Get on one of these phones and call Kasperik, Creighton, and Washington. See if they've talked to her."

He went back into Johnson's office and grabbed the phone. He called Mauk, but the sergeant said he was out. He would try to track him down.

He called Ba Thun. The valet answered, and after a brief argument, said he would wake the minister.

While he waited, another line lit up, and he punched the button.

"Carson."

"This is Colonel Mauk. I am in Moulmein."

"Stephanie Branigan is missing."

"I will be back in Yangon shortly, Mr. Carson, and will come directly to your office."

"Hurry, damn it! If you thought I'd gone hog-wild shooting up Daw Tan's place, you'd better find her damned quick, Colonel. Otherwise, I'm going to get mad."

Prome

Stephanie Branigan had become less frantic in the last hours.

She didn't know how much time had passed, but she thought that if they were going to kill her, they would already have done so.

She didn't know where she was, either. As soon as she had been pushed into the back of the van in the airport parking lot, she had been blindfolded, and it had not been removed since. Her wrists were bound together, and even the limited freedom of her arms was restricted by the fiberglass cast.

There had been a long ride in a medium-size boat. She remembered movement she associated with the sea—long rises and drops of swelling waves—and then many more hours in smoother waters. She assumed they had gone up some river.

The boat was long gone. At least, she had been removed from it, and marched into a nearby building. The air smelled of water and dampness. The pile of rags, or whatever it was, that she rested on was also damp. They were near water.

There were two men with her. When they conversed, they spoke in a language and dialect she didn't know. The woman who had first accosted her in the parking lot was not with them. She was beginning to think that the woman must be the chieftain, Nito Kaing.

A window was nearby, for she had felt the warmth of the sun during the day, but it was now night again. Twice she had been allowed to go to the bathroom, led into an evil-smelling room, and allowed to search in her darkness with her hands to find the toilet.

Twice she had been given water and rice cakes. One man had groped her and apparently had been rebuked by the other. She had been unmolested since.

The rest of the endless hours had passed in mindless solitude. She heard the men talking; she tried to concentrate on her plight; she attempted to free her hands; she counted numbers and devised complicated short stories to keep her mind from rebelling. A number of times, the fear welled up in her so unexpectedly, she nearly vomited.

She was lying on her side, unable to get comfortable because of the way her wrists were tied and the way the cast got in the way. She couldn't remember if she had ever fallen asleep, but thought that she had. Still, she felt overwhelmed by fatigue.

A door creaked.

And then a feminine voice, authorative, barking orders in that strange language.

Footsteps approached.

Hands grabbed her roughly and pulled her upright.

She struggled against them, felt her sleeve being ripped.

And then the needle.

Punctured the skin of her arm, in the crook of the elbow.

She screamed.

TWENTY-SIX

Myanmar army barracks, Yangon

Sixty-six hours after Branigan had disappeared, Lon Mauk had not accumulated one lead as to her location.

Or her grave.

He was of the opinion that her body, weighted with cement blocks, was in the slit at the bottom of the Rangoon River. Unless a ransom demand was in the offing, there was no earthly reason for her abductors, whoever they might be, to keep her alive.

Of course, that logic had been defied many times, especially by hostage takers in the Middle Eastern countries. Such cases as those made the reliance on precedent shaky at best.

His strongest suspicion was that Daw Tan's followers had taken her, in retaliation for Tan's murder. If so, it served only to prove that even Tan's minions—Kanbe or Thamaing, perhaps—were as misled as the world in believing that the government or the military had played a role in Tan's death.

Pamela Steele's articles, and she was getting a front-page byline in most of the international newspapers daily, were not helpful, either. While not spelled out, her implication was that the committee had had some say in Daw Tan's death and were hiding behind the alibi of some unexplained and unidentified suspect. Steele did say the suspect had gained entrance to Tan's cell in the guise of a relative—Mauk wondered where she had gotten that information—and surmised that the relative was female. Steele's story on the abduction of Stephanie Branigan had resulted in squeals of protest from everywhere. All of the media personalities who had now arrived in Yangon for the UltraTrain celebration were following up on Steele's leads and none too gently prodding Ba Thun and others on the committee for explanations. The explanations were not forthcoming.

This urged the newspaper and television correspondents into a frenzy of investigative digging. They were everywhere, underfoot, blocking the streets. On Mauk's recommendation, the barracks commander had banned them from admittance to the grounds of the army barracks. The air force had done the same at their airport facilities.

Also in a frenzy were the Americans, led by the chief fanatic Christopher Carson. The white vehicles of General Technologies and the blue-and-silver cars and trucks of UltraTrain roamed the streets and countryside, conducting their own searches for the missing woman. Mauk wondered that they got any work done, though he had been told that the rail line between Mandalay and Yangon was complete and undergoing testing.

All of this produced a great deal of pressure for the SLORC. The United Nations general secretary had suggested that an independent, international committee look into both Tan's death and Branigan's disappearance. The premier had rejected that idea out of hand.

The tensions on the committee, naturally, were passed on to subordinates. Ba Thun called Mauk four and five times a day, seeking information and berating him for his poor performance.

The reports stacked on Mauk's desk were of little importance in either improving his performance or in quenching Ba Thun's thirst for knowledge. The only one of consequence—the interrogation of Branigan's bodyguards—had not shed any light. The two men assigned to her had watched her take off in the morning with the chief roadbed engineer, then had retired to the restaurant in the airport's main terminal to await her return. And they had missed it. One man had seen the helicopter landing, but by the time they reached the General Technologies parking lot, she had disappeared. Stupidly, rather than reporting their malfeasance, they had spent the night and most of the morning searching for her at the compound and the UltraTrain installations.

The two men had been reassigned as infantrymen in the First Division.

Shoving the papers aside, Mauk stood and left his office. He settled his hat squarely on his head as he left the building and got into his Land Rover. He checked the backseat to make certain the box was still there. It was, and he was half-surprised. Thievery was on the rise, everywhere. Why should it not invade the army post?

There were reporters at the gate, but he revved the engine and shot through the gate and past them, turning onto Prome Road and heading for the airport. After parking in the crowded lot in front of General Technologies' operations building, he carried his large box and pushed his way through a half-dozen correspondents, who were being kept out of the building by two burly men. The wing insignia above their breast pockets suggested they were pilots.

They allowed him to enter after checking the contents of the box. Except for the helmet, it was all electronics, mystifying to Mauk and even to the pilots, possibly.

Donald Evans, the air fleet manager, met him.

"Good morning, Colonel."

"Would Mr. Carson be here?"

"I'm afraid not. He's got a chopper out searching along the river."

"Would you see that he gets this, please?" Mauk placed the box on the counter.

"Uh, what is it?"

"Some items I borrowed from our air force's supply. Mr. Carson is expecting them."

"I'll be glad to take them off your hands, Colonel."

"How about Mr. Montoya? Is he available?"

Evans's face screwed up in suspicion.

"I am aware of your Data Processing Center, Mr. Evans."

"Come on back."

Evans led him back to a rear office and banged on the door.
A young lady opened it.

"Colonel Mauk to see Carlos, Jackie."

She let him in with apparent misgivings and called to Montoya, who got up from a computer and crossed the room. Evans
stayed with them.

"Hello, Colonel."

"Have you been keeping logs on your primary surveillance
subjects?"

"Ah . . ."

"If I know that much, Mr. Montoya, you may assume that
Christopher Carson has made me a confidant."

Montoya looked to Evans.

Evans nodded.

"Yes, sir. Come over here and have a chair."

Montoya got a castered chair for him, and Mauk sat next to
the young Hispanic man while he tapped his keyboard. Evans
stood behind them, watching over Montoya's shoulder.

"What did you wish to know, Colonel?"

"I would like to see what calls have been placed to and from
Minister Ba Thun's office and residence."

Ba Thun had told him that he had tried innumerable times
to reach Khim Nol, but that Nol was not returning his calls.

Montoya's eyes showed some surprise that Mauk knew they
were monitoring Ba Thun.

"Over what period, Colonel?"

"Let us try the last three days."

Montoya tapped in the telephone numbers, then some other
codes, and a very long list appeared on the screen.

With his forefinger on the screen, Montoya slowly went
down the screen, identifying the calls.

"This main number is the YMCA . . . here is the YWCA . . .
these are extension numbers. There are a great many calls

placed from these two buildings. I assume it is because the reporters are all assigned to rooms at those two hotels and call the minister frequently. After the first couple calls, we stopped listening to those. Here is the premier's number . . . the interior minister . . . Khim Nol."

"How many calls to Nol?"

The man counted, scrolling the list up on the screen as he did. "Seven calls. According to this notation here, they were all short."

"He never talked to Nol?"

"No, sir. He left messages, but Nol has not called back."

"How about Shwe and Kaing?"

Again, Montoya counted.

"Three calls apiece. They haven't returned them, either."

So. The chieftains were ignoring Ba Thun. That was the reason why Ba Thun had not yet given him a definitive answer in the matter of identifying Nito Kaing to the media as his prime suspect. Without communication with Nol, the minister could not strike a bargain.

"What of Hyun Oh?"

"Chris just added him to our list a couple of days ago, Colonel. We weren't monitoring him directly before."

The earlier information concerning Oh had resulted from Khim Nol's call to Hyun Oh.

Montoya tapped the keyboard deftly, and a new list appeared.

"Let's see now . . . several calls to Seoul . . . a bunch around the country here. We haven't identified all of them, but many appear to be to persons who may be potential investors in local telephone companies. Two calls to U Ba Thun. One . . . two . . . five . . . ten . . . fifteen . . . looks like about twenty calls to different telephone exchanges. He was probably checking on construction, since they're all the newer exchanges."

"And that is all?"

"That's it, Colonel."

There was nothing in the least incriminating about this list. He would have liked to see a list of Carson's calls, but reason suggested he not even ask, much less assume that Carson was having his own telephone monitored.

"What of the Listening Posts?" he asked.

"Nothing significant, Colonel. Along the railway, we hear only the trains being tested and occasionally the movement of the First Division's patrols. The Listening Post at Daw Tan's place quit operating, probably damaged during the attack. At Shwe's, Kaing's and Nol's compounds, we've heard only the movement of vehicles and a few aircraft arriving or departing."

"Thank you, Mr. Montoya, Mr. Evans. I appreciate your assistance."

"Any time, Colonel," Evans responded for the two of them.

Mauk went back to his truck, dodging reporters and uttering the famous words, "No comment."

At the gate to the military post, as he slowed for the barrier to be raised, a woman reporter stuck a microphone in his open window and yelled at him, "Was it you who killed Daw Tan, Colonel?"

He resisted the impulse to strike out at her, gunned the engine, and raced into the safety of the grounds. By the time he climbed the short flight of steps to his orderly room, his fury had built sufficiently that he could no longer moderate his tone.

He yelled at the duty officer, "Lieutenant! Get on the telephone and find Minister Ba Thun. Do not stop calling until you have reached him."

It took twenty minutes.

When Ba Thun was finally on the line, he said, "Minister, I will no longer be called a murderer. I am going to name Nito Kaing."

"Colonel Mauk, I have not yet been able to reach Khim Nol."

"Let us assume that, even when you talk to him, he will not give up Kaing. What then? Do you know the students are marching again tonight? They have many complaints."

"We will upset many delicate balances," Ba Thun said.

"If the students and the jobless are moved to riot, if the

United Nations sends investigators, if the foreign workers strike, if the train does not run after your visitors arrive, how many balances will be upset? With all due respect, Minister, you must call a press conference. Or I will do so."

"Let me talk to the premier," Ba Thun conceded.

GTI compound, Yangon

The local television station carried the press conference, and Hyun Oh and Kim Sung-Young watched it together on the television set in the reception area.

After a long recital of reasons for maintaining the public peace, Minister U Ba Thun said, "The primary suspect in the murder of Chieftain Daw Tan, while he was in custody at the military-police detention facility, has been identified as Nito Kaing of Southern Shan State. An arrest warrant has been issued, and all military and police units have been notified to arrest her on sight. Her apprehension is considered imminent."

Ba Thun went on again to encourage all who listened to be moderate in their actions.

Oh suspected the announcement was directed chiefly to the outside world, which would not understand the immense difficulty in finding Nito Kaing in the jungles and mountains of Shan State. It was also directed toward the radical students, in the hope of quelling their enthusiasm for outrage during the march scheduled for tonight.

As far as Oh could tell, the students could care less about Daw Tan, but they were happy enough to use him as an example of governmental oppression. Ba Thun may have defused that particular stick of dynamite.

When the telecast ended, Oh said, "Let us go to work," got up, and went back to his office, followed by Sung-Young's suspicious eyes. The assistant director could not understand the change in his superior's demeanor, Oh was certain. In the last few days, he had become much more assertive, taking charge, ordering Sung-Young to perform his tasks with increased efficiency. The problem with Sung-Young was that he was merely an engineer with an accountant's duties; he did not understand the more arcane aspects of business.

Perhaps Mr. Pai, in reassessing Hyun Oh's worth, had realized that his knowledge of people and concepts was superior to Sung-Young's knowledge of numbers. Oh was a man of words and deals. In his humble opinion, it was words that made the world operate, not numbers. Judging people and formulating agreements with them achieved goals; numbers did not.

Perhaps, also, Mr. Pai had realized belatedly that Oh's awareness of the EASTGLOW laser project and its origins was an asset for Oh and a debit for Pai. The president of Hypai Industries could not very well dismiss Oh out of hand without jeopardizing EASTGLOW.

The machine had yet to operate as designed, according to the specifications in the plans, and that was for the lack of a true ruby of sufficient size. The Hypai engineers had made it work with an artificial ruby rod, but the power consumption was enormous in order to produce a laser beam, which the scientists said did not fulfill the output specified in the design. For nearly a year, the engineers had been clamoring for a Burmese ruby.

Oh thought that he had discovered the ideal stone—he had even louped it—but Mr. Chao had sold it to another. Now, he was down to hoping for a successful bid for the mining contract. He had turned the written proposal in to Ba Thun yesterday, then learned for the first time that there was another bidder in General Technologies Incorporated. Once again, Carson appeared to be on top of the issues.

That information was disheartening, but Oh had reviewed his proposal and thought that it had a fair chance of succeeding. At fifteen percent of production, the commission was not high, and he felt assured that it would be lower than any other submitted proposal.

He could not afford to be anything other than optimistic

about the mining proposal. If Hypai lost it, the EASTGLOW project was doomed.

In that event, his only hope of survival was his arrangement with Khim Nol. Hypai's assumption of the master contract would give him a respite for four or five years, time in which to further ingratiate himself with Mr. Pai. Oh consciously avoided the unpleasant thoughts related to his agreement with Nol. Carson's disappearance was distasteful, but necessary. In the same manner, he had attempted to keep his mind vacant of reflections on Stephanie Branigan, though he had been unsuccessful. The furor raised over her vanishing act was disconcerting. It would haunt him for a long time, he thought.

What eased his mind was the consideration of his future. He would rid himself of the ridiculously small apartment in the General Technologies compound and move to the Strand. He would get another Celica or perhaps a Lexus. He would . . .

Oh heard Carson's voice speaking to the secretary in the reception room.

Rising from his chair, he went around his desk to greet Carson as the man entered his office.

Stormed into it, rather.

Carson's face was suffused in anger. His blue eyes were almost silver in their intensity. The sockets were dark with fatigue.

"Mr. Carson—"

Carson stopped right in front of him, and stuck his face in Oh's, barely six inches away. Oh was offended.

"Mr. Oh, I'm tired of screwing around with you. I know you met with Daw Tan. I know you've been meeting Khim Nol. If I learn that you've done anything to hurt Stephanie, or if anything happens to that train on Monday, I'm coming back. I'll turn you upside down and rip your legs off like the wishbone of a chicken."

Oh gasped.

"I won't need evidence, either. Just a whisper will do it."

Carson spun around and charged out of the office.

Oh's legs collapsed. He tumbled sideways into a chair.

Menlo Park, California

"The cargo plane's here, sitting right out on the ramp, Mr. Abrams," Don Evans told him.

"And where's the cargo?"

"That, I can't help you with, sir. I didn't know anything about it."

"Where's Carson?"

"He's been searching for Branigan. Just an hour ago, he brought a chopper back and then took off for town. I didn't really get a chance to talk to him."

Abrams sighed. He picked up the scotch Alicia had mixed for him and took a long pull at it.

"Why can't anyone track him down?" he asked.

"Ah, the disappearance of Branigan has upset everyone. Our schedules are shot to hell. Mr. Abrams, he's not in the best of moods."

"Well, neither am I, goddamn it!"

"Uh, yes, sir."

"You just got yourself a new job, Evans. Find Carson and have him call me."

"Right away, sir!"

Abrams slammed the phone down.

From her chair on the other side of the lamp table, Alicia stared at him. The TV in the bookshelves on the opposite wall flickered soundlessly with some late, late show.

He stared back at her. "Carson's really done it this time."

"How long have you two been together?" she asked.

Sixteen years.

"Long enough that I should know better. He doesn't follow orders very well."

"But he gets the job done, every time," she pointed out.

"The board's involved this time, Alicia. Chris is playing with their toy. Given the R and D nature of it, it's about a fifty-million-dollar toy. I don't have a choice, as soon as they learn it's not back in the States."

"And Jack was killed. And this Branigan woman is missing."

"I'm mad, too."

"But not mad enough to buck the board?"

Abrams looked at his watch. Nearly midnight.

"I'll give him another twelve hours."

Keng Tung

It was daytime.

She knew that, though her mind felt foggy. She had been injected with some kind of drug several times.

The airplane ride had lasted several hours, but she couldn't be more precise than that. It had been, she thought, a twin-engined aircraft, though a small one. Branigan had been tied to a seat in the cabin, and while she was still blindfolded, the cabin just felt small to her.

The landing was uneven, bouncy, and after the plane rolled to a stop, she felt a blast of warm air hit her when the door was opened. The female voice spoke. Rough hands worked around her, releasing her from the seat, but not freeing her hands.

Her arm ached.

The man pulled her up from the seat, turned her toward the doorway, and prodded her forward. She was frightened, unable to see and not knowing how far to the ground it was.

Another set of hands, from outside the airplane, guided her down some steps, then forced her to walk across weedy ground to a car. She heard the door open, then struggled a little as she was pushed inside.

It was a short ride, then she was manhandled out of the car, up several steps, and into a building. She smelled the air and thought she was probably in the mountains. The inside of the house was cool and smelled of something strange, maybe incense. There were more voices.

The man grabbed her hands and towed her forward. Her shoes slapped on a wooden floor; she tripped as her toe caught a rug, and after several steps, she was back on a wood floor. Down a hallway, she thought.

A door opening.

The rough hands worked at her wrists.

They were suddenly free!

Then she was shoved, and she stumbled several times, trying to keep her balance.

The door closed with a solid bang behind her.

Branigan stood for several minutes, listening. She heard no movement.

A few times before, she had attempted to push her blindfold aside, and she had been slapped across the face hard. Now, she was hesitant to try to remove it despite the fact that the bonds had been removed from her wrists.

Tentatively she raised her left hand, and when nothing happened, got her left thumb under the edge of the blindfold and raised it away from her face, jerked it off her head.

She had closed her eyes in anticipation of bright light, but when she raised her lids a bit, found herself in semidarkness.

It was a nondescript room, perhaps twelve feet square. The window was shuttered, blocking out the light except for thin openings at the top and bottom. Behind her was the door, and she didn't even try the knob. There was a dead bolt above it, and she knew it would be locked. There was one narrow bed, made up with a pillow and blanket, a single chair, and a cheap bureau against one wall.

That was it.

Her cell.

She didn't even know what she was guilty of, but she was obviously being punished for it.

Holding her cast with her left hand, she crossed the room

and sat on the edge of the bed. Whatever had been used to sedate her was wearing off, and it only allowed her terror to surface. Branigan had never felt so isolated in her life. She had suffered crises before, and she had always been able to dredge up the will to face them and overcome them.

This was entirely alien. Unknown.

She thought she might even understand Carson's motives. This couldn't go on for much longer. And who could help her? Not the government, which was in collusion with these bastards.

Chris! Here I am! Help me. Please.

Her hands trembled when she thought that her life might mean very little to those who had taken her.

The bolt in the door clacked.

The door pushed open, letting in light from the corridor.

A very short man stepped inside, his face shadowed by the light from behind him. He was bald, and from the little she could see of his face, it seemed to be scarred badly.

Behind him came the woman from the parking lot. She was beautiful on a very petite scale.

She started to stand up.

"Sit!" he ordered.

She sat back.

He moved to stand at her left, and the woman crossed the room and stood on her right. She was carrying a heavy, gnarled stick, almost like a walking stick. Branigan couldn't decide who to look at. Her head moved left, right, then left again.

The man looked her over, but nothing in his face suggested whether he approved of her or not.

"I am Khim Nol," he said.

"What are you going to do with me?" Her voice sounded squeaky; she hadn't used it in a long time.

He didn't respond to her question, but said, "You will do as you are told. Otherwise . . ."

He nodded at the woman.

She swung the truncheon.

Branigan tried to turn into it, to deflect the blow with her cast, but it slammed into the fiberglass cast with a crack, which reverberated loudly against the plaster walls of the room.

The pain shot up her arm, and she nearly passed out.

She screamed and fell back on the bed, rolling onto her side, trying to cradle her arm.

When she could catch her breath, she looked at the cast. It was fractured across the top. The peak of pain eased, but her arm throbbed. It may have been broken again.

"You will do as you're told," Nol said again.

Fighting back tears unsuccessfully, Branigan said, "You're only going to kill me."

"Kill you? Of course not! You are my shield."

The porcelain-skinned woman laughed.

Data Processing Center, Yangon

At five in the morning on Saturday, Carson called Mauk. His call was directed to Mauk's quarters, and Carson realized he didn't even know where the man lived. Probably in one of the bungalows on the post reserved for officers. When he answered the phone, Carson asked him to come to the GTI operations building.

The place had become the center of the search activities and was packed with people. Pilots were in and out. A large number of UltraTrain personnel were helping in the search, as were InstaStructure, Hygienic Systems, and Hydrofoil Marine employees. Charles Washington was coordinating the ground search. Don Evans was launching helicopters as soon as they had been refueled and re-piloted.

Air activity for the main airport terminal was expected to increase substantially during the day as more of the invited guests arrived from outside the country and were transferred to military aircraft and conscripted local air-service planes for the trip to Mandalay.

Carlos Montoya and Kiki Olson were maintaining computer-generated maps posted in the operations room. They depicted areas that had been searched, were being searched, or were planned for search. Montoya was in contact with police and military units that, at Ba Thun's direction, were also involved.

The atmosphere of Yangon was not conducive to the rites of celebration over a damned train, Carson thought. The night before, two people had been killed and a dozen more injured when the student demonstration erupted in violence. Police and military patrols had been stepped up. The GTI compound and the airport headquarters had had their guard details augmented. In Mandalay, Prome, and Pegu, there had been mild demonstrations against government facilities, but they had been contained effectively.

While he waited for Mauk, Carson refilled his coffee cup and got a cinnamon roll. He had had plenty of coffee during the night, but only a couple hours of sleep on one of the thirty army cots Evans had set up back in the hangar.

Evans looked as fatigued as Carson felt.

"Chris, you called Abrams yet?"

"I'll get around to it."

"Shit, man! He told me directly!"

"Yeah. I'll call him."

Sometime. Now was not the time, however. He liked Abrams, but knew the man was under the thumb of the board. Carson didn't want any lectures, and he wasn't going to make any promises.

Until he found Branigan.

He also wasn't going to give up the Ruby Star until after that train covered four hundred miles to Yangon. If Branigan couldn't look out for her train, Carson would.

Mauk showed up looking fresh in crisp, starched khakis.

"Sorry I got you out of bed, Colonel."

"Have you been to bed, Mr. Carson?"

He ran his hand over the stubble on his cheeks. "Doesn't look like it, but I got a couple hours."

Carson waved the colonel around the counter and led him back to Montoya's domain.

"Hey, Carlos, let's run those tapes again."

Montoya set up the recorder, and Carson gave Mauk a set of headphones. He pulled another pair over his own ears.

When the tape was rewound, Carson gave Montoya a thumbs-up, and the reels began to turn.

He watched Mauk's face as he listened, for the third time, to aircraft engines.

After six or seven minutes of the same thing, Mauk pulled his headphones off.

"Airplanes," he said.

"All jets. Five of them landed."

"Where?"

"Khim Nol's private airstrip."

"When?"

"During the night. Between one and two o'clock."

Mauk's mouth worked, grinding his teeth, as he thought it over.

"It is not a normal occurrence, Mr. Carson?"

"Not that many planes all at once in the time we've had that Listening Post in place."

"May I use your telephone?"

"Help yourself."

Carson listened as Mauk called some Air Force colonel named Chit Nyunt. The two of them argued for a long time, and Mauk made some threats, listened, then hung up.

"Colonel Nyunt is the air-force intelligence officer. He will send an airplane to take a look at Nol's airfield. There is one in the vicinity, Nyunt said."

"It sounded to me as if he didn't want to," Carson said.

"He did not. But he will."

Forty minutes went by as they waited, Carson bringing Mauk up to speed on the search for Branigan.

Nyunt called back, and Mauk took it. They spoke for several

minutes, chattering in Burmese, then Mauk dropped the phone in its cradle.

"There are seven T-37 aircraft parked on the strip, in addition to several light twins, three helicopters, and five multiengine transports. There appears to be no activity other than routine maintenance taking place."

"You mention the T-37s specifically," Carson said.

"It is unusual for them to be together. Nol owns two, so the others must belong to Shwe and Kaing."

"Can these things be armed, Colonel?"

"They are not to be."

"Which wasn't the question."

"I have never looked at them closely, Mr. Carson. Quite likely, the answer is yes."

Now Mauk looked worried.

"Would Nol mount an attack against the government?"

"No."

"How about against one of our operations? If he hates them so much?"

"Not so obviously. Booby traps and timed explosives are one thing, Mr. Carson. Attacks by aircraft quite another."

"Something's up," Carson said. "I don't think we should wait to see what happens."

He wished he hadn't demounted the Ruby Star from the Skycrane.

Mauk was thinking along the same lines. "What of your secret weapon?"

"It would take a couple days to get it ready again. I've got it hidden right now."

"Minister Ba Thun is trying to talk to Khim Nol," Mauk said.

"But without success. You saw the phone logs, and Nol hasn't returned a call yet."

"I should think that that is unusual. I fear that a schism has developed between Ba Thun and Nol."

"Those T-37s wouldn't stand a chance against the air force,"

Carson said. "I think they're going after the rail line. Nol doesn't want the UltraTrain to run on Monday."

Mauk's head nodded his agreement, but his eyes were unfocused, looking far away.

"You have another idea, Colonel?"

Mauk shook his head, as if trying to clear his mind. "Nothing specific. I will go to Minister Ba Thun, and the premier if possible, and talk to them about a preemptive strike by the air force against Nol's aircraft. I do not think, however, that anything will come of it. The committee is already upset over my forcing the indictment of Nito Kaing. To press for yet more in an area of such fragile balances—already drastically disturbed—is a great deal for which to hope."

"All right. We'll continue monitoring the activity at the airstrip."

"Should there be an indication that the planes are leaving, please call me, and I will alert the air force."

Carson cocked his head.

"I do not wish the air force to know of your Listening Posts."

Carson sighed. It wasn't a good sign when one couldn't trust his own air force.

TWENTY-SEVEN

Twenty miles north of Pyinmana

The ceiling was low, around five thousand feet, and the threat of rain was ominous.

Carson kept the Gazelle centered over the pedestal guideway at 500 feet AGL. His forward speed was less than 50 miles an hour.

Dick Statler was in the left seat, and the motive-power chief, Craig Wilson, was in the back. Wilson had a portable radio and was in contact with the man operating the shuttle. Two of Mack Little's technology experts completed the complement of his passengers.

Several times, they were passed by military helicopters and transport craft taking some of the bigwigs to Mandalay. A few military planes patrolled the main line.

"All right," Wilson said, "on this next stretch, I want to open her up. That okay with you, Chris?"

"Punch it, Craig. I'll try to keep up."

Wilson gave the order via his portable radio to his operator on the work car, and the shuttle accelerated smoothly, pulling quickly away from them. From the air, the car's movement appeared utterly smooth. The acceleration was rapid, but didn't seem to disturb anything around the shuttle. It raced northward on the pedestal track, and Carson picked up forward speed in an attempt to stay with it, or slightly behind it so Statler and Wilson could observe.

"How fast did you tell him?" Carson asked.

"One seventy-five. I didn't want him to leave us behind."

They sailed along, following the rail line north, and while the two engineers studied the car and the guideway, Carson kept half his attention on the area surrounding the main line.

The military ground patrols seemed about evenly spaced, perhaps a mile to a mile-and-a-half apart. Most were motorized in that, while they guarded access routes to the track, they had armored personnel carriers or Jeeps available. Near the major bridges and road crossings, there were walking patrols.

As they passed over Yamethin, he noticed an encampment of tents on the edge of town. Near the tents were parked a dozen silver-and-blue trucks and heavy equipment.

"That's the third track crew I've seen camped along the track, Dick. I thought you'd pulled them off and sent them north."

"I've got five teams stationed along the way, Chris. Just in case we need to make an emergency repair. After we get the damned train to Yangon on Monday, I'll put them to work on the Taunggyi Division."

"That's what Stephanie would have done," Wilson said.

"I know," Statler said. "That's why I did it. Once that inaugural train run is part of history, I think the danger will die down."

Mention of Branigan made Carson's stomach churn. In a couple hours, four days would have elapsed since she had been taken. The last three of those days, since he had learned of her disappearance, had been anguish for him. He was certain there was something he could have done to prevent it.

He hadn't given up hope, though he thought that Mauk may have.

They were relatively certain she wasn't in Yangon, and military patrols in the far reaches of the country were passing out handbills and keeping their eyes open.

Supposedly.

Carson hated relying on others but had no other choices. GTI and subcontractor personnel at the outlying construction sites were still spending some of their off-duty time searching the roads and the byways. Chopper pilots transporting passengers and cargo were taking new routes in order to scan the countryside.

There had been no sightings and no reported leads, despite the $100,000 reward he had put up.

Headlights coming right over the median.

No place to go, and no way to control it.

Sliding backward.

Watching that pickup bearing down on him.

It was Highway 101 all over again. He felt as if he had no control, and yet knew there was something he should have done, or should be doing.

Ah, Steph, he thought, if only . . .

If only he hadn't spent so much time trying to be a policeman, instead of letting the cops do it. Jesus! He needed to see her again, if only to explain himself to her. Make promises. Make declarations.

"All right," Wilson said, "there's Thazi coming up. We'll slow it down to a hundred for the rest of the route in."

Carson matched the speed of the shuttle after Wilson radioed his order to the operator.

"That was all of the new stretch," Statler said. "I didn't see one glitch, did you, Craig?"

"Nary a one, Dick. No alarms went off in the shuttle, either."

One of the reasons Carson had offered to fly the railroad engineers on this survey was his own desire to examine the line in terms of military defense. The railroad followed the Sittang River valley all the way from Yangon to Mandalay, and the terrain was relatively flat. To the south, the distance between villages and towns was comparatively short—the population density was high.

As he continued to tag along after the shuttle, he noted that, between Thedaw and Thabyedaung, a distance of about thirteen miles, the main line was somewhat isolated. It pulled away from the highway on the left by four or five miles. On the right, the plateau country was a wild area of forests and peaks. And the border of Shan State was maybe fifteen miles away to the east. He noted that the army patrols were parked on the shoulders of the highway, rather than close to the rail line. He would mention that to Mauk.

The shuttle pulled into the Mandalay Yards, and Carson put down near the maintenance buildings for long enough to let Statler and Wilson disembark. Then he lifted off again and flew the short distance to the GTI heliport.

He shut down the turbine as he saw Mack Little approaching from the hangar.

Pushing open the door, he said, "You ready to work for a change, Mack?"

"Shit. You go joyriding while the good guys get their hands greasy. You get it?"

"I've got a box of junk that Mauk gave me."

One of the technicians in the back said, "I think we've got everything we need, Mack. I've been through the box."

Little leaned inside and peered into the box.

"Not state-of-the-art, is it, Ted?"

"Naw, but we can make it work. Everything else we've done is such a hodgepodge, it's amazing anything happens. We'll build us a miracle out of this stuff, too."

"Let's push this hummer into the hangar, then," Little said.

Carson helped move the Gazelle inside, then found a pair of coveralls.

"You're actually going to help?" Little said.

"I can turn a wrench. Besides, I'm flying the thing. I want to know if I'm going to kill myself."

"I think you're just going to get in the way." Little grinned.

He helped Little empty the box, laying the electronic components and wiring harnesses out on a workbench. He looked over the helmet, which was scratched and battered.

Little pointed out a logo stamped on a black box: British manufacture.

He read the label: Ferranti.

Carson said, "They make some good equipment. I saw some of it in action in the Gulf."

"Let's hope they build good Target Acquisition/Designators," Little said.

The phone on the wall rang, and after one of the technicians called to him, Carson walked over and took the receiver.

"Carson."

"This is Carlos."

God, they've found Stephanie.

"The seven jets left Keng Tung."

"You're sure?"

"Counted them myself."

"Any idea where they've gone?"

"No. I called Colonel Mauk and told him. He said he'd check with some guy named Nyunt and tell the guys guarding the main line to stay on their toes."

"Nyunt's air-force intelligence. Okay, Carlos, let me know if anything else develops."

He walked back to the Gazelle feeling as if he were missing something. He hadn't expected the T-37s to take off until Monday.

Something was wrong with the strategy he was building.

GTI compound, Yangon

There were no workers present on Sunday, and Hyun Oh had the office to himself. In the reception room, he heated water in the microwave, dropped a tea bag into the cup, and carried it and the *London Times* into his quiet office. His report for Mr. Pai rested on the corner of his desk. He had not yet completed it.

While the tea steeped, he spread the paper out on his desk and attempted to read.

Concentration was difficult. Since the confrontation with Carson, the state of his nerves had become erratic. He was not a physical person, and in one moment, he would shudder at the thought of Carson appearing in his doorway to make good his threat. In the next moment, he would absolutely *know* that there was nothing for Carson to learn.

But how could Carson know of the discussions with Tan and Nol?

Perhaps he should ask Mauk for protection from Carson.

Wait.

Mauk's bodyguards.

There was always a chance he had not eluded them before his meetings. Mauk might know of the zoo rendezvous with Tan or the chance dinner with Nol in Myitkyina.

Mauk was in collusion with Carson. The army officer approved of intimidation and mayhem.

Oh could not go to Lon Mauk for help.

And the telephone calls. He eyed the executive-model telephone call-director on his desk with suspicion. Would Mauk have tapped his telephones?

No. Oh was an expert—mostly an expert—on telephone systems. Mauk's people did not have the capability for tapping into sophisticated systems.

But Carson's specialists did have.

Again, Mauk and Carson were cooperating with each other.

What had he said on the telephone?

He could not remember. He made so many calls.

Nothing incriminating, of course.

Or was there something that could be misconstrued by the authorities as suggesting Oh's complicity.

No.

Those telephone calls might be recorded somewhere.

What had he *said?*

The last meeting with Nol. At the 2nd World War Cemetery. That was arranged by telephone. If Mauk had known of it, he could have been waiting. With boom microphones, he might have overheard their discussion.

His memory blanked out on him. He could not recall the details of the conversation with Nol.

While these thoughts chased each other through his brain, Oh's eyes scanned the newspaper, barely registering the content of the articles. Pamela Steele had a page-three story on the forthcoming celebration of the UltraTrain's completed link between the two principal cities. There was nothing scandalous or violent in the article, so it had not been considered front-page material. She listed most of the prominent attachés, representatives, and agents of foreign governments who were already in Myanmar for the festivities. Several heads of state were present—from India, Thailand, Australia, Sri Lanka, Japan, Indonesia, and Saudi Arabia. A contingent from the United Nations headquarters had arrived. The U.S. Secretary of State represented America. All of them, no doubt, were in attendance to judge, not only the UltraTrain's performance, but also the Union of Myanmar's progress on the issue of civil and human rights.

On page fifteen, near the bottom of the page, was a filler that he almost missed:

HIGH-TECH CONSULTANT ARRESTED

Donald Ming, 31, a Los Angeles, California, consultant in computer technology, was arrested at his Century City office on Friday. Ming is suspected of stealing trade secrets from several large American companies including Northrop, IBM, General Technologies, Hewlett-Packard, and Rockwell-Martin. Many of those companies hold Department of Defense contracts, and the Federal Bureau of Investigation has also entered the case.

Ming's office has been sealed, and his records have been seized by the district court. A source who wished to remain unidentified said that Ming is suspected of working for a number of Far East companies. When contacted at his office, General Technologies Incorporated president Dexter Abrams said, "If the allegations are true, GTI will certainly support the criminal prosecution as well as seeking remedies in the civil courts against any involved competitor." That sentiment was echoed by spokespersons from other companies.

Hyun Oh had never heard of Donald Ming before, but he instinctively knew that a connection between Ming and Hypai Industries would be determined. He also knew what the results of any investigation would be. Ming would be tossed aside to the authorities, a minion of some Hypai director operating independently of Mr. Pai's knowledge. The entire EASTGLOW scientific team would be sacrificed. Mr. Pai would be unaffected.

And if the investigation probed far enough to uncover Oh's pursuit of a mining contract in Myanmar, which had obvious ties to the EASTGLOW project, Oh would himself be discarded, perhaps turned over for criminal prosecution.

Or, if his conversation with Khim Nol was on tape somewhere, he could be arrested by Mauk and detained in Myanmar. The prospect was frightening.

He dropped the paper on the desk. He looked at his tea, still untouched.

Carson would soon come for him. Carson was bright enough to put all of this together.

Oh got up and went across the reception area to Sung-Young's office. He unlocked the door with his master key and went inside. Passing around the desk, he squatted before the vault and spun the combinations on the two tumblers. The door opened with a slurp of the rubber seal.

From the bottom shelf, he took the steel box labeled Petty Cash, and opened the lid. The stack of currency was pitifully small. Alarmed, he counted through it quickly.

There was supposed to be nearly fifty thousand dollars in the box.

In U.S. dollars, Thai *baht*, and Myanmar *kyat*, he counted less than five thousand dollars.

Kim Sung-Young had removed the rest of the cash, hidden it elsewhere. He knew it.

Frantically he searched through the drawers and pigeonholes of the safe, but discovered only legal documents. He went through the assistant director's desk drawers. Nothing.

He did not leave a receipt. Stuffing the bills into his pockets, Oh left the office and locked the door. He locked his own door and the front door as he left. He crossed the compound to the western entrance.

He would not go back to his room. There was nothing of importance there, anyway, except for his clothing. He could not be seen leaving the compound with luggage.

On Shwedagon Street, he flagged a taxi, and when it screeched to a stop in front of him, crawled into the back.

"Mingaladon Airport, the commercial terminal."

Keng Tung

It was still dark out when they came for Branigan. She thought it must be the early morning of Sunday. July 14.

She wasn't certain. Several times, she had lost her grasp on reality. Her arm ached steadily, and when the pain peaked, it was all she could do to think about anything else.

A man came up to her bed, grabbed her wrists, and jerked her upright.

A lance of pain shot up her arm.

She groaned.

The woman stood at the door. She grinned. She also held an old-fashioned barber's razor, opened, letting the shiny steel reflect the overhead light, and Branigan couldn't take her eyes off it.

My God! She's going to cut me. Chris! Where are you? Help me!

The fear rushed over her in heavy waves, which made her

sag back on the bed. The man pulled her up again, then bound her wrists together with nylon rope.

He got her to her feet, then jerking the rope, dragged her forward.

"No!"

"Be quiet!" the woman said. "I do not want to hear you."

Branigan planted her feet and dragged the man to a halt.

"You're Nito Kaing."

"And you are responsible for the death of my son, bitch."

"What! You're crazy!"

"Take her."

The man jerked the rope, sending the shards of pain shooting up her arm. Branigan grimaced against the pain.

It was the reverse of her arrival, though she was not blindfolded this time. She was taken to a car, then driven to the airfield. There, a helicopter waited with its engine idling, and she was pushed into the back of it. The man climbed into the back of it.

And they waited.

When Khim Nol appeared, he and the woman boarded. The woman sat next to Branigan, brandishing the razor. It was folded shut now, but that didn't make it less menacing.

The helicopter took off.

It didn't have its navigational lights on, and the space around them was dark enough that Branigan assumed there were clouds obliterating the stars. She hoped the pilot knew what he was doing.

Khim Nol and the woman were apparently talking to each other, but Branigan didn't have a headset and couldn't hear what they were saying.

It seemed like hours later that the helicopter began to descend. She tried to peer forward between the pilot's seats. She didn't know what kind of helicopter it was, but there was a lot of Plexiglas through which she could see, if there was anything to see.

A light flared on the ground, and the pilot veered to the right, toward it.

Moments later, with the engine shut down and her ears trying to recover from the prolonged roar of the engine, she was pulled from the cabin. In the dark, she couldn't see very much, but she thought one of the planes parked nearby was similar to the one she and Carson had seen just before they crashed.

They crossed the runway and she saw more planes, but they appeared to be badly damaged, their wings crushed and mangled and lying on the ground, the fuselages burned.

She had decided they weren't going to kill her yet, but she wished she knew where she was.

City Hall, Yangon

"I talked to Colonel Nyunt, Minister Ba Thun, but he does not know where the airplanes have gone. He says they are not airborne and have not appeared on any radar."

A long moment, then, "Does he know if they have been armed?"

"I asked that, but unfortunately, he had not ordered reconnaissance photos as I requested. The air force does not know the configuration of the trainers."

Ba Thun grunted.

Mauk waited. The commerce minister appeared distracted, as if he had to force himself to follow the course of the conversation. He stared at the files resting on his blotter.

Finally, with a minute shake of his head, he looked up, almost surprised to see Mauk still sitting opposite him.

"And what of Hyun Oh?"

"As I reported to you last night, he left the country on a flight for Bangkok. There was no advance notice of his trip. This morning, I learned from the Thai police that he transferred to an airline flight for Jakarta."

"And what do you make of this, Colonel?"

"He was conspicuous for his lack of luggage, Minister. For that, and other reasons, I do not expect him to return. I would not expect him to return to Seoul, either."

"Explain your other reasons, please."

"Carson told me, and I confirmed, that there is an investigation taking place in the United States relative to industrial espionage. There are indications that Hypai Industries—or some of its employees—may be involved. Whether or not Hyun Oh was a part of that, I do not know."

"There is more?"

"We know that Oh made contact on several occasions with Daw Tan and Khim Nol."

By the way Ba Thun's eyes widened, Mauk could tell he was surprised at that revelation.

"We do not know the topics discussed," Mauk continued, "but the probability is that they were unsavory. There was no evidence of wrongdoing, though the suspicion was present in my mind, at least."

"And you did something with your suspicion?"

"Ah . . . no, Minister. Mr. Carson confronted Oh in such a way as to let him know that we suspected him. The result, apparently, was Oh's flight from the country."

"You were aware of Carson's action beforehand?"

"We discussed it briefly, yes. I approved."

"And what did you suspect of Oh?"

"The truth is likely to remain unknown. My favorite theory is that Oh persuaded either Daw Tan or Khim Nol, or both of them, to assist him in discrediting General Technologies in some way, so as to assume the master contract for the modernization program. I hesitate to go so far as to say Oh would suggest that any of the principals of the companies involved be assassinated."

"But you feel the sabotage of microwave and railway facilities may have been masterminded by Oh?"

"Again, Minister, there is no evidence. My instinct tells me that Oh's conspiracy would be a logical explanation."

Ba Thun's eyes glittered under the fluorescent light now, bright as he followed Mauk's recital. He seemed genuinely interested in the hypothesis.

Mauk was disheartened.

"I will pass your instinctual reaction to the committee."

"As you wish, Minister. On another matter, so that I may provide security, what time did you intend to leave for Mandalay?"

"I will not be going to Mandalay, Colonel. I have decided to join the premier at Rangoon Station to oversee the reception preparations and to meet the train when it arrives."

"The premier will stay, also?"

"Yes. The rest of the committee will fly to Mandalay in the morning."

"Thank you, Minister. That is all I need to know."

Palo Alto, California

"You were supposed to call me a couple days ago," Abrams said. He fiddled with the pen set on his desk. He was nervous.

"I've been busy, Dex. I'm calling now."

"Evans told me that cargo plane is still on the ground."

"I imagine it is."

"Where is the Ruby Star?"

"It's safe. You know I'm not going to risk it."

Abrams let out a long sigh. "Jesus Christ, Chris! We've been together a long time. Don't do this to me."

"You know me well enough," Carson said. "Jack and Stephanie are gone. I'm damned well going to do something about it, and I need the laser to do it."

"You in love with her? Is that it?"

After a long pause, Carson said, "Yeah, Dex, I was. Am. Hell, I'm still in shock."

Abrams vacillated. It had taken Carson so long to get over

Marian's death. He was elated on the one hand that Carson had found someone else. And then for her to be killed . . .

He could understand the shock. But he had no way to fight the board. The San Francisco banker had set the guidelines, and he wanted them enforced.

"Twenty-four hours," Carson said, "then it'll be homeward bound on that 707."

"Can't do it. I've had nine calls from directors. This board won't stand for a fifty-million-dollar write-off if something goes wrong. Our profit picture for this year is so slim, that would put us forty-five mil in the red, Chris. Stockholder revolt."

"Nothing's going to happen to it."

"Absolutely, goddamned guaranteed, right?"

"Well . . ."

"That's what I thought. On the plane, within the hour, Chris. And I don't know if that will save you."

"Nope."

"Damn it!"

"Sorry, Dex. Do what you have to do."

"I need your resignation. Fax it to me."

"I'm not doing that, either."

Abrams looked at his watch. "It's nine-forty-five P.M., Sunday, your time. That's the effective time of your termination."

"See you around, Dex."

TWENTY-EIGHT

Central Station, Mandalay

It was a stand-up, buffet-type brunch, and the foods of a dozen Southeast Asian cultures were featured. Waiters in red jackets meandered through the jammed lobby of the station offering stemmed glasses of champagne to augment the orange juice, mango juice, coffee, milk, and tea. The atmosphere was festive. People smiled at each other, laughed. Conversational groupings formed, dissolved, reformed.

Wearing his best white tropical suit, Carson wandered around the echoing cavern of a room, smiling at people he didn't know, saying a brief hello to those he did. He liked the setting, and he liked the composition of the crowd. It was fully international.

He ran into a large number of UltraTrain and GTI people, but if they knew he'd been fired the night before, they didn't mention it to him. He had been provided a name tag, but since it identified him as the director of the Myanmar Project, he didn't wear it. After a few minutes, he figured out that the media people had been issued orange name tags. Most of them were congregated near the serving tables, stocking up on exotic egg dishes. He threaded his way through the mob until he was closer and spotted the distinctive figure of Pamela Steele, dressed as usual to the max of tropical fashion.

He stopped at the beverage table and picked up a mug of coffee, then moved in on her.

She had a large purse slung from one shoulder, a glass of

orange juice and a napkin in one hand, and a croissant in the other.

When she recognized him, she said, "Chris! Good morning!"

"Hello, Pamela."

She looked around at the people. "Wonderful turnout, don't you think?"

"You could probably get a dozen interesting interviews."

"I've been looking for your secretary of state."

"Unless you wanted to take a chance on getting a better story."

Her eyes snapped back to lock on his.

"You'll miss the train ride, and the odds of anything coming of it are about fifty-fifty."

"What's it about?" she asked.

"I'm not going to tell you. You're the observer. I want someone to record whatever events transpire."

She looked through the glass doors to the train platform. The train wasn't there yet.

"You used me to force the government to prosecute Daw Tan, didn't you?"

"Everyone around here seems to make the most of others. You don't think Daw Tan got what he deserved?"

She didn't answer.

"I should also tell you there's about a fifty-fifty chance of surviving a helicopter ride with me."

Her eyes came back to him, shining now with the possibilities.

"Let's go," she said.

She swigged down the rest of her juice and brought the croissant along.

The two of them worked their way through the crowd, headed for the main entrance.

"Have you seen Mauk around?" he asked.

"Not this morning."

Carson wanted to talk to the colonel, but hadn't been able to locate him anywhere.

Outside the station, the day was gloomy and cool. The overcast ran from horizon to horizon. Carson led her to the Jeep Wagoneer he had commandeered the night before, and they got in. He backed out of his parking slot and headed south on 78th Street, a traffic-clogged thoroughfare that eventually led to the airport, the GTI airfield, and the Mandalay Yards.

A large audience had already gathered along the main line leading out of town, though it was still three hours before the train was due to depart. Vendors with pushcarts were working the crowd, plying them with Burmese fast food.

"It's really a national celebration, isn't it?" Steele asked.

"They'll own the most advanced railroad in the world. It's something for a people to take pride in."

"And today cements that ownership?"

"It's a pretty damned good symbol," he said. He laid on the horn, hit the gas, and shot around several cars. He was trying to make some decent speed, and he shifted from lane to lane several times.

She turned sideways in the seat to look at him. "You seem different today."

"I do?"

"Somehow more . . . I don't know . . . carefree? Reckless?"

"I've been relieved of my cares," he told her but didn't elaborate.

They went past the entrance to the Mandalay Airport, then farther down the road, past the GTI helicopter port. Carson saw that six Stallions were parked there now, but wasn't concerned. They had been used to ferry in the last of the train passengers.

"I thought we were taking a helo," Steele said.

"In a little while. We've got to run down to the Yards first."

He parked outside the long structure of the primary maintenance building, and they went inside.

The stainless-steel and blue UltraTrain P-01 was parked on the closest track, shining under the skylights in the high ceiling.

It had been moved from Yangon early this morning without notable incident. Workmen moved in and out of the open doors, attending to the last details of cleaning and polishing.

Steele dug a camera out of her purse and took a couple shots. Carson headed for the main offices.

He found Statler and Wilson talking to engineers and foremen, and when he had their attention introduced them to Steele.

"Would you like an advance tour of the train?" Wilson asked. "I'm always willing to treat a beautiful lady to a free tour. For the promotion value, of course."

"Perhaps later," she said.

Wilson turned to Carson. "Sorry to hear about . . . well, you know."

"The word's out?"

"Yeah. There was a fax to all stations this morning, from Marty Prather."

Abrams wasn't wasting any time. But then, in his place, Carson wouldn't have waited, either. He could tell that Steele wanted to ask about it, but she restrained herself.

"Craig, would you trust me for about four more hours?"

Wilson asked suspiciously, "In what way?"

"That cargo car you loaned me?"

"Yeah?"

"I want you to put it on the front end of this train."

Wilson worked his teeth. "I'd have to pull off the head-end passenger car, then I'd be short eighty seats."

"Add an interior passenger car behind the cargo job."

"What's in the cargo car?"

"You heard about the little foray we took at Daw Tan's hideaway?"

"I've heard rumors."

"This is a purely defensive measure, Craig. Mack Little and a couple of his technicians will be aboard."

"That doesn't answer my question, Chris."

"It's a classified weapons system."

"Oh, shit! You think they're going to try something this afternoon?"

"I do."

Wilson looked at Statler. "Dick?"

The roadbed engineer said, "Stephanie would probably go along with it."

"All right," Wilson said, "we'll tack it on."

"We may not need it, but if we do, we've got it. One other thing."

"I might have known."

"The train's due to leave Central Station at one o'clock. Delay it an hour."

"Oh, for Christ's sake! That's real promotional, Chris. We need the black eye of not getting out on time, the first trip."

Carson explained what he knew of the T-37s and then his purpose. "I think it's important."

"Sounds damned good to me," Statler told his partner.

"What we'll do," Wilson said, "is add your car and an interior passenger car, then move the train into the station. We'll find us some canvas to cover that ungodly contraption on the roof of my beautiful car, and leave it in place until we pull out. I'll give everyone a tour of the entire train before we leave. I can make it last an hour. That way, it'll look planned."

Carson and Steele left the building and got back in the Jeep. A few minutes later, he parked near the hangar at GTI's field.

He shut off the engine, opened the door, and saw the reception committee coming.

"Ah, damn!"

"Problem?" Steele asked.

"I don't know."

They got out and went to meet the group. Martin Prather led them, followed by Don Evans, Charles Washington, and Colonel Lon Mauk.

Evans spoke first, "Damn, Chris! I don't like this a bit."

Carson said, "Charles, they brought you along because you're bigger than I am."

"I wondered why the hell I was here, Chris. I was supposed to take a train ride."

Prather told him, "This sure as hell isn't my idea, Chris. Abrams called me first thing this morning."

"You're the acting director?"

"Yes. And I don't like it a damned bit. I'm a staff person."

"You're supposed to tell me to go home?"

"You can go wherever you want, buddy. I've been told to get your keys, ID cards, and access cards."

"What is going on?" Steele asked.

"Don," Carson addressed the air fleet manager, "I want that Gazelle for one last flight."

"Ah, hell, Chris! I can't do it. I'm afraid you're grounded."

Carson looked to Mauk, who shrugged.

Man Na-su

Sometime in midmorning, Branigan's guard unlocked the door to the small cottage she had been confined in, bound her wrists again, and took her outside.

It was hot and steamy, and there was a thick haze in the sky.

From the barred window of the cottage, she had earlier seen that there was a lot of damage to the buildings and vehicles in the area. Some huts had burned to the ground, the large house on the far end had been partially burned, and several trucks appeared to have crashed and burned. Large chunks of the truck bodies had completely disappeared, as if they had evaporated. She had never seen that kind of damage before.

Given the destruction and the earlier stories she had heard about Carson's raid, she had assumed that she had been taken to Daw Tan's compound, which she thought was somewhere near the village of Man Na-su. Somehow, she felt better, just knowing where she was.

The knowledge didn't seem to improve her chances, though.

The guard made her walk the mile to the airstrip, dragging her along with the rope end, if she didn't move fast enough.

Branigan felt terrible. Her broken arm ached with a steady throb. She felt hot, and was certain she had a fever. She feared that an infection had set in somewhere. This morning, they hadn't bothered to feed her, and if she hadn't felt so rotten, she might have been hungry. She was wearing the same clothes in which she had been captured, and they were shredded and filthy. She'd have given her next year's salary for a shower. She hadn't seen a mirror, but knew her face was caked with dirt and grime.

Because of the pain in her arm, she hadn't slept well—fitfully for short periods, and her fatigue threatened to overwhelm her. During the past night, she had been close to despair several times, beginning to wonder if the effort at survival was worth the trouble it seemed to bring her. She had realized that, as soon as Khim Nol and Nito Kaing allowed her to see their faces, they had made the decision that she wouldn't live to tell anyone about it.

God, Chris! Where are you? I need you. You can be a cowboy now, I don't care.

At the airstrip, a great deal of activity was taking place. The black-painted jet airplanes were lined up in a row, and dozens of men were fitting them with missiles and bombs. The sight of the warplanes was ominous in the extreme.

A twin-engine airplane and two helicopters were also parked to the side of the runway. One of the helicopters she recognized now as an Aerospatiale Alouette, the one that had carried her here on Sunday morning. The second helicopter was a Bell JetRanger, she had flown in them many times. Like the jets, it was painted a matte black, and it carried no identifying numbers. Both of its side doors were slid fully open, revealing the interior of the rear compartment.

The guard took her to the JetRanger, boosted her into it, then followed her. He shoved her into the center of the backseat, then with the loose end of the rope binding her hands, tied one of her ankles to the seat frame.

As he worked with the rope, she got a glance at his wrist-watch.

It was eleven-thirty.

The guard finished with her, slid out of the cabin, and stood by the door.

She tried desperately to recall the maps and charts she had pored over with the engineering staff. Man Na-su was about 160 miles from Mandalay. In this helicopter, that was about an hour away. She thought of all the people gathered in Mandalay at this hour, ready to ride her train. *Her* train! Carson would be there.

Just an hour away.

She looked out the open side door toward the warplanes. How fast did they go? Four hundred miles an hour? A half hour from her train.

She knew that's what they were preparing for. They were going to attack her train. Branigan wanted to scream her frustration.

The train would not be attacked in Mandalay. It would take place on some lonely stretch of track south of the city. She could visualize the main line, having been over it so often.

South of Thabyedaung. Nearly two hundred miles from Man Na-su.

It was fifty-four miles from Mandalay to Thabyedaung. Barely fifteen minutes at 200 miles an hour.

One-fifteen in the afternoon. This helicopter could make the rendezvous if it left by 11:45. The jets would only need a half hour.

Thinking about the implications for seven hundred people on the train, Branigan felt more helpless than ever before. She tried working her hands, to loosen the rope, but the pain of her arm soon stopped her.

Chris! Save my train!

A Nissan Pathfinder pulled up next to the helicopter, disgorging Khim Nol, Nito Kaing, and two pilots. Nol and Kaing were both dressed in black, playing the bandit roles, Branigan thought. Nol wore a holstered pistol on a web belt. Kaing played with her razor.

The two of them climbed into the helicopter and sat on either side of Branigan. The pilots opened the front doors and clambered into their seats.

"I'm hungry," Branigan said.

Kaing smiled her doll's smile. "You will not be hungry for long."

Nol said something to her in their particular dialect, and Kaing quit smiling, and shut up.

The turbine engine whined, caught, and roared. Nol and Kaing pulled on headsets.

After several minutes, the helicopter rose straight up, dipped its nose to the southwest, and began to climb.

Eleven-forty-five, Branigan judged.

They had plenty of time.

Chris, I love you.

Save my train. Please.

GTI airfield, Mandalay

It had begun to rain, a slow steady drizzle, which promised to last for most of the day. Lon Mauk thought it typical of his country's rainy season, but less than optimistic for the grand celebration that was now less than an hour away.

It was one o'clock.

Carson had explained his tactics in regard to the time. If Khim Nol were indeed to attack the train, he would be planning on the publicized departure time of one o'clock. If he had selected the deserted stretch of track some one hundred kilometers south as his point of interception, he would launch in the aircraft in time to arrive at close to one-fifteen.

And they would encounter no UltraTrain.

It would cause some confusion for the pilots. Would they wait around for an hour?

Could they wait around for an hour?

If the airplanes had been moved to some hidden airfield in Laos or Thailand, their fuel loads would become a concern. The aircraft might well not have the capability to wait for the train if their return fuel allotment was threatened. With pilots becoming bored, and fuel becoming a premium, they could possibly abort the attack, or at the least, be less efficient when it came time to act.

Mauk appreciated Carson's plan. Tactically, it could prove masterful, especially in light of his conversations with, first, Colonel Chit Nyunt, then the air-force commandant.

With the lowering ceilings and the deteriorating weather, Nyunt had started recalling the air-force aircraft patrolling the main line. Mauk had objected strenuously, but to no avail. He had then gone over Nyunt's head, but the Air Force general refused to countermand the order. He would not risk valuable airplanes to the possibility of loss due to weather.

Mauk had called Ba Thun, but the minister would not intervene, and besides, Ba Thun had reasoned, the majority of the committee was in Mandalay and difficult to reach.

Mauk thought otherwise, but his suggestions were ignored.

Which left Carson's secondary plan, and Mauk was not certain how reliable that could be. It was difficult to place his faith in it.

It was especially difficult as Carson no longer had standing in his company, or in the country. By all rights, Mauk should send him to Yangon to embark on an airliner leaving the country

He had not yet mentioned that part of his duty to Carson.

On the other side of the hangar, staying out of the rain, Carson, Evans, Steele, and Washington made a desultory group They were gathered in chairs around an overturned crate, drinking coffee. Mauk had been walking the perimeter of the hangar listless and worried.

Martin Prather, the apparent successor to the ousted Carson had left for Central Station. He was going to ride the train as the representative of General Technologies. Mauk assumed he also represented UltraTrain, in the absence of Stephanie Branigan.

Whenever he thought about Branigan, Mauk was depressed and discouraged. He felt as if he had abrogated his responsibilities. If he had detailed more, and better, men to her security, she would not have fallen into the clutches of Khim Nol.

He was assured by now that Khim Nol was behind this scheme. The chieftain had never returned Ba Thun's calls. The jet aircraft had massed at his private airfield.

When the telephone rang, and one of the technicians called his name, Mauk went to a phone hanging on the wall and picked it up.

"Colonel Mauk, this is Carlos Montoya."

"Yes, Mr. Montoya."

"I didn't know who to call because of the shake-up in the administration."

"I am glad you decided on me," Mauk said. "Do you have new information?"

"Not really, but I thought of something. After the raid on Daw Tan's compound, we lost use of the Listening Post."

"Yes."

"What if those Cessna T-37s were moved over there? We wouldn't have heard them land."

"Mr. Montoya, that is an excellent deduction. I thank you."

Mauk hung up, went back to the group around the packing box, and reported Montoya's suggestion.

"Damn," Donald Evans said. "That would put them a hell of a lot closer. Fuel won't be a problem."

Carson said, "They're in the air now."

Steele asked, "Isn't anyone going to *do* anything?"

Rangoon Station, Yangon

U Ba Thun made his second inspection tour of the ground floor and second floor of the station. The linen on the tables gleamed. The wine and water glasses sparkled. The heavy silver place settings bespoke an elegance not often seen in Yangon. The platoon of waiters in red waistcoats stood patiently by.

The premier and his two aides had made the same inspection tour and were now standing out on the upper-level platform. It was, fortunately, protected from the rain. Ba Thun thought that the premier was acting much younger. He was excited and proud.

He rode the escalator back to the ground floor and spoke to the station manager about the wines and the champagne, emphasizing that the bottles were not to be opened until the train pulled into the station.

Then he walked over to the main entrance and stood by the glass doors. He looked back at the large clock that loomed over the lobby. Its hands stood at 1:12.

In a matter of minutes . . .

The station manager came trotting over to him.

"Minister, the train is delayed!"

"What! Why is this?"

"The message said simply that they were performing a tour of the train. It will leave at two o'clock."

"I detest these last-minute changes!"

"Yes, Excellency."

"But that is precisely why I did not want the wines opened prematurely."

The manager went back to his tasks, leaving Ba Thun to stare out at the rain. Its intensity seemed to have increased.

The gloom of the afternoon invaded the lobby of the station, making it seem much darker than it was. He would have to tell the manager to turn on additional lights.

Ba Thun began to worry about events other than nature's precipitation. He wondered if Khim Nol would be able to react to the delay.

And he forcefully reassured himself that the old chieftain was quite resourceful.

There would be no problem.

And at 2:15 P.M. on July 15, the obstinate members of the SLORC—particularly the interior minister and the treasury minister—would cease to be obstinate.

Then there would only be the premier to deal with.

Seventy kilometers south of Maymyo

The JetRanger had been circling over the desolate mountains and forests for a long time. Branigan didn't understand why. She had simply been elated when, peering past the pilot's seat, she had seen the chronometer on the instrument panel. It was 1:45 P.M.

The UltraTrain would be nearing Pyinmana, now, soon to be out of reach of the airplanes. At two hundred miles an hour, or two hundred and fifty, if necessary, it could certainly outrun the helicopter. The jet aircraft, which she had seen circling above them, would be getting low on fuel. A few minutes more, and she felt confident they could not make the chase to the train and still get back.

They were flying low over the peaks, and she had seen only one road to set as a landmark. The aircraft above them were barely discernible in the low clouds and blankets of rain. Khim Nol had partially closed the side doors, but because of the rotors and the slow forward speed, very little moisture entered the cabin.

Branigan sat with her shoulders hunched forward, with her broken arm in her lap, trying to ease the pressure on it. It was cold in the cabin, but neither Nol or Kaing seemed aware of it.

She wondered what had gone wrong with their plan.

Forty minutes earlier, the jets had swept past them, heading west, but had soon returned to begin circling. She had noticed that all of the aircraft still carried their weapons, and the sight had given her hope.

Nol and Kaing had argued—silently to her—for a long time,

then settled into a sullen silence. The woman played with the razor, opening and closing the shining blade. Twice, when she had seen Branigan watching her, she had grinned. In anticipation?

She didn't know what had happened, but she knew something was wrong.

They continued to circle. Going nowhere, doing nothing, waiting.

Waiting for what?

Nol shifted next to her, and from the corner of her eye, Branigan watched him talking over his headset. He smiled grimly.

Said something.

The helicopter suddenly broke out of the circle and began speeding west.

Branigan couldn't stand it anymore and yelled at him, "What's going on?"

The lopsided grin in his scarred face appeared obscene. "We are going to look at your train," he yelled back. "And then I will ask my friends to join me."

With a stubby forefinger, he pointed upward.

At the weapons-laden jet airplanes.

The train hadn't started on time!

That was the problem.

Branigan groaned.

Chris! Get off the train. Please!

GTI airfield, Mandalay

In the end, Lon Mauk had nationalized the Gazelle, commandeering it for the use of the Union of Myanmar Army, and taking the responsibility out of Evans's and Prather's hands. Everyone seemed relieved by the decision, except that Mauk, Washington, and Evans all demanded a ride. Prather had been content to take the Jeep into Mandalay and get on the train. Evans rode as copilot, since he was qualified. Washington rode as the muscle they might need, and Mauk was present as commander of the flight. He nearly banned Steele, but Carson defended her presence as an objective observer and recorder. She sat in the center seat in the back, Mauk and Washington on either side of her.

Carson had told them all they were subject to a potential tragedy, but no one backed out.

He had lifted off at 1:50 P.M. in a steady rain. The ceiling was down to about three thousand feet, and visibility was less than two miles. He found the main line and immediately turned south as he climbed to 2,000 feet AGL.

On the intercom, he said, "Everyone stay alert. We're looking for anything with wings coming out of the east."

Pulling the headset off, he hung it on the hook behind him. From the floor, he picked up the TAD helmet and settled it on his head, then snapped the chin strap in place. Stabbing the connector of the communications cord into the jack on the panel, he was back on the aircraft's communications system. The umbilical cord to the TAD panel was already connected.

Switching the radio to the frequency he had agreed on with Little, Carson touched the transmit stud. "Mack, do you read me?"

"Gotcha, Chris."

"Marty with you?"

"He's back in the passenger cars now, but he told us all about it."

"You know you don't have to do anything for me."

"The hell with it. I'll kick Abrams's butt when I get home."

"What's your status?"

"They closed the doors at one-fifty-eight. I've got one-fifty-nine right now."

Carson maintained 100 knots forward airspeed. He searched the mountains to his left, but saw nothing moving. Checking his cabin, he saw that everyone else was also watching the mountains.

At precisely two o'clock, Little reported, "We're under way,

Chris. Wilson says we'll hold fifty miles an hour to the Mandalay Yards, then he's kicking it up to a hundred and sixty."

At that speed, Carson could stay with the train. Any faster, loaded the way he was, and he would fall behind.

"If we spot any hostiles, tell him to take it to the max. We want you to be hard to hit."

"I *want* to be hard to hit, believe me."

"How's the Ruby going to perform?" Carson asked.

"Who knows? I've got a full three-hundred-sixty-degree traverse and seventy degrees of elevation. The computer's tied into you, but I can take over manually, if I need to."

Carson kept checking the rearview mirror, watching for the train. While he waited, he activated the TAD transmitter. They had tested it last night, but he called Little and said, "I want a TAD test."

"Gotcha. Send anytime."

The transmitter was separate from the helicopter's navigation and voice radios. It was mounted under the rear seat, with the antenna taped to the fuselage.

Carson hit the Test Sequence button on the auxiliary controls mounted under his instrument panel. A red light flickered.

"Affirmative," Little said. "We've got a five by five signal."

"That's step one," Carson told him.

He finally saw the train, and he sideslipped the helicopter for a few seconds so his passengers could get a look at it.

"Beautiful!" Evans said.

"That's almost as good-looking as one of my boats," Washington conceded.

The silver-and-blue train whisked smoothly through the rain-drenched day, snaking through the slight curves with grace. Though he was high above it, Carson could see the incongruous attachment to the top of the lead car. The fifteen-foot-long laser on its tripod appeared completely out of place.

"It is moving very fast," Mauk said.

"Only a hundred and sixty, they tell me," Carson said.

He straightened out his line of flight, and as the train moved under him, picked up speed to match it.

Little said on the radio, "I see you, Chris."

"Ditto. Keep your eyes open."

They raced southward in tandem, with Evans calling off the towns. "Kyaukse . . . Minzu . . . Myittha . . ."

"After we pass Thabyedaung, that's the optimum area," Carson said.

"Optimum for whom?" Washington asked.

Several minutes later, that village passed below. The mountains encroached on the left. The highway swung off to the right. The day felt as if it darkened.

"There they are!" Steele yelped.

"Damn! Where?" Evans echoed.

"You've got sharp eyes, honey," Washington said. "I think you fighter pilot-types would say eight o'clock low, Chris."

Carson went into a steep left bank, turning to the east as he looked for the hostile aircraft. He found them really low, clearing the foothills by less than five hundred feet, he judged. They were staying close to the ground and out of any radar coverage.

"Here we go, Mack!"

"It's getting loud in here, Chris! I'm bringing all generators up to full output! Go! Go! Go!"

"There are seven of them!" Evans called out.

"Call 'em for me as I go," Carson said.

The closest aircraft was a dark streak above the green hills. The rain made it look slippery, and its speed of some 400 miles an hour, combined with Carson's closure speed of 170, made time accelerate unnaturally. He guessed the plane at five miles distance.

He kicked in the Target Acquisition/Designator and pulled the helmet's targeting visor down. He could still see through the visor, but now he could also see the infrared beam projected by the movable eye of the TAD unit mounted under the nose of the Gazelle. When he moved his head, the beam moved with it, guided by the helmet.

Carson immediately traversed the red beam right and down, caught the T-37 in its path. The opposing pilot wouldn't see a thing. He locked it in place by pressing the button taped to the head of his control stick. The transmitter instantly sent the co-ordinate and range information to the computer aboard the train, and the electronic brain interpreted place, time, and speed in milliseconds, then aimed the laser.

"Fire one, Mack!"

"Gotcha!"

From below and behind him, the laser beam arced across the flat land toward the foothills. In the rain, the sudden pulse of ruby light was utterly fascinating. The raindrops refracted and reflected the light into crimson waves that radiated outward from the core of the beam. Ahead of him, the whole gloomy afternoon bloomed a deep blood red.

"My God!" Steele screamed.

The laser found its target, and a wing sheared off of the T-37. The fuselage began tumbling immediately. Carson didn't watch for it to impact the earth.

"Come left!" Evans called.

Carson swung his helmet to the left, but couldn't find the next target right away. The color echoes of the first laser blast were dying away, but still interfering with his infrared beam.

"Down! Down!"

He pulled his chin down.

There it was!

Lock in!

"Fire, Mack!"

Another brilliant display of cerise light followed, rolling across the valley.

"Now up and right!" Evans said.

Carson found it faster this time, locked in, and ordered Little to fire.

The laser beam cut the third Cessna in half, right down the length of the fuselage. The flash of red spread across the valley like spilling blood. Carson wondered what the people on the train were thinking.

By now, the four remaining aircraft were within a mile of him. He didn't see how he was going to get all of them.

He discovered the next one before Evans had a chance to warn him. Its pilot had seen him and was attempting to pass under him. The hostile aviators might have figured out by now that the lone Gazelle had something to do with the disaster they were facing.

He locked it in.

"Fire!"

Zap!

Instant dead airplane, the pieces of the fuselage and wings tumbling and spreading as they emerged from the flash point. Some of the fighter's ordnance may have detonated also.

The raindrops carried the ruby color for a fraction of time after the laser shut down.

"They're turning tail!" Evans called.

Carson guessed that the opposing pilots, perhaps still groggy after having to wait an hour after they had anticipated combat, were in shock at the sudden and dramatic loss of more than half their complement. The three remaining planes had all rolled into tight turns and were pulling away to the southeast.

He found one with the designator and locked it in.

"Fire!"

The laser spit death and destruction.

"They're running, Chris!" Steele called out, suddenly appalled.

"And they might come back."

The sixth fell into the beam of the infrared designator.

Locked in.

Fire.

Six down.

And the seventh dived out of sight behind the foothills.

Carson slowed to a standstill, then did a full 360-degree turn. He scanned the sky between the ground and the low clouds.

"See anything, Don?"

"No. Go around again. It's hard to see."

"Mack," Carson said on the radio, "you can back down your generators."

"Will do."

"Hey!" Washington said. "The train's stopped."

"Mack, what are you doing?"

"Craig Wilson says we're on hold for a minute. We don't want to leave the area in case you need us."

"You've got seven hundred people to worry about."

"They're enjoying the show, I think," Little said. "Hell, man, I've never seen anything like it."

The nose of the chopper came around to the east again.

"There!" Steele yelled. She had her camera at the ready and was shooting everything in sight.

"Damned fine eyes," Washington said. "It's another chopper."

Carson located it.

Two miles away, coming fast and low.

"Not afraid of us," Evans said.

Carson put the nose down and picked up forward speed, losing altitude fast to meet it head-on.

"Move that train, Mack!"

"Not if you've got another hostile."

"You've got a thirty-mile range with the Ruby. Hit it!"

"We're going."

Within a mile of the other helicopter and down to 1,000 feet AGL, Carson identified it.

"It's a JetRanger. Black."

"That will be Khim Nol's," Mauk said.

"Is he crazy? Coming on like this?"

"He may be extremely disappointed in his fighter aircraft," Mauk said. "And yes, he may be crazy."

Carson aligned the infrared beam on the fast-approaching helo.

"Power up your generators, Mack."

"Coming up. Let me know."

The JetRanger's navigation lights began to blink erratically.

"Anyone here remember your Morse code?" Carson asked.

"I think he's telling us to hold fire," Evans suggested.

Carson hesitated, and as he did so, slowed his forward speed.

The other pilot matched him, and they closed on each other slowly and warily.

The JetRanger slowed to a hover, seven hundred feet off the ground, and turned broadside to him.

Carson flipped the toggle for his landing light.

The bright white beam lit up the side of the Bell helicopter. The side door was wide open.

"Jesus!" Evans yelled.

Carson shoved up his targeting visor so he could see clearly. He continued to close on the enemy.

Quarter-mile.

Two hundred yards.

"It's Stephanie!" Washington said.

Carson had already made the ID. His heart leaped.

She looked to be in bad shape. Her face was wan and streaked in the bright light. Nol and another woman sat on either side of her. The woman held some elongated object close to Branigan's face.

"The son of a bitch!" Carson yelled.

"Easy, Chris," Evans told him. "There's a rocket pod mounted on that chopper."

Carson pulled the visor down, lined up the infrared beam on the turbine exhaust, and thumbed the transmit switch.

"Surgical, Matt."

"Surgical?"

"As thin a beam as you can get, and go light on the power. I just want to disable an engine."

"Got it."

"Go."

It was just a dash of light, a ruby bolt that shot across the darkened sky and slapped at the JetRanger's exhaust. It trailed a wake of rippling color.

The engine immediately began to splutter.

Carson hoped the guy was a decent pilot.

Whoever he was, he immediately went into autorotation and slipped into a steep dive.

Carson cut hard to the left and followed him down.

"Everybody be ready to pile out," he ordered.

The JetRanger hit the ground at a steep angle, hard, and its skids plowed up the rain-softened ground. One skid collapsed, it canted to the right, the rotors kicking up dirt and mud and breaking up.

Carson landed sixty feet away, and was out of his helmet and harness before the Gazelle settled on her gear. He shoved the door open and slid out, Mauk right behind him.

He slipped and slid in the muddy, weed-choked field as he ran.

Nol and the woman, with Branigan held between them, climbed from the JetRanger's wrecked cabin. They appeared unsteady. The woman had a razor.

Carson slid to a stop fifteen feet away from them. Mauk came up on his right side. On his left, Washington came to a halt and whispered to him, "Let's not do anything rash, Chris."

"Are you all right, Steph?"

There was such a look of relief on her face, he thought the prognosis was good.

"Chris—"

"Be quiet," the woman said.

Mauk spoke up. "What now, Khim Nol?"

"I believe we are at stalemate, Colonel," Nol said, grinning foolishly.

His pilots clambered out of the helo behind him, one of them helping the other, whose face was mashed and gushing blood.

Branigan sagged, as if trying to fall, but the woman held her tight, the razor pressed up under her chin.

"A stalemate," Mauk said, "is not to be allowed this time, Khim Nol. The lady with us is a reporter, and the world will know of your treachery."

"My treachery! It is the government giving away our country."

"Still, you are to consider yourself under arrest."

"Miss Branigan will have to die for that to be accomplished, Colonel."

"Then," Mauk said, "that is the way it is to be."

Carson glanced at the colonel and saw him pull his Browning automatic from its holster.

Khim Nol unsnapped a military holster on his right hip and pulled his own gun.

"Hey, guys!" Washington said.

Pamela Steele, off to Carson's right, was snapping pictures as fast as her automatic winder allowed.

The rain continued to fall. Carson was drenched. The rain ran off his forehead and into his eyes.

"I've got an idea," Carson said.

Everyone looked at him.

Carson turned to Mauk and asked sotto voce, "Who's the woman?"

"Nito Kaing."

"Miss Kaing," Carson said. "How would you like to take a walk?"

"A walk?" she said. Her tone said the suggestion bewildered her.

"Yes." Carson pointed to the foothills and mountains behind her. "All by yourself. Or better yet, take the two pilots with you."

The pilots looked as if they liked the idea. The one was brushing blood out of his eyes with his sleeve.

So did Kaing.

"By myself? Unmolested?"

"It may be a long walk, but I'll bet you make it."

Nol was dumbstruck. His gun hand hung loosely at his side as he looked first at Carson, then at Kaing.

Kaing dropped her arms, freeing Branigan.

Branigan lurched away, tried to run, slipped and fell to the muddy earth.

Kaing turned and began to run toward the forest.

Mauk raised his pistol, but Carson blocked his forearm with his own.

Nol, entranced for the moment by the new treachery, hesitated, then raised his own pistol toward the prone Branigan. Unsure of himself, and what threatened him the most, he spun and aimed toward the running Kaing.

By then, like a linebacker accustomed to running in the mud, Washington slammed into him so hard that Nol was jolted into the side of the JetRanger's fuselage. His gun hand slapped the open door, and the pistol went flying.

Carson didn't see it.

He was on his knees next to Branigan, trying to help her up. Steele was right beside him.

Branigan was crying.

TWENTY-NINE

Two kilometers north of Thedaw

The helicopter made two trips. On the first, Carson, Branigan, Washington, and Steele were flown to the train. On the second trip, Evans picked up Mauk and Nol, who was in handcuffs.

Evans seemed to know what he was doing with the helicopter, and he landed near the head of the train. He reached across the left seat and unlatched the door, shoving it open.

Mauk crawled out, then reached back and grabbed Nol's arm. He pulled him out, not worrying about how rough he might have been. The old man seemed deflated by what had transpired, and he offered no resistance.

Yelling over the volume of the idling turbine engine, Mauk said, "Thank you, Mr. Evans."

"Anytime, Colonel. It's been a magic day."

"Yes. It has been."

With Nol's arm clutched in his hand, Mauk marched him across the field toward the steep embankment leading up to the railbed. It was a struggle getting the man up the incline. The rock and earth were slippery. When they achieved the concrete of the track, he pushed Nol ahead of him toward a hatchway that had been opened in the side of the car.

There were steps there, and the two of them climbed into the car. The man named Statler grabbed Nol roughly.

"I could take care of this bastard for you, Colonel."

"Perhaps it would be best if you did not," Mauk said.

He was no more on board then the steps were retracted, the door closed, and the train under way.

Mauk was impressed with the smoothness of the ride.

Statler spoke to one of the men standing in attendance, and Nol was taken back, forced to sit on the floor, and tied with a length of nylon rope to what appeared to be a pallet supporting a large number of diesel generators.

Mauk suppressed the thought that the government had been lied to, and the train was powered by diesel engines rather than electricity and magnets.

There were about seven meters of space ahead of the pallet of generators, and it seemed crowded with all who were in the car. Carson, Washington, and the man named Wilson all tended to Stephanie Branigan. She was in the left-side seat of the two seats available. There were others he did not know. Mack Little's technicians, he supposed. Statler was in the right seat, apparently running the train. The rain pelted the windshield, rolling up the steeply slanted Plexiglas to leave it clear. The countryside slipped past with dizzying speed.

He was sopping wet and covered with mud, and he slipped out of his uniform blouse, tossing it on top of a still-hot diesel engine for the generator. His white undershirt stuck wetly to his ribs.

Squatting in front of Nol, he studied the man's face.

It seemed to reflect a bizarre combination of rage and resignation.

"It will be just like Daw Tan," he said. "Because of the world's interest, the government cannot afford to let you escape. If in the balance, it is you who must lose face, or the SLORC who must lose face, you may anticipate the outcome."

"I have money," Nol said.

"Yes. That is the same offer Daw Tan made. Yet Daw Tan is dead."

"Nito Kaing killed him, not I."

"It is the same difference, old man. And Nito Kaing? She has what she wanted, does she not?"

"What is that?"

"Her freedom and your empire. Can you imagine that she will not move quickly to fill the vacuum you leave behind? With the power she will accumulate, she may well strike a bargain with Yangon in regard to her indictment."

The image deflated Nol even further. His shoulders sagged and his bony old chest contracted.

"We have," Nol said, "lived in harmony for many years, Lon Mauk."

"Then why did you choose to change it?"

"It was not my doing."

"I see. Then who?"

"U Ba Thun, of course."

Mauk had begun to suspect it, but only as late as yesterday when Ba Thun had become so interested in Mauk's hypothesis that Hyun Oh was the mastermind of the scheme. It would suit Ba Thun's purpose to have a scapegoat.

Then, too, as he and Carson had once discussed, he suspected that many betrayals were taking place at the same time. Oh had his plan. Daw Tan had his, and Ba Thun his own. They all coincided in some ways, but the outcomes were projected according to each man's goals. And in the end, Nito Kaing triumphed.

"You may save yourself from a hangman's noose, old man, and go on to live in solitary confinement for the years left to you if you can tell me why the minister would choose such a course."

"He told me but one reason, and that was to discredit the Americans, to put them off schedule, and to reap profits in penalties."

"But you know of another?"

"I only suspect. The rest of the committee was to be on the train."

"Leaving Ba Thun as the sole man in power?"

"I assumed that from the beginning, but I could work with him."

Mauk stood up and walked forward to the control station. It amazed him that he could walk so steadily in the moving train. When he looked down at the Instrument panel, a digital readout displayed in blue letters: 223.

"That is the speed?" he asked Statler.

"I'm trying to make up some time, Colonel. We got way behind, back there."

"Do you have a telephone, Mr. Statler?"

"Sure do."

He reached down beside his seat with his right hand and lifted a handset. Mauk stepped behind the seat and took it from him.

He had to ask information for the number of Rangoon Station.

And he had to wait several minutes before Ba Thun came to the phone.

"Minister, this is Colonel Mauk."

"Yes, Mauk. What is it? Is the train to be late again?"

"No, I don't think so. They tell me they are making up the time now."

Silence on the other end.

"Minister?"

"I am here."

"I have placed Khim Nol under arrest."

"You have not!"

"Indeed, I have. He is telling me interesting stories. I am, in fact, now going to the back of the train to talk to the members of the committee about these amazing tales."

He hung up the telephone.

Mauk assumed that, by the time the train reached Yangon, Minister U Ba Thun would have followed in the footsteps of Hyun Oh.

It did not matter. The committee had long arms and capable

hands, should they decide to retrieve him from wherever he might go in the world.

Lon Mauk was satisfied.

One mile north of Mahlwagon Station

The mud had dried in big splotches on Carson's best white tropical suit. Like Mauk, he had shed the suit coat and his shirt.

In front of him as he leaned on the back of the seat, Branigan was wearing Craig Wilson's safari jacket, a blanket, and not much else. Charles Washington had wrapped nearly a full roll of duct tape around her broken cast in an attempt to stabilize it. She held it gingerly in her lap. With her free left hand, she held onto Carson's hand over the back of the seat, as if it were her last grip on life. She squeezed it regularly, and he squeezed back.

Also regularly, she leaned her head back and looked up at him. He had washed her face with an old towel and a bucket of rainwater. His job hadn't been very effective, but she looked damned good to him.

"I'm not letting go of you again," he said.

She smiled. "Any particular reason?"

"It's love, I guess."

"Can you explain it to Merilee?"

"Yeah, I can."

"Good."

"One thing, though. I got fired."

"Fired?"

"I'm unemployed."

"You know, after all that's happened, Abrams will want you back."

"Tough. Dex had his chance." Carson didn't even care if Abrams got his mining contract, but he probably would. He was tired of playing double-sided corporate games.

Maybe he'd become a jungle guide, or something.

"I need an assistant. You want to work for me? Deputy director?"

Could he do that? Give up all the control he was so used to?

"I wouldn't buy Hypai's magnets," he told her.

"We'd go with your recommendation."

"Okay. I'll work for you."

"I love you, Chris."

The train shot past Mahlwagon Station, beginning to slow as it entered the outskirts of Yangon. Despite the rain, everything about Yangon looked fresh and clean.

"Watch the scenery," he said. "That's the twenty-first century you're seeing."

THE AUTHOR

William H. Lovejoy is a Vietnam veteran and former English professor, college president, and college system chief fiscal officer. He is a member of the adjunct faculties of the University of Northern Colorado and Metropolitan State College of Denver and lives in northern Colorado where he is at work on his next novel.